"All the fun of pulp adventure, filtered through a twenty-first century lens. Helms isn't content simply to play in the genre; she questions it, complicates it, adds layers it didn't have eighty years ago. Missy's journey to become Mr Mystic isn't the usual heroic training montage — but it's a hell of a lot of fun."

   Marie Brennan, author of A Natural History of Dragons

"A tough, witty young woman who inherited her superhero grandfather's powers barrels through a rollicking *Big Trouble in Little China*-esque tale filled with magic, monsters and wisecracks. I loved it."

   Alex Bledsoe, author of The Sword Edged Blonde

"*Dragons of Heaven* combines superheroes, romance, ancient mythological China, and does it right. The worldbuilding is stunning, and Missy's challenges feel incredibly real as do her reactions to amazing worlds she's put in. In fighting against the machinations of overly honorable yet incredibly nefarious ancient dragons, its clear she's the best chance humanity's got."

   Cassie Alexander, author of the Edie Spence series

ALYC HELMS

The Dragons of Heaven

ANGRY
ROBOT

ANGRY ROBOT
An imprint of Watkins Media Ltd

Lace Market House,
54-56 High Pavement,
Nottingham,
NG1 1HW
UK

angryrobotbooks.com
twitter.com/angryrobotbooks
Run for the shadows

An Angry Robot paperback original 2015
1

Copyright © Alyc Helms 2015

Alyc Helms asserts the moral right to be
identified as the author of this work.

A catalogue record for this book is available
from the British Library.

ISBN 978 0 85766 432 7
EBook ISBN 978 0 85766 434 1

Set in Meridien by Epub Services.
Printed by 4edge Ltd.

For Jason Pisano, Storyteller

ONE

Mystic in the City

Now

"It's all over for you, Mr Mystic."

The boy leveled his gun sideways at me in a fair imitation of the hip-hop videos he'd been raised on. His hoodie gleamed with the polished-cotton newness of recent purchase. His lip curled like that of a thousand cinematic thugs before him. Suburban white boys should stick to watching films about gangstas, not try to emulate them.

"We chased off them Asians, and now we're gonna ice you, old man. Once you're out of the picture, the Dogpatch'll belong to my crew. Ain't no one gonna get in our way." He paused. The five yes-boys surrounding him crossed their arms and directed chin-nods at me. I scanned the catwalk above us for movement. Nothing. I sighed and resigned myself to playing for more time.

"My dear boy," I said to the leader in my most reasonable tones – the kind calculated to annoy. "Do you honestly believe that I came here unprepared? Do give me an ounce of credit. I've been in the adventure hero business since before you lot were in leading strings."

"In what? What were we in?"

"Leading – oh, never mind. The point is, you haven't caught

7

me unawares, and the longer you stand there holding that very heavy pistol, the longer the police have to move into position."

I lowered my hands, uncowed. The boys shifted in a ripple of whispers, unnerved by my deviation from script. I was betting that their young leader was high on pop culture sensibility and low on common sense. The gun he had trained on me shook; the muzzle lowered an inch. I didn't bother to conceal my smile; the shadows cast by the brim of my fedora would do that for me.

"So, the question is: are you going to soliloquize more on your triumph, or are you going to escape now and hope you can get away?"

The gun wavered, as did the boy, but neither withdrew. The presence of his five cronies acted as a bolster to keep the leader from backing off. Better nudge him along.

"By all means, take your time deciding. It's your neck the noose is tightening around."

The muzzle lowered another inch, but then the boy dredged up a dose of righteous fury from somewhere. He tensed, and the gun rose with a jerk. I spared a moment to pray that the trigger was a stiff one.

"I'm not falling for your shit, Obi-Wan. I've heard about you. They say you have the power to control men's minds n' shit. Well, not me, motherfucker."

So much for stalling. The police support I'd hoped for was nowhere in sight. Time to call on other allies. The room darkened around us. The crew shifted; their shadows did not.

"I believe you're thinking of the Shadow. I'm afraid my skills are far less noteworthy, though the confusion is understandable given what I can do."

The boy jerked as he realized his shadow was no longer following him. Then he panicked.

"You can die is what you can do, asshole!" His arm tensed, and his eyes clenched tight. Likely the boy had never fired at anything but bottles and air. The tell gave me time to drop to the ground before the gun went off above my head.

I released my hold on the darkness surrounding us. The shadows attacked.

Black shapes thick as smoke rose in an eddy around the wannabe gangstas. The boys scattered in a confusion of shouts, running in all directions and drawing weapons as they did so. The leader's gun went off twice more before he disappeared into the vortex of shifting shadow. His weapon skittered across the cement of the warehouse floor to rest inches before my nose. I stared at its still-smoking muzzle, smelled the stench of cordite. I rose to a crouch and darted after the leader, skirting the gun – nasty, loud, oily things; I refused to have anything to do with them.

The other boys ran for the warehouse entrance, firing at the shadows in pursuit, but they were not my main concern. Their leader launched himself up the catwalk risers two at a time, a roiling sea of shadow-forms close on his heels. I followed, wading through the shadows. The boy's footsteps rattled the catwalk as he bolted for the multi-paned windows that stood propped open to the night beyond. The fog had crawled over the peninsula earlier in the evening. There was no visibility to speak of, and the aluminum rooftops would be slick and treacherous.

I didn't relish the idea of chasing this boy down in a daring *le parkour* escape. I whispered a command, and the shadows flooded ahead and surged up in front of the boy. He stumbled and fell to his knees. The metal catwalk groaned and shuddered beneath us.

"Get away! Get them away!" He batted at the shadows, his voice breaking. Nobody likes confronting their childhood terrors – the things that lurked under our beds when we were young – but his fear lacked the distance of maturity. I revised my age estimate down a few years. His parents were probably worried sick.

I waved away the knot of shadows with another whispered command, leaving the boy huddled on the catwalk, sobbing to himself.

"Now, don't you wish you'd left when you had the chance?" I tried pulling him to his feet. He resisted deadweight. I locked my arms around his chest and heaved. That's when my tardy cavalry burst through the doors, weapons and lights bristling in all directions.

"San Francisco PD. Drop your weapons!"

I froze, squinting against the lights. The other aspiring bad-asses – mere boys no older than the one I held – surrendered with a clatter of firearms hitting cement. The lights chased away all the shadows save those cast by my fedora, but too late. The police had seen the monsters I'd brought forth.

Lovely. That would add another two hours to my deposition.

The police scattered through the warehouse, securing it with procedural thoroughness. Several of them climbed up to the catwalk, weapons trained on the boy I held. "Masters, release the perp and back away. We'll take things from here."

My prisoner took the opportunity to shove away from me, scrabbling across the grating to huddle against a support. He kept his eyes on me rather than the approaching cops, as though I were the greater danger. I heard a few whispers from the spooked officers before their leader shushed them.

"It's all right," I said. "He's in no condition to harm anyone."

"Pat him down." The command came from Officer Cordero, the officer-in-charge of this little bust. I worried that the police might be daft enough to include me in that command, but seeing my shadows had scared them honest. They moved straight to the boy.

"You took your time arriving." I pulled my fedora a little lower, coaxing forth more shadows to conceal my features. The front of my dark suit was covered with grit from my clinch with the warehouse floor. I brushed the dust away as if it caused me more affront than the police's tardy rescue. There would have been no call to scare the boy if Cordero had brought his men in sooner.

"I'm not losing another arrest because of some judge's bench notion of probable cause, and the only thing we had before the gunshots was a Prius out front that was reported stolen."

Cordero settled at my side, keeping an eye on the patdown. He grunted as the boy's hoodie was thrown back, revealing what I'd already heard in his voice.

"He looks awfully young and white to be the head of the Shadow Dragon Triad's San Francisco branch," Cordero drawled. "I thought you said Lao Chan was going to be here."

"He was supposed to be."

"Then who is this... kid?"

"Billy Westmont," supplied one of the frisking officers, who had just opened the boy's wallet. "Potrero address. Just got his learner's permit last week, looks like." The officer gave the boy a condescending smile. "Hey kid, don't you know you're supposed to have an adult with you when you boost cars?"

"It's my mom's," Billy muttered. The two frisking officers traded an eyeroll before reading young Billy his Miranda.

"He's a red herring," I explained as Billy was led off. I had lost my taste for this night's business. "Lao Chan must have gotten wind of the bust and moved his people elsewhere. I'd wager these boys just happened to squat in the wrong place at the wrong time."

"Well, maybe Billy here knows something. About the Shadow Dragons, where Lao Chan moved his base. Something." Cordero gestured to the boy with a jerk of his head. "Can you question him? Y'know, use your power to cloud men's minds to make him talk."

Why did people insist on mistaking me for a fictional character? "Even if I could, I fear it wouldn't be ethical."

"Guess we'll have to make him piss himself the old-fashioned way." Cordero leaned over the catwalk railing to call down orders to his people, the normal procedure that accompanied a police bust. My shoulders twitched; bureaucracy and I had never been the best of friends.

"Officer Cordero, if that is all, I'll be going. I'll send you word if I hear more on Lao Chan."

"We'll need your statement," he reminded me.

"I'll have my lawyer send my affadavit to the DA's office."

Before he could give a response, I stepped back towards the propped-open windows – poor young Billy's means of escape. The shadows welled up around me and I slipped out into the night. Behind me, I heard Billy whimper and the cops mutter to themselves. Well, the rest of the bust might have gone pear-shaped, but at least my exit was up to par.

It looked like a carnival had set up on the street below, the flash of red and blue from the squad cars reflecting off the black-slicked pavement. Yet, no calliope music accompanied the lights, just the static of radios and the drone of dispatchers and the occasional bleat of truncated sirens. So much sound and fury, and all the police were going to get for it was Billy and his gang of Eminem fanboys. They would not be happy.

Not wanting to be snippy at someone less stoic than Cordero, I avoided the street and fled across the industrial rooftops.

I was like a shadow myself, slipping along tin-rippled awnings and between squat air conditioning units. The fog enveloped me. Water beaded on the dark wool of my tailored suit and the felted brim of my fedora. I fought to find traction as I darted through the obstacle course, but not even the challenge of the terrain could distract me from my frustration.

I had cocked things up rather spectacularly this night, and I needed to suss out why. How had I been duped into chasing down poor Billy Westmont from Potrero Hill? Why wasn't Lao Chan where he was supposed to have been? A leak on Cordero's team? Some slip-up on my own part during surveillance? We hadn't dared warn Lao Chan by starting warrant proceedings, which was why Cordero had been willing to let me dangle in the face of danger until he got his exigent circumstances.

I slid down a fire-escape to the narrow street where I'd parked my motorcycle, reviewing every aspect of my investigation for some flaw, when a blast of heat and force blew me from the ladder.

I hit the cinderblock wall of the building. My head cracked sideways into it. Too stunned to scrabble for purchase, I plummeted to the street below. Came down hard on hands and knees, barely avoiding cracking my head again. Concussions are not funny.

Smoke clogged the air. I coughed and blinked, trying to clear at least one of my senses. My ears were ringing, and the world was orange.

Slumping down to one hip, I pushed back against the wall. My hand brushed against soft fabric. I looked down. My hat. I set it gingerly atop my aching head. Habit, but the brim helped cut out some of the orange, or maybe my vision was finally clearing. A ball of flame had appeared where the Triumph had been. I struggled to piece everything together. Smoke. Flame. Concussive blast. An explosion.

"Those bastards blew up my ride!" I took my time marveling over that as the flames danced down. Little remained to feed them once the accelerant had burned away.

Using the bulk of the cinderblock wall, I pushed myself to my feet and took a few steps towards the smoking husk. The frame was still there, but everything that made it more than a mechanical skeleton had been burned away: the midnight blue of the chassis, the sleek leather of seats and saddlebags. Even my half helmet had been burned onto the husk like a charred carbuncle on the Triumph's ass.

I gaped uselessly. I'd had that bike since I became Mr Mystic. It was as much a part of me as the hat and the shadows. In the strange, fluid realm of identity, the Triumph was an anchor.

Its loss shook me more than the explosion had.

Lao Chan, it had to be. I searched around for some kind of clue, but he hadn't left me a note or helpful bit of graffiti, and demolition forensics wasn't precisely my field. Still, the simplest explanation favored the crime boss. Something had tipped him about tonight, with enough time for him to clear out of the warehouse unseen by surveillance. Little wonder he'd be looking for some payback for all the fuss.

And here I was, standing at ground zero for him to take more potshots at. I had to get out of here. I had to get home.

I made it as far as the mouth of the alley, stumbling as my knees threatened to give out. My body ached from its meeting with the concrete. Groaning, I lowered myself to the curb. I took out my cell phone and dialed the top person on my contact list.

I was getting too old for this kind of excitement.

A quarter hour later, a car drove up. I hadn't risen from my very comfortable curbside seat, and I didn't bother now. The driver burst out of the door and rushed towards me. He was in his mid-thirties, handsome in the manner of a young professional, and still clad in a dress shirt and slacks despite the hour. My lawyer. It was a sad statement on my affairs that he was my first call in such a situation, but I didn't trust many people with my secrets.

"Mis–"

"Not yet," I snapped, holding up one hand as if that could stop his words. "Not here."

He gawked at my raised hand as if not sure what was meant by it. I jerked my arm when he didn't move. "A little help here, if you please, Jack? I'm not as spry as I used to be."

He blinked, then reached down and helped me up, supporting my weight when I leaned into him. We maneuvered me into the passenger seat, and I struggled with the seatbelt until he had returned to the wheel. He steered us back towards the city proper.

"Where would you like me to take you?" he asked, reminding me why I kept him on retainer. It's hard to put a price on pragmatism.

"Home. But I believe your offices would be wiser. I still have an affidavit to give, after all." The Citizen Vigilante laws in California were particularly strict about such things, and I wasn't going to be the one to spoil what little legal protection people like me had left. The corporate-sponsored heroes could afford to be lax; I could not.

Jack fell silent under the pretense of navigating the streets through the dark and the fog. Water beaded on his windshield, not enough to use the wipers, just enough to annoy me into wishing he would.

"Are you sure the emergency roo–"

"I'm sure." My head had cleared while I waited for his arrival. I was in pain, but my confusion was gone, replaced by anger. Jack's fingers tightened on the steering wheel. He frowned and said nothing in the most pointed manner possible. I relented. "I'll have Shimizu look me over after we're done. Promise."

"Are you going to tell me what happened?"

"That is the point of an affidavit, so I'm told."

"That wasn't what I was talking about." He waited. When I didn't offer anything, he tried again. "I take it the bust didn't go well?"

"It didn't go at all. Lao Chan wasn't there. Just some boys with delusions of gangsterhood."

"And you hurt yourself how? Falling off a rooftop? Please tell me we're not going to have to sue the city for not maintaining a safe climbing environment."

That startled a chuckle from me, and pain shot through my chest. I cringed and prayed that no ribs were cracked. Jack spared me another concerned look, but the issue of hospitals had been settled. He returned to glaring at the road.

"Sorry," I said when the pain had receded. I looked out the passenger window. We were heading into North Beach, where Jack lived. He preferred to work out of his home, away from the large downtown firm he worked for. We passed the Pagoda Palace, one of Lao Chan's many holdings, and a guilty reminder that Jack was involved whether I liked it or not. As much as I might want to protect him from the worst, he deserved to know what he was getting into.

"Lao Chan wasn't there, but he knew I was behind it. He left me a message." Jack arched a questioning brow. I sighed. "He blew up my motorcycle."

Jack's knuckles whitened on the steering wheel. "Why? Why just your bike?"

"He didn't have time for more would be my guess. He had to move his operations quickly. Finding my bike must have been chance; he seized it as a warning of opportunity, to let me know I've gone too far."

"You've interfered in his business before. What makes tonight any different?" Jack asked. He pulled in to a tiny garage at the base of a twee little townhouse, indistinguishable from the line of Victorian townhouses that ran the block. The garage door rolled open, the entry so narrow that he came within centimeters of scraping the sides of his car.

I used the excuse of levering myself out of the car to avoid his question. The truth was, I didn't know. It would have been just as easy to detonate the bike after I was on it, or pick me off while I was dazed from the explosion. I'd been left alive, when Lao Chan had no reason to do so. It was too convenient to be luck.

The garage door closed behind us. I let myself into the house and climbed the narrow staircase to his downstairs office area.

Jack had spent a lot of time restoring the Victorian elegance of the interior. The light from several wall sconces warmed the woodwork and the antiques that lined the entry. The beveled glass on the front door at the head of the hallway showed his name in reverse: Jonathan Q Wentworth III, Esq.

Jack's mostly-geriatric clientele preferred this blurred divide between service and friendship. But then, I suppose I wasn't any different. Poor Jack. He was in no way the kind of person who should have to deal with my kind of person.

And yet, he opened the door to his study, ushering me through when pain would have left me leaning against the newel post. I made my way to his most comfortable armchair.

My hat band was a circle of iron pressing into my skull. I tossed the fedora to the floor and released the shadows I used to obscure my face. My head still pounded like it was trapped in a vise. I ran my hands over my head, tearing out pins and ripping off my wig. A thin, nylon cap landed next to my fedora. My red hair remained tightly braided against my scalp, but the pounding in my skull was receding as the worst constriction was removed.

Jack leaned against the closed office door, an irritated frown on his face. He crossed his arms. "All right. We're safe. What the hell is going on, Missy?"

I slumped in the armchair and out of my role as Mr Mystic. "Fuck if I know, Jack."

TWO

Big Trouble

Then

Nobody becomes an adventure hero by accident. For me, it started with a revival showing of *Big Trouble in Little China* at the opening of the rebuilt Pagoda Palace in North Beach. *Big Trouble* ranked as one of my favorite movies of all time, and I roped a crew into going on the strength of my enthusiasm. Who can pass up the chance to see Kurt Russell as Jack Burton? Plus, spunky Kim Cattrall. Yowza!

The reopening of the Pagoda was event enough in its own right – the victory of San Francisco eclecticism over the demands of encroaching gentrification and civil engineering. That didn't stop the new ownerthrees from trying to cash in on Argent age nostalgia. A local acrobatic troop from Chinatown entertained the crowd out front, and the mezzanine gallery boasted a small exhibit on the Chinese experience in San Francisco, courtesy of the Chinese Museum of Culture. It was a flavor display, not a formal curated collection, but the cases still boasted sturdy alloy locks. The mingling audience overshadowed it all. Costumes ran the gamut of characters from the film, including a bevy of girls in cheap cheongsams and green-tinted contact lenses, and at least one sewer monster. The Pagoda looked like an extras casting call for Kung Fu Action Cinema.

My crew – a motley collection of buskers, burners, and struggling artists – hadn't gone to cosplay lengths. We spent our lives standing out, so none of us felt compelled to hog the spotlight tonight. We were here to see the film, revel in the spectacle, and pepper our conversations with our favorite snippets of dialogue. We arrived early enough to secure two rows of seats, and we perched on them in every way except the one they were intended for as we waited for the film to start.

I sat on the back of my chair, my battered Docs planted on the arms, and tossed quips in broken Cantonese with Andrew Han. He wasn't part of my street-performer crew – we studied gung fu at the same *kwoon* in Chinatown – but he was the only other person among us who spoke Cantonese, so I was helping him show off. It worked like gangbusters. One of my contortionist friends, Vess, perched half on Andrew's lap, coaxing him to teach her naughty foreign phrases. What can I say? I make a damn fine wingman.

Andrew's new popularity left me on the social fringe. I shifted on my seatback, gauging the conversations nearby to find one I could nudge into, but I was at the end of the aisle, and my options were limited. A pretty little gothic Lolita sat alone across the aisle from me. Her black-on-black brocade frock coat was a snappy fashion choice, but she looked a little lost and more than a little lonely in the crowd.

She caught me looking and gave me a nervous smile. I couldn't leave her hanging. I smiled back. "Cute outfit."

"You like it? Thanks." The soft twinge of the Midwest in her accent threw me for a moment. Shades of Mike from *Fargo*. The pause turned awkward, and the girl looked away. I'd been performing half my life; putting myself out there had become habit, but I knew what it was like when you didn't quite know how to talk to strangers. I twisted on my seat back to face her.

"And I totally covet your boots."

She propped them on the seat in front of her so we could

both admire them better. "I got them custom. They're my favorites. Really comfortable. They were my gift to myself for finishing my residency."

"You're a doctor?" She didn't seem the stethoscope type, except maybe as part of a steampunk ensemble.

"I'm in public health. I volunteer at the free clinic on Post."

"That's pretty hardcore."

Her boots hit the floor with a soft *thump*, and she straightened back up. "Well, I don't know about that. I just started, so I haven't done much yet. And I don't think they're going to be throwing me any parades back home."

"Where's home?"

"Oskaloosa, Iowa." She grimaced in apology.

Well, that explained the accent. The name sounded familiar, but it took me a moment to place it. "Isn't that Skyrocket's hometown?"

"Hence the lack of parades for me. When a town has a real hero, they don't have much love left for bleeding heart activists like me. Besides, I kill babies. Crack babies. With AIDS. Real heroes don't do that." She spoke like she was quoting – like she was relieved to be kicking that hometown dust from her creepers. She shook her head and offered another smile. "I'm sorry. You're not an Ace fangirl, are you?"

Loaded question, that. I pretended nonchalance and gave her the response I would have given six months past. "Me? Naw. You won't find many around here who are."

"I think that's one of the weirdest things about being on the coast. Back home, people go crazy over Skyrocket. He polls more popular than the local sports teams, except when they're winning. Out here, I've met folks who haven't even heard of him."

I leaned forward, bracing my elbows on my knees. "Do you think they're relevant anymore? The Argent Aces? I mean, they had their place fifty years ago, but things have changed."

She looked down, fingers plucking at the brocade of her coat.

"I don't know. I complained a lot back home, but Oskaloosa wouldn't be the same without Skyrocket. Out here, you just don't need the Aces in the same way."

"Well, it's not like we're completely without heroes in San Francisco," I pointed out. "There's Mistra."

"Who?"

Her question deflated me; I shrugged as if it hadn't. "Some new Ace. She started showing up about six months ago."

"Bully for her, going up against Mr Mystic's legacy like that. Not too smart, picking that name. This city loved that old man. Whoever she is, she should get a new alias and a better PR firm."

I checked my exasperation. She had no notion she'd just rubbed a raw nerve. "But there you go! That's the problem I was talking about. Either the heroes are corporate shills or they're outdated and out of touch. Sure, this city loved Mr Mystic back in the Argent Age. You know why? Cause he supported McCarthyism and Japanese internment camps! He was so gung-ho American that he wanted to kick out anyone who didn't fit his definition."

"I thought he was a Brit."

"Who became a naturalized citizen," I countered. "Converts make the worst fanatics. The only reason this city loves him so much now is because everyone thinks he was a closeted homosexual."

"Well, wasn't he?"

I choked on my denial. The world knew Mr Mystic was Mitchell Masters, and it knew he'd disappeared a few years back. I couldn't say anything without revealing I might know more. I vented my frustration with a huff. "I don't know, and I don't think it matters. It doesn't negate the other things he stood for. Are those the only options? Sell out to almighty dollar or carry on a tainted legacy?"

"I don't think it has to be like that. Take Skyrocket. The old one was a white supremacist. I've seen pictures of him from before World War II, shaking the hand of the local Grand Dragon. But my cousin dated him for a while – the new one, not the old one. I got to meet him a few times, and he was really something. He's changing what Skyrocket stands for. People treat each other better, knowing he's around. He's not just living out some Forties American Dream with the race and sexual politics swept under the table. It's more like he encourages people to embrace what the Forties wanted to be. That's what I think adventure heroes can offer. They're... inspirational. You know, like one person *can* make a difference."

I blinked. I'd spent the past six months polling everyone I knew for their views on adventure heroes and got disillusion across the board, but there was something in her earnestness that echoed my own yearning for a less complex world where what you did mattered. I cocked my head. "Who are you, masked woman, advocate for uninsured patients and underappreciated Aces?"

She laughed and reached a hand across the aisle. "I'm Shimizu. Gail Shimizu, but I go by my last name 'cause I hate my first."

"Missy. And I don't use my last name for pretty much the same reason. Sorry if I got a little intense on you."

"Hey, don't apologize for being passionate. In my line of work, I don't see enough of it. Apathy is worse than any supervillain."

The lights flickered and dimmed.

"And that's my cue to shut-up." I slid down to sit properly in my seat and slanted her a rakish grin. "Are you ready?"

"Ready?" she growled, though there was laughter in it. "I was born ready."

The lights cut out, the screen flashed to life, and I sat back, happy to escape to the easy Good vs Evil of Jack Burton's Chinatown.

•••

Our group scattered after the film. We lost Shimizu to the specter of work, but she gave me her card and made me promise – with a minimum of arm-twisting – to show her around all the best secondhand stores. The rest of my friends split three directions on where to grab food for the film postmortem. I would have joined Andrew and the dim sum crowd, but it was late, and I had other obligations. I waved them farewell as they tromped off in the direction of the Dragon Gate, then I slipped into the alley behind the theater.

The alley was typical of San Francisco: bright, upscale shops not a block away, but here all was dank and urine-scented, with homeless people nesting in stoops. The emergency exit was just as I'd left it – rolled up bit of cardboard keeping the latch from fully catching. I slipped inside and used my pinkie to pry the cardboard free so some keen-eyed employee wouldn't notice it and decide to look for intruders.

There were plenty of shadows backstage for me to manage a quick costume change. If I was determined to continue with this idiotic crusade, I was going to have to figure out a better way to handle the costume issue. Or else not go out with friends on a "work night".

Checking to make sure the house was empty, I shrugged on my backpack and crept up the side aisle. With each step I took, I slid a little more into the shadows. I hated this part and approached it with all the trepidation of a swimmer entering cold water.

No. Not cold water. Slimy, leech-ridden, eel-infested waters. That's what shadow felt like to me: a living thing wrapping about my limbs like it would devour me if it could just get a firm enough grip.

I shuddered at the thought and shook a little too free of the shadows' grip.

"Hello?" came a voice from the projection booth. The silhouette of a head obscured the window. I pressed back deeper into the shadows, pulled them about me like a safe blanket, let them test and taste me, just so long as they obscured me from the curious projectionist.

The head disappeared, and there came the sounds of laughter and ghost noises.

That was fine. Let them think the strange flicker in the shadows was a ghost, if it would make them leave more quickly. I slipped out of the house and into the lobby.

A few more employees gabbed at the concession stand with the last stragglers of the audience. They didn't notice me as I skimmed along the front doors and into the free-standing box-office. Just another shadow of a car passing by outside.

It was the best vantage I could hope for. I couldn't hang about outside. My quarry had been watching the theater for a week and would have a good notion about what belonged and what didn't. With the police scaring the street people into the alleys, I was in the not-belonging category.

I crouched in the box office, searching Washington Square across the way. There. She was just a shadow among the trees, leaning up against a burned out park lamp, but I had an affinity for seeing into shadows. She wore her dark hair pulled back into a thick plait that hung past her waist. Her face was like a mask, all sculpted features and arched dark brows. Somewhere in Mumbai, a Bollywood casting director was crying that this woman had chosen a life of crime instead of superstardom. Her black clothes stood out in a dark blot against the softer shadows of the park. On previous nights she had been settled onto a bench, drinking some steaming liquid from a thermos, but tonight she stood tense and ready. My waiting was over. Whatever she was planning, tonight was the night for it. I settled in and waited for her to move.

A few months ago, if you'd told me I was going to be charging around at night spying on nefarious characters and foiling heists, I would have laughed my ass off. Granted, until now the best I'd managed was to stop a few muggings and one impromptu dog-fight, but none of this had been part of my life plan.

You wouldn't know that to see me now: running around in a costume, using my shadow powers for the greater good. That Shimizu girl had put her finger on it: rail against the Citizen Vigilante laws all you wanted, there was something deeply satisfying about going out and making a difference in the world.

The thrill warmed me against the damp of the night as I prepared for my first encounter with the kind of crime that adventure heroes were meant to fight. Finally, I was doing something worthwhile with my gifts.

The interior theater lights went out, and to my left came the clunk of locks and the murmur of people chatting as the manager and staff closed up for the night. As they disappeared into the BART tunnel down the street, the woman in the park stirred, lifting a pair of binoculars the size of opera glasses. Green lights flashed along the top edge. The binoculars were digital, some kind of night vision. I ducked lower and held still. It meant I couldn't see what she was looking at, but better not to be seen myself. When I poked my head up again, the space by the lamppost was empty. I scanned the trees, the shadows that were pierced by the headlights of each passing car, but the seconds ticked by and I couldn't spot her. With increasing unease, I pressed my cheek to the box office window and scanned the street for any sign of movement; still nothing. Dammit, how had I missed her?

I dithered for a moment before pushing open the box office door and peeking out into the theater.

The lobby was lit by dim lights from the concession stand and the amber glow of street lamps from outside. My thief was nowhere in sight. I knew the theater's layout as well as any visitor, but not knowing what my thief was after meant

I wasn't sure where to go. I hated being so new and clueless. For the thousandth time, I considered ditching my legacy and going back to being a simple street magician who was too busy trying to find a flop to worry about fighting crime.

I didn't want to give up. Couldn't. I could manage this; I just needed help.

I closed my eyes and concentrated again on the Shadow Realms. This time, instead of stepping into shadow, I pulled something out of it. The mass was sticky and unformed, more like tar than taffy, and it clutched at my mind with little claws of darkness, scrabbling for purchase. I whispered a name, shaping the darkness before it sent me into a panic. This was another thing I feared I'd never grow used to – calling creatures from the shadow. The claws released my mind, and the scrabbling that only I could hear was replaced by the real scrape of claws on the lobby carpet.

"Templeton." I sighed with relief. The rat, about the size of a terrier and composed of shadow, snuffled around my feet.

"Hello, Missy," he whispered. His snuffling ranged further afield, along the base of the concession counter and up the paneled sides as high as he could reach on hind legs.

"Hey, Templeton." I kept my voice low. "Would you mind giving me a hand with something?"

"Of course," Templeton said, but curiosity outweighed his ability to focus on a conversation. He continued to snuffle around the concession counter, rounding the corner and going straight for the popcorn machine. "What smells so good?"

"Get back here," I hissed, following him behind the counter. I was about to yank him away from the industrial popper when I heard a sound from the street. Footsteps. Someone was coming.

I crouched low and peered around the corner of the counter, shushing Templeton. Just in time. A new shadow approached the main doors, a dark shape against the frosted glass. The silhouette twisted to look over its shoulder, then bent to fiddle with the latch on the main doors. A few moments later there was a soft *ka-chunk* and the door pushed open. The figure slipped in and tucked two thin slivers of metal into a pouch at her belt. I was impressed. As a magician, I knew my way around a set of lock picks, but I could never have popped a tumbler that fast. She was a pro.

She was also not the woman I'd been watching all week. This one had a solid, athletic build, and her heritage wasn't as easy to peg. She wore her dark hair pulled back in a braid, but a few frizzed curls had pulled free. She walked with a loose and easy stride, daring the world to question why she was breaking into a closed theater at night.

So, my mysterious lurker had an accomplice. And I had two bad guys to deal with instead of just one. I should have called the cops. What the hell did I think I was doing? Who did I think I was?

Ignorant of my presence, much less my minor existential crisis, the woman spared only a brief glance around the lobby before sauntering up the stairs to the mezzanine. Too late to call in anyone now. I left my hiding place and followed her up.

"Hello, Asha." The newcomer's voice breaking the quiet made me flinch. I crept up the last few steps and peeked over the balustrade. The Indian woman stood in front of an open display case from the Chinese exhibition, a slender tube of dark wood held in one hand. The newcomer stood a few paces ahead of me, stance wide as she leveled the muzzle of a small firearm at the other woman.

"Just put the Sutra on the floor and kick it over," said the lady with the gun. So, not conspirators. Competitors.

The Indian woman cocked her head and arched one of those perfect brows. "Really, Abby? Do you really want me to treat such a prize so poorly? I could just as easily walk it over. You have the gun, after all. You're in control." Something in the rolling cadence of her accent made the words mocking.

Gun-Lady – Abby – tightened her grip and firmed her stance. "I'm not letting you anywhere near me. Not after last time."

"Last time… was that Prague?"

"Warsaw."

"Of course. I get those East European cities confused. So cold and comfortless."

"I'm not going to be drawn into your banter, either. You're trapped. There isn't any unalloyed metal up here; I checked. Now hand over the Sutra."

"That leads us to a small conflict. You see, my employers want it badly."

"You'll just have to disappoint them."

"Ah, but I hate to disappoint such – persuasive – gentlemen." Asha took a step to the side. And another.

"The Sutra." *Ka-click* went some part of the gun that I assumed was the hammer. "Now."

Asha stopped sidling at the sound. Her searching glance flicked in my direction. Her shoulders relaxed as she spotted me, and a slow smile lifted one corner of her mouth.

"I am sorry, but I can't bring myself to treat such a treasure so poorly. Why not have your little friend come forward to take it."

"My wha–?" Abby might not have fallen for the ploy, but I jerked back in surprise at being pulled into the confrontation. Abby caught my movement at the edge of her vision and turned, the gun's muzzle training on me. Reacting on instinct to the threat of that ugly shape, I vaulted the balustrade. I ducked under her guard and came up between her outstretched arms, thrusting them open with the momentum of rising. The gun flew out of her grasp, hitting the wall behind me and tumbling down the stairs in a series of thunks.

Abby grabbed for me. I wrapped my arms around hers. She was bigger and stronger than me, but she was more the barroom brawling type. We ended up face-to-face, grappling for the upper hand.

"A ninja? Is that what you're supposed to be?" Abby went for an arm-lock, and then another when I relaxed and flowed through her first attempt.

"I'm Mistra, and I'm not letting either of you walk off with that... uh... scroll case thingy."

"Kid, back down. You have no idea what you've gotten into."

Aikido wasn't my main form, but Abby seemed a lot less scary without her gun. I could redirect her attempted holds all night. "Looks pretty clear to me: a couple of thieves squabbling over a bit of shiny."

The shadows behind me shifted. Not toward me. Away. Asha was using our distraction to sneak off.

"Templeton, stop her!"

Claws scrabbled on carpet, followed by a piercing shriek. Abby looked up to see what had frightened the other woman. I swept her legs out from under her, sending her down with a shove to the sternum, then vaulted back over the balustrade to the main staircase below. Asha cowered against the banister, the scroll case clutched to her chest.

"Just hand it over, lady, and no one gets hurt," I said in my best threaten-the-villain voice. It needed some work. Templeton advanced a pace, which was much more effective. I'd have to ask him how he perfected that rabid look. Shadow foam dripped from his muzzle.

"Keep your *asura* away from me," Asha said, a hitch of terror in her voice. With one hand, she reached for, missed, then grabbed the banister. She clutched it to her back, as if the anchor could somehow save her from our combined threat.

"Hand it over, and I'll call him off." I held out my hand and tried to look like the more reasonable and comforting of her two options.

She backed up another step. Her hand found the copper

fixture that held the banister to the wall. Her posture relaxed. She twirled the scroll case in her hand. "I don't think I will."

"No! Don't let her escape!" Abby dove down the stairs for her fallen gun. Asha rippled as though she were reflected through a shimmer of desert heat, and her form blurred into cobalt blue smoke. A gun fired, deafening in the confines of the theater. The wall behind where Asha had stood exploded in a spray of plaster chips. The pillar of smoke had already dissipated, sucked into the copper fixture. I thought I saw a reflection of Asha's laughing face reversed in the curve of the copper, but then she was gone.

Something twinged in my left shoulder. Thinking one of the plaster chips had nicked me, I lifted a hand to it. It came away covered in blood. A lot of blood. I sat down.

Templeton nuzzled my hip. "Missy, are you all right? You're leaking." I tried to answer, but I was having difficulty staying upright.

"Oh my god." A wad of fabric was pressed to my shoulder. "Kid? Kid, speak to me."

"Huh?" I looked at her. The lines of her features were sharp, each stroke clean and bold. She was too strong for pretty. Handsome. Striking. Those were the right words. She looked like an amazon – like an Ace.

"I messed up, didn't I?" I asked her, looking at the blood covering my hand so I wouldn't have to face her.

"You're going into shock. What's your name?"

I shook my head, or tried to. It might have been more of a wobble.

"Your name, kid. Name," she insisted.

"Can't," I managed. "Secret identity."

"Oh, for the love of – you! Rat-thing. Your mistress has been hurt. I need to get her help. Can you tell me her name, where she lives, anything?"

"Missy isn't my mistress; she's my friend. I serve the Conclave of Shadow."

Their exchange helped to bring me back a bit. I'd been hurt, she said. I'd been–

"You shot me." I'd been shot. I opened and closed my hand. The blood was bright red. Sticky. And there seemed to be a lot of it.

Like an anvil in a Wile E Coyote cartoon, the pain came crashing down on me. A high whine lodged in the back of my throat, a sound that scared me even more than the blood because I couldn't seem to staunch it.

Abby pressed her makeshift compress harder, which didn't help the pain or the keening. "I just grazed... the bullet must have... Shit. Can you get up? I need to get you to a hospital."

That broke through. I swallowed the whine and shook my head. "No. No hospitals."

"Look, kid. Uh, Missy." She grimaced; I sympathized. My name didn't make me sound any older. "You're hurt. You're losing blood, and I'm not that kind of doctor. I respect you trying to do the whole Argent Ace thing, but–"

"No hospitals. No insurance." I fumbled for my backpack and handed her a card, getting blood all over both. "Free clinic. Twenty-four hour trauma clinic. On Post." A field of cotton had sprouted inside my head. It clogged my ears, mouth, and thought processes, but it seemed to be absorbing the pain.

"Well, at least it's close." She hefted me up. Templeton pressed against my knees, which did nothing for my balance.

"Templeton." My voice sounded faint and far away. I cleared my throat. "Go home. I'll be fine. Go home."

With a hangdog expression, he snuffled once more at the ground, then stepped into the shadows of the stairwell and was gone.

"Right. Let's get you to this clinic. I hope they can handle walk-in bullet wounds."

I hoped so too. Poor Shimizu. This would teach her to strike up a conversation with a complete stranger.

There's nothing like medical-grade painkillers to give you vivid dreams.

I knew my grandfather was Mr Mystic, but he'd retired by the time I came along. The tales of his hero days were no more or less real than the ones he read to me about Narnia or Prydain, and I would play at being an Argent Ace the same way I would play at being Inigo Montoya or Jack Burton.

I was wearing my grandfather's hat, which meant I was either Mr Mystic or Indiana Jones. Given the maze of couch cushions I was crawling through and the ancient pearl necklace dangling from my belt, my money was on Indy.

A monster of shadow leapt out at me and I ran, with it fast on my heels, jumping from cushion to cushion as the floor turned to lava, then to a river full of ice floes, then to the only solid footholds in an avalanche. I made the final, impossible leap to the cushion that marked the peak of the mountain. The shadow wasn't as agile. It tumbled into a bottomless abyss, caterwauling all the way down. My grandfather dragged my dangling body to safety, taking my hat and settling it on his head.

"Where are we going?" I asked.

"I thought you were leading this expedition."

"You have the hat."

"Then it must be bedtime." He tucked me in, and I didn't complain. Bedtime was story time.

"Tell me about the dragon maiden," I begged, rubbing the strand of pearls along my lips. I loved their smoothness, how they warmed to my touch and gleamed like Lady Amalthea's star.

"Wouldn't you rather hear about how your grandmother and I fell in love?" he asked. That was the story he preferred to tell.

I shook my head. "No. That's boring 'cause it really happened. I want to hear the dragon story."

"Are you saying that one is more interesting because it didn't happen?"

"Well, duh," I countered with all the rhetorical skill at my disposal.

"What if I said it was real, Miss Missy? What then?"

"Don't be silly. Dragons don't exist. Now tell the story and tell it right."

"As you wish," he said. "Once upon a time, a young and foolish man journeyed to the roof of the world because he wanted to be a hero. He climbed all day and all night. For three days he climbed, and on the third evening, near collapsing from the cold, he came to the gates of Shambhala."

We sat on my bed as it floated above the clouds, watching a younger version of my grandfather climbing to the roof of the world. "That's heaven, right?"

"Heaven has many names. Now, the dragons who lived there were upset by his presumption. They only allowed him to find the gates so that they might send him on his way."

"Except for Lung Huang, right?" I knew this story so well, it was almost like I was telling it to myself.

"Except for Lung Huang. She admired the young man, and she agreed to train him against the wishes of her siblings. She left heaven and took her champion to a remote valley, knowing that she would never be allowed to return."

"Poor Lung Huang. She gave up everything..."

The story scattered again, like a pearl necklace breaking. An older and more experienced Mitchell Masters received a farewell gift of a string of pearls from his dragon-lover at the same time that a young and brash Mitchell Masters clashed with his teacher, fighting his attraction. My grandmother beamed out from a wedding photo wearing the same pearls, while beside her my grandfather kissed a tall, slender girl whose dark hair coiled around them both like a living thing.

The beads of the story rolled every which way. I chased them across my bed, using my grandfather's hat to keep them from spilling over the edges and into the abyss. They clacked against each other in the hat, all out of order like my grandfather's story. What came after was reinscribed and gave new meaning to what came before – an oral palimpsest. How many times had I heard him tell that story but never heard the truth in it?

"Grandfather, what's happening?" I curled up in the center of the bed, my eyes shut tight. I floated on a sea of shadow, waves rising up to grab at me. Something awful was being held at bay by the light shining off the pearls, and all I had to guide me was the story.

"Shh. It's all right. It's only magic." He reached for me, and I thought he was going to pull a quarter from my ear, an old trick that never failed to charm me. Instead, he pulled a never-ending crimson scarf from my shoulder. He pulled and pulled until I feared I'd go with it.

"Grandfather, it hurts," I whimpered.

"It's all right, Missy. I've nearly got all of it."

"Kid? Hey, Missy?"

I groaned as light blossomed behind my eyelids, illuminating my darkened inner landscape to a pre-dawn umber. I cracked one lid at the sensory intrusion.

"Hey." A woman bleared into view. I knew that strong-featured face. I blinked open both eyes, hoping that would help my recollection. She didn't look all that pleased to see me.

"Abby?" I guessed.

"That's right."

I broke away from the intensity of her gaze. I've never dealt well with people being angry at me.

Somebody had tucked me in nice and snug under a wine-purple velvet duvet. The bed sported a high canopy of black netting, and the rest of the room was decorated in a mixture of arsenic and old lace.

"Not to sound cliché, but where am I?"

"My apartment," said a voice from the doorway. Shimizu stood there, wearing a set of scrubs with little black and blue anime cats scampering over them.

"Cool scrubs," was all I could think to say.

"Thanks. My mom makes them for me."

"Cool mom," I murmured, distracted by my attempts to figure out what was going on. I felt like I should know, but the old brain engine wasn't firing on all cylinders. "Why am I here?"

Abby crossed her arms, frowning at me like this was all my fault. "You caught a stray round in the shoulder. The bullet went through the meat, but there was a lot of debris in there. Shimizu here cleaned you out and patched you up."

"I was worried there might be lead in the paint," Shimizu explained with a grimace. "That theater is so old, and they're not always careful about that kind of thing when they renovate."

It took a moment to figure out what they were talking about. I tensed as I remembered, but I only felt the slightest twinge from my shoulder.

"I feel OK," I said in wonder. I risked flexing my shoulder and found only a distant, pervasive ache. "Shouldn't it hurt more?"

Shimizu grinned. "Oh, it will. Tomorrow."

Abby was still glaring, her lips set into a flat line. "We didn't want to leave you at the clinic, and we didn't know where you lived, so we brought you here." Her eyes narrowed as she leaned forward. "So, does Mr Mystic know that you're stealing his shtick?"

I darted a warning glance in Shimizu's direction. She just grinned and plopped down on the end of the bed. "You're Mistra. Abby told me, but I think I might have figured it out on my own if she hadn't. The shadows were getting pretty hinky while I was cleaning your wound."

"I had to beat several of them down," Abby added. She was not smiling.

I ducked my head. "I'm still having some control issues."

"You're having a few more issues than that." Abby slammed both hands down on the bed, trapping me. "What the hell were you thinking, butting into my business? Because of you, Asha got away, the Sutra is gone, and I have to get Argent's legal department to step in and soothe things with the local blues."

"So... you *are* an Ace."

"Of course I am. What did you think I was?"

"I thought you were one of the bad guys. I saw you break into the theater."

Abby's mouth worked. There might even have been a throbbing vein or two. Shimizu's eyes darted back and forth between us, but she kept silent.

"Look, kid–"

"Missy," I corrected. Yes, I'd fucked up, but I didn't deserve to be talked down to like an erring child.

"*Kid.*" She frowned. "You've obviously got some unusual talents, and I respect that you want to use them for the greater good, but being an Ace is about more than just putting on a fancy outfit and fighting crime. It requires care and planning and having a fucking clue about what you're doing. Most folks don't get into this gig unless they have either serious psychological issues or a deep-seated vendetta."

"Which is it for you?" I asked.

"The vendetta. And you just let my nemesis get away, so I'd be more careful about pissing me off, if I were you."

I nodded.

"Now, I'll have legal fix things without bringing you into it. In return I want you to consider two pieces of advice. First, get out now. You don't have what it takes to be an Ace, and believe me, you don't want to have it. You got me?"

I nodded again, but that wasn't advice I intended to take. "And the second?" I asked.

Abby pushed off the bed, huffing in exasperation. I guess my intentions were pretty transparent. "Get your own shtick. Mystic's part of the old guard, but I met him a few times before he retired. He comes across as a dapper British gentleman, but that old Limey can be a mean fucking bastard. You do *not* want him to come out of hiding to beat you down." She shouldered a small brown satchel. Nodding once to Shimizu, she strode out of the room. Shimizu and I both flinched as the front door slammed.

"I think I pissed her off." I said into the silence.

Shimizu burst out laughing. "You think?"

Three days later found me dragging my feet as I approached a row of restored Victorian townhouses in North Beach. Shimizu had insisted that I stay so she could make sure I didn't drop dead of lead poisoning. I think she also may have been a bit lonely. I was OK with that. The three day convalescence turned into an extended slumber party, which helped my shaken confidence.

I knew what I needed to do. Now, I just needed to convince Jack. He was the only person who knew about my connection to Mr Mystic, and as executor of my grandfather's estate, he held the purse strings.

The door opened before I could even knock. Not an auspicious beginning.

"Where the hell have you been?" Jack had shucked his coat and tie – or perhaps he never wore them when working from home. The sleeves of his shirt were rolled up. He crossed his arms and leaned against the jamb, still glaring. He couldn't fool me. He'd been worried. His eyes flicked over the sling that kept my arm pinned to my side, and the glare softened.

"Dammit Missy, why didn't you call?"

I had a host of excuses, but the truth was that I hadn't been accountable to anyone but myself for ages. Calling him hadn't even occurred to me – not an answer I could give.

"I'm sorry?" I offered, knowing it wasn't enough.

He sighed, and his jaw clenched and unclenched, then he uncrossed his arms and stood aside to usher me in.

"I was about to have dinner. Mac'n'cheese. There's enough for you if you want." Food was Jack's main form of emotional expression. Mac'n'cheese. Comfort food. He *had* been worried.

"You don't strike me as the mac'n'cheese sort." I followed him back to the kitchen, a cheery room with shining porcelain fixtures from the early part of the twentieth century. Yellow daisies dotted the white curtains over the sink. Jack stood in front of a retro white stove, scooping something out of corning ware. It did not look like any mac'n'cheese I'd ever seen. I sat at a little round table. Jack glared at me over his shoulder.

"Don't think I'm letting you off the hook just because I'm feeding you. What happened to you? Last I knew, you were staking out the theater. What happened to your arm?"

Telling him I'd been shot would derail all other conversation topics, and I'd come with an agenda. "Things didn't go as planned," I said. "I pulled a muscle and got in the way of the good guys."

Jack set a plate in front of me. There was macaroni, and there was cheese, but that's where the resemblance to the familiar boxed variety ended. Jack's mac'n'cheese flowed out in a thick, creamy mass from underneath a cracked brown crust. The cheese was the color of fresh cream, with chunks of tomato and some thinly-sliced pinkish meat that I couldn't identify.

"Is this bacon?" I prodded at it with my fork.

"Prosciutto," he said as he sat across from me. At my look, he shrugged. "What?"

"This is not mac'n'cheese. This is some frou-frou dish masquerading as mac'n'cheese."

"It is so mac'n'cheese."

"Really? What kind of cheese did you use?"

"Look, just because the cheese wasn't toxic orange and from a tin-lined pack doesn't mean it isn't mac'n'cheese."

"Nice evasion," I said. "What kind?"

"Gorgonzola and gruyere with crème fraiche." He refused to meet my eyes.

"Aha! I thought so!" I crowed. I took a triumphant bite, and damn if it wasn't the best mac'n'cheese I'd ever tasted.

"Nice evasion," Jack parroted while I was lost in cheesy bliss. "So, mind telling me the real reason you've shown up three days late with your arm in a sling?"

"I'm not cut out for this, Jack."

"Glory, hallelujah! The girl finally speaks some sense."

I ignored him. He'd been trying to get me to stop almost from the moment he found me. "I thought having super powers and being Mr Mystic's granddaughter would be enough, you know? That the Argent Ace legacy was in my blood or something. But it's not. I realize that now."

"No shame in walking away from this, Missy. Most people wouldn't even have tried in the first place. It's too dangerous. Your grandfather knew what he was doing. You don't. Maybe he would have trained you if he'd stuck around, but..." Jack trailed off. Mitchell's abandonment was a sore point with me, one we'd wordlessly agreed to avoid. Jack was convinced my grandfather had his reasons for leaving. I couldn't imagine a reason good enough for what I'd had to go through after he'd gone.

"You're right," I said into the awkward silence. I shook off the glums, conviction and volume returning as I spoke. "He did have training, and he didn't get it by sitting around on his ass or jumping straight into the thick of things."

It was Jack's turn to look wary. "I'm not going to like wherever this is heading, am I?"

No, he wouldn't. But a girl's gotta do what a girl's gotta do.

"I'm gonna need money. And a passport. Oh, and my grandmother's pearls. They're still in the safety deposit box, right? I'll definitely need those." I straightened my shoulders, winced at the sharp twinge the movement caused. "I'm going to China."

THREE

The Great Wall

Now

Tsung Investment Capital's main offices were on the 36th floor of the Transamerica Pyramid in the heart of San Francisco's financial district. The reception area was all sleek lines, ebony moldings, and walls of dove gray with seating in leather-and-chrome. The receptionist wore the deceptive mien of a pretty girl in the bookish vein: dark-rimmed glasses and retro-librarian cardigan. It was a front. Cerberus guarding Hades didn't do his job half so well.

"I am sorry, Mr Masters, but Mr Tsung has only just returned from Shanghai and isn't available to see new clients today," she said, the steel beginning to show through the velvet of her voice. It was possible that I was being a level of pushy she hadn't been trained to deal with.

"I will be happy to wait as long as it takes. Your chairs are exceedingly comfortable. Could I trouble you for another cup of tea?" I wondered if she'd plied me with tea so Tsung could slip out while I was in the restroom. But I'd been plied by greater masters than her. I was betting that she'd break before I did. I'd seen her buzz enough people in at this point that I could probably figure out the mechanism if she would just abandon her post.

She smiled at me, a very pointed sort of smile that would earn her a trip to the dentist if she kept it up. Before she could think of another polite way to tell me to piss off, another woman who could have been her older sister emerged through the guarded doorway.

"Mr Masters? I apologize for your wait. Mr Tsung will see you now. May I take your coat and hat?"

Only years of cultivating an unflappable mien kept my jaw from dropping. I hadn't really expected anyone to cave. My stubbornness grew from my fury at the verdict on my motorcycle: unsalvageable. David Tsung wasn't much of a target, but he was the only one I had.

I touched the brim of my hat. The receptionist had offered the same, and rationally I knew it was only good manners, but it felt for all the world like they were offering to strip me of my armor before a duel. My hat in particular always left me in a quandary. Etiquette dictated that I remove it indoors, but I relied on the shadow it cast – augmented by my own powers – to conceal my face.

"No, I'll keep them, thank you."

"Of course. Can I get you something to drink? Tea? Water?" More tea. Interesting that she didn't offer coffee, but I presumed it was due to the international nature of the business. In most parts of the world, tea was the drink of the civilized palate.

"Nothing for me, but thank you all the same."

We arrived at a conference room, one windowed wall exposing the interior to the view of anyone passing: an aquarium for the sharks of the business world. The assistant opened the door and ushered me through. The shark inside stood to greet me.

"Mitchell Masters? David Tsung. It's an honor to meet you, sir."

David Tsung was Lao Chan's new *Cho Hai*, the public face of the Shadow Dragons in San Francisco. Any official business went through him, and most unofficial business as well. As faces went, it was a good one. Mid-thirties, fit and handsome, Brooks Brothers suit, an MBA from Wharton, and regular mentions in all the major periodicals frequented by the Wall Street set. He wasn't just the face of the Triad. His was the face of international business in the twenty-first century.

I shook his hand, taken aback by the enthusiasm of his greeting, and then sat at his gesture. Compounded with his assistant's cordial treatment, I was starting to wonder if they knew my reason for being here.

Apparently not. "It's wise of you to take advantage of the current downturn to diversify your assets. I've taken the liberty of running a basic analysis of your holdings on public record."

He pushed a sleek bound folder across to me. I laid my hands on it, blinking down at the little logo in the corner: the silhouette of a turned shoulder and tilted-down fedora in profile. It looked too tailored to be stock art; had they made it just for me?

If they had, it meant that newly-returned or not, David Tsung knew I'd be seeking him out, and he'd had enough time to put such a portfolio together. The information in the binder was either a lure or a warning. Be our ally, and we can make you rich; go against us, and we can destroy you.

I pushed the binder back towards my host.

"I apologize for the misunderstanding, Mr Tsung. I'm not here to discuss my investments, but rather to arrange a meeting with the head of your board of directors. I have urgent business with Lao Chan."

"I am sorry, Mr Masters. Truly sorry. Mr Chan is in the midst of some important negotiations and won't be available until they are completed. It may take several days. I hope no insult is taken."

Of course he would hope that. It was possible he didn't know about my motorcycle or the Dogpatch bust. Possible he'd been shunted off to Shanghai for that very reason. A *Cho Hai* wouldn't get his hands dirty with a Triad's illegal work, but he was vital for maintaining face. I'd assumed Mr Tsung had risen to such a prominent position at such a young age because he was being groomed to take over, but did that mean he was in the loop, or deliberately kept out of it?

"No insult, of course," I assured, trying to read beyond Tsung's apologetic smile. "But Mr Chan did send me a clear message that we had urgent business."

I couldn't come right out and accuse Tsung's boss of attacking me. That would be rude. Lao Chan had done me the favor of not killing me, so by his reckoning, I should now be in his debt. I'd lived in China for years, and I still struggled with all the nuances of *guanxi*.

David Tsung registered polite confusion at my claim. "I am surprised that he would take the time away from his current business to do so. Do you have a copy of this message?"

No, you smug bastard. Because my vintage Triumph is a burned, twisted husk in some junkyard now. But I didn't say that.

"I'm afraid I neglected to bring it with me," I replied.

Tsung's confusion turned troubled but sympathetic. He was so good at this that I wondered if his undergrad degree might be in theater. "You understand my quandary. I'm certain that if he has business with you, he will be in contact once this current matter is seen to. I'd advise you to be patient."

I rose. Touched the brim of my fedora. Stonewalling was stonewalling, no matter how politely it was phrased. "I suppose I have no choice, then. Please inform him that I await his convenience."

We shook hands, said our polite goodbyes, and the receptionist was kind enough to help an old man all the way down the elevator and out the lobby doors. There would be no lingering in the hopes of trailing her boss to some sort of clandestine meeting. And even if I could, stalking isn't condoned by the vigilante laws. Not even a connection with Argent could get me out of that trouble.

But like hell was I going to be patient. If Lao Chan had business going on that was more important than his vengeance against me for the Dogpatch incident, I wasn't going to wait until he was ready to deal with me. I'd just have to get to him some other way.

"What am I doing wrong?" I wailed. I usually had my solo training sessions with Johnny Cho on Sunday mornings, but Tsung's stonewalling had me so frustrated that I'd asked for a fit-in after his Lil'Ninja class. He was being extra hard on me for interrupting his Saturday afternoon.

"You're dropping your shoulder."

"No, I know that. I mean, what am I – ooof!" The world spun cockeyed. I sailed through the air and landed hard on the mat – hard enough that I had to struggle for breath for several moments.

A face swam into view as I stared up at the roof of the studio, cocky grin under a thatch of spiky bleached hair threaded with streaks of azure blue. The bleached part was damaged and yellow as straw. I saw kids like him slumping around the manga shops all the time, but unlike most guys who tried to rock the Street Fighter aesthetic, Johnny Cho had the power to back it up.

Johnny was a guardian of Chinatown. Well, San Francisco's Chinatown. All Chinatowns had guardians. It was a legacy inheritance thing, though that didn't explain how a Korean guy got the gig.

Johnny hadn't aged a day in all the time I'd known him, and a bit of asking around revealed that it might have been a lot longer than that. I sometimes wondered just how much of Chinatown's history Johnny had seen. Sure, he looked like a cosplayer's wet dream these days, but he wore the look, it didn't wear him. I could just as easily see him in a *changshan* and a coolie hat. Not the braided queue, though. Johnny was a rebel to the bone.

He offered me a hand up. I took it, knowing it might be another trap.

It was. He yanked me off-center, but I was ready for it. I flowed with the momentum, faking a stumble. Johnny kicked out to give my ass a nudge – he subscribed to the school that said a little friendly humiliation was a necessary part of training. I spun about, catching his foot with my free hand and sweeping his supporting leg from under him. I threw his foot up, and he tumbled back. Almost as quickly, he kipped up to his feet, grinning.

"That's better." He nodded his approval of my renewed caution. "Even if I did let you have that one."

"I'm distracted. Help me find Lao Chan, and I'll do better." We circled each other. It was my turn to lead-in, but I was more interested in talking than in sparring.

He shook his head, clicking his tongue. "After what Mr Mystic pulled in the Dogpatch? You're *laowai*, and you bring *laowai* into our business. I'm not going to help you with that."

"Our business?"

"Chinatown."

"Come off it. You don't like the Shadow Dragons any more than I do. They're shipping girls, Johnny. They blew up my bike."

"I'm taking care of the trafficking. Sucks about your motorcycle, though."

All the sympathy of someone who could teleport most anyplace he wanted to go. I grounded my stance, dug in my feet, centered my hips. "I'll make you a deal. I down you for real, you help me find a solid lead."

It was wishful thinking, me being able to take him down, but maybe having that carrot to strive for would improve my game.

Johnny's brows rose, but he nodded. "Sure. You down me before I down you."

"Now, wait a–" I didn't have time to protest. He rushed me, shoulder catching me mid-thigh. He flipped me into a fireman's carry as he fell back, so that I'd land beneath him.

I hit the mat with a double *oof*, one for the mat, and one for him as he landed atop me. I was breathless for the second time in as many minutes.

Johnny rolled off me, propping up on his elbows to wait while I caught my breath.

"No fair! What was that? I wasn't even ready," I complained.

"It's called a teaching moment. The world doesn't wait for you to be ready, and it doesn't play by your rules." He flicked my nose. "You need to review your Sun-Tzu. You aren't ready to tackle Lao Chan. You're definitely not ready for his boss to take notice of you. Don't take the fight to them until you're certain of your win."

He stood and offered me his hand again. I didn't take it. I kipped up on my own, glaring. I grabbed a towel, wiping sweat off my face, then limped toward the edge of the mat. I still had a few aches from the motorcycle incident. I *had* been certain. That bust should have gone like clockwork, which meant there was an unknown that hadn't been accounted for. And it gnawed at me.

Johnny frowned. "We're not done."

"I am. I'm distracted by this thing with Lao Chan, and having you condescend to me isn't helping." I flumped to the floor and into a series of cool-down stretches.

Johnny sat opposite me in lotus, no longer the cocky street-punk that I could mouth back to. This was my *sifu*.

"I said I was dealing with the trafficking thing. Come to our usual session tomorrow and I'll see what I can turn up about where you miscalculated."

I looked up at him sideways from under one arm as I leaned

over to touch my toes. "Take me with you?"

"No." He stood and snapped his towel at me. "And if you try to follow me, I'll just hop around Chinatown until I lose you."

I beamed at his departing back. My *sifu* was a good *sifu*.

"Need a refill on potstickers and *cheong fun*," I called as I rolled an empty dim sum trolley back into the kitchen and checked the next one to make sure it was fresh. Refilling carts was Andrew's job. He was Doris's eldest and heir to her dim sum empire. He took cart management very seriously.

Johnny hadn't shown for our Sunday morning session, which would have worried me more if he weren't the biggest stick in Chinatown. Either he was avoiding me, or he was still busy "dealing" with the trafficking issue. Either way, all I could do was wait at the bottom of the *kwoon* stairs.

Then Doris caught me waiting, and before I knew it I'd been roped into filling in for her daughters and nieces, who were off at some kind of Girl Scout Jamboree thing.

Because the Pearl was family-owned, with Doris as chef and consigliore, it didn't operate in the traditional fashion. There were no standard waitstaff, no outsiders coming in to rent carts, hoping to pocket the difference between what they paid and what they pushed. Instead, the kids of the extended family drew their spending money from what they could earn during the weekend rush. At least a dozen child labor laws were being broken, but nobody was going to mess up a good thing by reporting it.

Especially not the kids. Cart jockeying among them was twice as cutthroat as in a normal dim sum setup.

"That one's mine," said KC, a fourteen year old beanpole with a crooked grin. He hip-checked me into the wall and made off with my cart.

"Ow?" I complained, rubbing my side. Andrew laughed. At me.

"You've lost your edge, Missy. Few years ago, you'd have flipped him over your shoulder for that cart."

"What was in it?"

"Shrimp *siu mai*, spare ribs, and *bao*."

Some of the bestsellers. Of course. Cart like that would never come back with leftovers.

I shrugged. "Let him have it. Don't really need the money anymore. Just give me the phoenix talons cart." The Pearl catered to the tourist crowd on the weekends, none of whom found chicken feet appealing, but Doris was a purist, so she kept making them.

Andrew shook his head and nudged another cart toward me. "Completely lost your edge."

I wheeled out my cart. Andrew had taken pity on me and given me a more palatable dessert selection. I rolled from table to table, inured to the looks of surprise I got when the customers realized I was as white as they were. Tourists.

My cart sold before I'd finished two circuits of the room. It was getting late enough that the crowd had thinned, and most of the folks left were lingering over tea and dessert.

KC must have decided that more work was a waste of his valuable time, too. He leaned over the hostess desk to chat up Lin, one of the few employees who wasn't a member of the extended family. She was another one of Doris's foundlings, like me. Nobody spoke about Lin's story, which right away said it was a bad one. But three years under Doris Han's rough coddling had done a lot to chase the haunted look from Lin's eyes.

Like now, for example. She looked more bemused than intimidated as KC yammered at her. She had ten years on him, but that didn't stop the boy from trying.

I was about to leave him to his crash-and-burn – Lin could handle herself – when I caught a snippet of conversation that didn't sound like flirting at all.

"What did you say?" I asked, keeping my voice down and checking to make sure no customers were nearby.

KC preened at being the focus of attention from *two* pretty girls. He'd kill me if he realized I just wanted to ruffle his hair for being so adorable.

"Those guys at the table in the corner. They're 49s."

"They're football fans?" Lin asked. KC and I both shot her incredulous looks. How had she worked here for three years without picking up the slang?

"49s are Hung Society. Triad," I clarified when she still looked confused. "Mostly the low-level bully-boy types. General membership."

KC jumped on the chance to impress Lin with his extensive knowledge. "Yeah. See, they have all these numerological codes for the ranks. Like the *Shan Chu*, that's the dude in charge, he's–"

"You don't know they're 49s," I interrupted. Yeah, it was a cock-block. I didn't care. This was too important. Lin was too old for him, anyways.

"I saw em flashing signs when their friends showed up. And then again when this other guy came and gave them all red business cards." He leaned over a whispered in the loudest possible aside to Lin, "That means there's a meeting."

"Or coupons for a massage. Hawkers sneak in here all the time," I said. Lin nodded at this more likely explanation. After all, she was the one who had to try and keep the hawkers out.

I was a complete ass for downplaying what KC had seen, but I'd have to make it up to him later. The party in the corner was breaking up. I had to extricate. Quick. I pushed my cart back to the kitchen and told Andrew – by virtue of taking off my red server's apron – that I was done for the day. I swerved past Doris to give her a hug on my way out of the kitchen.

"Johnny back?" she asked, assuming that was the reason for my rush. With the lunch crowd thinning, she didn't need my labor anymore.

"Yeah," I said, not wanting to waste time explaining. Johnny would be back when he got back. Those guys, if they really were four-nines, were already on the move.

Out the side door, I sprinted down the alleyway. No time to become Mr Mystic. I'd have to trail them as I was.

I rounded the corner to the main street just as the group of young men – four of them – were passing. I skidded to a halt to avoid running right into them, earning several glares from the forty-nines and not a few grumbles from the people behind me.

"Sorry! Sorry." I held up my hands and smiled, trying to look innocuous. The young men didn't care. They continued on their way, laughing in Cantonese about the stupid *laowai* tourist with no tits.

I frowned, cheeks hot. Feminine pride warred with practicality. At least they weren't suspicious of me?

I followed them at a more sedate pace, promising myself that if the afternoon ended in a fight, I was going to whup each of their asses.

The afternoon passed in a haze of boring. The guys stopped in several emporiums, but they were window shopping, not extorting. They tried on coolie hats, played with fans, ogled girls. I couldn't get close enough to make out what they were saying without fear of them recognizing me as the *laowai* from earlier, but they code-switched freely between English and Cantonese. Local boys, then. Immigrants only spoke English when they had to.

They meandered along until they reached the narrow entry of a massage parlor – the Garden of Willows. They paused at the door, looking around. I hid behind a street pole covered in flyers: complimentary facial with massage, housecleaning and gardening, a "have-you-seen-me" poster with a pale chow-chow being ridden by a chubby toddler. I studied the missing dog until the boys went in. Then I made myself feel better by banging my head against a nearby doorway. I'd wasted my entire afternoon; that's what I got for listening to the claims of a fourteen-year-old boy who was trying to impress a girl.

I was *not* going to wait around for my marks to have their "happy ending".

I turned to go and spied David Tsung walking down the street toward me. I ducked back into a shop doorway, waving off the woman who perked up and started trying to sell me a jade... something. I had no idea what, and I didn't care.

Tsung passed within a few feet of me, eyes sliding right past as he idly perused the shopfront windows. Of course he wouldn't know me. Why would he connect the gothy redhead lurking in the doorway of a jewelry shop with Mitchell Masters? I breathed a sigh of relief, then caught my breath almost as quickly.

David Tsung entered the Garden of Willows.

I considered and tossed out several plans for how to infiltrate the massage parlor myself, from calling down a police bust – I had no cause – to sneaking in Charlie's Angels-style using a sexy *cheongsam* and my dazzling beauty. Problem was, I didn't have the dress, and I doubted I had enough of the beauty. I'm no slouch, but I ain't no Cameron Diaz.

I settled on going round back and seeing what the rear façade had to offer. Somebody had left an upper-story window cracked, and it was easy enough to scale the fire escape and slip through.

Which left me in a narrow closet that had been repurposed as a bedroom, if the mattress wedged into the space was any indication. I picked my way across the rumpled bedding and opened the door a crack, peeking out.

The corridor was bare except for a line of narrow wood doors painted the same institutional green as the walls and a few faded pictures. Given the parlor downstairs, I decided it might be better not to speculate who these rooms were for. I could come back and gather enough evidence to warrant a bust. Places like this were the hydra's heads. I was after the heart.

At the front of the building, the hall opened up into a more opulent lobby. The wood floors were polished and not scarred, the walls painted scarlet and the moldings gilded. A black gate guarded an elevator shaft. Down or up? I opted for the stairs and went down.

I expected only one level to the ground floor. It's San Francisco. Nobody sane does basements here. But the stairwell boasted a heavy fire door opposite the street exit. I scanned the frame; it wasn't alarmed. A noise above that sounded like a door opening decided me. I pulled open the fire door, revealing an unlit staircase descending into darkness.

It is a sad statement on my life that on seeing that, I sighed with relief. Most people fear dark places. I find them comforting.

I slipped into the shadows, my shoulders relaxing at the extra cover. Straddling the divide between worlds isn't true invisibility. People can still bump into me, and bright lights will chase the shadows away and leave me standing there with a stupid look on my face. Anyone feeling particularly vicious can mow me down with a spray of gunfire. Slower weapons are less of an issue; they give me enough time to get out of the way or cross into the Shadow Realms.

But I have a healthy respect – read: fear – of the Shadow Realms, and I wouldn't risk crossing over in this place. If this were some sort of Triad stronghold – and why else would David Tsung be here, besides the obvious? – then they would have protections. Lao Chan's Incense Master was no slouch at the sorcery side of things, and the denizens of the Shadow Realms flocked to ritual spaces, feeding on the inevitable energy bleed. Here be monsters? I didn't want to find out.

The stairway opened up onto another hallway: long, and made crooked by water-damaged boxes stacked along both sides. Bare, florescent bulbs flickered at epileptic speed, so dim that it hardly felt like they were doing their job. Not that I needed the light to see. I was offended on principle.

I crept through the maze, passing boxes stamped with every dialect I knew, and a few I didn't.

Lucky cats? Who needed twelve boxes of beckoning lucky cats? Seriously.

The hallway opened up on a storeroom, or what might have once been a storeroom. The mold of long sitting boxes patterned the floor, but they'd all been cleared away to make room for four large kennel cages like you could get at any Petco, one at each corner of the room.

Johnny sprawled in the far cage, bleached-blond and electric blue hair a dead giveaway.

"Shit." I kept enough presence of mind to scan the room before rushing across it. Empty, if you didn't count the animal occupants of the other cages.

"*Sifu*!" I pulled back with a yelp as the bars burned me. I sucked on my fingers. Electrified? But then how come Johnny wasn't crispy bacon?

He rolled over with a groan, eyes fluttering open and closed. His irises crossed and wandered. I couldn't tell if they were dilated. Beaten, then. Or drugged.

I checked the cage for some kind of connection or cord leading away. Nothing. My hands hovered over the mesh. I could touch it again, if I had to, but it would hurt like fuck-all. My fingers were already red and pulsing pain. "I can't open the door."

He groaned again and pushed himself up to sitting. A few more blinks, and he managed to keep his eyes focused on me. "Warded."

Oh. Well, duh. Should have thought of that.

"Can you pop out?"

"They're. Warded." Johnny's enunciation of each word was its own reprimand.

"How do I break the wards?"

He tried standing, but the top of the cage wasn't quite high enough. He settled to his knees, rubbed his face and ruffled his hair. "Not sure."

"I could help you," hissed a voice from my left. I twisted to face the cage in that corner. An emerald-patterned boa slid down from a single forked branch that had been propped across the cage for her comfort. The draped loops of her body rustled and slid as she sought her way to the bare mesh floor of her kennel.

A snake talking to me, and I didn't even blink. My life.

"And I suppose you want out, too?" I asked.

"Thank you, Xuan Wu," Johnny said at the same time, giving the snake a respectful bow. "Forgive my student for her rudeness."

Xuan Wu? That was a guardian's title. "I thought *you* were Guardian of Chinatown," I whispered.

"I am *a* guardian of Chinatown. Have some manners."

Manners. I could do manners. I headed over to the snake's cage. In the cage opposite the snake's, a large, red-tailed hawk ruffled her feathers and let out a soft, curious cry. The dog in the other cage raised her head with a throaty whine. It took me a moment to place that bristling coat of pale fur. The chow from the poster.

They'd kidnapped some kid's dog? Now that was just low.

Grumbling about dognappers, I bowed before the snake's cage as I would to Johnny. "You said you could help, Xuan Wu?"

"There is a key in the shape of a knife. You must wash it with your own blood and touch it to the wards that bind us. That is all."

That was all. "And where is this key?" I asked, pretty sure I wasn't going to like the answer.

"The *Shan Chu* has it." The *Shan Chu*. Lao Chan.

"Great."

Any other complaint I might have made was interrupted by the creek of the fire door echoing down the hallway. Johnny fell to a prone position, and the snake slithered up to its branch. I looked back at the hallway. The only way in was the only way out. There wasn't enough cover to hide in the room.

Yay me for not needing cover. I flattened against the wall behind the snake's cage, deepening the shadows there even as I phased into them. Not all the way into the Shadow Realms. Just far enough to not be noticed.

The headache-inducing fluorescents flickered off, replaced by a steady, yellow glow from the mouth of the hallway. A single file line of figures entered, the first two carrying paper lanterns hanging from tripods. Two more lantern bearers brought up the rear. My 49s, looking very serious about their lantern-carrying duties.

Most of the men wore business suits, but a few had opted for red-on-black embroidered robes. I spotted David Tsung among the suited members, sneaking a peek at his smart phone. I recognized a few of the other attendees, all respected businessmen and leaders of the community. But no Lao Chan.

My dim sum buddies set their tripods down, one between each cage, spreading the light more evenly. How annoying. One of the robed men set down a folding card table. The other two set down a large plastic tub and started pulling out props: a cloth to cover the table, a red banner with "*Fan q'ing – fuk ming*" in black letters, a red tupperware bowl filled with rice, a stack of robes that they started handing out to the others while the first robed man arranged candles, and other props on the makeshift altar.

Must be the Incense Master, the official sorcerer for the Shadow Dragon Triad. I slid along the wall, dragging the shadows with me, and leaned in to get a better peek at his box of supplies, but I didn't see a knife or anything key-like. So much for hoping.

One of the assistants turned at a command from the Incense Master, nearly bumping into me as he put the depleted pile of robes on the edge of the table. I lurched back to avoid a collision, my hand knocking one of the lantern tripods. Not hard, just enough to make one of the legs grate against the cement floor and set the lamp to swinging. The apprentice, the Incense Master, and several others looked in my direction. I pulled back deeper into Shadow, far enough that I could hear the howling of the Shadow Realms like a rush of blood between my ears, and feel the tug of a hundred questing tendrils. It was like standing on a steep slope. I struggled to keep my footing, to not fall back completely. I could escape there, but I'd almost rather try my luck against two dozen triads. Most of them looked pretty harmless. There's nothing harmless about the Shadow Realms.

Before anyone could investigate further, the chow started barking. The red hawk stirred, flapping her wings and screeching. The snake hissed, which wasn't much in the way of sound and fury compared to his companions, but a nice try nonetheless. The din echoed loud enough to burst eardrums in the confines of the basement.

Johnny sat up. That got everyone's attention. I slid away from the altar and back behind the snake's cage.

"Where is Lao Chan?" Johnny asked, as pleasant as if he hadn't been drugged, kidnapped, and warded into a cage. Nobody could pull off cool like Johnny.

Nobody except Lao Chan.

"I am here." Even the dog and the hawk – and the snake – quieted as the *Shan Chu* of the Shadow Dragon Triad spoke from the hallway.

He wore robes open over his charcoal suit. They were blue and black, heavy with embroidered dragons. A wide sash wrapped around his waist, a sheathed knife hanging down from it.

Score! Now to get to him.

Another tripod blocked my way. It wobbled as I squeezed past. Without getting caught, I amended. The hawk flapped and screed unhappily. The chow paced, growling and snapping at the nearest men. Johnny kept talking as I inched along the wall to the opening where Lao Chan stood.

"There appears to be a misunderstanding. Someone drugged me and left me – all of us – in these cages. I am honored that you have come to rectify the matter yourself, *Shan Chu.*"

I'd never heard Johnny play the self-effacement game. This was the guy who prided himself on out trash-talking twelve-year-olds on XBox Live. Lao Chan didn't seem to notice anything off about it. He left the hallway, approached Johnny's kennel.

Damn. I backtracked past the wobbly tripod and behind the snake's cage. If I could get to Lao Chan, I could get to the knife, no problem. I'd filched off harder targets than him.

If I could get to him.

"There has been no misunderstanding. I am sorry for your discomfort, *Sifu.* You and the other Guardians." He bowed to each cage in turn. "But you will all see that this is for the good of Chinatown. For our protection."

"Then why did you not ask?" snapped the dog. One man yelped and the others backed away from her cage.

Noobs. Even I understood that the guardians weren't normal animals.

Which was why, when one of the robed acolytes interrupted the standoff with a wary, "Shan Chu, Xuan Wu is doing something," I was smart enough not to look in the snake's direction to see what that something was.

Most of the others were not that smart. They craned their necks to see around their fellow triads. One by one, their jaws grew slack and their eyelids sagged half-closed. They started to sway back and forth, heads bobbing in time with the snake's.

Except Lao Chan, who still faced Johnny. Perfect distraction.

I crept closer, but still not close enough. Thanks to the lanterns, the shadows didn't extend to the center of the room. I'd have to come out. Expose myself.

"Tell Xuan Wu to stop," Lao Chan said. Johnny gave a one-shouldered shrug and resumed his sitting position. I crept around the back of his cage, so I'd be on the right side for the swipe. Everyone except Lao Chan was entranced now, swaying in time with the snake like some beginning belly-dancing class.

Lao Chan checked his watch and sighed. "I wish you would be more cooperative, *Sifu* Cho, but as you will not." He reached over to the table, nearly punching me in the chest as he grabbed an unused robe.

No time for much finesse. I reached out into the light and yanked the knife free. Flipped it one handed, ran my thumb across the blade and slammed the blooded knife and my hand against the mesh of Johnny's kennel. Heat and light flashed, enough to make Lao Chan and I both flinch away. I sank back into the shadows, ready to flee into the Shadow Realms if this didn't work out.

The flare of light dimmed, revealing an empty kennel. I'd been training with Johnny long enough that I knew what to expect next.

Lao Chan did not. He *urked* with surprise when Johnny appeared behind him and caught him up in a body hold. While Lao Chan struggled, Johnny jerked his head at me.

Get the others. Right.

The flash of light had broken the mass hypnosis induced by the snake. Several of the younger, fitter attendees threw off their robes and lowered into fighting stances. Johnny turned and backed up, using Lao Chan like a shield.

"Now. Why don't you explain to me how this is for the good of Chinatown?"

Lao Chan ignored the question. "Somebody else is here. Helping him. Find h–*urk!*"

I couldn't go back the way I'd come, so I continued around the room, slamming the knife against the hawk's kennel. I would have preferred the chow, now barking herself hoarse, but the bird was the next in line. Another flash of light, and she was free. She blinked out of her cage and reappeared above the line of fighters advancing on Johnny and his captive. She swooped down at them like Hitchcock's best extra. They raised their arms to shield their faces and eyes from her talons. One dared to swat at her. A beat of those great wings, a sickening crack, and the man was on the floor, clutching his arm to his chest.

I used the distraction to circle to the chow's cage, sacrificing stealth for speed. Bad call. Someone caught my arm as it emerged from shadow and used my surprise and their momentum to slam me back against the wall.

David Tsung. He peered through the concentrated shadow, eyes widening as though he could see my face.

But that should be impossible. The shadows should have made that impossible. Shouldn't they?

No time to worry. I opened up that ever-present conduit to the Shadow Realms, and pseudopods of darkness erupted from the wall behind me, suckered like octopus tentacles. They lashed around Tsung's arms and legs; he released me with a shout. I ducked out of the way, and the pseudopods slammed him into the wall, once, twice, as though they were trying to drag him back with them. A third time, and he went limp. The pseudopods slid back into the wall until they were only shadow again, one of them giving me a little wave as it disappeared.

I hate it when the shadows get cheeky. Like I need the reminder that there's some kind of sentience there.

David Tsung slid to the floor, his groans attracting the attention of several triads who weren't dealing with Johnny or the hawk. What I needed was another distraction. I slammed the knife against the mesh of the chow's kennel.

There is no skirmish that won't be made more confusing by the addition of a large, barking dog. Especially when that dog can grow to the size of a pony, with jaws as wide as a great white's and teeth to match.

Utter pandemonium. I slid over to the snake's cage and pressed the knife to it. The flash of light was almost anticlimactic amid the chaos caused by the other guardians and the flailing triads.

"Let's get you out of here. Follow me." The snake slithered back to the box-filled hallway. I skulked behind, casting a glance over my shoulder.

"Shouldn't we help?"

Though it didn't look like Johnny and friends needed much help now that they were free. The Triads did, but I wasn't inclined to assist them.

"This is Chinatown business," said the snake, leading me up the stairs. The fire door swung open of its own accord. "You should stay out of it." And then he slithered back down the stairs to rejoin the fight.

Ungrateful little hisser.

I waited out on the street, but Johnny didn't follow me out; he didn't have to. As Guardian of Chinatown, he had the run of the place. Literally. He could tap in to the ley lines, or whatever it was he used, and be wherever he wanted to be within the confines of the Dragon Gates. It was akin to my connection with the Shadow Realms. Except a lot cooler. And safer.

So I went back to the *kwoon*, let myself in, and waited.

It was a long wait. I tidied the equipment area, frightened dust-bunnies out from under the free-standing lockers, and tried to meditate, which had the opposite effect of what I was going for and just set me to pacing. Outside, it grew dark.

It was a *very* long wait, but that didn't stop Johnny from starting in as soon as he arrived. He burst through the door and came storming into the practice space.

"You are a special kind of stupid, Missy Masters. What were you about, coming after me? Did you even have a plan?"

I gaped. Yelling was not what I'd expected, but I held my ground, ignoring the way he loomed over me. Johnny intimidated the hell out of me, but that was a matter of power and skill: he had more. Chest thrusting didn't cut it with me. I had more. Barely.

"The plan was reconnaissance. I didn't come after you. I was following some kids who turned out to be the lantern-carrying fellows. Didn't have much else do to, since you didn't show up for practice this morning. You're welcome by the way."

Now he remembered to be a little gracious. He rubbed the back of his neck. "Thank you."

"Better."

"Even though I'm not sure you bumbling in and freeing us was the best thing."

"Why? What did you learn from Lao Chan?"

"I didn't learn anything from him, except that he's even more pissed at you now."

"Me?" Shit. David Tsung had recognized me somehow.

"Mr Mystic. That's who he thinks was there." Johnny turned from me, putting away the mop and broom I hadn't gotten around to storing myself. Classic stalling tactic. He wasn't going to share anything else.

I grabbed his arm. "Johnny, will you just tell me what's going on?"

The universe was determined to deny me the answer to that question. A crash from the street interrupted us, followed by a siren, and the whistle and crack-boom of fireworks.

"What the hell?" Johnny pushed past me and drew the shade on one of the narrow, floor-to-ceiling windows that lined the street-facing wall of the *kwoon*. I followed and peered over his shoulder.

Hell was right. People flooded out into the streets, draped out of upper-story windows, and called at each other in a babel of dialects.

The crash was easily explained. Some enterprising souls were getting their loot on. The window of the big souvenir emporium across the street had been shattered into Spiderglass, several men emptying the contents of the emporium into shopping carts with all the organization of a fire brigade. Not local boys, if the hair nets and wife-beaters were anything to go by. And besides, the store had to be under Triad protection. Nobody local would dare touch it.

Still, what the hell did they think they were going to do with piles of colorful brocade silks? Give them to their mothers and sisters and aunts as Christmas gifts?

I peered up at Johnny. "You want me to meet you down there or just wait up here? There's a lot of them."

"Might as well head down. We need to find out what's going on after I school those punks."

Johnny closed his eyes, and I took a step back. Both gestures were unnecessary to what came next, but they gave it the proper gravitas.

Except... nothing happened.

"Johnny?" Johnny *should* have been able to pop away from the studio and rise up from the pavement below for his planned pwnage. Unless something was wrong.

"Something is wrong." Johnny's whisper echoed my thoughts. "China is... not there."

I stumbled back another step. "What? How? Why?" Impossible!

"My connection. It's just... glancing off. Like there's something in the way." Another crash rose from the street, followed by a woman shouting. We both looked. Doris Han had emerged on the stoop of the Dragon's Pearl to harangue the boys across the way. The boys circled up and stalked toward her, which broke Johnny and I both out of our shock.

"Later. We can figure this out later." He hopped out the window and dropped down the fire escape to land between the looters and Doris.

"You know the stairs aren't just there for decoration," I called, and then followed him down the fire escape.

There were too many men for them to be impressed by our acrobatics, but Doris was happy to see us. She backed up into the Pearl's doorway as the looters shifted to face Johnny and me.

"You got a problem, Mr Miyagi?" A Virgin Mary tattoo wept on the muscled forearm of the speaker. I winced as he cracked his neck left and right. Awful sound.

Johnny ignored the question. Sort of. Seemed he was still in a teaching mood. "Missy, what do I say about pre-fight banter?"

I almost pitied the looters. If they hadn't already gone wrong trying to loot the emporium across the street from Johnny's studio, then their spokesman had sealed the deal when he opened his mouth. Call Johnny Bruce Lee. Call him Jackie Chan or even Dragonball-Z. But don't ever call him Mr Miyagi.

"That it's a good time to take off your watch so it doesn't break during the fight?"

"No." *Wham* went looter number one as Johnny blurred into motion, grabbing him by the Virgin Mary and flipping the attached body over. The man convulsed on the pavement, struggling for air. The other looters looked almost as shocked as their friend. They backed away from Johnny. Well, and who could blame them? Johnny was out of their league. "Don't bother with it unless you're good at it."

Johnny hauled the downed man up and shoved him toward his buddies. "Anyone else want to give old 'Miyagi' a try?"

Nobody did, not even the ones with the tell-tale bulges of weapons under their wife-beaters. They scattered. I golf-clapped. "Have you ever been in a fight that lasted longer than ten seconds?" He hadn't even broken a sweat.

Johnny's eyes flicked away. He rubbed the back of his neck. "Not a real one. Not in a long time. I prefer this kind of fight. They're easier to walk away from."

"Hey, guys?" Andrew's voice interrupted us from the doorway of the Pearl. The entire Han clan had gathered behind Doris, including the girls. I guess the Girl Scout thing was over.

Andrew beckoned us in. "You're going to want to see this."

"This" was the television, but it turns out that there's a lot of space between seeing something and understanding it.

Doris was the first to break our silence. "How… how is this even possible?"

The talking heads continued to yammer Orwellian newspeak: saying much, meaning nothing. They couldn't answer Doris's question any more than Johnny or I could. We'd been huddled around the flat screen in her living room for I couldn't begin to guess how long, gaping in silent disbelief apart from the occasional "oh god" When faced with the incomprehensible, language didn't just become inadequate. Sometimes it broke down completely.

It said a lot about what a rock Doris was that she could manage any kind of coherence. "This has to be a joke, right? A hoax?" She turned to Johnny, then to me, the only other adults – since her baby, Andrew, didn't count and never would.

Stage one: denial.

I shook my head. I didn't have an answer, but I knew it wasn't a joke. Johnny's connection to China was blocked, and now we knew why.

"…Repeat, some sort of barrier has gone up, encircling the entire nation of China. We're getting initial reports from correspondents in Taiwan, India, the Philippines, and Kazakhstan that this… this… force field… does in fact seem to be blocking the whole of China, including Tibet and Hong Kong. We don't yet have any…"

"I don't think it's a hoax, Mrs Han," Johnny said, turning away from the streaming commentary. Some enterprising soul had already thrown together some shock graphics asking *"Great Wall or Great War?"* I hoped there was a special hell for people like that, stirring the pot when the crisis was less than an hour old.

"Then... How? How could something like this be possible?"

Johnny didn't have a chance to answer. Andrew already had his laptop open and seemed to be getting information more quickly than the network news fellow.

"There's a blogger here in Thailand who says it's dangerous but not fatal. Some farmers sent their chickens running into it. They bounced off. Singed a few feathers, but they're mostly fine. There's pictures."

We left the television and crowded around his Mac. The pics were cell phone quality: a broad-faced Thai farmer holding up a hen with a bare, singed patch of feathers on her breast. An arrow laid over the images pointed to a supposed shimmer behind the farmer's shoulder that I could imagine seeing if I stared long enough.

The page blanked away, replaced by another one.

"Hey!" I protested. Andrew shushed me.

"These guys are live-blogging the whole thing. They're geology students from Laos, just happened to be near the border doing some surveys on electromagnetic variation. They're running tests with their equipment."

"Any results?" I asked, trying to read over his shoulder. The technical terms were flying fast and furious as one of the students recorded their findings.

"Whatever it is, it's not electromagnetic," Andrew said, skimming back over the record. "Not even measurable by most of their equipment, though they had some recording stations on the other side, and now they can't get a signal. So it's cutting off communication."

Another window popped up, showing video of a shipping barge. I leaned to one side, as if that could let me see the window that had been obscured. "What are you–"

"Watch," Andrew said. I did, trying to make sense of what I was seeing. A minute passed in silence before any of us figured it out.

"Oh god," I whispered as we watched the front end of the barge crumple like a tin can. The video was silent, taken from too great a distance to tell how the people on the barge fared. In some ways, that was worse.

Behind us, the television kept spewing its form of news: "...Emergency meeting of the United Nations. The Chinese representative to the UN has released a joint statement signed by the Chinese ambassador to the United States and several other prominent Chinese officials denying any knowledge of or collusion in the creation of this New Great Wall, and requesting the aid of the world community to find the terrorists responsible..."

"There's a site here that says it's India's fault 'cause they're jealous of China," said one of Andrew's younger sisters, who had followed her brother's example and pulled out her tablet.

"Michelle, put that away!" Doris snapped.

"But Andrew–"

"We don't need gossip and fear. India didn't do this. It's inhuman."

Johnny caught my eye again. We both knew that Doris had meant "inhumane", that she couldn't conceive of a person who could do something so evil – something so sure to cause worldwide panic and war and collapse. But Johnny and I knew of a wider world. We knew there could be explanations that went beyond the scientific. And we knew that if this was magic, Doris was absolutely right. No human sorcerer could have created a ward on this scale.

I touched Johnny's elbow and pulled him away, leaving the

Hans to huddle around Andrew and his laptop like refugees around a garbage-bin fire.

"What was the ritual Lao Chan was trying to do?"

"It didn't cause this. Couldn't have. Caging a bunch of local guardians..." Johnny shook his head. "It couldn't create a ward that strong. Besides, you stopped it."

True, but I refused to believe the timing was coincidence. So what had I stopped? How was it linked?

"I should go," I said, little more than a movement of lips. "You-know-who should be a presence out there tonight."

"Yes, because Mr Mystic is known for his fair and balanced attitude toward China."

Given the state of his world at the moment, I could forgive Johnny the sharpness of that comment. "And in this case, that might be a good thing. He's positioned to speak to both sides. Maybe he can nudge the warmongering extremists somewhere closer to center."

Which was possibly true, but wasn't why I needed to leave. I couldn't sit around and do nothing. Finding Lao Chan had just become my top priority. Maybe San Francisco's Incense Master didn't have the power to do this, but the head of the Shadow Dragons? Yeah, this had his stink all over it.

FOUR
Up a Hill

Then

Jim and Jill were on their honeymoon. They were from LA. Tanned and fit. Jim was an editor at one of the studios, and Jill taught t'ai chi and power yoga. As the only other person under fifty on the tour, I became something of a lifeline for Jill. I got to hear about their wedding in excruciating detail. Jill referred to herself as Bridejilla, which made *her* laugh, Jim wince, and me want to vomit blood.

It might be assumed from this that I didn't like Jim and Jill. On the contrary. I loved them. When everyone else was visiting whatever indigenous attraction deemed appropriate by our tour guide, Jill would drag Jim and I to yet another obscure little shrine that even the locals probably didn't know about. Over tea and rice, Jill would practice her broken Mandarin with the confused owners, while Jim and I kept up a running commentary on what they might be talking about, based on gestures and my equally shoddy understanding of Cantonese. Like all good Americans, Jim only spoke one language – English – but he had a wicked sense of humor, and he adored his new bride.

Our sleek tour bus drove into the Huanglong valley just as the morning sun burned away the mist. I pressed my face to the window, rubbing it with the cuff of my coat in a vain attempt for a better view. No amount of rubbing would erase the cloud of scratches on the Plexiglass. I fidgeted in my seat the entire twisted ride up to the valley, and I was in the aisle the moment we pulled to a stop at the base of the valley. I had to make my escape before–

"Missy!" Jill's call grabbed me moments before she did. She was slight, but daily yoga meant that every slight inch of her was superhero strong. There would be no escape.

Oblivious to my intent, Jill slung her day-pack over her shoulder and pulled me down the aisle and out of the bus.

"Good idea, getting out of here before we run into the geriatric bog," she said. "We need to get a move on if we want to have any quality time at the tea house and still make it back before the bus leaves."

I sighed. This is what I got for letting myself get dragged along on Jill's other field trips. I had no good excuse for ditching her on this one.

"Tea house?" I pretended like I didn't know her alternative itinerary inside-out. "Actually, I was thinking I'd go with the group today. After all, seeing the pools and poking around the three temples, that's pretty much why I came to China." A half-truth. I'd come to the Huanglong valley because of my grandfather's stories and journal entries. I wasn't sure how I was going to find a dragon based on this sketchy evidence, but I figured the Buddhist monastery was a better place to start asking than some obscure little tea house.

Jill waved away my protest, "You can go there tomorrow after we leave." I'd told her of my plan to jump ship in Huanglong; the last thing I wanted was her and Jim raising a fuss over my disappearance. "Today's our last day together, so today you're mine. Besides, the cousins said they wanted to come, which means Gunther is coming too. It's the cool-people group. You want to be part of the cool-people group, don't you?"

The cousins were Anita and Claire from Suffolk, seventy years if they were a day. Gunther was a retired businessman from Hong Kong. He was sweet on Claire, which would have been adorable, except...

"He still hasn't figured out that they're gay?"

Jill shrugged. "Different era. He's used to women traveling together. Probably doesn't think anything of it. Anyways, he says he wants to keep Jim company. Save him from too much frou-ferrah."

"He actually used the term frou-ferrah, didn't he?"

"Maybe it's German? Frou?"

I chuckled and let myself be dragged along. Sure, I was antsy to get started on my search, but the promise of watching Gunther trying to manly it up with tech-geek Jim was too good to resist. One more day wouldn't kill me.

"We're lost."

Heads turned at my pronouncement. Gunther lowered his topographical map. Jim stopped waving his cell around in the vain hope of reception. The cousins nodded, and Jill grinned as if getting lost was just the beginning of a grand adventure.

"Maybe we should head back? We don't want to miss the bus," Jim ventured, earning a frown from his bride.

"We can't do that. We're almost there, I'm sure of it," Jill said. "We just passed the shrine they mentioned in the directions."

"I have not seen this fork we are supposed to follow," Gunther said.

"To be fair, dear, we've passed three shrines." Anita looked to Claire for support, but Claire just shrugged.

"I don't mind being lost. It's a lovely day, and we have time enough to head back before we get left behind."

Jill's grin brightened at this tacit support, and Gunther nodded, though the slump in his shoulders said he dearly wished to side with Jim and Anita, rather than the object of his affections. As one, all eyes turned to me.

"What's your vote, Missy?"

Uh... when did this become my decision? "We're voting?"

"Of course," Jill said. "Me and Claire are for forging ahead, and Gunther's with us. Jim and Anita are for wussing out and heading back."

"Hey!" Jim said.

I hitched my pack, wishing I could put it down. Wishing I wasn't still recovering from being shot so I could swap it to the other shoulder. "But even if I vote for going back, it's still a tie."

"Sure, but as Bridejilla, I get to cast any tie-breaking vote." Overbearing bullies should always be this charming.

I snorted. "So, it doesn't really matter which way I vote."

"Course it does. You want to be on the winning side, right? Not with the wuss brigade under Captain Jim."

"You're going to pay for this later, Jill. In I-told-you-so's."

"Nope, you are. When we find the teahouse, you're treating us all to lunch."

"And when we don't, I'll buy you a nice helping of crow, instead."

"All right!" I said before the cute got any thicker. "We still got some morning daylight to burn, and we've missed the monastery tour, so I say onward ho!" I pointed in the direction I was pretty sure we were headed; it was the only other direction to go besides the one we'd come from. With varied degrees of enthusiasm, the rest of our group trooped out.

A half-hour later, that enthusiasm was as beat down as the rest of us.

"I think that's the same shrine we passed before," Claire said. She and Anita kept flagging behind. I guess being spry at seventy only took you so far. Even I was having trouble keeping up with the power-house that was Jill. Both my shoulders were aching.

"Which one?" Anita asked with a glance at Jill. Nobody could do pointed and polite like the Brits. "We've passed several."

"Not sure. All of them, maybe?"

"Has anyone thought to leave an offering? We could check for it." Heads shook at my question.

"I think it's time we headed back," Jim said, taking Jill's hand to stave off her disappointment. She opened her mouth to protest, but then she caught the glances Jim and I both gave the older member of our crew. Anita leaned against a nearby rock taking sips from a water bottle. Gunther mopped sweat from his brow with a soiled kerchief, his face red from either flushing or burning. Hard to tell. Claire poked around the dense foliage that lined the trail. It took me a moment to realize she must be looking for a private spot to take a piss.

"I suppose you're right," Jill said. "I'm just so bummed. I really wanted to see this place. It's been here since... well, forever."

"We'll go to two places that have been around forever when we get back to Chengdu. Promise." Jim slid his arm around her waist and kissed her temple. Anita and Gunther hid relieved looks as Jim guided Jill back the way we'd come.

"Wait!" Claire's excited cry emerged from the forest. A few moments later, her head popped into view. She beamed at Jill, blue eyes bright. My aching shoulders twitched with foreboding.

"I found something! I think I found it!"

Jill slipped out from under Jim's arm and skipped over to Claire before he could stop her. He sighed and followed.

"I saw a little trail," Claire explained as we gathered, "so I went down it a way to see if I could... er... to see where it led. And there's a neat little cottage tucked back there in a glade."

"I knew it was here!" Jill crowed, flashing Jim a triumphant look. She waved at the shrine behind us. "I bet that *is* the same one we've been passing, and we've just been going in circles this whole time."

"Which is the beginning of her argument for why we have

time to stay because it's not as far to get back as we think," Jim announced to no one in particular. "So we might as well save her the breath and go along now."

Claire and Anita were already gabbing about Claire's find, heads bowed close together. Gunther nodded along with an avuncular smile. Jim slipped his hand through Jill's and let her drag him through the trees.

I paused at the edge of the track. Something was... off. It was similar to the feeling I got when I stepped into shadow, a tenuous gravity tugging at me that seemed innocuous, but wasn't.

"Missy, you coming?" Jill's voice drifted back to me.

"Y-yeah," I called back, trying to shake off the feeling. It had clamped onto the nape of my neck and wouldn't budge. I pivoted and glanced back at the little shrine. Our way marker.

I travel light. I don't carry a bunch of crap around with me unless it's necessary crap, so it took me a moment to dig a suitable offering out of my pack. I had my grandmother's pearls, but they were going back to the dragon, assuming she existed. Assuming I could find her.

But being a magician meant I always kept a few trinkets on me for sleight-of-hand tricks. I'd picked up the scarves at a souvenir kiosk in Shanghai. They were thin silk, red and green, and stamped with gold foil carp. Cheap, but pretty in a flashy sort of way. I knotted them together and tied them around a limb of one of the little trees flanking the shrine. They fluttered in the light breeze.

I knelt before the shrine like it was the mat at my *kwoon*. "Uh. Ms Lung Huang? Hi. This is your valley, so I'm hoping this is your shrine. I'm Missy. Missy Masters. You knew my grandfather. Anyways, I have a bad feeling about whatever's going on. So, if you're listening and could offer any guidance, that would be great. Uh. Thanks!"

Totally inadequate, but the offering was meant to assuage

my paranoia as much as anything. Rising from my crouch, I shrugged on my backpack and trudged into the forest.

The clearing Claire had found wasn't more than fifty yards from the track, but the foliage grew so dense that I wasn't surprised we'd missed it. Claire must have really wanted her privacy to have wandered so far.

Scant sunlight pierced the gloom of the canopy. The clearing was limned green, like the Emerald City before Dorothy removed her spectacles. I wrinkled my nose against the moldy smell, which was punctuated by a sharp, rancid stench from the half-rotted pile of refuse edging up against the side of a shack that huddled in the middle of the clearing.

There was nothing quaint or appealing about the shack. The walls were a patchwork of rough wooden planks, cobbled stone, and corrugated tin. The structure listed to one side; the roof looked like it was about to slide into the compost heap.

"Missy, come meet the owners!" Jill waved me to the entry, where everyone had gathered. They parted as I approached, revealing a bent old hag and her equally bent... husband? Man-servant? Troll? I like to think I'm egalitarian about my standards of beauty, but these folk would have been outliers on almost any scale.

The woman reached out a clawed hand to grasp mine. She had some sort of skin ailment that turned her flesh scabrous and even more greenish in the dim light. Up close, she smelled worse than the trash pile. I expected missing teeth when she smiled, but instead was treated to gleaming rows of teeth, serrated like a shark's. I glanced around at my friends, but everyone else smiled along with her as if nothing was amiss.

"Jill tells me you find us on the Internet. This is good. You follow directions, you find us. We make you tea. Come inside."

Non-plussed, I let myself be dragged into the hovel. Of all the anomalies, the fact that she spoke understandable, if broken, English was the most unsettling. Jill and the rest followed us in, all of them still grinning like Stepford tourists.

The inside of the hovel was bigger than it should have been, but that's about all it had going for it. The stench of rancid garbage and moldy mushrooms hit me square in the gag reflex. I closed my mouth and tried not to breathe too much. A cloud of gnats rose into the air at our entry, their individual forms visible only when they flew near the single lantern that hung from the loft crossbeam. The corners of the room remained in shadow, but with my improved vision I could see... things. Moving. I wasn't sure what, and I didn't want to know.

"Oh, how lovely!" the cousins exclaimed together. It was eerie, how similar they looked, hands clasped to their chests, dopey smiles on their faces.

"Sit, please. I will make tea." The old woman waved us to a long, low table flanked by ratty cushions. The man-thing trundled past us and settled into one of the corners to glower at us. He licked his lips, and I caught a glimpse of teeth, sharp like the woman's.

"Jim," I hissed as he moved to his seat. "Don't you think we should leave soon? You don't want to miss the bus, do you?"

"Hm?" His smile faltered for the briefest moment, then returned. "Oh, it's no worry. Mrs Hu says we have plenty of time."

My friends settled at the table, blind to the skittering of insects, the creepiness of the whole situation. This was not good.

"Have a seat, dear, while I make the tea." Mrs Hu's tone this time was a little less sweet.

I clutched the strap of my backpack and edged toward the door. "If you don't mind, I thought I'd take a look around outside before tea. Stretch my legs a bit." As if I hadn't just spent the whole morning walking. The hag's beady eyes narrowed. "I thought I spied a garden around the side. I'd love to take a closer look at it." That mollified her. Whatever illusion the old hag had created, it must have included a garden. Probably where the compost heap sat rotting. I slipped out before she could stop me.

I didn't go far. I trudged over to the trash heap and pretended to admire it while my mind raced.

"You'd be best served by leaving them to their fates."

Jerking around, I scanned the brush to see who had interrupted my growing panic. I caught a flash of russet at the edge of my vision. I looked up

Perched on one of the mossy eaves, pink tongue lolling between sharp canines and black lips, sat an amber-eyed fox. She – at least, the voice had been female – had the same predator's grin as the old hag's in the hut.

"OK, this is going to sound crazy, but did you just speak to me?" I asked the fox.

She didn't respond for several moments, just panted at me and blinked like a dumb animal, then: "Oh, you don't know how tempting it was to keep quiet and let you think you'd gone mad."

My knees nearly gave out when she spoke, canine jaw moving in ways no canine jaw was meant to move. Happily, my knees held, otherwise I would have been rolling in rancid compost. I gathered up the shreds of my composure and shut my mouth before a fly decided to go exploring.

"You're... a *kitsune*?"

She growled low in her throat. "*Huxian*, please." A tail flicked with a flash of white, and my eyes were drawn to three other tails that lay dormant. Four tails. That didn't bode well. "Now, may we stop wasting time? I'd like to guide you away from this festering pit so I can go back to my much more interesting and important business."

I took a step back. "Why would you help me?" Whatever she called herself, she wore the guise of a trickster. And she talked like a trickster. And only idiots trusted tricksters. Right?

"Why, indeed?" The *huxian* cocked her head, golden gaze unblinking. When I blinked, she turned her back on me, all four tails thumping impatiently. "You asked for help, and I was sent. I suppose you may ask for different help and see what comes next."

"But… my friends." That was my biggest concern. I could deal later with the weirdness of talking foxes and evil hags who wanted to eat me. After all, this was what I'd come to China to find.

The vixen nuzzled at some imaginary dirt on her paw, lapping it clean before she deigned to answer. "They're lost. There's no way to break the *yaoguai*'s curse from the outside. Count yourself lucky that you were protected, and let's go." She hopped to the ground and trotted across the clearing. She paused and glanced over her shoulder, one paw raised, when I didn't follow.

"What will she do to them?" I asked.

"What do you think?" It was impressive, how much derision could be put into a look, especially in a long-nosed canid face. But she was right to be disdainful. I'd seen those pointed teeth. I knew what they were for.

"I'm not leaving them."

Her whiskers quivered as she frowned. "Take it from one who knows this world better than you: your friends are already lost."

"But they're not dead yet." I turned back to the door. As I reached for the cracked plank that hung askew on the frame, the fox behind me spoke.

"Wait." She let out an exasperated huff. "If you're really set on trying to save them, you'll have to set aside Lung Huang's protection. The yaoguai's illusions have to be fought from within."

I gave her a pathetic, hopeful look. Trickster or not, she clearly had a better idea of what was going on than I did. And she seemed more willing to help than she pretended. "How do I do that?"

"Fighting them from within? I doubt you're bright enough. But to cast aside the protection, just eat whatever she gives you. That should be strong enough to break the ward. Assuming you can choke it down."

Having seen the inside of the hovel, I had to admit I shared the fox's doubts. "And then what?"

"And then you're on your own. I'll wait for you at the shrine. If you're able to make your way there, I'll guide you back to mortal realms."

"I don't suppose you'd be willing to help me defeat her..." I asked, giving the fox my friendliest smile. Her return smile wasn't so friendly.

"Happily." She darted forward and nipped me. Hard.

"Ow!" I jerked back, cradling my hand. Her sharp canines had grazed the skin, leaving two angry, red scrapes along the back. "What. The hell?" That's what I got for trusting foxes.

"You're welcome," she said with a sharp, yipping laugh. And with a flick of her tails, she disappeared into the trees.

I took several deep breaths, preparing myself for re-entry. Pasting a big smile on my face, I opened the door and entered.

"Missy! You're just in time. The tea's ready. Mrs Hu was just about to go get you."

"Is everything all right?" Mrs Hu cut off Jill's enthusiastic greeting. Her lip curled, and the thing in the corner shifted its glare to me.

"Wonderful. You have a lovely garden. So peaceful."

"You are ready for tea now?" she snapped. The suspicion hadn't budged. Well, I guess there was one way to gain her trust. I nodded and took my seat next to Jim, bracing myself for what would come next.

The cousins ooh-ed and ah-ed as Mrs Hu plunked the cups and pot on the bare table. Even Gunther looked impressed, and Jill was in awe. I tamped down on the irrational envy that my friends might be witnessing the illusion of a formal tea ceremony being performed by a master.

Swampy-looking water sloshed over the sides of our cups as Mrs Hu poured out. Yellow foam floated on the surface, and I thought I spied... yup. Those were larvae of some kind. Something I'd learned during my brief stint on the streets: if you were hungry enough, you could eat just about anything. Problem was, I wasn't hungry. Not this hungry. I swallowed down my bile as I stared into my cup.

While Mrs Hu poured, her man-thing plunked plates in front of us. Each one sported a fibrous leaf smeared with mud. The spread looked like the tea parties I used to throw for my grandfather in our garden: muddy water and leaf-surprise. Unlike my grandfather, I couldn't get away with pretend sipping.

"Well, eat," Mrs Hu snapped. Knowing I'd lose my nerve if I had to watch the others chowing down, I snatched up one of the mud-leaves. Maybe the hag would mistake my haste for eagerness.

Before I could think too much about what I was doing, I bit down. I had a fleeting sense of tasting compost, things long dead and rotting, iron, grit, and the juicy pop of earthworms, and then it was gone. The earthiness turned sweet like yams, the pop became the crunch of dough fried to a light crisp. I pulled the treat away, looking at it in astonishment. I wasn't sure why I expected it to taste bad. Red bean paste pancakes were my favorite.

I put the pancake down and lifted my tea, taking a deep breath of the floral brew. Not jasmine, that would have been trite.

"What is this? Chrysanthemum?" I asked, sipping from the delicate cup.

"Lotus blossom, dear," Mrs Hu responded, her eyes bright.

She winked and bent over me, her whisper loud enough for all to hear, "but don't tell my secret, or all the other tea houses will run me out of business."

"Not likely," Claire said, leaning forward to talk past Gunther's bulk. "I don't think I've ever seen a nicer tea than this. Don't you agree, Anita?"

"Oh yes. I wish we could lure you to Suffolk, Mrs Hu. Lucy would turn green with envy."

Lucille is the head of the Ladies' Auxiliary," Claire said. "She's Anita's arch nemesis."

I nodded along with the others as Mrs Hu bustled around us, refreshing the treats with cheerful industry.

Cradling my cup, I settled into the warmth of camaraderie, happy to let my attention drift between conversations. The cousins and Gunther debated the merits of obscure poets – or, at least, poets I'd never heard of, so maybe not that obscure. Mr Hu dozed in a chair in the corner, while Jill and Mrs Hu exchanged herbal tonic recipes. Like me, Jim seemed content to play observer to the conversations. Except his brow was furrowed.

"Jim? What's wrong?"

He smiled, but it faded again into a frown. His eyes darted about, like he was looking for something that he thought should be there, but wasn't. "I don't know. Nothing. Right?"

I didn't want Mrs Hu to see his distraction and take unintended insult, so I nudged him to face me, lowering my head so the others wouldn't catch my whisper. "Jim?"

"I just... there's something..." He paused, chewing on his lip. "About buses? I'm not sure." He glanced down at my hand on his arm, and his vague distress sharpened. "Missy, what happened to your hand?"

"Huh?" I glanced down as well. Two long, red scrapes marred my skin. "Huh. I wonder when that happened. It must have been..." I tried to think, but it was fuzzy. I shrugged. It couldn't have been that important.

"It was when you were in the garden."

"Garden?" I echoed. "I don't remember any garden."

"You don't..." Jim trailed off as Mrs Hu appeared between us to fill our cups. Jill plopped down on my other side to extol the virtues of some hot pebble wrap she'd just learned about from our hostess.

"Bad continuity," Jim kept mumbling, his sharp eyes darting about the room. He took a sip of his tea, then grimaced as if he'd tasted something foul. I tested mine before turning to Jill with a half-shrug. Jim was weird. The tea tasted fine to me.

Our cozy party gabbed well past dark, but Mrs Hu was kind enough to offer us lodging in the loft above. Nothing fancy, she warned, just some old hammocks strung between the beams. We happily accepted whatever she could offer. I had just managed to nod off in spite of the hammock's creaking and swaying when Jim's poke startled me awake. I jumped, and my stomach lurched as my swaying bed threatened to overturn me. I struggled onto my side.

"Shouldn't you be dangling next to your bride?"

"Continuity errors," he whispered, as if this explained everything.

"Huh?" I said, because it didn't.

"Anita is allergic to nuts, but she ate the nutcake, and when I asked her about it, she said it wasn't nutcake at all, it was fudge."

"Somebody's a nutcake," I muttered, but he ignored me. He was on a roll.

"Jill's vegan, but she ate one of Gunther's sausages. You have scrapes on your hand, but you don't remember going out to the garden."

Jim ran a hand through mussed hair. The look he gave me was almost mad. Pleading. "Something is wrong. We missed the bus."

"Jim." I struggled to sit up, then abandoned the effort in defeat as my aching shoulder protested. The hammock swayed, refusing to grant me purchase. "Go back to bed. We'll talk about this with the others in the morning."

"No!" he hissed. "They want to believe everything is fine. You knew differently. You knew, and then you came back, and you didn't know anymore." He grabbed my wrist, shaking it. "What bit you? What's happening? Why can't you remember? And why doesn't it bother you that you can't?"

"I..." He had a point. Every time I tried to think about the scrapes, or what had brought us here, or why I wasn't able to recall these things, my thoughts broke into a million fragments, all distractions. I remembered being shot, could still feel it like a sore muscle, but I couldn't recall how I'd gotten the fresh scrapes on my hand, or where I was, or how I'd gotten there.

"I can't think," I whispered, the beginnings of panic crawling up my throat.

Jim nodded. I struggled to rise again, but the hammock held me fast. The more I struggled, the more the mesh tightened around me. "Help me!"

Jim tried to steady the hammock, but my struggles left me cocooned in the netting. With a curse, he pulled something out of his pocket. A tiny blade snicked open, and he began cutting through the individual strands. A hole widened at the bottom of the net, and I wormed my way out, falling onto my injured shoulder. My yelp pierced the cobweb-festooned rafters.

"You OK?" Jim hoisted me to my feet. I dusted myself off, shooting an irritated glance at the hammock. I froze at what I saw.

"Jim..." his name was more strangled whisper than anything.

"I see it. I don't believe it, but I see it."

The hammock had morphed into a thick wrap of grey, sticky webbing, too much like something a spider would weave around its prey for my tastes. I shuddered and swiped my arms again to brush away phantom remnants of the webbing.

"We have to free the others." Jim turned, and I realized mine wasn't the only cocoon. Dim light flashed off his pocketknife, and I caught sight of a familiar fleur-de-lis logo on the side.

"Always be prepared," he said with a self-deprecating smile and a two fingered salute before he went to work on Jill's pod.

Waking up entrapped and having to struggle free did a lot to convince the others that something was wrong. Enough to start unraveling the hag's illusions. I'd spent a few moments puking in the corner of the loft after recalling what I must have eaten, but the others were spared that memory. They were seeing the truth for the first time, and they were cowed by it. Even Jill had set aside her bouncy optimism, shoulders sagging as she huddled against her husband's side.

"How did you know?" she whispered to him as we spied on the room below. It looked empty, but the hag and her man-servant had to be somewhere. I wanted to know where before I led us back to the shrine.

"Continuity errors," he repeated. His mantra.

"Jim, this isn't a movie. Life doesn't have continuity errors."

"Exactly."

"What do you think she was going to do with us?" Claire asked. She clung to Anita.

Gunther was shaken enough not to care. "Hansel und Gretel," he said, his florid complexion gone pasty.

"Gunther?" Anita touched the back of his hand. He flinched.

"When I was a boy, I would always have the same nightmare since my nana read to me the story of Hansel und Gretel. I have not dreamed that dream in many years, but I dreamed it tonight." He wiped a hand over the haunted look in his eyes, then nodded at Jim and me. "The witch is gone. I say we go now, before she returns and tosses us in her oven."

Anita and Claire nodded; Jill reached for the rickety ladder.

"Wait," I said as Jim steadied the ladder and Gunther helped

Claire follow Jill down, then Anita. Nobody paid me any mind. "She could be anywhere."

"Well, she's not here. Besides, she's just one old lady," Jim said. "Jill could probably take her. Hell, *I* could probably take her."

"Notice he rates my ability to kick ass above his own," Jill called up.

"I call it like I see it." Jim climbed down. "Why do you think I married you? I needed a stalwart protector."

"This is a bad idea," I muttered, following Jim.

Anita cracked the door and peeked out into the night. "I think it's clear," she whispered over her shoulder.

"Allow me to go first," Gunther offered, pulling her back. He opened the door and charged out before any of us could stop him.

"I guess we're going then. Ladies?" Jim linked arms with Anita and Claire as though they were going on a Sunday stroll and led them out after Gunther. I glanced over at Jill when she sighed. A sappy grin had replaced her anxious frown. Any woman seeing that look would feel a pang of envy, so I didn't feel too guilty about mine.

"He plays fantasy football with the guys at work. He thinks magic is just special effects or mass delusion, and that the things Argent Aces can do is just corporate hype. And the main reason my mother likes him is because he's the first guy I brought home who didn't reek of patchouli."

I grinned. I knew what she meant. Scratch the surface, and Jim was a keeper. "You're a lucky, lucky girl."

Her sappy grin faded. Her knuckles were white on the door frame. "Only if we survive."

"Then let's move."

Darkness shrouded the clearing. What little moonlight there might have been couldn't pierce the canopy. Ahead of us, Gunther stumbled and cursed.

"Which way?" he muttered, eyes wide and unblinking. His head swiveled as he searched for some path.

"Here, let me." I could see in the dark almost as well as the day, one of the perks of my inherited powers. I moved past Gunther, taking his hand. "Link hands everyone."

I struck out through the trees in the direction the *huxian* had taken. The train of people behind me shied and jumped at the darkness around us, but I could see the shadows for what they were: just shadows. Wherever our hostess had disappeared to, she wasn't here.

"Are you sure this is the way?" Gunther asked. His hand was clammy, his grip finger-crushing.

"As sure as I can be. We need to get back to the shrine. There's a... guide there who will take us back."

"What?" "Back to the monastery?" "What guide?" "How do you know?"

I grimaced at the barrage of questions, in part because answering them would require too much exposition, and in part because the raised voices would give away our position. Not that the hag needed any help.

"Look, let's just get to the shrine. I'll explain once we're – oof!"

"Missy!"

My hand was torn from Gunther's as something the size and shape of a Pittsburgh linebacker charged into me, lifting me and slamming me into the trunk of a tree. Pain arced down my arm. I doubled over my attacker's shoulder, struggling for breath.

"Run," I tried to gasp, but it was just a soundless movement of lips. The linebacker ground me into the tree, giving me a good idea of what a literal rock/hard place situation felt like. My friends huddled together in the middle of the path, trying to make out what had become of me. Beyond them, her toothy smile gleaming razor-sharp to my eyes, stood the *yaoguai*.

"Run!" I found enough air to croak the command. I set my

dangling feet against the trunk, wormed my forearms against the shoulders of the meaty giant, and kicked back with all my strength. It wasn't clean or graceful, but the hag's ogre was top-heavy. He stumbled back far enough to release me from the pin. I fell hard on my hip and rolled to one side, rising to a crouch. I drew a breath to yell at my still-dithering friends when the ogre opened his mouth in a hideous bellow.

It wasn't the sound that was awful. It was the yawning chasm of green, glowing nothingness. I shied away from the blast of heat and the stench of sulfur, shielding my eyes from the glaring light. It flooded the clearing, giving the others their first look at what had been threatening us.

If this was the thing the hag had kept hulking in the corner, it had *grown* since we went to bed. Its skin glistened in the green light, moist surface and shiny grey-brown underneath, like mud packed into entrails. Knobby protrusions – truncated horns of some sort – jutted out over beady, black eyes. The creature was all torso and muscled arms, cartoonishly so. If the cartoon in question was made by Rob Zombie.

One of the cousins squeaked in fear, and the demon-thing swiveled at the sound of easier prey. He took a step in their direction.

"I said run!" I snapped a kick at the back of the demon's knee. It stumbled hard to one side. Roaring again, it tore up two huge clods of dirt and hurled them at me. I skipped to the side of one and ducked under the other, spinning into a kick aimed at the monster's jaw.

I cried out at the impact. It was like kicking a slab of granite. Only my boots saved me from a broken foot. Thank Doc Martin for steel toes.

My cry spurred the others to action. Gunther wrapped an arm around each cousin and crashed ahead into the brush. "Go! We go!" Jim had his arms around Jill, restraining her from rushing to help me.

"Get her out of here!" I shouted. The demon rose, shaking his head and blinking. Well, at least my kick had hurt him too. He rubbed a meaty fist against his jaw, wiping away a dribble of glowing green ichor that I hoped was blood. The ichor hissed and smoked where it hit the ground.

"You should worry for yourself." The demon's mouth moved, but it was the hag's voice that emerged. My gaze flicked back to her, still huddled in the shadows of the brush. Both of her hands were raised, fingers twisting in a familiar pattern. It took me a moment to place it. Puppetry. I'd seen marionetteers work the sticks just so.

Her left hand twitched and the demon responded with a devastating roundhouse. I tried to dance out of the way, but his fist clipped me on my good shoulder with the force of a truck, slamming me face-first into the dirt. I tried to roll up to my feet, but the world lurched, and I only managed to flop onto my back. I curled my knees to my chest and thrust up with both feet as the demon loomed into view, catching him under the chin with my heels. His head snapped up and he stumbled away, letting loose another roar. Acidic ichor flew in a spray, hissing with little tracers of smoke wherever it landed. I smelled burning rubber and leather. My Docs weren't going to survive this, even if I did.

"You, you're doing this!" Jill cried, worming free of Jim. Snatching up a deadfall branch, she flailed away at the hag. A good thing for me. The demon halted mid-lunge, jerking around in a macabre dance. More ichor flew. I considered kipping up to my feet, but I wasn't sure I had it in me. I rolled upright, doing my best to avoid the acidic blood.

"Go away, stupid girl!" Unlike her minion, the hag wasn't all that sturdy. Jill and her branch were routing the old witch. Unfortunately.

Snarling at Jill, the hag thrust out her hands. She spat something in a Chinese dialect I didn't recognize. The demon lurched away from me and stumbled toward his mistress and her attacker.

"Jill, look out!" I jumped on the demon's back. With my arm barred across his thick neck, I tried to steer him aside or knock him out. My shoulder ached as I called on muscles I'd left recuperating too long. Acid-blood burned through the sleeve of my coat, down to my arm underneath. I clenched my teeth against the fire and tugged harder, but my yanking did no good. The demon juggernauted at Jill.

Jim tried to pull his bride away, but Jill stood stiff with fear, branch held out in futile defense. The hag cackled and flicked her fingers. The demon threw me from its back. I slammed shoulder-first into the hard ground, and for the second time in as many minutes I was left struggling to breathe around pain blooming like a red lotus through my back and chest.

I closed my eyes. Get up, get up, get *up*. My body was having none of it. I was helpless to help Jill. Helpless to do anything except breathe in shallow whimpers.

No. Not entirely helpless. Not sure what else to do, not sure it would work, I reached deep beyond the pain, beyond my fear, and ripped something out of the shadows. Not Templeton. Something I'd never encountered before. Something without form. Something… not nice.

I'd never allowed the shadows such a free rein. They poured into the forest, inky blackness rising on all sides of us. I heard several shouts and cries of terror. Not just Jim and Jill, but Gunther and the cousins as well. And the hag.

I concentrated on her voice, urging the tide of shadow to overwhelm her. Finish her. Destroy her. I could feel their claws tearing into her soft, wrinkled flesh, like they were my own hands. Shadow wrapped itself around her face in a smothering embrace, muffling her cries. Her screams grew frantic, then weak. Then, all was silence.

I lay there, waiting for the shadows to turn on me and

devour me as well, but they fled out into the woods, dispersing until I could no longer sense them. My harsh breathing broke the silence left behind.

I heard a tread, the crunch of deadfall needles.

"Missy?" Jill's voice, trembling and unsure. I tried to sit up and found to my surprise that I could.

"What was that? What happened?" Jill clutched her branch to her chest, half weapon, half security blanket. Jim stood close behind her, holding the backpack I hadn't realized I'd dropped. He was pale; his tan floated on the surface of his skin like an oil slick.

"What happened to the demon?" I struggled gracelessly to my feet, waving away assistance because I didn't want anyone yanking on my arm.

"The demon... collapsed. Into a pile of leaves and mud." Jim frowned, then muttered, "I can't believe I just said that. I can't believe any of this magic crap is real."

Jill dropped her branch and turned into his arms. "I suppose now would be a bad time to tell you I told you so?" His shirt muffled her words.

"Grounds for divorce," he replied, then belied his threat by hugging her and pressing a kiss to the top of her head.

"But," Jill pulled away and twisted in his arms so she could look between us. "The other things. Those shadow monsters. Where did those come from?"

"I don't care," Jim said. "I say we just get out of here before they come back."

I nodded along with Jim, not ready to explain my own role in the night's terrors. "I think I heard the others that way. Hopefully, they made it to the shrine."

In silent consensus, we plunged through the trees in the direction I'd pointed, bursting out onto the path only moments later. My nausea eased as I caught sight of Gunther, Anita, and Claire by the shrine. Beside them, a russet vixen thumped her tails in the dirt.

"Ah. Good. You made it. About time. These three refused to leave without you."

"The fox talks," Jim muttered. "Of course it does. Why am I even surprised?"

"She's the guide I mentioned. Without her, we never would have gotten out."

Jim glanced at me, then down at my hand. "She's what bit you?"

I nodded.

"Can we please go back now?" Claire whispered. Anita soothed her with soft kisses along her brow. Gunther didn't so much as blink. Huh. Maybe he did know.

"I think that's a great idea," Jill said. She glanced to either side of the shrine. Where there had been one path, two now branched out. Jill hesitated. "Uh... which way?"

The *huxian* rose to her feet. "That is the question, isn't it? One path leads back to the monastery and the mortal realms. The other leads deeper into the spirit world and ends at the top of the mountain."

"Well, you're the guide," Jim said. "Which one leads back to the monastery? I think I speak for everyone here when I say that none of us wants anything more to do with this place."

The fox cocked her head at me, amber eyes boring into mine. She grinned at the conundrum she'd just served me. Damn trickster spirits.

"I do."

Now the fox wasn't the only one staring at me, although the looks on my friends' faces ranged from surprised to "are you fucking mental?"

"Lung Huang?" I asked the *huxian*, just to make sure.

"Even so."

"What's the catch?"

Her withers twitched in an animal shrug, "No catch, but I

am only one creature. I cannot be a guide down both paths."

Of course. My grandfather had told me enough stories about these kinds of dilemmas to know what my options were. "So I have to choose. Their safe return or my mission."

She didn't respond, but Jim had recovered from his shock and was happy to fill the silence. "Missy, you can't seriously be considering staying in this place."

"I have to." I took my pack from him, let it drag at my side. Fuck if I was putting any weight on my shoulders. "It's why I came here."

"You're not really a folklore student researching local dragon lore, are you?" Jill asked.

I shook my head. I couldn't sacrifice their safety. I'd already put them in enough danger. "*Huxian*. Please guide them back. I'll find my own way up the mountain."

"Missy, no." Jill touched my arm. Gently. She must have seen how I'd been favoring it. "We'll be fine. It can't be that far. We can find our way back safely." I glanced at the rest of the group. From their expressions, none of them shared Jill's conviction.

"Come back with us," Jim offered instead. "Those shadow things are still out there, and who knows what else?" He shook his head. "And you're hurt. Nothing can be worth putting your life at risk like this."

Gunther and the cousins nodded in agreement. Jill's chin jutted, and she huffed as if she wanted to argue with Jim's assertion, but she stayed silent.

"I know what I'm doing." Which was a lie, but they didn't need to know that. I glanced back at the fox. Her black whiskers twitched. "Take care of them?"

"As I was charged to." The fox rose and loped down the right-hand trail.

"Go," I said, giving Jill a quick hug and Jim a reassuring shoulder squeeze. "Before she manages to get too far ahead.

I'll look you up when I get back to the States. Promise."

Before I could lose my nerve, I turned to the other path and trudged my way up the mountain.

FIVE
Inverse Effectiveness

Now

Shimizu wasn't answering her cell. She wasn't at the co-op, either.

"Have you tried the clinic? She's always there," said Patrick, our resident grad student and medical marijuana grower. Even when everyone else was gone, I could always find him in the huge solarium at the back of the shared house on Russian Hill, working on his dissertation. He'd taken over the entire couch with journal articles, books, and hand-written notes. Save a tree; kill a grad student.

"They're not picking up." The clinic never did when they were in crisis mode. Even a tremor over 4.0 meant their phones were ignored for at least an hour. I tried Shimuzu's phone again. Straight to voice mail. "Damn."

"What's going on?" Vess wandered into the common room with one long arm draped over her head. Stretching her traps. Vess was always stretching something.

"Shimizu's missing." Patrick moved a stack of journal articles aside to make room for her.

Vess flopped down, pulling one leg up behind her shoulder. "Missing how? I just saw her this morning."

"You haven't heard about the shit with China? Didn't your

twitter feed download what's going on right to your brain?"

"I wish," Vess snorted, throwing her towel at Patrick. She was still hoping for a singularity that involved her becoming a cyborg. "I was meditating. Why, what's up with China?"

She pulled out her smart phone and fiddled with it, but before it could tell her the world was going to hell, Mason and Luis charged in and did the honors.

"Did you hear what's going on in Oakland?" Luis asked, brandishing his tablet. The screen flipped from portrait to landscape and back too quickly to make sense of it.

"Oakland?" Patrick opened his laptop, which he'd shut when I'd come in frantic and looking for Shimizu. "You mean China?"

Luis shook his head. "No, dude. Oakland. Check it."

"Have you guys heard from Shimizu," I asked while Patrick Googled the local news.

Luis swiped at his tablet. "She's on a date."

As one, the house turned to gape at Luis. Well, at least I wasn't the only one who hadn't known.

"She didn't tell us?" Mason might as well have said *you* for all the accusation in his voice. The way he was glaring at Luis, somebody was sleeping on the couch tonight.

Luis shrugged. Only a true stoic could date Mason and survive the drama attached. "It's not a date-date. More a meeting-to-confirm-you're-not-a-psycho date. Some girl she met online."

"Ha! Got something." Patrick's grin faded into horror. "Holy shit." Behind the pretty young reporter, hordes of people crowded the Alameda ferry terminal, cops in riot gear holding them back.

We groaned as a group. "Shimizu took the ferry, didn't she? Chicken and Waffles?" I didn't need Luis's confirming nod. Of course she did. It was her favorite first date. According to Shimizu, somebody who couldn't appreciate good chicken and waffles wasn't worth dating. And her favorite chicken and waffles place was off Jack London Square in Oakland. Right where the newscaster was covering the proto-riot. Spitting distance from Chinatown.

"I'm heading over there." In this crisis, getting across the bay was going to be a bitch, even with the leased replacement bike Jack had gotten for me.

"Are we Avengers-assembling?" Patrick asked. The other co-op members didn't know about Mr Mystic, but sometimes I wondered about Patrick. Whether it was from being smart, or often being high, he had an uncanny insight into things I'd rather keep secret. But he didn't talk, and that was what mattered.

I shook my head. "I'll head down there. You guys stay safe. I'll call when I find her."

"I don't see what the fuss is about," Mason said, taking Luis's hand – relenting on his cold shoulder almost as soon as he gave it. "Shimizu's not Chinese. Hell, she's barely Japanese. Her family's been here longer than mine."

"And almost as long as mine," Luis said. "But I still get asked for my green card and told to learn English."

Vess looked up from her Twitter feed. "Yeah, people are going to stop and wonder about that Iowa accent while they hate crime all over her. Missy, there's another thing. Whatever's going on in China, it's affected Oakland. There's one of those force field things around their Chinatown."

She handed me her phone. I scanned the feed. "Shit."

Whatever they'd been trying in San Francisco, it looked like they'd succeeded in Oakland. I did some hashtag hopping. And New York. Los Angeles, Manila, London, Sydney. Every recognized Chinatown in the world was reporting a wall similar to the one around China.

Except for San Francisco.

Double shit.

•••

I left, assuring the house I'd bring Shimizu back safe, then doubled back to the alley that ran alongside the Russian Hill Victorian and snuck into the first-floor rooms I shared with Shimizu. I forced myself not to rush through my transformation into Mr Mystic. The likelihood that Shimizu was in danger increased with every moment I delayed, but being Mr Mystic was about more than just keeping my identity safe. Even if the whole world discovered he was just Missy Masters in disguise, I'd still pull him about me. Mystic was cool and methodical. He thought things through. He remembered his Sun-Tzu. He didn't trust to luck and wits. At some point along the way, becoming my grandfather had started to feel as right as being myself.

And besides, he was an icon. People saw him, and they calmed down. Bad guys lost the will to fight. When people looked at me-as-Missy, they just peered over my shoulder, looking for the real threat.

Or, as Shimizu said when we first came up with the crazy idea: "Nobody surrenders to the Dread Pirate Westley."

Braiding my hair flat and tacking down the wig took the longest. It was a thing of vanity that I refused to cut my hair or dye it black. I rationalized that it made my head look bigger, which added to the impression that I was larger than I was. Also, it meant my hat stayed on in a tussle. That was key. Without the shadows cast by my hat, deepened to a twilight dimness that foiled rods and cones, anyone might see through my disguise.

But in almost three years, nobody had.

The physical transformation was also a mental one. I'd practiced expressions; spoke to myself until my scatty rattle of verbiage smoothed into dry, urbane British wit – with the accent to match. It was a role, but after so long, I slipped into it like a well-tailored suit.

People flocked to fan forums dedicated to speculation about Mr Mystic's return to active duty after years of retirement –

Mitchell Masters was pushing 70, after all. Some theorized that I was ageless due to my Eastern Kung Fu and meditative practices, others that I was a Legacy: some young man who had taken over the role while the old Mystic coached and guided me from his stronghold in the Cave of Mysteries. Nobody speculated that the Legacy might be a long-lost granddaughter. My grandfather had done his best to keep me secret and safe. Not even the most dedicated fans knew of Missy Masters.

Yes, I frequent the fan forums. I'm allowed my small pleasures.

The clothes were made to move in. My wool suit had gussets and plackets inserted to give me full range of movement without spoiling the lines. Double-breasted, thin pinstripes, starched collar harkening back to a silver age when clothes made the man, and style was a statement of moral fortitude. Soft leather half-boots, gloves to match, and a trench coat because at one point Mystic had been a spokesman for London Fog, and the look had stuck.

The hat was my finishing touch. I appreciated it for its pulp thematics as much as for the way it helped hide my features. Without his hat, Indiana Jones was just Harrison Ford in a costume. I settled the fedora on my head, swiped my fingers along the brim in a crisp gesture. I deepened the shadows around my face as I did so, and I became Mr Mystic.

They hadn't yet closed the Bay Bridge by the time I rode over it, but the traffic was doing a fair job at shutting things down all on its own. The Ducati had better pick-up than the Triumph, but it didn't handle as well. I occupied myself putting her through her paces. No use fretting over what I'd find in Oakland until I got there and could assess the situation on the ground.

I threaded through stopped cars, the world lit red by the constant brake lights. I kept an eye out for disgruntled motorists who might find it amusing to swerve into my path or clothesline me with whatever came to hand. People scoff, but such things are more common than my faith in the goodness of humanity likes to examine. I received more than my share of glares and horn blasts as I whizzed by inching SUVs and Priuses.

That was the appeal of the motorcycle for me. The dangers and the perks were the self-same thing.

The police were a presence the moment I exited the 880, diverting traffic and curiosity seekers away from Chinatown. I went with the flow, since it took me where I needed to go. Down Market and along the Embarcadero. The crowd outside the ferry terminal had worsened since the newscast, with people jostling and pushing towards the closed ferries: tourists antsy to get home, locals anxious to get out, and almost as many police in riot gear as there were civilians. Oakland never reacted when it could overreact.

There was a buzz in the air, the kind that just waited for a spark.

Little I could do here. I touched my helmet to the few shouts of recognition I received, ignored the flash of cell phones snapping a photograph, and wove south between cars and the growing crowds of people pushing out onto the Embarcadero.

I made it as far as the corner of Jack London before the crowds got too thick to ride through. I parked.

How was I ever supposed to locate Shimizu in this mob? I pushed through, abandoning my *excuse mes* and *pardon mes* after the first dozen or so human obstructions.

If I'd had my phone on ring, I never should have heard it. Good thing I kept it on vibrate. There was no quiet place to take the call. It was all I could do not to get trammeled by the crowd. I plugged one ear and resolved myself to shouting.

"Shimizu?"

"What the hell are you up to? I just called Patrick, and he said you came across to look for me."

"Well, then, I suppose your question is redundant, since you already know what I'm about."

"Why are you talking like that?"

Somebody shoved into me. I shoved back. The entire crowd was being herded like cattle up Broadway, away from the ferry and the more upscale shops around Jack London. I covered one ear and let myself go with the flow. "Why do you think?" I bit out.

"Oh. Oh! Are you serious? You *changed* before coming to get me?"

"I do wish you'd decide if you're upset that I came, or merely that I delayed slightly in coming."

"Ooh, who's a pissy old man?"

"Shut up and tell me where you are."

"Broadway and 4th."

"What the devil are you doing up there? Nevermind. Wait and I'll come to you." An easy enough promise, since the crowd was pushing in that direction. Getting her back to my bike would be the hard part.

After a few more triangulating phone calls, and a good deal of shoving, Shimizu and I managed to rendezvous a block further northeast from her original location, underneath the 880 overpass. Getting back to my bike was unlikely. The best we could manage was going with the flow, which seemed determined to push us closer to the city and Chinatown. I hadn't seen any reaction from the police myself, but others in the crowd were reporting the use of pepper spray, batons, and kettling nets.

If that was true, it was only a matter of time before the tear gas and rubber bullets came out.

"This is bad," Shimizu said, looking up. Bodies and cement blocked us on all sides. The underpass stank of car fumes, urine, and fear.

"Yes it is." I kept my arm about her waist. "I don't think we're going to be able to make it back to the bike."

"Some rescue."

"Hush, I haven't completed it yet. You don't critique a maestro halfway through a composition."

"This is why people prefer Skyrocket and think you're a has-been. He'd have had me out of here by now, no excuses."

"I'll put a rocket pack on my Christmas list."

The banter helped relieve the anxiety as we were pushed further and further along Broadway. We both took a deep breath as we came out the other side of the underpass and back into open air. A line of cops with orange kettling nets blocked off the side streets, keeping us moving along the main thoroughfare. At least half the crowd had cell phones out, brandished like cameras – hoping to catch their fifteen minutes of fame with some police violence to post on YouTube.

And then, at no cue I could discern, the police gave it to them.

Shrieks arose in reaction to the *whump* of canisters being launched, and smoke plumes followed. Shimizu and I, and the entire group we'd been shuffling along with, was shoved forward into the line of cops.

The police were not happy about being shoved closer to what I presumed was the invisible barrier around Oakland's Chinatown. They shoved back with their batons and their nets. I wrapped my arms closer around Shimizu, both so as not to lose her, and to protect her from elbows, fists, and batons.

The crowd surged again, pressing us up against the police and moving us all closer to the barrier. The same kind of barrier that had singed hapless chickens in Indonesia and crumpled shipping barges. Who knew what effect being mashed up against it would have? I didn't want to find out. We pushed back, not just Shimizu and I, but everyone under threat of being crushed. No good. The streetside crowd had too much collective mass, meanwhile the police between us and the barrier did their best to keep us all from being crushed and killed against its invisible force.

This could only end badly. I shouted against Shimizu's ear. "Hold on!"

Fearing I might regret it, I pulled us both into the Shadow Realms.

The rush of blood roared in my ears as I staggered forward and fell to my knees. Everything was so quiet here after the madness on the other side. And dark, and calm. No flashing red lights or smoke or confusion. Just a dark and twisted landscape and a moon like a great eye glaring down at us.

Shimizu gasped. The moon blinked.

Oh. No. That really was an eye.

My grip slid down to Shimizu's hand. "Run."

Stumbling to my feet, I pulled her after me into a labyrinth of twisted columns. The creature behind us shrieked like a Nazgûl on steroids. Shimizu's hand in mine was cold and slick.

A rush like the flapping of bat wings sounded above us. I ducked and rolled, pulling Shimizu down with me. She hadn't known to roll. She splayed out on the ground. Another shriek and rush of wind. The monster was coming around for a second pass.

Perhaps coming here had been a bad idea after all.

"Can we go back to the riot?" Shimizu asked, as I helped her to her feet. We huddled back against one of the towering columns.

"I need some source of light." The darkness here wasn't absolute – not to me – but whatever part of itself our attacker had blinked, it was now closed. No more glaring moon. The ambient light wasn't nearly enough to escape the gravitational pull of the Shadow Realms.

"I have something."

I could just make out her bent silhouette as she dug through her bag, looking for something. "Cell phone will be dead by now," I told her. "And lighters don't give enough light. I usually carry sparklers, but..."

She shushed me and kept digging. The creature's shriek

drowned out the rattle of pens and cosmetics.

A sharp crack and an eerie glow. Shimizu's face lit from below, like a children's campfire tale. If the campfire were blue and purple.

"Will this work?"

"Do I even want to know why you have glowsticks?" I asked, to cover my self-disgust. Glowsticks. Why hadn't I ever thought of that? I wrapped my arms around her and dove into the light, just as the something flappity snapped its jaws around where we had stood.

We came across in an alleyway, rolling over asphalt. A few looters yelped at our appearance, leaving a half-empty produce truck abandoned at its loading dock.

"We're in Chinatown," Shimizu whispered, looking up at the signs that were mostly in Cantonese. They were dark; no eye-straining neon. So were the streetlights, and all the windows. Shimizu's glowsticks were the only light in the world.

Of course. Cut off from electricity as well as everything else. Probably water, too. What about sewage?

Somebody, or a lot of somebodies, had not thought this through.

"How did we get into Chinatown? I thought that barrier thing–"

"Doesn't cross over into the Shadow Realms, it would seem." I stood, brushed myself off, and repositioned my hat, making sure the shadows around my face were still in place. I helped Shimizu to her feet. "Which isn't right. I've never run into a ward that didn't extend across the veil. Especially not a ward of this size, strength, and complexity."

I made for the opening of the alleyway. Shimizu followed. "I guess the world is going to have to start believing in this magic stuff now," she said, voice shaky and high. For all that she was my closest friend, Shimizu didn't often get glimpses into Mr Mystic's world.

"Why?" I hesitated at the mouth of the alleyway. The streets were mostly empty apart from a few people scurrying by with their heads down. Oakland's Chinatown was quiet and afraid. "Consider how many people don't believe in global climate change or evolution, and there's much more evidence for those things. Besides, the spin doctors are already working *their* magic. Blaming this on some kind of force field technology. People tend to believe what they want to believe and then accept the evidence that supports it."

Shimizu pressed against my back, peering around my shoulder. "I didn't realize Mr Mystic was such a pessimist?"

"That was cynicism, not pessimism."

"Either way, it's annoying. What now? Cross over somewhere safer and try to get back to your bike?" From the waver in her voice, she didn't like the idea of re-entering the Shadow Realms much better than I did.

"We could." We were inside now, and Oakland's Chinatown wasn't nearly as large or as well-organized as San Francisco's. If I could find the right people, exert the right leverage, I could find out where they'd taken their guardians and free them like I'd freed Johnny.

Assuming any of this was connected to the ritual I'd foiled at The Garden of Willows.

"You're killing me with that hesitation thing," Shimizu said, poking me.

"I think I may be able to destroy the wall here."

"Oh." Shimizu let out a shaky breath. "Then we should do that."

"Should we? Right now, this area is protected." And Xuan Wu's admonition to mind my own business still stung, reminding me that I would always be the interloper where China was concerned.

Shimizu flicked my ear. "Right now, this area is without services. Do you know how long it takes for dysentery and cholera and other sanitation diseases to develop? Not long. China's big enough to have infrastructure. Oakland isn't."

"We take down the ward, those riots could spill over. They'll need more police to keep the peace, and many people will wonder why Oakland and San Francisco are unaffected, but nowhere else. We're talking Homeland Security and internment camps."

Even as I ticked off the reasons I shouldn't meddle, I was on the move. Shimizu followed close behind. None of the scared tourists scurrying in the direction of Broadway paid us any mind.

"You're going to help, though. Right?"

"Yes, because it's one thing to stay out of China's business, but this isn't China. It's Oakland, and these are American citizens being held captive in their own city. We'll suss out China later. Come along." I dragged her across the street, dodging a few stray tourists.

"Where are we going?"

I pointed at the darkened shop sign for an apothecary. "It occurs to me that even villains have to buy their ritual candles somewhere."

I'd figured right. The apothecary turned out to be the Incense Master for the Oakland branch of the Shadow Dragons, and not at all pleased that the ritual Lao Chan had sent him had interrupted Cake Boss.

"Idiot," muttered Oakland's guardian, a wiry woman of middling years who told us to call her Judy. I was fairly sure I recognized her from Doris Han's monthly *pai gow* night. After I'd explained the breadth of the crisis, she'd agreed that down was better than up where the ward was concerned. She clutched a fluffy red hen to her chest while I freed the other two guardians: a sleek, red-point Siamese cat and Mrs Liang's fourth grade pet turtle, if the painted letters on his shell were any indication.

"He was just following orders," I said, feeling almost bad for the apothecary, who still couldn't get Cake Boss even now that his cable was working. Every channel had someone reporting on the New Wall Crisis.

"Not him." She tucked the hen under her arm and took the turtle from me. The cat stalked out of the storeroom, butt held high and tail twitching with feline disdain. "Lao Chan. I bet he didn't know any better than Zufong here what the ritual would do."

"You don't think it came from him?"

Judy had mastered that same look that Doris often gave her brood. The one that could make any human being feel twelve again. "If they managed this in Oakland and the other Chinatowns, then they did the same ritual in China. Do you really think even the Triads have the power to capture and hold China's guardians?"

No. I didn't. But I'd been hoping my suspicions were wrong. Three years had gone by, and I still wasn't ready to face my past. Hell and damnation.

"Why you? And Johnny? I follow the others: red bird, black turtle, white tiger, but you–"

"Dragon. Guardian of the East. All the city guardians have a dragon ancestor."

That answered that. Whoever had done this in China had to have the power to capture a dragon.

And not just any dragon.

"I need to talk to Johnny again," I said, taking deep breaths to control the fury and the fear and the trembling that came with. No doubt now who'd done this. I would end him and anyone who had helped him.

"You should talk to Lao Chan," Doris grumbled.

"I can't find Lao Chan."

"Is that all? Here."

She thrust the chicken into my arms, handed the turtle

to Shimizu, and tore a page out of the apothecary's ledger, scribbling out an address. "There. And when you go, tell him no moon cakes for him this New Years. Lock me in a cage, will he? Hmph."

Moon cakes. I refrained from telling her that I doubted any conversation I had with Lao Chan would touch on moon cakes. I exchanged the chicken for the address. Glanced at Shimizu, who was making googly-faces at the turtle. She lowered him and shrugged. "Well, I'm definitely not the kind of back-up you're going to need. Go get Johnny and Andrew. I'll be fine here. There's a clinic on Webster that I've done some work for in the past. Probably could use another pair of hands."

"We will keep an eye on her."

Shimizu nearly dropped the turtle when he spoke. His little feet swam about in the air, as if that could save him from a fall.

I snorted a laugh at the look on Shimizu's face, the humor breaking through my head-pounding fury.

Too many families. I had too many families, and I had to figure out how to protect them all. Which meant sometimes trusting them to take care of themselves.

"Stay safe," I told her, bypassing the turtle to give her a hug.

"The turtle talked," she squeaked.

"So he did. Welcome to my world."

I turned and strode out of the apothecary. My world. Time to save it.

San Francisco's Chinatown was not as I'd left it. Bush Street running past the Dragon Gate was no longer lit by electric paper lanterns and strings of fairy lights; instead, there was the red and blue strobe of a police blockade. It stretched down to Stockton and snaked up the western edge of Chinatown. The governor hadn't yet called in the National Guard, but it was only a matter of time. People were frightened, and when people are frightened, they tend to do stupid things – like go to war against their own citizenry.

Too many bodies and flashing lights to slip past them in the shadows. Instead, I headed up Dashiell Hammett Street, skirting the edge of the district and looking for another path through.

Unlike the police, I wasn't limited to a single plane. I looked up, evaluating the possibilities: distance between fire escapes, convenient overhangs, that sort of thing. Jack's constant jibes about safe climbing environments weren't far off. Urban running is not for the faint of heart, and I'd taken my share of tumbles over the past few years. I wouldn't be swinging Spiderman-style between high rises. Just leaping to my death across a street-wide chasm of potential pain.

Hadn't somebody once told me that people who choose to become adventure heroes have serious psychological issues? Why hadn't I listened?

I slipped into the deeper shadows cast by the buildings. San Francisco's architecture lent itself to rooftop running; I had my pick of fire escapes. I mounted one, clattering my way to the top story and hauling myself onto the flat rooftop.

The first leap is always the hardest. Once you get into the rhythm of the running, fear goes out the door. Momentum hurls you forward when common sense might scream *Stop, you fool!* The secret of flying is forgetting to fall.

We should all learn so much from cartoons.

I took a deep breath, centered my chi, and sprinted at the chasm between buildings. I used a small utility box as my springboard to the squat air conditioning unit abutting the roof's edge. The thin metal casing buckled under my foot as I launched myself into free space. I had no spare thought to worry about the noise. My entire being was focused on the decorative swoop of the rooftop across the way. It curved out to me in welcome. I strained to catch it, because the alternative was...

My grip strained as momentum threatened to rip tendons

and muscle and bone. I swung my legs and used the change in vector to heave myself up over the curved awning. I hung over it, a bit of laundry left out to dry, and stared down at the street far below. Good lord, I was a madman to have risked that.

But a madman now in Chinatown. I hauled myself up and slipped along the edge of the rooftop. I couldn't descend to the streets just yet. The police might spot me, or less savory elements looking to make trouble.

I slid down another fire escape, made a smaller, easier leap – barely a hop, really – across a narrow alleyway, and then a drop and roll onto another, lower rooftop. I came up with one hand atop my head. My hat remained in place. Brushing dust and city grime from my coat, I watched the building across the street with narrowed gaze.

The Pearl was closed, the windows dark. So was Johnny's studio, but that didn't mean anything. Doris Han would be holed up with her brood in their third floor apartment. Johnny would be out patrolling, but he'd know when someone broke in.

Or would he? How much of his guardianship depended on his now-blocked connection to China?

I lowered myself off the rooftop, crawling down the face of the tacky consortium that had served as my perch and dropping into the empty street. Somebody had already put plywood over the window that Virgin Mary and his friends had smashed earlier that day.

I crept past the Pearl's kitchen door in case Doris had decided to cook away her anxiety – woman could hear questionable comings and goings from twenty paces – and slipped into the studio.

I needn't have worried about waiting for Johnny. He was already there, kneeling at the head of the mat and limned by the faint light coming in from the streetside windows.

"Mr Mystic," he said in greeting before I could blurt my

business, warning me with those two words that we were not alone. I looked to the other end of the mat. A man knelt in the same position as Johnny, concealed by the shadows. I knew him.

David Tsung.

"I didn't expect to see you again, Mr Tsung."

He stared at me as though the darkness were no more impediment to him than it was to me. He shook his head. "Incredible."

Johnny fell back on his butt with a groan. "Well, this is fucking inconvenient. What are you doing here?"

I hesitated, not sure who I should be watching: my gaping enemy or my *sifu*, who was currently pulling at his hair spikes like he only did when I'd annoyed him.

"I think that is a matter best discussed in private."

"She even has the accent down," Tsung murmured. "How long have you been pulling this off?"

She? And the way he blinked and stared, with the same incredulous recognition as in the Garden of Willows.

I threw my hat at Johnny and dropped my act. "You gave me away?"

"You did that, Masters. He saw you in the basement, getting your shadow on. I've just wasted the past twenty minutes trying to convince him that he was mistaken, and you barge in."

"How?" I demanded. Johnny ignored me in favor of rubbing his face. I turned on Tsung. "How? And while you're at it, give me one good reason why I should let you walk out of here with my secret."

My empty threat made him snort. "You won't kill me. Everyone knows Mr Mystic has developed a conscience since his return." He held up his hands when I took a step toward him. The only thing that was saving him from an ass-kicking at this point was that I still had my shoes on and didn't dare cross the mat to get to him.

"I don't have to kill you. The Shadow Realms are lovely this time of year. Could just send you there." Another nearly-empty threat. The Shadow Realms were never lovely.

For some reason, Johnny thought this was hilarious, chuckling and coughing behind his hands.

"I won't talk," Tsung said. "I'm not here as your enemy. If you are who I think you are, I've been looking for you for days – since I got back from Shanghai."

I crossed my arms. "And who am I supposed to be?"

"I think you might be Mitchell Masters's granddaughter. I think you're *Lung Xin Niang*."

I swayed where I stood. Sat, before I embarrassed myself by falling over and cracking my head on the hard wood of the door frame. Johnny collected himself and tossed my hat back at me.

"You never told me," he said with a hint of underlying accusation. Not for the connection with my grandfather; Johnny had been my *sifu* since toddling days. For the other.

"It was never…" I shook my head. Pretended to be fascinated by my hat to keep the tears at bay. "It's not something I like to talk about." And especially not now. Not with Tsung here. "It's complicated."

I put on the hat to give myself a moment to process, a moment to be someone else. Tsung. The New Wall. Focus. "What do you want with me? With *Lung Xin Niang*?"

"I was sent to bring you – her – an invitation."

Like pulling teeth. "*What* invitation?"

"This." He took something out of his coat pocket and slid it across the mat – something hard, bundled in silk. I had to lean far over to get it. I unwrapped the silk and scootched back with a yelp, flinging the contents away like a snake.

The dull wood-carving knife thunked to the mat. Johnny picked it up. Turned it over in his hands and arched a brow at me.

"Careful," I said. I knew that knife, and it was a lot more dangerous than it seemed. Which meant Tsung probably was as well. "How did you get that?"

"I stole it. From the head of the Shadow Dragons. My master sent me to bring it to you. She said you're our best option for sorting out what's going on."

I didn't believe him. "The head of the Shadow Dragons isn't so easy to steal from."

Tsung raised a brow. "You would know, wouldn't you?"

I looked away first.

Johnny snatched up the silk and re-wrapped the knife. "Just how many do you call 'master,' Tsung?"

Tsung flinched. "Song Yulan approved of my coming, if that's what you mean."

Song Yulan. Shanghai's guardian, just as Johnny was for San Francisco or Judy for Oakland. There was a lot more to the daggers Johnny and David Tsung were glaring at each other than I could figure out just by watching. "I'd like Exposition for five hundred, Alex."

Johnny rose to his feet. Tsung followed suit, and I scrambled to mine so I wouldn't be the only one left sitting. Perhaps there was going to be a fight after all.

Johnny handed me the knife. "Mr Tsung was Song Yulan's apprentice until he left to go work for family. And now it appears he has changed allegiances again."

Family. Which meant "dragon" if he'd been in training to become a guardian. My hands trembled as I tucked the knife away in my coat. "You're working for Lung Di." It explained Tsung's prominence in the Shadow Dragons. It explained the knife and the ability to see through shadows. And the penchant for betrayal and shady dealing.

"Was. He's gone too far with this ward, which is why I was sent to bring you that." He nodded at my breast pocket. "It's the key, the master key. Free China's guardians, and the other wards will go down like dominoes."

It didn't make sense. "Why bring this to me? Why not free the guardians yourself? Perhaps *before* the wards went up and sent the world into a panic? "

"I... can't."

I snorted.

"Come to Shanghai. My master will explain–"

"I don't think anyone is going anywhere at present," said Johnny, peering out the window. I skirted the perimeter of the mat and looked out. Several dark sedans had pulled up, blocking the street at either end, and shadowy forms waited on the rooftop across the way, cradling large, dull-surfaced assault rifles.

"Of course. Now Lao Chan wants to talk." He could be here for Johnny, but I doubted it. Someone had seen me enter the building and made a call.

"He has orders not to kill you. Mr Mystic, I mean." Tsung said, coming up on my other side. "Now I know why."

That explained my continued existence after the motorcycle incident. "Orders from whom?"

David Tsung looked at me like I'd eaten stupid for breakfast. Right. Lung Di.

"Just checking." I tugged on the brim of my hat and deepened the shadows around my face. "Shall we see what Lao Chan wants?"

The alleyway that ran alongside the Pearl was dark. A lone street lamp lit the street out front, its chemical-orange glow fighting a losing battle with the darkness. This was a different Chinatown than the one I knew – gaudy lights and tourist traps on the one face, arcane family networks and community drama on the other.

This was the third face. The Triad's Chinatown.

As if in response to my thought, a footstep scuffed from

behind a sheltered stoop. Deliberate. Letting us know someone was there. A signal to the rest to come forth. Shadows that weren't shadows moved.

Lao Chan stepped into the light of the street lamp; the Incense Master from the basement of the Garden of Willows stood at his side. The lamplight strengthened. It pushed back the shadows, leaving the men standing in a glowing amber nimbus.

"Mr Masters. I see Mr Tsung has found you after all. How... industrious of him. Especially since he indicated earlier that you might be an imposter."

"Did he?" I glared at David Tsung. So much for not giving me up.

"I was wrong, *Shan Chu*," he said, bowing to Lao Chan. "I am now confident in Mr Masters's identity, and I have passed along Mr Long's invitation."

Mr Long's invitation? How many different lies was Tsung telling?

Lao Chan folded his hands and regarded Tsung coldly, as though he wondered the same thing. I ventured a few steps closer to him. The nimbus of light carried the damp smell of *pu-erh* tea, pungent and earthy. I tried to touch the shadows around me, but my connection to darkness slipped from my grasp. Even the shadows that concealed my face felt thin and insubstantial. I stopped. Lao Chan and his Incense Master were still several meters away, cocooned in their street light. Another ward. Had to be.

"It is well enough for you to be satisfied, but I am not. I think perhaps a demonstration of proof is in order." He straightened the starched white cuffs under his dark suit sleeves and refolded his hands.

There was no purpose to the gesture. Lao Chan was impeccably dressed and he knew it.

It was a signal.

I let instinct take over, turning to block the first strike almost before I knew it. I guided the fist past me, pulled the attacker off balance, and used his body as leverage to spring up and bring an elbow strike down on the back of his neck. He was too eager to please his master – overconfident. He went down with a soft grunt. The rest wouldn't be so easy.

They streamed from the doorways and alleys where they'd been waiting, silent save for the flutter of their dark cotton tunics, faces covered as a means of intimidation. They formed a semicircle of various stances, leaving a wide open space with me in the center.

"Don't interfere," Lao Chan snapped when Johnny and Tsung tensed and moved to cover my back. Tsung stepped back up to the sidewalk, obeying. I'd expected that. But so did Johnny. I glared at him for his betrayal, but he was too busy watching Lao Chan with narrowed eyes.

Fine. It was a test. He'd been ordered not to kill me, if Tsung was to be believed. Perhaps beating me up was Lao Chan's way of regaining the face he'd lost from the failed bust and the disrupted ritual.

I'd faced worse adversaries in worse conditions. I took a centering breath, shifted my legs, and lowered into a fighting stance. Better a dozen attackers than just one, I supposed, if the inverse effectiveness rule was to be believed. I waited for them to strike.

Unlike their cinematic brethren, they didn't pay me the courtesy of attacking one by one, nor were they foolish enough to attack *en masse*. They clustered in three groups of four, each cluster blocking a path to escape. I concentrated my focus on my front and right flank. The cluster to my left mistook this for inattention and launched their assault.

Perhaps this would be easier than I'd feared.

The middle attacker, thicker-set than the others, charged for my back. His fellows came around my sides. I was meant to

meet the large one's attack, but that was an amateur's tactic. I
went low with a leg sweep, catching the attacker on my right
unawares as he tried to circle around me. Forward roll under
the outstretched arms of my main opponent, then up with a
low kick to the back of his knee. The knee popped, and he
collapsed with the first scream of the fight.

Before I could regroup, the one on my left came at me with
a series of short, quick jabs to my gut. I fought the urge to curl
around the pain, tightened my abdomen, and tried to redirect
the blows. I missed as many as I caught. He drove me back
into his partner, who had recovered from my sweep. I slipped
through his arms as he tried to grapple me, spinning to one
side to shift the angle of their approach.

They weren't comfortable fighting side-by-side. The grappler
reached for me again, but the close-fighter got in his way. I
caught the grappler's arm, wrapped it into a lock under my
own, and struck his exposed throat with the heel of my hand.
He went down choking, right into the path of my third attacker.

With his footing off, the third relented on his attacks. I did
not. Lowering my center, I skirted the obstacles of my downed
opponents. He turned to meet me, throwing off his own
center. I feinted to one side, and he moved to block. Dropping
to one knee, I snapped out a kick to his exposed solar-plexus.
He didn't have enough air to cry out as he collapsed next to
his fellows.

I looked for the fourth – there had been four, hadn't there?
– but a shift of movement behind me warned that the second
wave was coming. A body struck my back, rolling us out of the
pile of moaning fighters. My side scraped along pavement, my
breath gone for a moment.

I kicked out to flip my attacker off me, but he rolled away.
Someone else's foot came down into my exposed center. I
fought the urge to puke, retained enough presence of mind to
grab hold of the leg. Using it as leverage, I pulled my second

attacker down and windmilled myself up. I mimicked his stomp, but aimed higher. The bones of his clavicle cracked under the sole of my boot.

I had no time to be queasy about that. The assailant who'd tackled me had paired with his buddy. They lunged at me with a series of coordinated spins, kicks, and punches. I blocked and diverted, but with both of them coming I couldn't spare a moment for a counterattack. They drove me back until one of the kicks broke through. It connected solidly mid-chest, sending me lurching backwards.

I hit a wall of light that burned like acid fire along my back – Lao Chan's wards. The pain saved me. Rather than collapsing to my knees, I launched away like a scalded cat, stumbling into my startled attackers. We went down in a tangle of limbs. I locked legs around one and proceeded to kick him in the face until I heard bones crack. I rendered the other one unconscious with several good, old-fashioned head-butts. Not pretty, but it worked.

I wiped blood from my face and rolled up to my feet. My back burned and my chest ached, but the adrenaline had kicked in; I hardly noticed the pain.

Like the two before, the third group didn't grant me a moment to catch my breath. They circled me in a blur of movement, a series of spinning jumps and kicks so fast they were hard to follow. I didn't have to. If you've ever seen someone thrust a length of rebar into the spokes of a moving bicycle, then you have a rough idea of what happens when you deliver a high kick to someone mid-spin.

Of course, the outcome isn't always pretty for the rebar, either. I snapped out a kick at one of the leaping attackers, catching him hard at the hip joint mid-spin. He lost the trajectory, came tumbling down wrong, and cracked his head on the pavement. I tried to pull back, but my leg got caught in his flight, twisting me off balance and bringing me down hard on one knee.

I collapsed to one side, which is the only thing that saved me from the kick aimed at my head. I rolled in the direction of my collapse, using the momentum to push myself up. Each time I went down, getting up became harder. How many left?

These two at least. The one who had missed kicking my head circled me, looking for an opening. The other didn't wait, launching into a flashy kick. Somebody had dabbled in Taekwondo and liked to show off.

I ducked underneath, leaping up after he sailed over me, and delivered my own kick into his back. The extra momentum was more than he knew what to do with. His form dropped and his arms and legs wheeled as he slammed face-first into Lao Chan's wall of light. It was somewhat edifying to hear him scream where I had not.

I turned to face my final opponent. He started in with a series of quick arm strikes, but they lacked strength. I blocked and redirected until he grew impatient and went for another kick. I shifted around it. Catching his leg, I locked it against my side and dropped to the ground. His only option was to follow me down or risk a dislocated knee. He chose poorly.

Leaving the last of my attackers moaning on the ground, clutching at his joint, I staggered up and faced Lao Chan. He smiled. Genial. Pleasant. Not what I expected from him when nine of his men had failed to kill me in less than a minute.

Wait. Nine. Hadn't I counted twelve at the beginning?

Something shuffled behind me. With a sigh, I turned to face the three I'd missed. They held their stances without eagerness or hesitation. In every line of their bodies was the control that came from years of training. These were the masters. I'd wager it was their students I'd just taken out. Lovely.

Fresh, I could perhaps hold my own against one of them. Now, I had not the slightest chance.

I took a breath, two, then shifted back into my stance. Better to go out fighting.

"Enough."

The three masters flowed to attention. I hesitated. Perhaps the reprieve was another trap, but if so, what was the point? Straightening, I turned to face Lao Chan. He looked at David Tsung. I realized it was Tsung who'd spoken. Tsung who'd stopped the fight.

"Are you satisfied?" Tsung asked. "He's no imposter."

The older man nodded. "So it would seem. I have never seen you fight, Mr Masters. You are very skilled."

"Not skilled enough."

Lao Chan frowned. "You took down nine of my best men."

"But you brought twelve."

"So I did. You would do well to remember this lesson when you go to see Mr Long: when it comes to anticipating a conflict, I am the student; he is the master." A dark Lexus pulled up beside Lao Chan, followed by a black, windowless van. The light from the street lamp dimmed back to its normal amber glow. The pungent, earthy smell had dissipated. A driver got out of the Lexus and opened the door for his boss, while a crew of dark-clad figures loaded my downed assailants into the van.

"At first, I was put out by your interference in my business," Lao Chan said to me over the roof of the car. "But then I realized that you deserved my pity, not my antagonism. Mr Long commands much… *respect*. I believe you will be rewarded amply for the trouble you have caused me over the past few years. I leave you in Mr Tsung's excellent care."

I stood in the middle of the street, watching the tail-lights flash red before the car turned the corner. The van followed. Possibly, I was gaping. Johnny Cho was pinching the bridge of his nose. Again. He did that a lot with me.

"So. China." David Tsung joined me in the street. He was neither gaping nor looking for a wall to bang his head against. If anything, he was smirking. "Any idea how we're supposed to get there?"

SIX

Enter the Dragon

Then

I dreamed of snow, the kind you never see growing up in coastal California: blizzard thick, muffles sight and sound until it's just you in a cocoon of white. I struggled against it, but it wrapped itself around me until I couldn't breathe.

I woke up fighting my blankets. It took me several moments of confusion to realize I was acting like an idiot, that the percale and eiderdown comforter *wasn't* attacking. A rich coverlet of red, green, and gold brocade spread in rumpled folds across my feet, and carved wooden panels on all sides latticed the sunlight streaming into the room. I stared up at the wooden canopy for a few moments and then wriggled my toes. I couldn't see them, but it felt like I still had all ten.

I was in a room. I had no idea how I'd gotten here.

I remembered leaving Jim and Jill and the others, but after the snow started falling around dusk, things got a little fuzzy. Had I been dreaming of snow, or was that part real? Did I find this bed on my own? Had I collapsed in the snow and been rescued? Was this just another illusion of the *yaoguai*?

I shoved aside the covers at that unsettling thought, peering through the latticework as though it offered any sort of protection.

The red, green, and gold of the bedclothes continued throughout the room, framed by dark, carved woods. The length of one wall had painted shutters thrown open to the outdoors. In the distance rose the snowy peaks of other mountains. Thick clouds obscured everything below; the blizzard I'd dreamed about was still going, or another like it. It didn't touch the tranquility up here above the clouds.

A mural ran the length of the opposite wall, depicting a series of stylized gardens cupped in the hollow core of a mountain peak: paradise on earth. Seven figures stood in the gardens, sad and somber, while one waited just outside, reaching toward the gates and his companions. Another figure, shrouded in darkness, glowered at them from far below.

I was alone, but there were signs that someone else had recently been in the room. A basin of water, fresh lotus petals floating on the surface, sat in a stand near the bed. The water was still warm enough to be steaming. The steam mixed with a ribbon of smoke rising from an incense burner on the stand. I took a cautious breath, then a deeper one. Sandalwood. The scent settled my initial panic. If Lung Huang was giving me warm water and incense, then she probably didn't have immediate plans to eat me.

Probably. My experience with the *yaoguai* was fresh enough to give me pause.

Not wanting to be caught lying down if the dragon *did* want to eat me, I slipped out of bed. My forearm, where the demon's acidic blood had burned me, was wrapped in gauze, and somebody had stripped me and put me in a light shift of undyed silk. Minimal embroidery decorated the neck and hem. I took a closer look. Or... not so minimal. A chain of red and gold carp leapt out of green waters, their tiny bodies and the spray of their antics picked out in minute detail.

Unlike the sandalwood, the intricacy unnerved me. Wandering girls who woke to fairy tale environments rarely fared well, and in Chinese folklore, mortals who dallied with spirits usually ended up worse off than they'd started.

Why had I come here, again?

My hand strayed to my throat. She'd left me my pearls. I didn't know what to make of the gesture. They felt tight around my neck. Strangling.

I bit down on a growl. Enough dithering. No point working myself into a tizzy until I ran into something worth tizzying over.

A large wardrobe with carved jade facing stood next to the washstand. I pulled the doors open and found a blinding array of brocade silk. It was too much. I pawed through the silks until I reached the back of the wardrobe. It was deep enough that I half expected to run across fir trees and a lamppost. Instead I found another layer of simpler robes hanging on hooks. Well, simpler by comparison. I pulled out a robe of pale green silk embroidered with pink blossoms. It only came to my knees, but there were dove-grey trousers to go underneath. I liked the color combination. It made me feel cool. Composed. Calm. The opposite of how I really felt.

I dug out a pair of white socks and black cloth shoes, then dressed and bound my hair back in a thick French braid. I'd impale myself if I tried to work with the array of hairsticks in the box on the washstand.

I stepped out of the room and onto a walkway, grabbing for the carved railing as vertigo threatened to send me stumbling. Lung Huang's home-in-exile sat atop the Minshan range. The buildings nestled at different levels climbing up to the peak, connected by wooden stairs and walkways. The roof points curved up toward heaven, painted in reds and greens and gilded along the edges. Crimson banners with tassels of green and gold fluttered in a light breeze. Lung Huang's home reminded me of a cheerful holly bush rooted deep in crags where less tenacious plants wouldn't grow.

I took several breaths and released my white-knuckled grip on the railing.

The stairway nearest me led down to a series of terraced gardens. Small wooden benches, stone carvings, and reflecting pools were interspersed among the cultivated topiary. I spied a flash of steam and viridian at one edge where the gardens dropped off into clouds, one of the travertine pools that the Huanglong valley was so well-known for. The steps leading down to the gardens were wide and shallow, built of the same dark wood as the building frames and walkways. Off to one side, a tiny pagoda had been erected on a flat spar of karst. The frame was open to the light breezes. I couldn't tell from where I stood, but I bet that on clear days you might actually be able to see forever.

And that's when I spied my host.

She sat on a bench at the base of the stairs, her back to me, so still that she had become one with the landscape. *She* had no qualms about the clothes being too flashy. She wore an embroidered robe of red, green, and gold brocade. It should have looked opulent and overdone. It didn't.

Her black hair flowed free down her back. And kept flowing. And then flowed some more. It coiled in a serpentine tail on the ground behind her. In the light breeze, there should have been wispies. Lord knew I was already sporting some of my own. But Lung Huang's hair wouldn't dare be so unruly.

I took a breath. She had to know I was here, but she didn't turn, didn't tense, didn't shift one finger out of that perfect, meditative posture.

Right, then. With another breath, I headed down the steps, pausing when I reached the bottom. I stood directly behind the bench, and still she didn't move.

Uh...

"Miss Lung Huang? Thank you for welcoming me into your home." My Cantonese wasn't great; my fingers tended to twitch and swoop like a pop diva's, tracing out the tonal shifts that my voice only sometimes followed, but it had to be better than English, right?

She stirred. She turned.

Oh. Crap.

"I mean... Mister?"

For whoever he was, he was definitely a *him*. There was no way he was human, either. His eyes swirled a depthless black, flecks of red, green, and gold flashing. His face was smooth, unwrinkled. Ageless. And expressionless as he watched me struggle to not look like a carp gasping for air.

I snapped my mouth shut until I could think of something to say. It wasn't even that my Cantonese was failing me. I couldn't come up with anything in English, either. The coil of hair flicked and settled around his feet once more. If it were a tail, I would have said it was a gesture of mild impatience.

If it were a tail.

"You're Lung Huang?"

"I am." His voice was as impressive as the rest of him, a deep, rich baritone that many an actor would kill for.

And once again... male.

"You're a man."

One brow arched. It was just a twitch of movement, but it made me feel as stupid as my blurted statement had been. "Am I?"

Thank god I'd grown up in San Francisco, where fluid genders weren't uncommon. I winced and smiled an apology. Way to start off on the wrong foot, dumbass.

"You're a Dragon."

He nodded. The brow settled. "Better."

We both fell silent until I realized it was my turn again. It was conversation by rote, call-and-response. If this kept up, my chances were shot. He'd be tossing me down the mountainside before I could ask him anything important.

I reached behind my neck and unfastened my pearls, letting them pool in my hand. I caressed a thumb over them, their nacre rich and warm, reminding me of love lost but never forgotten. My grandfather's love.

But of course, that's not what they represented. I held them out. "I came to return these to you."

"Why?" He folded his hands in his sleeves, looking down at the pearls, but he made no move to take them.

"They don't belong to me. My grandfather told me about you. About your... relationship." The ramifications were only starting to sink in. The queer community would explode if this ever were confirmed. "He's gone now. I don't know where. Maybe dead. Probably dead."

And Lung Huang didn't need my life story. Chances were he knew better than I what had become of Mitchell Masters. I forged ahead before I could get bogged down. "He gave these to me before he left. When I realized everything he told me was true, I figured that you should have them back."

Lung Huang frowned, the slightest twitch of lips. Like the eyebrow, it was enough to crush me with censure. What had I said to upset him?

"That is not why you came here."

Oh. Right. I licked my lips. "Not the only reason. I came hoping you would train me as you trained him."

"Mitchell Masters was *Lung Bao Hu Zhe*. My Champion. I had no choice but to train him. Honor demanded. What are you to me?"

I felt stupid, standing there with the pearls held out between us. He still hadn't taken them, but he had given me an opening. The pearls clicked between my fingers. "I'm his granddaughter, and I mean to take up his legacy. But I'm as clueless about how to do it as he was when he came to you. So doesn't honor demand that you train me like you trained him?"

"You are not *Lung Bao Hu Zhe*. You have little *guanxi* with me." He took the pearls, turning them over to inspect them. "Why do you wish to become what your grandfather was?"

Months of asking myself that same question gave me a ready answer. "Because I want to make a difference in the world."

"So that the world will celebrate you as a hero?" He didn't look up. The pearls clicked against each other as he twined them through his fingers.

I dodged pitfall number one easily. This wasn't about pride. I didn't *want* people to know who had helped them. I just wanted to help. "I don't want fame. I just want to make the world a better place."

"You wish to shape the world into what you think it should be?"

Yes. Wait. "No..." I dragged the denial out to give myself a moment to think. "I can't control what other people do, but I can protect people who can't protect themselves."

"The sage practices not-doing."

"Like you not-did when you sent the *huxian* to save me from the *yaoguai*?"

His eyes flicked up from their contemplation of the pearls, deep as starlit void. I looked down. Me and my smart mouth.

"Why do you wish to follow your grandfather's path?" he asked again.

"Why did you help me against the *yaoguai*?"

"You presume the two motivations are related?"

"I don't think you like standing aside and watching when you know you can help. That's why you're here and not in Shambhala."

He stilled and I took a step back, wondering if I'd just gone too far.

"Perhaps you are right. But in the doing of a thing, the how and the why matters. If you do not understand this in yourself, compromise will weaken you, and you will cause more harm than you fix." With a nod, he handed the pearls back to me.

"These were a gift, and the love they represent has not died; it lives on in you. They are yours to keep."

I grinned at the victory, my stomach doing flips. He'd agreed!

"However," he said, folding his hands back in his sleeves. "You have made quite a mess, and I am disinclined to take a student who is so inconsiderate, especially after I have helped them."

"A mess?" I echoed. What, had I left too many snow angels during my climb through the blizzard?

"Your demons, the ones you unleashed on the *yaoguai*. They have spread throughout my valley, and they are wreaking more havoc than she ever did."

Oh. Crap. I fidgeted, tugging at my own sleeves in a parody of his calm posture. Good going, Masters. "I'll clean them up," I offered, even as I realized that I had no idea how to do that, or how long it would take. What else could I say?

Lung Huang took a step toward me, too close. He searched my face for I don't know what. I fought the urge to step back. Americans: we like our space.

"You will. If I agree to train you during your stay, then you must agree to remain until every shadow has been laid to rest."

In other words, no pulling a Luke Skywalker and rushing off to save Han and Leia. "Agreed," I said.

"Very well, Melissa Masters." He reached out and took my hands, the pearls pressing into my fingers, warmer than they had any right to be. It was an oddly formal, almost ritual gesture. "I will undertake your training."

Another wave of vertigo washed over me. I swayed, and his hands dropped to catch me at the elbows, the first real expression crossing his features: concern. I smiled to show I was all right. The world had already righted itself.

"Call me Missy."

He nodded. "And you may call me Jian Huo."

•••

Lung Huang – Jian Huo, I guess he was now – led me to the pagoda, where a table had been laid out. He remained silent as servants brought us tea and bowls of rice and steaming vegetables. The servants were human-shaped, but they moved like something else in a human costume. The composition of their faces was off, the proportions of their bodies, the fluidity of their movements. It was easier to look at the dragon across from me than it was to watch them go about their business.

Not much easier, with him looking back at me with that eternal gaze. I poked at my rice and greens. Guess I was going to be eating healthy while I was here.

"Why did you call them demons?" I asked when I couldn't take the silence any longer. Jian Huo took a slow sip of his tea, then another.

"It is what they are." He set the cup down, folded his hands in his sleeves. He settled in as if he could sit there for all eternity.

"Is everything in the Shadow Realms a demon?" I asked, thinking of Templeton and the few other denizens I'd met who didn't scare me silly.

Jian Huo pursed his lips, eyes narrowing. "What did your grandfather tell you of your gifts?"

I didn't know the Cantonese word for "bupkiss", so I used the American version and got another raised brow for my efforts. The corner of his mouth twitched whenever he did that. I was going to start collecting those raised brows. They made him not quite so intimidating. How many had he given me so far? Three? Four? Hell, I'd have to start my count with this one.

"That was poorly done of him."

"He didn't know I'd inherit his powers," I said, surprising myself more than the dragon across from me. I never stood up for Mitchell.

"Didn't he?" His tone suggested that my grandfather had known very well. Right. That was why I didn't make a practice of defending the man. He had been a secretive bastard.

"It falls to me, then," Jian Huo said. The silence that followed those words stretched on until I realized it wasn't just a pause for dramatic effect.

"OK," I prodded, but Jian Huo gave a minute shake of his head, unfolded his hands, and stood.

"You are not ready to understand. Finish your meal. Find me in the library when you are through. Your Cantonese is atrocious. We will improve it."

"But... what about cleaning up the shadows?" Hadn't he said they were wreaking havoc? I didn't want to be responsible for any more havoc than I'd already caused.

Another eyebrow lift. I had no clue what I'd said to earn that one.

"You are not ready for that, either." He pulled his robes close and swept past me, sandalwood-scented hair trailing behind him.

Well... peachy.

"'The Tao that can be told is not the eternal Tao'," I recited. Months of constant study, of digging into every text Jian Huo put before me, comprehending, analyzing, critiquing, contextualizing, and discussing until late in the evenings, had honed my Cantonese beyond passable. My Mandarin was coming along, and I had even started to pick up some of the other major regional dialects. The mountaintop temple had become my home. I'd befriended most of the servants, and once they were comfortable with me, they reverted to their natural, amorphous forms with relief. And Jian Huo no longer intimidated me. Mostly, he annoyed the shit out of me.

Like now, because, despite all my progress, we kept returning to this first book, this first line. His response was always the same.

"No. You do not yet have it."

My jaw set. I would get this. I *would*. I tried again. "The Tao that–"

"Repeating your mistake brings you no closer to rectifying it."

"What mistake?" I shoved the scroll aside. He allowed me to read from a modern translation rather than the original he'd first handed me. It was only better in that I could be a bit more careless with the materials. Struggling through Classical Chinese was kind of like struggling through Chaucer.

We'd spent a week on Chaucer.

He repeated the line in rich, rolling tones. I couldn't hear any difference from what I'd just said, except my voice didn't have that echo of eternity in it.

I sat back on my heels, rubbing my face. "I'm just not getting it."

"That is obvious."

"I mean, I'm not even getting what to get."

"As you might say, 'Again with the obvious'."

I peeked through my fingers to glare at him. A smile threatened to break through, but no eyebrow lift, so it didn't count for my collection. "I'm a bad influence on you."

"I believe I will survive the ordeal."

"I might not," I muttered.

He inclined his head. Jian Huo hadn't said as much, but I suspected we weren't going to start hunting shadows until I broke this puzzle. I was antsy to get started.

"Is this like a Karate Kid thing, where the answer is different than what I think it is?"

"I know little of karate, but I believe it is clear that the answer is not what you think it is, or you would have succeeded in one of your ten-thousand attempts."

"There haven't been that many," I grumbled.

"As you say." He rose, his coil of hair tumbling out of his lap. I breathed deeply of the sandalwood that washed over me. *That* earned me the eyebrow twitch I'd been gunning for. Shit.

I'd been caught. Usually I managed to be more subtle.

"Set it aside for now. Walk the gardens. Drink tea. Practice your hanfu." I grimaced at this last. The issue of how I dressed was a constant struggle. I kept going for the unadorned robes at the back of my wardrobe, much to Jian Huo's chagrin. But he never pressed the issue. Maybe because he dressed fancy enough for the both of us.

Those rich robes rustled as he left the room. He paused at the doorway, regarding me with eyes of endless black. "It will come to you in time. You are a good student."

He left me gaping in a wake of sandalwood. Jian Huo was a patient teacher, but not an effusive one. A compliment like that from him was as precious as a pearl.

I hopped up and all but skipped my way down to the gardens.

When I'd first come to the mountaintop temple, I'd thought it was a lonely place, deserted by all save Lung Huang and a few spirit servants. I couldn't have been more wrong. Nobody else lived here, but the through traffic was constant. Supplicants came to ask the Guardian of the East for aid: minor spirits, the occasional monk, the even more occasional farmer or businessman. Sometimes the greater spirits dropped by. Feng Huang, the Phoenix Guardian of the South, came on a weekly basis to play *wei-qi* with Jian Huo. She'd deigned to play me once. The game lasted less than five minutes. Jian Huo observed that this was another subject to be added to the growing list of things I needed to learn.

Don't ask me what *wei-qi* had to do with hunting down shadows or taking up my grandfather's legacy. We hadn't gotten that far yet.

Sometimes, our visitors were messengers. My steps slowed, the skip faltering, as I spied a familiar flash of russet. It could be that it was a different fox each time, but the way she watched me, with mocking amber eyes, made me doubt it.

Besides, how many foxes had four tails?

Those tails flicked as I approached. I bowed in return on the off chance that she meant it as a greeting. Jian Huo had taken a lot of care to beat some manners into my skull, so it was a good chance to practice.

"*Huxian*. It is a pleasure to see you again. Lung Huang is above. I do not believe he is occupied."

"Thank you, *Miqian*, but I am not here to see Lung Huang. I am here to see *Lung Xue*."

Another thing I'd learned here: spirits have many names and titles, and what they call each other – or in the case of powerful spirits like Jian Huo, what they *allowed* you to call them – said a lot about your standing in the world. *Huxian* had taken to calling me "silk purse", and I couldn't decide if she meant it as an insult or a backhanded compliment.

"There aren't any other dragons here." I was still shaky on the ancient dialect that the spirits used for their honorifics, but Lung was a word I knew.

Huxian laughed, mocking and merry.

"That's you, idiot. You're *Lung Xue*, his student."

Oh. "And you're here to see me?" I was busy boggling over having a title. It made it all seem so... official. "Why?"

She half-turned toward the gardens, tails flicking. This gesture I could guess. She wanted me to walk with her. I did.

She led me out of the gardens, down toward the mountain path that led back into the valley. I paused at the gates, reluctant to follow the fox past them. It was cold down here, much colder than the gardens and house above. That change in temperature told me that stepping past that threshold was more than just a matter of a few steps.

The fox paused, turned, and cocked her head at me. "Well? Come along."

"Why can't we talk here?"

"Because I wish to speak in private. It is only a few more steps."

The saccharine tone decided me. I took a step back. "I'm not allowed to leave. Anything you have to say, you can say here."

She sighed and settled on her haunches. "My, he *does* have you on a short leash. Very well, *Miqian*. But I meant no harm. It is truth, that I only wished to speak in private. Lung Huang *is* his realm. He knows all that passes within."

I didn't believe one word that came out of her smiling muzzle. I crossed my arms, folding my hands into my sleeves, as much because it was cold down here as because I was not happy that she'd almost tricked me.

"What do you want to talk about?"

"There are demons plaguing the valley. Lung Huang knows this, and I believe you do as well."

She had been there when I called the shadows. She knew I knew. I did my best imitation of Jian Huo's skeptical eyebrow. "And?"

"We have been forbidden from dealing with them ourselves."

That got me. My hands dropped to my sides and I gaped at her. "Why would he do that?"

"You wish me to guess at the motivation of dragons?" She laughed. "Perhaps it is that the longer we are troubled by these demons, the more we will be in your debt when you stop them. Perhaps it is that they are your responsibility. Or perhaps it is because the eyes of Heaven have fallen upon you."

"Wh-huh?" And I thought she'd flummoxed me before.

"Lung Huang has taken another student. That has stirred curiosity in the gardens of Shambhala, but those visitors who come here have no interest in speaking of you, or else no impetus to do so, or else nothing useful to report."

"Who's interested?" I prodded.

"His siblings, the Nine Guardians. Well… eight, for Lung Huang is exiled here." Her ears flattened. "Well, seven, for who knows where the prodigal has gone to ground."

"Why do they care about me?" Jian Huo's siblings were gods, for all intents and purposes. So was Jian Huo, but I tried not to think about that. It was too daunting, and it made my schoolgirl crush feel blasphemous, which was a different magnitude of wrong than the squick that it went to when I recalled he'd been my grandfather's lover.

But that connection to my grandfather explained why Jian Huo might take an interest in me. The other guardians? It made my shoulders twitch.

Huxian agreed with my confusion, if her malicious little grin was anything to go by. "Lung Huang suffered exile the last time he took a student. A *laowai*. He still suffers it. But that at least could be explained. Lung Huang had a duty to train his Champion. A man already proven."

"And I'm not?"

"That is what they wish to determine, and perhaps why Lung Huang wishes you to be the one to defeat the demons you unleashed."

"So this is all some kind of a test?"

She yipped a laugh. "*This* is a conversation. And a warning. You have brought the eyes of Heaven down upon you, and the valley suffers while you struggle with the first line of the Tao." The look she gave me might almost be called sympathetic. "It cannot be a comfortable prospect, to be under such scrutiny."

"Yeah," I agreed. I was not feeling in charity with her. "Thanks for the warning."

"It is only polite." As if that was her reason for telling me. She turned and trotted down the mountain path. I watched her go until she disappeared around a bend with a flick of white and russet.

I found Jian Huo in the pagoda, sipping tea and looking down on the valley. It was clouded over most days, but today the sun shone mellow gold, dappling the snowy hillside and sparkling off the aqua and viridian pools that wended along the valley's length. I could just make out the rear temple, nestled at the foot of the glacial crevasse and the head of the valley. I couldn't see the tour buses from here.

Jian Huo didn't acknowledge me. I could never decide if I was meant to speak right off, or if this was some game of Jian Huo's to see how long I could wait him out before I broke. From the little smile I sometimes caught on his face, I suspected the latter.

I didn't give him long this time. "I'm going down into the valley tomorrow."

He turned. Set down his cup. Gestured for me to sit. "How was your meeting with the *huxian*?"

Oh, he could be infuriating. "Didn't you hear what I just said?"

"I did. Your mistake is in assuming I have been keeping you from doing so."

I choked on the beginnings of several curse words before managing a coherent sentence. "You said I wasn't ready!"

"People suffer, and you are the author of that. Will you make them wait until you are ready?"

"But Sun Tzu says... And there's the Tao... and... aren't I supposed to be learning about right reasons and practicing 'not-doing'."

"Is that what you call your current inaction?"

I almost hit him, right then. Would have, but for the twitch of his eyebrow. Something about *this* was amusing him?

Hell if I could tell what.

"Fine. Then tomorrow I'm heading down into the valley," I snapped.

He lifted his cup and took another sip of his tea. "Dress warmly."

I left before I did something stupid, like dump the teapot over his head.

Pissed I might be, but I took Jian Huo's advice and dressed in layers – enough to keep me snug, but not so much that I looked like the kid from *A Christmas Story*. After all, I might need to move and fight. I had only the one experience with calling these kinds of monsters from shadow, and none at all with sending them back. Templeton didn't count. As shadows went, he was a fluffy-bunny.

Jian Huo waited for me at the gate.

"Come to kiss me goodbye?" My irritation made me daring and snarky.

"I regret I must forgo the pleasure. I am coming with you."

"You are?" In all my months here, he'd never left his mountaintop sanctuary.

He stepped to one side and gestured for me to precede him down the path. "I would be a poor teacher if I did not."

"In other words, somebody has to haul my sorry ass home when it gets handed to me?"

"Oh no. I will expect you to make the climb yourself."

I couldn't tell if he was serious, or if my snark was rubbing off on him. Worse, what if it had been there all along, and I was only now getting glimpses of it?

No, that just wouldn't be fair. Fascination I could deal with, but if I started *liking* him, I was doomed.

You're not your grandfather, I promised myself as I stepped through the gates.

The path at the gates was clean of snow, but the drifts piled up not far down the mountain. After a few minutes, I wished I'd stacked on more layers. *Fuck,* it was cold. I tensed against the wind that cut through my clothes. I'd forgotten that it would still be winter beyond the protections of Lung Huang's pocket sanctuary.

"C-couldn't you just f-fly us d-down?" I asked Jian Huo as I led the way down the path. At least, I thought it was the path. The snow was piled up knee-high here, where it hadn't drifted deeper. For all I knew, I was about to lead us over an unstable edge.

He'd stop me before I did that. Wouldn't he?

"I could. I will not."

I shot a glance back at him before I realized he was replying to my words and not my thoughts. He had a knack for that. "I am so going to sneeze on you when I catch cold," I muttered.

"Colder temperatures do not cause viral infections," he said. I tamped down on the temptation to lob a snowball at him. The last thing I wanted was him retaliating. Trudging through the drifts was just starting to warm me up, and a serving of slush down the back of my neck would undo all my hard work.

"I am so going to catch a cold so I can sneeze on you."

He chuckled, a rumble like a thunderstorm. I didn't have a chance to savor my victory. I stumbled to a halt as my shadow-sensitive eyes caught a flash of movement ahead.

"Is that…" I whispered, then trailed off as the glimmer of darkness responded. Not to my words. Couldn't be that, because we'd been bantering loud enough to be heard over the wind. No, it responded to my *notice*, constricting upon itself and slinking crossways over the path at not much faster than a crawling pace, as though it could creep away unnoticed.

No chance. Now that I'd spotted it, I realized I could feel it in other ways: the twitch at the back of my shoulders that I thought was a reaction to the temperature, the flutter in my stomach that I'd assumed was due to Jian Huo demonstrating a sense of humor.

"Do you see now what I mean when I say 'demon'?"

I didn't, but I'd let that lack of perception unnerve me later when I had time to think about it. Sure, the shadow felt unnatural, the metaphysical equivalent of milk gone off, but it was mostly harmless: a cold, starving thing trapped away from home and terrified of the pale sunlight. It might have stayed huddled behind that drift all day if we hadn't come along and spooked it.

"Poor thing," I said, holding out my hand and taking a few steps off the path.

That's when it attacked.

Darkness slammed into me, pushing me back on my ass. I yelped as snow slid under my collar, and the shadow took that opportunity to wrap around my face and fill my mouth. The world went dark and quiet. I fought back, tried to grab hold of something to give myself leverage against it, but my mittened grasp passed right through the shadow, and I ended up giving myself a face full of snow.

The shadow constricted tighter as I sputtered and choked for air. It clung like a plastic liner laid over a swimming pool. I staggered to my feet, trying to tear myself free. I remembered the *yaoguai's* fading screams when the shadows had smothered the life from her. She couldn't fight them, and neither could I. The thing choking me was insubstantial, just air and darkness that got stronger the more I struggled.

Think. I didn't need to fight this. I was its master. I'd called it from the darkness, and I could send it back.

I reached out for my connection to the Shadow Realms. As though it sensed the opening, the creature convulsed tighter, wrenching me off my own axis. I stumbled a few more steps, spun about, and shunted the shadow into the darkness with such force that I fell back.

And back. And then down, as gravity came into play. I flailed against the air, as insubstantial as shadow, eyes watering at the sudden brightness and disorientation that came with flipping end-over-end in free-fall. The mountainside whizzed past me, swapping places with the sky and the ground and then the sky again.

Something large and sinuous caught me. My stomach continued to drop for several moments, though the mountain and the sky returned to their natural positions. Everything still rushed past, but my vector had changed.

I dangled from golden claws. Something red, green, and gold flashed at the periphery of my vision, but I didn't dare twist around to look at the creature that carried me. Not in mid-air. Not when the grip of those claws felt so loose and the ground whizzed past far below. We crested the ridge, breaking through the cloud cover that blanketed the valley and nudged up against the peaks in a thick, stratus layer.

Jian Huo set me down on the broad lawn in the center of the gardens. I collapsed to my knees, gulping deep breaths and fighting the urge to puke.

"Th-thanks," I managed to stutter when my heartbeat had calmed to merely racing. My mittened hands clutched at the grass as if that could save me from what had already happened. I couldn't make myself look around, look up. All I wanted to see in that moment was the ground solidly beneath me.

"Of course," Jian Huo said, coming around me and stooping into view. He was man-shaped again. The long tail of his hair snaked behind him, little wisps of storm and cloud drifting up from the dark strands to be blown away by a breeze. "Pancakes make for terrible students, so I'm told."

I managed a smile, tried to chuckle. It came out more like a hiccup. "Yeah, well... you should see the other guy."

Jian Huo smiled. An actual, honest-to-goodness smile. My belly did another of those flippy things, and I told myself it was just an after-effect of my aborted attempt at base-jumping.

"Even so." His smile twitched and he made a sound somewhere between a cough and a snort. Two or three more of those, and he was laughing.

At me, I was pretty sure. "What?" I said, less charmed than I'd been a moment before.

"Poor thing?" he gasped, which set him to laughing harder. He rose, arms wrapped around his middle in a vain attempt to hold it in.

"Poor thing!" he repeated, "and then..." He jigged about in a pantomime mockery of the shadow's attack and my life-and-death struggle, before falling off an invisible cliff with a look of comical horror. He landed safely on the grass, laughing even harder. "P-poor... thing..."

I responded the only way I could. I stripped off my wet mittens and lobbed them at his head.

Dragons were assholes.

"That's ten," I said, dusting my hands off as though they'd gotten dirty. They hadn't, but it was what you did when you completed an important task, and it wasn't like anyone else was going to congratulate me. "We have to be whittling them down. I was pretty out of it, but I can't imagine I summoned more than a dozen shadows. Unless they're breeding."

In contrast to the excitement of my first try, my subsequent forays down into the valley had verged on boring. Track a shadow, spook it from hiding, chuck it back into the Shadow Realms. Glare at Jian Huo if I managed to catch him smirking and murmuring "poor thing".

He'd managed to contain himself this time. In fact, he seemed less inclined towards humor today. He scanned the shadows more closely than I did and gave the clumps of bracken a wide berth. "These demons are not bound as mortals are. They can shred themselves into legion, or come together in one monstrous gestalt."

"So, kinda like breeding. Great. How will I know when they're all gone?"

That got his attention. "Are you so ready to leave? Have you found the answers to the questions that brought you here?"

He sounded almost as though he wanted me to stay. Well, maybe he did. Except for Feng Huang, he didn't get a lot of recreational company. Maybe he was lonely.

"No," I reassured him. "But, you know, a running tally would be nice."

"I will tell you when you have defeated the last," he said, but it was an absent-minded promise. Something beyond my shoulder had caught his attention. His eyes narrowed.

"Thanks," I muttered. "You're a real... pal..." I drifted off as my attention was caught by the same something. I don't know how it felt to him, but for me it was a familiar twitch crawling up the back of my neck, a queasiness in my belly.

"We should return home," Jian Huo said, taking a step back the way we'd come.

I held out a stalling hand. "Hold on. I can take this one."

"Missy..."

I ignored him, taking a few cautious steps around a copse of evergreens and brambles grown too thick to walk through. I'd learned my lesson from the first one; I wasn't going to get jumped.

The shadow awaited me on the other side. This one was more than just a few wisps of darkness. It hulked like a linebacker, and it took me a few seconds to realize that the shadow had formed itself into a parody of the *yaoguai's* demon.

An inky pseudopod in the shape of a fist swung out at me. I ducked low and swept out a leg, wondering if it would even work, or if this shadow was as insubstantial as the others.

My foot hooked something, and the shadow fell back into the brambles, little wisps bleeding off it as the thorns tore into whatever passed for flesh.

Practicality warred with my desire to finally square off against something I could pummel. Practicality won. I didn't need to beat this thing into the ground; I just needed to send it back from whence it came.

I kicked the creature in the chest-area, knocking it further into the thicket at the same time I opened my connection to the Shadow Realms.

It should have worked. It *did* work, but the damn thing caught my ankle and pulled me off balance, dragging me in after it. I flipped over and grabbed for anything of substance to hold me in the real world, but the shadow had dragged me too far across.

The clearing turned dark and colorless, like a film negative. The root I grabbed for slipped through my fingers. The tidal pull of the Shadow Realms took hold of me, and as I slipped further in, the forest twisted into a nightmare caricature. The demon scrabbled up my body, back toward the light.

"Jian Huo!" I screamed, because he had to be there still. He'd saved me from falling. He would save me from this.

But there was nothing. No response. I couldn't see him, couldn't sense him. There was just darkness that even my eyes had trouble penetrating, and trees howling laughter at me, and claws raking down my back as the shadow I'd been fighting pulled me down further in its attempt to reach the light.

Right. Deal with that thing first, preferably before more arrived. I rolled over and planted both feet square in the creature's midsection. If it made a sound, I couldn't hear it over the gibbering trees, but it did stop clawing at me. I did a backward roll up to my knees, then rose to a crouch, not pressing my attack in favor of getting my bearings.

The world had gone cock-eyed – Shadow geographies never quite match the mortal terrain – but I spied a stripe of lighter darkness just beyond the shadow creature that coincided with a break in the trees back in the real world. That was my best chance for a way out, assuming I could wrench myself free. The deeper you sank into the Shadow Realms, the harder it was to break away from the gravity of the place. You needed light, and that thin strip was all I had.

The creature lunged for me. I danced around it, crying out when its claws ripped through my sleeve and across my left shoulder. I slammed my elbow back into its face, hearing a crunching noise where there shouldn't have been anything to crunch. It echoed my cry of pain, and I repeated the elbow strike twice more for good measure. I couldn't let it get ahold of me and piggyback out into the real world.

The creature stumbled, and I took my chance, charging at

that strip of not-quite-as-dark and grabbing for it like a rope.

The forest flashed back into being around me, so bright that it blinded me. I hit something that had enough give to send us both tumbling to the ground. Jian Huo. He caught me in a painfully tight embrace, painful mostly because of the damage the shadow creature had done.

"Shoulder. Shoulder!" I protested, cringing away in an attempt to make the pain not hurt. First I get shot, and now this. My shoulder was not having a good year.

Jian Huo sat up, still holding me, but only loosely so he could examine the gashes through the shredded silk of my robe. I craned my neck to see them and was disappointed. They burned like they were bone deep, but all I could see was four long, red scrapes, like I'd been attacked by a kitten.

"Have you no sense? When I say we leave, it is for your own safety. Did it never occur to you that a stronger shadow could pull you back across with it? The connection you tap goes both ways, and to a place I dare not follow." Jian Huo's hands clenched, his forearms tensed as though he'd like nothing more than to shake me. "Don't you ever do something so foolish again!"

"I didn't know," I said, but it was a weak defense. He'd said stop, and I'd ignored him. "It was only another shadow creature. I thought–"

"What do you think it is, this thing you call the Shadow Realms?"

Well, I knew it wasn't shadow. Not in the scientific sense of being an obstruction of light. That was just shorthand, an easy-to-spew-out explanation to describe something that defied the laws of physics.

Jian Huo's lips flattened into a line when I couldn't answer. "Even so. You do not understand." His grip relaxed. "'The ten-thousand things are born of being; being is born of not-being'."

My confusion was probably obvious, but I said "Huh?"

anyways, just in case he'd missed it.

"The place you call the Shadow Realms is a cushion between states of being, the buffer that separates all that is this place from all that is another place. It also divides all that is from all that *isn't*. The stuff of not-being."

Jian Huo was a master of many things; it seemed exposition was not one of them. I shifted, wishing I could just enjoy being this close to him, surrounded by the scent of sandalwood, but my need to understand trumped my libido. "So how was I supposed to know that the Shadow Realms would try to eat me just now? That's never happened before."

"Because we are close to my realm." His fingers traced along my scrapes, cooling the abraded skin. Absently, I figured. His gaze was caught at some point beyond my shoulder. "What do you think we guardians are guarding against? At the beginning of creation, we nine set ourselves as sentinels to guard the divide between all that is and all that isn't. You have only ever walked the borderlands between your world and the place you call Shadow; whereas my realm touches much closer to the frontiers of the divide." His brow furrowed and his flattened lips tugged into a frown. "There are other places that are closer still."

He jerked, coming back from wherever had made him so pensive. His grip tightened. "You must promise never to touch that place while you are here. You are not strong enough to face it."

I nodded my agreement. Between the awfulness of being sucked away and Jian Huo's dire glower, there was no way I was going to try something like that again.

"Good."

And then he pulled me into an embrace. Nothing to it, just a concerned master hugging his startled student. I returned the hug, and it stretched on longer than a hug between master and student should.

Jian Huo stiffened, pulled back with something that sounded almost like a clearing of his throat.

"It is getting late, and you should soak those scrapes in the spring before they become infected," he said, rising and helping me up. He didn't linger over holding my hands as he had over the hug. He turned away, and, for once, he was the one who led the way back. I trailed behind in silence, wondering what the hell had just happened.

An hour soaking in the hot springs cleared my head on the matter, making me brave enough that I decided not to avoid dinner that evening. Not that Jian Huo would have let me. We were reading Su Shi that week, a particular favorite of his. He would have hunted me down if I had skipped out on our after-dinner critique.

Better for all involved if I demonstrated more emotional maturity than a twelve-year-old.

"Jian Huo, we need to talk." I said after the dinner dishes had been pushed aside.

"Were we not just doing that?"

"Not about salt monopolies during the Song Dynasty. About. Uh…" Now that I'd come to the edge, I couldn't seem to make myself jump. Jian Huo took care of the matter for me.

"You wish to know if I am attracted to you."

I gaped. And here I'd been expecting an hour of conversation that danced around the subject. Why did he choose now to be direct? I closed my mouth and nodded. "Yeah."

We sat in silence, me waiting for Jian Huo to continue, and Jian Huo… well… who can say what he was thinking? My turn to prod.

"Well?"

"Well what?"

"Is it true?"

He turned and leveled a look at me. I had no trouble at all

reading that. The intensity of it twisted my gut... and places lower and more interesting. My internal Keanu Reeves took the opportunity to slip out. "Whoa."

Jian Huo blinked. The intensity of the moment before was gone. He turned back to watching the moonlight play silver over the travertine pools that snaked down the valley. "Even so."

My brain scrambled to give my mouth better material. "Bu– wha– hah... Why?"

My brain failed at life.

One shoulder hitched, dark hair shirring across brocade at the movement. "Who can say what sparks such things or why they fan to flame? You amuse me. You intrigue me. You are not unintelligent, despite your tendency to rush ahead and to prattle nonsense. Indeed, I believe those qualities may be part of your charm, but, in the main, it is because you were right. We both are very bad at practicing not-doing. So it was with your grandfather. So it is with you."

"Please don't tell me this is about reliving your affair with Mitchell," I blurted. Because... ew.

"I agreed to train your grandfather because honor bound me to do so. What passed between us was... complicated. I agreed to train you out of choice, and what has grown between us is unique."

Amazing, how few words he had to use to make me want to melt.

"What do we do?" I asked, because the training montage that was my life had just taken a turn for the interesting.

"We do nothing."

And I thought I was confused before. So close, and yet... I pursed my lips, considering the best way to seduce him. He was ancient. Nothing I could devise would surprise him. Might as well not even try for subtlety. I sucked at it anyways.

Decision made, I drew my legs out from under the table that

sat between us and crawled around it. It wasn't some amazing sex-kitten-tigress crawl. More of a "get this damn table out of my way" crawl. Jian Huo cocked his head, brow twitching at my progress.

"Why nothing? If you're into me, and I'm into you..."

His eyes flicked down. I followed his gaze. The "V" of my robe gaped open, revealing... not much, really. But revealing nonetheless.

Jian Huo reached out and tugged my robe closed. "And here I had hoped our reading and discussions had improved your understanding along with your grasp of the language. I will be clear: you are my student. It would not be honorable to take advantage."

I sat back on my heels with a huff, our knees almost touching. "I don't recall signing an academic code of conduct. The only thing I agreed to was not to leave until these shadow things aren't a danger."

"Nevertheless, as long as you are *Lung Xue*, it would not be honorable," he insisted.

"Aren't there circumstantial exceptions?"

The burble of sound that came from him might have been a chuckle, but it was a resigned one. Jian Huo had given up before starting. That just wasn't in my character.

"What possible circumstances could forgive taking such advantage?"

I bit my lip and looked down at the rich brocade that stretched taut over his knees. I reached out to trace the form of one of the little carp that gamboled across the surface. This was me, being subtle. He didn't push my hand away. "What about the old 'we got drunk and tumbled into bed together' excuse? That's a classic. You like the classics."

"On tea?" He had a point. Jian Huo practically drowned me in the stuff in a vain effort to improve my palate. Blacks, greens, oolongs, whites. It made me have to pee, and sometimes woke me up in the mornings or kept me awake in the evenings, but so far I hadn't ever copped a buzz off of it.

"Point taken. What about the old 'I snuck into your bed in the middle of the night and you just thought you were dreaming' excuse? Releases you from all culpability."

"I do not dream so deeply that I cannot discern the truth of you from my nightly imaginings."

My finger paused in its tracing. Wait. Did that mean that he'd already considered this – us – in carnal detail? I looked up. That *look* was back, the one that was almost embarrassing in its intimacy. I couldn't hold it; my gaze dropped again. I flattened my palm against his knee, fingers curving around to brush the pile of hair that coiled beside him. And once I'd had that brief contact with silk, it wasn't enough. His hair fascinated me, and if he kept saying "no", who knew when I'd have another chance like this?

I slid my fingers deep, losing them in the black. My hand trailed down through the strands, and it was like touching Shadow, if Shadow were something thrilling rather than terrifying. So not like Shadow at all, really. More like a thunderstorm.

I marveled at the tiny shocks and cool damp that played along my fingers. It was just hair. How could "just hair" feel like this? Jian Huo had fallen silent. "How about the old 'What was I supposed to do, your honor? You should see the way she eats a banana' defense?"

He caught my wrist, pulled my hand from his hair. I looked up and was snared by his eyes. Nothing mortal there. Dragon. And for reasons that made no sense, he wanted me.

Jian Huo lowered my hand to rest on my lap. That hunger in his eyes receded, packed away with a control I would never have been able to manage. "The eyes of heaven are upon us, but even if they weren't, I wouldn't take you to my bed. You are my student. Would you ask me to dishonor that bond?"

Well, hell.

"No," I conceded, scooting back so that distance could stand for willpower, because I didn't have much of the latter at the moment. His breathing eased. I hadn't even noticed it was strained. It made me feel a little better, that I wasn't the only one finding this hard.

"Fine. We can do it your way. But if you were looking for an incentive to get me to work harder, boy did you ever find it. Those shadows better watch out."

Jian Huo rose. I folded my hands in my sleeves, fingers digging into each opposite elbow to keep myself from grabbing him again, or from touching the coil of hair that tumbled past me with his movement.

"Let us hope that is the case." He nodded, and I don't think it was my imagination that his movements were more abrupt than usual as he strode away, leaving me alone in the pagoda.

"The Tao that can be told is not the eternal Tao."

"The dragon that can be seduced is not the eternal dragon," I muttered in response.

Time had passed. It was hard keeping track how much in this place, where the days bled into each other. Cantonese, Mandarin, a smattering of other languages and dialects. Literature, calligraphy, politics, history, *wei-qi*, though I never improved enough in that to give Jian Huo any kind of challenge. Gung fu, which I did improve at. This week was British folklore and the literary movements based on it. I'd barreled my way through Briggs, happy to be reading in English again, and then we'd circled back to the Pre-Raphaelites.

But wherever my education wandered, it always came back to the Tao. Always the fucking Tao. I knew at this point it wasn't a pronunciation thing, but hell if I could figure out what it was. I would though. I *would*. My libido depended on it.

"Even so," Jian Huo said, unperturbed. It took me a moment

to realize he was replying to my words, and not my thoughts. He was pretty good at ignoring my disgruntled rumblings, just as I was good at pretending not to notice the few times I'd caught him watching me in ways a Master probably shouldn't be watching his student. They were rare moments, but they were reassuring. I hadn't imagined that night in the pagoda.

I'd gone over interpretations ten thousand times; once more might just kill me. I tried anyways.

"It's like infinity in mathematics." We'd been working on math, too. If nothing else, time with my Dragon Master was great prep for my GED. "It's not a rational number. You can't calculate or express it, so you add a limiter, like infinity minus one. But that's not infinity. It's just a math game you play to try to calculate using an incalculable concept."

Jian Huo sat at his desk, enameling a tiny gold carp with green and red pigments. One hand held his sleeve back, the other poised the applicator. Everything about him – his *hanfu*, his posture, the dark fall of his hair, and the serenity of his face – looked like a painting itself. He paused in the act of dabbing the carp's eye into being, tilted his profile toward me.

"The eternal Tao is not mathematic."

"I didn't say it was. It's a simile."

"Metaphor."

"Whatever. What I'm saying is, I *get* it. There's this... all this stuff of creation." I thumped the floor boards, flipped the hem of my short robe. "And that's the Ten Thousand Things. But then there's something bigger that encompasses all those things and is also *more*. God, Brahma, Unity, the Creator. All those names are incomplete reflections that can't name the whole, because even the names are still part of the Ten Thousand Things, and the whole is nameless. You can't use something within a system to describe something that transcends the system. That'd be like a two-dimensional creature trying to describe space."

"So you have said, and many other variations of the same."
He set his brush down and examined the little carp. It looked
fine to me, ready for firing. He must have concurred. He lifted
the mount, carp and all, and rose to his feet with a rustle
of brocade.

Another failed attempt. Another crash and burn. I threw
up my hands. "Then I give up. I quit. I'm not going to get it. I
might as well pack my bags and leave tomorrow. I can't get it,
'cause it's not something that can be got."

He stilled. Turned toward me. The carp wobbled on its
mount. He steadied it so the paste wouldn't be jarred before
firing. "You... quit?"

"Yeah." I folded my arms, chin jutting. I wasn't really
serious, but it felt good, even as a small act of rebellion.

"What of the shadows?"

"How are they different? You said yourself, they can be
legion as easily as they can be one." I blinked, realizing this was
just another impossible puzzle he'd set me to solve. Asshole. I
glared at him, my face growing warm. "It can't be done, which
you knew from the beginning. I'll never defeat them all."

"Why?"

Sometimes it felt like he didn't even listen. "You said yourself:
they're part of the buffer zone. I was doomed to lose the
moment I summoned them. I can fight a thousand shadows,
but there'll always be one more because they're shadows, they
can't be enumerated like things of this world can. And I can
repeat the words of the Tao ten thousand times, but I'm doomed
to fail the moment I open my mouth to speak. I'm not going to
get it because the thing to be gotten isn't something that can
be expressed. So if I'm doomed to fail before I start, what's the
point? I'm just wasting everyone's time. Right?"

"Wrong. But... it is a beginning. Now we may move on to
the next line. 'The name that can be named is not the eternal
name'."

My arms flopped to my sides. "You're shitting me."

"After we have finished with the Tao, we'll move to the writings of Kong Zi. Unless you truly plan to, er… 'pack your bags and leave tomorrow'?"

"No. I'll stay." What had just happened there? Had I passed? Why? Because I quit? A double dozen questions jockeyed for asking, but Jian Huo had turned to leave.

"Then we will continue our discussion over dinner, after I have fired this. I am eager to hear your thoughts on Rossetti. Finish your calligraphy."

I glared at him as he departed, but he failed to drop dead in his tracks. Stupid immortal creatures.

The table was set with our usual, plain fare, but in the center sat a large bowl of fruit. Jian Huo's nod to Rossetti's *The Goblin Market*, no doubt, but screw him if he thought that would deter me. I snatched up a banana and cocked a brow, daring him to say something. He didn't rise to my challenge.

"Rossetti. I suspect you have much to say–"

"She's a sensual, religiously-repressed woman who might have had a thing for her sister," I said, peeling my banana. It was a bold and spurious claim, the kind that Jian Huo usually enjoyed helping me dismantle in favor of a more nuanced reading. I looked up when he didn't respond.

He held a peach plucked from the bowl, checking it over, feeling its firmness, fingers rubbing the fuzz on its skin. He lowered his face to it, inhaling deeply, as if the sweet scent were the most intoxicating fragrance in the world.

My first bite of banana turned to sawdust in my mouth.

He never looked at me; all his attention focused on the peach. The tip of his tongue darted out to test the soft, fuzzy surface, slipping along the seam of the double-globed fruit; then his lips wrapped around the peach and he bit into it.

I dropped my banana.

Something niggled at the back of my mind, some distant memory, but watching him eat the peach distracted me from chasing that memory down. After the first deep bite, he took his time to savor the fruit, sometimes nibbling at the edges, sometimes taking more substantial bites – sucking and licking away the juices. He took an eternity to eat that damn peach, and I felt dirtier and dirtier as I watched him do it. I've never been a food-and-sex person, but, damn, that was one hell of a peach.

When he was done cleaning the juice from his fingers, he placed the pit on the tray and looked up at me. No way – no *way* – was he as innocent as he looked. Not after that performance. It just wasn't possible. Or if it was possible, it wasn't fair. "How did you like your banana?"

I spied it resting, forlorn and browning, next to my hip. I nudged it under the table.

"Fine. Fine," I said. It wasn't a lie, because I had enjoyed the first few moments of my first bite. "But I'm not really that hungry. I might just stick to rice for tonight." And let's hope you do too, I thought. Let's face it, there's nothing sexy about rice.

"You do not desire more fruit?" I didn't like the way he was eying the strawberries. That was just what my libido needed.

"No, I'm good," I squeaked, looking for a distraction. Any distraction. "Where's the tea?" Because the bowl of fruity temptation sat where the teapot usually did.

There was no tea, it turned out, but there was wine. Plum wine, rice wine, grape wine, even some mead. Jian Huo took to filling my mug freely as he explained about vintages and barrel times and things I didn't really care about as long as I was warmed by the wine and his presence. I ended up drinking more than I ate.

It made for a more heated discussion than usual as we dissected the poem.

"…I'm just saying, '*Laura, come and kiss me… Lick me, squeeze me, suck my juices*'. Can you tell me she wasn't writing about… what it sounds like she was writing about?"

"You are misquoting." He tapped my nose in reprimand. I scrunched it at him and bit down on a yawn. I didn't want dinner to end. "Do not do that. And of course she was writing about that. Does that mean she can't have been writing about other things as well? Or that the love she was exploring was sexual rather than sisterly?"

"She dedicated the poem to her sister. Just saying."

"You are not 'just saying'. You are trying to escape responsibility for supporting your claim." He was right, and he'd make me pay for it tomorrow. Jian Huo had little patience for intellectual laziness.

I started to reply, but it got lost in another yawn – a full, jaw-popping one, though I remembered enough manners to cover my mouth.

"It is late." He ducked his head, sheepish, like we were kids on a date who had broken curfew. "I should not have kept you awake for so long. Do you feel like sleeping now?"

"Are you offering to take me to bed?" I leaned into him with a playful leer, which faded as I realized what I'd just said, and how gauche I sounded.

"I am."

I did a double-take, then a few more, certain that I'd heard him wrong – certain that his assent was an alcohol-induced hallucination. He cupped the back of my head, coaxing me closer. Too close to avoid meeting his gaze, and who can handle gazing into eternity for long? My eyes slid shut, and his lips pressed to mine. I tasted plum wine and white rice and maybe the echo of a peach in his kiss.

Jian Huo kissed like he did everything: studied and reserved, a thorough exploration of all that a kiss between us could be. I suppose he would say I kissed like *I* did everything.

More enthusiasm than skill, and always impetuous. I was the one to push us to the next step. With a groan, I pressed closer, flinging one leg over his lap to straddle him. He leaned back as our center of gravity changed, which brought us into even more intimate contact. Heat flared from my groin to my breasts and, oh god, it had been too long since I'd felt anything but my own hand pressed between my legs. I needed more. Wrapping my hands around the lapels of his robe, I stood, pulling him up with me. He grasped at my waist to steady us both, and his mouth moved off mine to nuzzle the crook of my neck.

"Where are we going?" he whispered, sending shivers through me.

"My room," I gasped, "unless you want to have a go right here in the pagoda."

"Very well." His hands had snaked inside my robe, which was making it much harder for me to think basic logistics.

"Uh... very well to which? My room or here?"

"Your room," he chuckled. "I have no desire to bed you on bare wood."

We fumbled our way along the walkways, only stopping once when he thrust me up against the railing. I responded by wrapping my legs around his waist, and we spent some time exploring the possibilities of verticality, but the promise of a bed beckoned us onward, and we reached my room.

I disengaged long enough to turn around and try to figure out how to work a door. As I did so, the worry that I'd been successfully ignoring blossomed. My hand froze on the door.

"Wait," I said. He answered by wrapping his arms around me from behind, with his hands splayed across my bare midriff. He nuzzled the nape of my neck.

"Have you decided on the pagoda after all?" he asked.

"No." I struggled to think as his hand wandered higher. "Wait, Jian Huo. Earlier today. The nameless line..."

"Yes." His other hand wandered lower. For a moment, all I could think about was peaches.

"And…" I struggled to keep focused on my derailing train of thought. "After the Tao, we've got Confucius?"

"Master Kong, yes. Is this so vital that we need to discuss it right now?" His fingers were pinching and squeezing and OH. Good. Mother. Monkeys. Of…

My misfiring synapses insisted this was important for some reason. I struggled to figure it out, and then it hit me. I wrenched from his hands and fell forward against the door, gasping for breath and sanity.

"We can't do this," I said, breathing hard into the screen. The silence that followed stretched on and on and on.

"I'm sorry. I'm sorry. I'm sorry." I squeezed my eyes shut and tried to make my thoughts make sense. "I know I'm the worst kind of a tease, and I never, never, ever meant things to go this far. I mean, not until I wasn't your student anymore, and we were allowed to go this far." I pulled my robe closed around me and turned to face him, slumping against the door with my eyes still lowered. "I said we'd do it your way. I would never try to make you… I would never ask you to sacrifice your honor." I looked up at him then. "I'm so sorry."

He kept his hands to himself through my incoherent explanation, but there wasn't any anger or rage in him, just surprise and a kind of curious reserve.

"So you want me to leave?"

"Yes. I mean, no, of course not." I shook my head. "But I think you should."

"You're certain?"

God, no. "Yes."

"Missy." He took my hand. "Today you made yourself an empty vessel, where before you were full. But in learning you were empty, you also learned that you can never be full. You will always be a student of the Tao. I've reached the limits of my patience, and I think you have too. We can end this all tonight, right now. Are you sure you want me to leave?"

Always? I gulped but steeled myself for what must be done. Fucking Joan of Arc on her way to the stake did not have my conviction. The eyes of heaven were upon us. No way would I let him dishonor himself. No way would I make him give up what little he had left for me. I wasn't my grandfather.

"I'm sure." I kissed him somewhere in the vicinity of his cheek. "Now go. Git. Skeedaddle." I made a shooing motion with my hands, then shot him a pleading gaze. "Quick. Before I change my mind."

With that, I escaped into my room and slid the door shut in his face.

I had the worst time ever getting to sleep. I threw off my robe and grabbed my night-shift, but the soft material caught on my sensitized skin, and I knew that the extra fabric would just be a distraction. I slid nude between the covers and considered taking care of myself, but that wasn't what I wanted. Instead I beat the pillow, tossed and turned, tried to hypnotize myself, and did everything but count sheep before exhaustion and the leftover effects of the wine claimed me, and I feel into slumber.

A soft noise roused me, but I still meandered in the realm between sleeping and waking until the noise repeated. I opened my eyes to see the room in shadow, the only light a bare gleam from a crescent moon, displaced by the latticework shutters. The sound came from beyond, from a shadow on the other side of the sliding door.

"Jian Huo?" I rose from the bed, dragging the coverlet with me rather than wasting time finding my robe.

The door slid open, wide enough to allow Jian Huo to slip through, but he remained waiting at the threshold, looking as rumpled as I felt. "May I come in?"

This was a bad idea. I nodded anyway. "What are you doing here?"

He entered, closed the door behind him. Smiled. "I'm not here. This is a dream." He closed the distance between us, lifting both hands to my face. Confused, I let him pull me in for a kiss, yet again savoring the taste and feel of him, until rationality asserted itself. I pulled away, and his hands dropped to my shoulders.

"Wait, no. It isn't. Why are you doing this? Please don't make me send you away again." I closed my eyes as we engaged in a tug of war for the covers. "I don't know if I can."

"There is no need to," he said. "This is not real. It is a dream."

"No, it isn't," I responded in frustration, pulling away from his grasp with the covers in tow. "It is real, and there is every need to, because I'm still your student."

"I never agreed to take you back." He stepped on the tail end of my covers, halting my retreat.

"Wha–?" My grip on the covers fell slack, and he gained a couple inches of ground before I managed to pull them back up.

"You quit today. I did not agree to take you back."

"You said I was still your student. Tonight. You said it." I had relived our stumble from the pagoda to my room several times. I recalled exactly what had been said and done. Hence the not being able to sleep.

"I said you were a student of the Tao." Much too late to be of any use, the niggling thought I'd had earlier in the evening slapped me across the face with its relevance.

"Bananas... the wine... this 'dream'." I listed the events of the evening. His lips twitched as he fought to hold back a smile. I gaped. He thought duping me was *funny*?

"You have some very strange notions about how to perform a seduction. I only thought to satisfy them, now that I am free to do so."

"You're trying to get off on a technicality?" He grinned at

my unintended *double entendre*. I was not in such a smiling mood. "You... you... you son of a pig!"

I yanked the covers out from under his feet. He fell back, rolling on the floor, laughter cracking through the room like the rumbling of a storm. I circled him, covers trailing behind me.

"Stop that laughing, you overgrown lizard! I can't believe that you've been setting this up all evening... and I... I... Gah!" Tears coursed down his cheeks now. "And then tonight you just let me think I was being all self-sacrificing and martyring, and you knew this entire time that we could have been going at it like bunnies, and you just let me... stop that laughing you... you... carp with delusions of grandeur!"

I snapped my covers in his general direction, more out of frustration than with any intent to do actual harm. His hand shot out and caught them, bringing me tumbling down on top of him, covers and all. His arms wrapped around me, and his chuckles died away as he contained my struggles.

"I am sorry," he offered when I subsided. "It was never my intention that the joke should go on this long, or that it should have gone so wrong." His smile gentled and he loosened one arm from around me, bringing his hand up to run his fingers across my brows, my cheek, my lips. I tried to hold on to my frown, but how could I when he touched me like that? And being naked and lying on top of him didn't help.

"Yeah, well, it would serve you right if I tossed you out on your ear right now," I said, squirming as he traced circles up my spine.

"You realize that now that you are free, you may leave whenever you wish?"

"Are you kidding me?" I buried my nose in sandalwood-scented hair. "I'm not going anywhere now."

SEVEN
Aces High

Now

"Missy?" Shimizu tapped on the edge of my bedroom doorway, then pushed the door open without waiting for a response.

I mumbled something unintelligible to make her think I was still asleep and shifted to pull the covers over my head. That made me groan in earnest. I ached all over from the fight with Lao Chan's men. That was the pain that had woken me, but it was Lao Chan's parting-shot and David Tsung's shady-dealing that kept me hiding under my covers. I just wanted the world to go away for a few more hours.

The world might obey my unspoken wish; Shimizu didn't.

"Missy? You OK?"

"I'm dying. Go away."

"At least you're not dead. C'mon, time to get up. The world's falling apart. There's hero stuff to do." She threw the covers back before I could tighten my grip. Her breath caught as she got her first look at me.

"Oh my god."

I uncurled from my pillbug roll. My long T-shirt had ridden up, leaving all my bruises exposed for Shimizu to cluck at. "It's not as bad as it looks."

"Jesus!" She set down the mug she'd been holding, going

from roommate mode to doctor mode in an instant. "You were fine when you left Oakland. What happened?"

"Is that tea?" I asked, ignoring her concern for more important things. She pushed the mug out of reach and grabbed my left ankle.

"It's my tea. If you want your own, you have to prove you're functional by putting on clothes and getting it yourself." She rotated my ankle, then moved up to my knee to test my range of mobility. I only hissed and winced a few times.

"I can get tea in my jammies," I said, because throwing on pants seemed like too much of an effort.

"Jack's here. He wants to talk to you." She'd moved to my other leg, bending the knee that I'd twisted. Knees weren't meant to twist. They were hinge-joints, as Shimizu was fond of reminding me. The furrow between Shimizu's brow deepened.

"Jack can talk to me in my jammies." But the news got me moving. I was strict about keeping Missy's life separate from Mr Mystic's. If Jack had come to the co-op, it must be important.

Shimizu backed away as I sat up and swung my legs over the edge of the bed. She grabbed a pair of yoga pants from my dresser and tossed them at my face. "At least put these on. Neither of us is going to be able to pay attention if we have to look at those bruises. How many fingers?"

"Isn't it a little late to be testing for concussion?" I managed to pull on the pants with a minimum of painful bending.

"Well, if *someone* didn't insist on coming home injured and falling straight into bed..."

"You hadn't gotten home yet."

With a tetching noise, she helped me stand up and make my way toward the door. Momentum kept me going. "Next time, leave me a note. Better yet, don't let there be a next time."

I hobbled up the stairs to the main floor, not making any promises. There would be a next time, and I wouldn't bother her unless it was vital. I knew my limits. As much as I ached this morning, I'd be fine in a few days. They were just surface aches, giving me something to think about that wasn't the knife sitting in a bundle of silk on my dresser.

"Jesus!" Jack said as I entered the kitchen.

"No, just Missy." I gave up walking and sank onto a chair.

Shimizu gave Jack a "you talk to her" look as she passed him on her way to the counter. I hoped it was to take pity on me and make me tea. He nodded and sat in the chair across from me.

"I hope this is one of those cases where I should see the other guy?"

"Guys," I corrected before I could catch myself.

"Plural?"

"Nine. Wait, no. Twelve. Damn. Made that mistake last night, too."

"You fought twelve men?" Jack's question was slow. Skeptical. Possibly I had a history of exaggerating my exploits just to shock him. Not this time, though.

"I fought nine. There were twelve. You see the problem now?"

"Lao Chan let you live?" Jack was quick, I'll give him that. That was twice now that I should have died at Lao Chan's hands, but hadn't. "Why?"

"His boss, Mr Long, wants to see me. In Shanghai."

Shimizu's teaspoon clattered on the counter. "Mr Long? Is that your–"

"No." I said, before she could invoke painful memories. This whole China business was hard enough without thinking about what I'd lost the last time I'd been there. Jack and Shimizu exchanged another look at my curt denial. This was the other reason I didn't let my worlds mix. They tended to gang up on me when they did.

Jack took the lead. "Does this have anything to do with whatever you were doing in Oakland last night?"

"How did you know about that?"

"It's all over YouTube. Videos of Mr Mystic disappearing at the edge of the Wall shortly before it went down. I've been fielding calls all night, but somebody turned her cell phone off."

"She came to find me." Shimizu handed me a mug, and I drank in the warmth. Some kind of jasmine sencha, sharp enough to jolt my brain into working, but the floral element smoothing over any rough edges. I gave her a grateful smile. Best. Roommate. Ever.

"And the wall around Oakland just happened to go down while she – excuse me, while Mr Mystic was there? How did you even get in?"

I avoided the snarky part of his question. "The Shadow Realms aren't just a copy of our own world. Geographies don't align in the same way. Whatever the New Wall is, it doesn't extend across the veil."

"So that's how you expect to get into China to see this Mr Long?"

I wondered if Jack took classes in frowning, or if it came natural.

Shimizu curled up in a chair of her own. "Crossing over was dangerous. What if there are more of those things from last night?"

"Things?"

I ignored Jack. "It is. And there will be, or worse things. I'll just have to be faster than they are."

"Take lots of glowsticks. I have a box."

I laughed, then choked it back. Laughing hurt. "I have to figure out how to get there first."

"About that." Jack rooted through his coat pocket.

"Hm?" I sipped my tea. It was almost too hot, but the warmth provided another jolt to my synapses.

"This came by courier this morning." Jack pulled out a tri-folded letter. Just the letter, no envelope. Jack opened all of Mr Mystic's correspondence. The dove-grey stationary rustled with the sound of high-quality paper. I caught a flash of silver foil at the upper corner. A logo in crisp, Art Deco lines.

I took the letter, opening it to confirm my suspicions. "What does Argent want with me?"

Jack's lips twisted into a grimace that might have been meant as a smile. "It's a short letter, Missy. You could read it."

"A meeting. Sylvia Dunbarton is in town. I got that. Why does she want to see Mr Mystic?"

"Maybe she saw him skulking around Oakland on YouTube. Like the rest of the world. How should I know?"

I waved the letter at him. "You're you. You know things. What, you think I keep you around for your clean-cut good looks?"

"No. My cooking. And I know things about things I know. This is Argent, Missy. I have as much chance of figuring out their motives as you do defeating twelve Triad."

"I managed nine," I muttered. Didn't anybody respect that nine wasn't too shabby?

Jack crossed his arms. "I rest my case."

"I don't see what Argent has to do with this." Mostly because I didn't want to. It was going into the pile of things I didn't want to deal with, on top of David Tsung, Mr Long, and the past I'd left behind in China.

Shimizu took the letter from my unresisting grip, reading it for herself. "Your grandfather used to work for Argent? They have whole divisions dedicated to research. If they know about the Shadow Realms, maybe they know you can get across. Figured out you were responsible for saving Oakland?"

"They also have a better information network than the CIA, so they might know about this Mr Long's invitation," Jack said. Between the two of them, they were making it really hard for me to keep my head in the sand. Couldn't I get a morning off and enjoy my tea and my aches in peace?

"So what if they do know," I mumbled against the rim of my

mug. "I'm not working with Argent."

"You just said you need to get overseas somehow," Shimizu said. "It's not like you can just hop the next trans-Pacific flight."

"But–"

Jack gripped my forearm before I could hide behind my tea mug. "Missy, I know how you feel about Argent." Jack should. He'd heard me rant about it often enough. "But the world isn't black and white. This New Wall, all the other affected Chinatowns, don't you get the scope of this crisis? Every corner of the world is affected. They've only just started compiling lists of tourists and expats who were in China when the Wall went up. The numbers already put every other hostage crisis to shame."

"And not that I'm a die-hard capitalist, but how long can they keep the markets closed?" Shimizu snorted. "Hell, Patrick listed his new iPad on Ebay this morning, and the bidding is already enough to let him take a semester off teaching."

I splurted tea. "What? What does that have to do with this?"

Shimizu wiped the table. "Not like Apple is going to be able to get their parts from Foxcorp anymore. If this goes on, you're talking the collapse of the tech industry. And all the jobs that go with it. This isn't the fourteenth century. China can't just declare *Hai Jin* and cut itself off from the world."

Jack took over the badger-express. "It's only going to get worse the longer it goes on. Sometimes doing something for the greater good requires compromise – a little bit of sleeping with the enemy."

I covered my head as they battered at me from both sides. Jack pulled my hands away, forcing me to face him. "You're the one who wanted to be a hero. Now's the time to step up. Shimizu has a point. If you tried to go through official channels, you'd probably get a one-way ticket to Gitmo. Argent can get you to Shanghai. And fast. You don't have another option. Am I wrong?"

He was wrong, on almost every count. The ends didn't justify the means. The how and the why of doing a thing mattered. Sleeping with the enemy was just asking for karmic STDs, and Argent was as crooked as Lombard Street. Everything about this situation screamed "It's a Trap!" in Admiral Ackbar tones.

But someone had to go to China and take down this wall, and I seemed to be the best person for the job. Mitchell Masters had extensive resources, but they didn't pack the kind of economic or political punch to get me to China. Argent did.

I opened the letter again. Reread the tiny block of text. Did anyone ever come clean out of a deal with the devil?

I crumpled the paper into a ball. Didn't matter. That New Wall needed to go down.

"Fine. Mr Mystic will go to Argent."

The Argent Corporation tapped into the nostalgia of another age, and, as CEO, Sylvia Dunbarton had nurtured that into a cult of personality. She epitomized studio-era Hollywood glamour coupled with old-money British aristocracy. She knew the power of her image, and she used it. But that was just surface. Everything she did had at least five purposes.

Which was why I didn't trust her motives for leaving me cooling my heels in the lobby of the Fairmont.

I'd been waiting long enough to attract several second glances and a few surreptitious phone pictures when the Grande Dame of Argent appeared, flanked by two men in identical dark suits.

She wore a smart, tailored jacket and pencil skirt in charcoal herringbone, her silver hair cut in a sleek bob and her oxford heels clicking crisply on the marble flooring. Grey fox lined her gloves and collar, but there was something about her air that would have given pause to the most ardent PETA activist. She looked like a character from a Wodehouse novel, but I knew her – or knew of her – and she was far more canny and unsettling.

"Lady Basingstoke. A pleasure, as always." I rose, sketching a small bow. The wait had sparked a simmering irritation, but appearances must be maintained.

"Titles, Mitchell?" She took my hands, kissing the air above each cheek. "It has been a long time, but I thought we were better friends than that."

"I did not wish to presume," I murmured, pulling away. "As you say, it has been a long time, and I couldn't be sure you'd forgiven me."

"For not saying word one since your return? For turning your nose up at Argent and going it on your own? No, I shan't forgive you for that, but I'm certain you have your reasons." She rapped me on the arm. The gesture needed a fan, but she somehow made it work without one.

"Reprimand accepted. Why did you wish to see me?"

There it was, the flash of steel in her pewter-grey eyes. She smiled, but it didn't quite reach them. "Right down to business?"

"I am a busy man, and as you might be aware, my city is in something of a pother."

"The world is in a pother. But then, you always were a bit myopic about such things. Come, let's not trade barbs unless there's tea to soothe the wounds. They make a passable cuppa here. Join me."

The last was a command rather than a question, and the way she took my arm and led me off, the both of us flanked by her guards, brooked no refusal.

Without a doubt, Sylvia Dunbarton, Lady Basingstoke, Grande Dame of the Argent Aces, was even more recognizable than Mr Mystic, even in my home city. As we made our way through the lobby to the hotel dining room, Sylvia's purpose for not meeting me in her suite became clear. Heads turned. Phones snapped pictures and took video. Tweets flew. Within moments, half the city knew. Mitchell Masters was reconciling with Argent, news at eleven. How do you know? The internets say it is so.

The hotel had been kind enough to cordon off a small section of the restaurant for our use alone, but that only drew more eyes. We were clearly visible – on display, even – to the other patrons enjoying their afternoon tea. I pried my arm out from under Sylvia's grasp to pull out her chair. The guards tensed as I leaned close to murmur in her ear.

"I presume there's more purpose to your invitation than that little PR junket?"

She smiled up at me, response equally cool. "Please. Argent hardly needs you. If I cared to have you back on our rosters, you'd be back."

She laid her serviette across one knee, waited for me to take my seat, and then lifted the teapot. She poured like a master, or at least one to the manor born. My irritation built as she prepared my tea. She stirred in milk and sugar with nary the clink of a spoon, then handed me the cup and saucer. I took a sip, but it did little to soothe my foul mood at being played.

"What do you want?"

"China."

"I think the Chinese might object."

The corner of her mouth twitched, a tiny crack in her façade. "Rumor has it that you're responsible for Oakland being free, and possibly San Francisco as well?"

That little rise at the end. She was fishing. Her information network wasn't all it was rumored to be, then. "So you do get your intel from YouTube."

"We're not the only ones. You've gone from being a quaint bit of nostalgia to a hot commodity in the intelligence community."

"And you called dibs?"

"You'd prefer I left you to the wolves? Argent's claim means that others won't be asserting theirs. Besides, you do owe us rather a lot."

I couldn't argue with that. Not because it was true, but because I didn't know if it was true. Mitchell Masters's notes on Argent had been rather thin on detail. Argent's secrets remained secret. I toyed with the brim of my fedora, worn indoors despite propriety. And yet still I felt exposed to Sylvia's sharp eyes. She knew Mr Mystic, but did she know him well enough to mark me as an imposter? Why had I agreed to this meeting again?

"It might be that I have the means to end this – *if* I can get to Shanghai – but I won't allow you to jeopardize this chance. You take me and my contact in, you drop us with gear outside the New Wall, maybe one of the islands off the coast, you let me assess the situation on the ground and handle it my way. That's it."

Sylvia's smile tightened. "I hardly think so. At the very least, I need more information. How did you get across into Oakland? How did you take down the New Wall? Is it technology or sorcery? Is the Chinese government responsible for this? That's the consensus in Turtle Bay, and I could do with some solid evidence to refute it. I don't think you comprehend just how close some fingers are to that button."

"Is there really a button, Sylvia?"

"This isn't a laughing matter, Mitchell."

"No. It isn't." I sighed and pushed aside my tea. Let Sylvia be insulted. We both had something the other wanted, but my something was more valuable. "The CPC isn't behind this."

She jumped on that. "You know who is."

"I do. And not even Argent is strong enough to touch him."

"Evidence?"

"My word. Just tell whoever is asking that it's an underground interest. Then get me across the Pacific and drop me off the coast of Shanghai. Preferably with a parachute and a raft of some sort. I'll find my way from there."

Sylvia refreshed my tea for the benefit of the several reporters that crowded the archway leading to the lobby. Watching her assess, assimilate, and calculate was a tiring business, though that might have been the bruises talking.

"You can take others across with you, yes? You're taking your contact? If we brought forces along–"

"No, Sylvia."

"But a small, tactical team. My best Aces–"

"I said 'No'." She had gracious doggedness down, but few could beat me for implacable when I put my mind to it. "I'll be taking one person. My go-between. I have no intention of antagonizing people who already don't look kindly on me, and I especially don't want to take more Westerners in without the Chinese government's permission. You may be confident in your ability to deal with the ramifications of that. I'm not. You send me with one pilot, and I'm not taking any of your people across with me."

Sylvia eyed me for several moments, but I could read nothing of what she was thinking. Then her eyes raised heavenward and she gave a tiny shake of her head. "Impossible man. You always did turn up queer where China was concerned. Fine. A pilot. My best. I'll even make sure to give you a parachute that works."

Argent's private airfield was an hour southeast of the bay, surrounded by fields of spinach, strawberries, and broccoli, guessing from the stink. One would hardly think it was October, here in the middle of California's bread-basket.

I made David Tsung drive.

"Are you sure this is a good idea?" he asked, breaking our self-imposed silence as we were guided through what I hoped was the final set of security gates after our identifications had been checked and checked again. Annoying, but better than being forced to fight a dozen men to prove who we were.

No, I wasn't still a little bitter about Lao Chan's test. I winced and stretched out my knee, grown stiff during the drive.

"I am fairly certain this is a horrible idea, but I'm afraid I see no other options. We'll airdrop into one of the accessible coastal islands and take a raft across. You know how to paddle, right?"

"Shouldn't you be asking me if I know how to parachute?"

I liked David Tsung less each moment I was with him. Possibly because I suspected those glances he kept stealing were aimed at my chest, as if that were the most unbelievable element of my guise. "Perhaps your people should have considered issues of transportation before instigating this mess," I snapped, crossing my arms.

"My people?" He returned his attention to driving, creeping down a line of silver-grey hangars tall enough to block the view of the rest of the base. I couldn't read his eyes behind his sunglasses, but his lips pursed into a flat line and his knuckles whitened on the steering wheel. "You seem quick to – holy shit!"

The car lurched to a stop as we rounded another corner and came out onto the airfield. Tsung's hand shot out to check my forward momentum. The seatbelt caught and jerked me back. I strained against it, craning my neck to peer up at what had startled him.

An angel in gold armor and flowing white robes rode the thermals above us on widespread wings. She led a squad of troops wearing jetpacks through a series of aerial drills.

Tsung twisted to one side as much as I did to keep the angel in sight, lowering his sunglasses even though it meant squinting against the daylight. "Is that–"

"La Reina de Los Angeles. Yes," I said, as if it were perfectly normal to see the heavenly host at a training base in central California. I straightened when Tsung and I nearly bumped heads trying to keep the woman in sight. Releasing my restraint, I opened the car door and got out. Ostensibly to stretch my legs, but also to take in the full scope of Argent's operations, unhindered by the chassis.

It was a daunting sight.

La Reina and her jetpacked warriors were the only troops to take to the skies, but they formed only a small contingent of Argent's amassing might. Along the length of the tarmac, units in standard-issue fatigues drilled, wearing the silver-grey berets and arm-bands of Argent's ground forces. In the grassy field across the runway, a cavalry troop rode maneuvers, led by two figures in mail. To anyone else, they might have looked like reenactors from Medieval Times, but there was no mistaking those twin winged helmets of silver and gold.

"Mayhawk and Summerhawk," I said to my companion, nodding at each rider in turn.

"Of the Round Table?" Tsung's sunglasses – and his cool – were back in place. "Doesn't that qualify as foreign operatives on American soil?"

"Camp Argent has special dispensation as the private holding of a supranational organization," said a crisp voice behind us. I turned. Sylvia Dunbarton and her entourage had snuck up on us while we were gaping. She stood in the doorway of the hangar, flanked by two dark-suited men with earpieces, sunglasses, and blank faces, and a younger version of herself who must have been a personal assistant of some sort.

I suffered through Sylvia's cheek kisses. "I thought they spent all their time searching for their Arthur."

"They agreed that the world's hour of greatest need trumped Brittania's."

"Lovely." The whole show made me more grumpy. I didn't want to become involved in things at this level. It was too big and too complicated. There were no right answers here, just making the best of a bad situation. "Please tell me you're not amassing an army for an attack on China once the New Wall goes down?"

"An Army? This is a peacekeeping force."

"Pardon me if I can't tell the difference."

"Stop being tiresome and introduce me to Mr Tsung."

I shouldn't have been at all surprised that she'd discovered his identity. She'd likely known even before we hit the first security gate.

"David Tsung, Sylvia Dunbarton." They nodded, but there were no cheek-kisses for Mr Tsung. Must be a special torture she reserved just for me.

"So these are my passengers?" drawled a young man as he emerged from the shadows of the hangar.

"And here's your pilot. You know Tom, yes?"

Clean-cut, all-American poster boy for the Aces – he'd smiled down at me from more than one box of Wheaties, but photographs muted his ineffable charm. Tom Carter was a walking campaign for the Silver Age, and he didn't disappoint. He wore a beat-up WWII bomber jacket and loose khaki pants. His sky-blue button-down, complete with crisp white undershirt peeking at the collar, echoed the blue of his eyes. A playful breeze toyed with the ends of his hair. He was leading-man pretty, and everyone knew it. Why else would Sylvia thrust him so often in the spotlight? I knew Tom. Everyone did, though most people knew him as Skyrocket.

I offered my hand, and he took it and shook it once. A man's shake.

"Not in this incarnation. It is a pleasure to finally meet you, my boy. Samuel would be proud."

Sam. His grandfather. The original Skyrocket. Back in the day, Sam and Mr Mystic had been good friends and sometimes friendly rivals. Forums speculated more, but I'd never found any proof of it. Also, Sam Carter's homophobia had been as sincere as his racism and sexism.

Tom smiled, teeth white and straight. I pondered whether Colgate had him under contract, too. If they didn't, they were idiots. "No, he wouldn't, sir. But you're kind to say so." His soft drawl was an echo of Shimizu's. Pure, corn-fed Oskaloosa, Iowa.

No question, Tom was the total package. The PR reason Sylvia could get away with her private army and her special dispensations. I gritted my teeth so my smile wouldn't falter.

Sylvia looked to be doing the same. "Don't believe it, Tom. Mitchell is many things, but kind isn't one of them. Sam *would* be proud of the way you've carried on his legacy. We should all be so lucky in our progeny."

Only the fact that she didn't look at me when she said it kept me from blanching. That, and the sight of Tom's loose and easy smile tightening, just at the corner of his mouth and eyes.

Now we were all smiling, and none of us meant it.

Lovely.

"The *Kestrel*'s fueled and ready to go, ma'am. Is it just Mr Masters and Mr Tsung, or will you be flying with us?"

"No, Mitchell was adamant about going alone, and I have meetings with the security council. Someone has to keep the dogs on their leashes and to make sure their tails wag properly after you boys save the world. I leave Mr Mystic in your capable hands, my dear. Good hunting, Mitchell. I expect you'll have this all sorted within a week." She patted Tom's arm, then my cheek, like the boys she'd just called us.

She clicked across the tarmac in the direction of the control tower, trailing blank-faced bodyguards and a fresh-faced assistant in her wake.

Tom turned back to me, his smile subdued, but genial once more. He gave a rueful chuckle. "She's quite a character, isn't she? A firecracker, as my grandpap might say." He led us around to the hangar door.

"I believe Samuel would have used more choice language, of a kind not fit for mixed company."

Tom grimaced. "Yeah, well..." He used the excuse of

punching in a security code on the door pad to hide his pause. "He may have had his flaws, but he had a good heart."

I suffered a pang of sympathy. Poor Tom. Skyrocket had been a man of his time, for both good and ill. It had to be hard, fighting to recover the tarnished legacy of a grandfather he'd loved and respected, even as he knew Samuel had been in the wrong. At least my own legacy of prejudice was overshadowed by the rumors of Mr Mystic's presumed homosexuality. Though he shouldn't have been given a pass on the basis of that.

But then, I didn't have many illusions about the kind of bastard Mitchell Masters was.

I was?

Hell. I pulled down the brim of my fedora and fussed with the shadows, reminding myself who I was. It was Tsung's fault. His presence made me self-conscious. Even when he kept silent, I couldn't shake the feeling of being evaluated.

This was why I worked alone.

"He was a good man and a good friend, and though it guts me to admit it, Sylvia is right. He would be proud. Samuel was the last person to admit that he was wrong, but he was often the first person to realize it."

Tom laughed and pushed open the hangar door. "Now isn't that the God's honest truth. Cussed as mules, the both of us."

Tsung and I followed him into the hangar. My steps faltered as I took in our transportation.

"We're flying across the Pacific in... that?"

I'll say this for Argent, they work their branding. Sylvia Dunbarton's cultivated studio-system glamour was just one facet of that marcasite jewel. There was Skyrocket's WWII charm, the Antiquarian's Howard Carter persona... and now this.

The *Kestrel* gleamed a burnished silver from the curve of her snub nose to the arch of her slender tail. Evenly-spaced rivets were the only interruption to her sleek lines. There weren't even engines tucked under the wings, or windows to mar the length of the fuselage. She looked like Howard Hughes's wet dream, and not at all air-worthy.

Tom, bless him, grinned at my skepticism. "She's a beauty, isn't she? Flies like a dream."

"She… flies?" How?

He answered my unasked question with a shrug. "Same tech as my rocket pack. Stuff my grandpap helped develop, though they've gone way beyond that, now. Argent's tech people… those guys are whip smart. Could probably solve world hunger." He frowned. "If world hunger could be solved with aviation technology, I guess."

If there were more power in solving world hunger than in letting it strategically continue. But a seam opened at the rear of the *Kestrel*, interrupting any sour comment I was inclined to make. A gangplank lowered to the ground. Tom hopped up the slope and held out a hand to help me up. I ignored it. I was old, not *decrepit*.

The ramp led to the cargo bay and jump deck. Tom gestured to a pile of gear held in place with netting.

"'Chutes and suits are back here, plus a supply drop and an inflatable raft. You can suit up later, I reckon." He opened a pressurized door and led us through a small cabin and to the cockpit. Everything was primed and lit. Maybe he'd done his pre-flight check before our arrival. Though I was still skeptical about the flight aspect. There were *no engines*. How could the blasted thing fly with no engines?

Tom sat in the padded flightseat and flicked switches on the console, doing lord-only-knew what. "Should have us in the air in about twenty minutes. It's pretty spacious back in the cabin. Just make yourself comfy. Have a drink. A snack. Grab a seat up here and chat if you feel like it. It's a milk run until we hit Chinese airspace. The company'd be nice."

Tsung took the co-pilot's seat. I shook my head. Between

the glances Tsung kept shooting at me and Tom's youthful vigor, I was beginning to feel every year of my presumed age. "Perhaps later, when things get interesting. I think I'll try to sleep just now."

Tom chuckled as I returned to the passenger cabin. "Those old-guard types are all the same," he told Tsung, as if I couldn't hear him. "Sleep when they can, cause who knows when they'll have the chance again, right?"

"So it would seem," David Tsung murmured.

I settled into a chair I suspected was Sylvia's favorite and pulled my hat down over my face. I feared those words would prove to be prophetic.

"So, why did you leave Argent?"

I'd woken from my nap and headed back to pull my jumpsuit and parachute on over my clothes. I exchanged my fedora for a helmet, and stashed it in a bundle that included my trench coat and the knife. I'd jump with them, but be damned if I was taking that woodcarving knife to the leg because I'd landed wrong.

I took David Tsung's abandoned co-pilot seat while he went back to change. From the extended weight of silence that had descended as Tom and I watched the blue go by, he'd been trying to figure out how to blurt that question for a good while.

"Technically, I didn't." Even more technically, I didn't know. There were gaps the size of the English Channel in Mr Mystic's journal entries regarding Argent. "I had matters to see to, and seeing to them took longer than expected. When I came back, I simply neglected to contact the agency. We'd both changed so much in the interim, there didn't seem to be a point."

"But you don't like them."

"'Them' is a collective of individuals, some of whom I like very well. But no. On the whole I do not approve of the course that some of those individuals have charted for Argent."

"But we do good work." Tom had an earnestness that couldn't be feigned – another reason he made such a good spokesman. I had no doubt he believed in Argent's mission statement. "We do drives for charities, act as ambassadors and peacekeepers all over the world. And when some terrorist with a few magic tricks up his sleeve or a couple of fancy gadgets comes along, bent on world domination, we're there to stop him."

"You know, there's some who argue that the existence of Argent invites such opposition. That if you didn't exist, neither would they, and the world would be a safer place all around."

"Well, that's just stupid talk."

I chuckled. Tom's eloquence was all the more effective for being homespun. "I'm inclined to agree."

"I mean, what do those folks think? If we weren't around, those terrorists would still be out causing trouble, and we might not even know about it."

I placed a steadying hand on his shoulder. "As I said, I agree. But the corollary to that argument is that as a result, Argent has been given broad, unchecked powers. They've become a force to be reckoned with, on a par with any nation. Witness the fact that in this current crisis, Argent has a seat at the table. A private corporation, with nobody to answer to, no mandate from any people. That is what troubles me."

"There's shareholders."

"Who care about the bottom line, which is hardly the kind of a line a hero should be drawing in the sand, wouldn't you agree?"

But Tom's strength as a spokesman was that he believed in his heart what he couldn't quantify in his head.

"We do good work," he insisted. "And we get things done. You have to admit that, at least. You wouldn't be here now if it weren't true."

"Lord, you're much like your grandfather," I said, as much to change the topic as anything.

"Thanks. I – Jesus H!" The *Kestrel* rocked as a muffled *whump* sounded from somewhere outside. Tom pulled the control yoke, sending us into a steep climb. I tumbled from my seat. A cry and a thunk came from the back as David Tsung and gravity made their acquaintance.

"You all right, sir?" Tom's hand shot down to help me up. I waved it away.

"Fine. I'm fine. Keep… driving. Or what have you. Tsung, you all right?" I glanced back down the length of the windowless fuselage. David Tsung was suited-up and scowling. He crawled up the aisle and strapped in to the cushy seat I'd abandoned.

"I'm fine. What the hell was that?"

I had no clue, but Tsung's idea was a good one. I clambered back into the co-pilot's seat and strapped myself in. "Tom?"

"Hold on." Seeing us safely belted, Tom nudged the *Kestrel* into a dive. My stomach flipped as I slammed into the restraints; I closed my eyes to fight back nausea. Correct that. Not a dive. A *Kestrel* dive. I wanted to demand what the tactical logic of that was, but I was too busy struggling to keep my lunch.

"We got two bogeys at six and eight."

"Bogeys? Do you seriously call them that?"

"I'm old school." Another grin. Another moment of stomach flipping terror as he did something that only belonged in an airshow. I recalled liking flying, once upon a time, and on a flimsier craft than this. But then, I'd trusted that pilot with my life. I barely knew Tom.

"Are they after us specifically, do you think?" I asked through gritted teeth, "Or just taking potshots at whatever they're running across?"

"Don't know." He flicked some switches on the console. "They're speaking gobbledygook." Another switch, and Mandarin poured from the cockpit speakers.

Perhaps Tom wasn't completely free of his grandfather's ethnocentrism.

"Shenyang J-15s off the *Liaoning*," Tsung said for Tom's benefit as the pilots chattered with their controller. "Sounds like they've got orders to herd anything they see into an early demise."

Tom shook his head. "They must have been blue water when the Wall went up. Can't get Argent command on the com. We're too close to the New Wall."

Even worse. "How close?" The footage of that cargo hulk crunching into the Wall like a tin can had become one of the signifying images of the current crisis. What would the New Wall do to a plane?

A few more switches flipped, and another rocking *whump* from outside. The control yoke rattled in Tom's grip, and for a moment he struggled to keep it steady. "Closer than we were a few minutes ago. They're herding us toward it. Shit. Shit."

"We have to jump," I said.

Tsung, who'd been leaning as far forward as his restraints and our aerial acrobatics would allow, choked on a laugh. "Are you crazy, old man? What's to stop them from taking us out, chutes and all, and then herding the evidence into the ward?"

"I ain't abandoning ship," Tom said with a firming of that lantern-jaw. "Not letting them get ahold of her tech."

"You have to take us across to the Shadow Realms," Tsung said to me.

"Who is the crazy one now?" If Tsung knew the Shadow Realms as well as I suspected he did, he had to know the effect they'd have on the *Kestrel*'s engines. "We'll be dead in the water... sky... within a few moments."

"We'll have long enough for all three of us to jump, nobody will get access to Argent's tech, and we can cross back over once we're on the ground."

Assuming nothing found us and ate us first. "It's too dangerous."

"This is more dangerous. Take us across."

"You are mad if you think I'm going to."

"Take. Us. Across." And unspoken behind Tsung's glare: *If you don't, I will.*

As much as I didn't wish to cross over, I wanted even less to be dragged across by someone else. What if he wasn't as powerful as I was? What if he lacked my control?

"Mr Masters, sir? I don't usually disrespect my elders, but if you don't do as the man says, I *will* pop you one when this is over. Assuming we survive."

"Fine," I snapped, leaving the rest of what I wanted to say hanging. *Don't say I didn't warn you.* "When I say go, put out the interior lights. You'll only have a few moments of power before the Realms start draining it. Can you make it to the bay to jump?"

"I'll make it. You two head back. I'll see what I can do to give us some space before pointing us in the right direction."

Any further arguments I might have made were silenced by another *whump* and a burst of alarms from the console. Tom cursed and struggled with the yoke.

I unstrapped and followed David Tsung to the jump bay as the *Kestrel* bucked and swayed and threatened to send me bouncing back towards the cockpit.

"This is a seriously bad idea," I muttered to Tsung, grabbing my little satchel and holding on to a carabiner so I wouldn't go hurtling out the back of the plane before I was ready to hurtle myself.

"You're just saying that because nobody likes us over there."

"You fellas ready, or you want some private time?" Tom called.

"I just assumed you needed to kiss your girl goodbye," I shouted back. "Give the word. We're ready when you are."

"I'll remember you were making fun, Old Man. OK, go!"

The lights went out and the rear bay opened. I rocked back at the change in pressure and the wind, squinting my eyes as they started to water, and wishing I could cover my ears. The cold sunlight slanted into the jump bay, washing up the curve of one wall, but the rest of the windowless fuselage was in darkness. I gathered up all the shadow like net webbing, braced myself, and pulled.

It was like pulling on a brace holding back an avalanche. I didn't so much take us across as that the *Kestrel* barreled into the darkness.

The sunlight cut out, as did the deafening sound of the wind. We were cocooned in a void so absolute that for a moment I feared I'd somehow killed us all, and this was death.

No. *Cogito ergo sum*. I bolstered myself with that thought.

And then I didn't need to, because equilibrium made my stomach drop, like I was going over the edge of a roller coaster.

The carabiner strap cut into my wrist, keeping me from tumbling.

I drew in a breath, an incipient scream. It broke the silence, then more breathing from my right. Tsung.

"Are we falling?" My question came only a little higher than my usual tones. Darkness within, darkness without, and no sound of air or engines to explain the odd, weightless feeling. I gripped the strap, the only thing solid in this void.

The silence was broken by the sound of someone stumbling their way behind me. Tom. "We've lost power. No instruments. No engines. We make it across?"

"The darkness doesn't give it away?"

"The New Wall. We make it across the New Wall?"

"I've no way to tell."

"Right-o. Follow me." Another click, followed by an explosion of light. Skyrocket flashed past us, the flare of his rocketpack blinding me. But it also gave me a direction to follow. I released my grip on the strap and managed a graceless run into freefall. Pulled my chute immediately because who knew how much altitude we'd lost in the darkness. I clenched my eyes as wind and gravity returned. Something flapped above me. I looked up in case it was a raptor or something worse. It rippled and spread, a slightly paler shade of dark. Then it caught, and my stomach lurched as I was pulled up short.

I rocked back and forth under the pale cloud of darkness, like an infant in a rough cradle, falling through the void. No, not falling. At least, not entirely. Now that I could see in every direction, I spied the lambent curve of the horizon, a few pockets of luminescence dotting the shadow landscape below, and above me, the cloud resolved into the pale rectangle of a parachute.

And then, off below me, a flash so bright it burned my retinas, and thunder concussive enough to make me flinch.

The *Kestrel*, making her final landing.

EIGHT
Family Matters

Then

My feet and back were killing me. I spared a longing look at an empty bench on the other side of the garden, but I couldn't escape until I finished with the Shanghai contingent. I'd greeted Guardian Song Yulan and a host of lesser temple spirits from Shanghai, which just left me with Fang Shih, a spirit who escaped categorization, and who seemed determined to talk my ear off in a dialect I could barely follow. Keeping my groan purely mental, I returned to my silent catalogue of his features.

Fang Shih's eyes bulged out over a flat, pushed-up, piggy nose, and his mouth stretched wide open in a perpetual snarl, which was useful for showing off his many rows of teeth. His burly head sat on an even burlier pair of shoulders, but then his body narrowed to cartoonish thinness and ended in a pair of delicate trotters. He swayed back and forth with such regular rhythm that I was starting to get motion sick.

Fang Shih paused; he must have finished his formal address. I smiled and bowed, thanking him with a similar formality, which included a string of memorized honorifics. His bulgy eyes bulged larger. Guardian Song Yulan placed a restraining hand on Fang Shih's massive shoulder.

"I do not believe she meant it like that," she said in Shanghaiaccented Mandarin. I nodded, afraid to speak and make things worse. Whatever I'd mispronounced, I definitely didn't mean it. My mind blanked on the proper way to say "Please don't curse me back into the stone age."

Jian Huo appeared at my side, his hand settling at the small of my back. He spoke in a series of whines and growls that I assumed was Fang Shih's native speech. I smiled and bowed and tried to look apologetic.

Whatever Jian Huo said, it worked. Fang Shih roared and grabbed my hands, pumping them up and down several times, baring every tooth they had and nodding its ridiculously-sized head. It was like receiving a blessing from a Jim Henson Muppet. Still roaring, Fang Shih allowed Song Yulan to lead their party off, leaving Jian Huo and myself in a small pocket of solitude for the first time that day. He smoothed my wispies, brow furrowed.

"Are you well?" he asked. "That mistake was not like you."

"How bad was it?" Though I was too exhausted to care.

"You called him a dung heap."

I shot Jian Huo a skeptical look, certain that he was messing with me. I didn't get so much as a brow twitch. He was serious. I tried to muster some horror, but I choked on a laugh instead.

Jian Huo frowned. "You find the possibility of angering a Fang Shih amusing? Their curses are legendary." He might have gone on, but my laughter cut short as a spasm of pain twisted my lower back. Disapproval became concern. "Are you well?"

"I'm fine," I said, waving away his concern. "It's just that my back aches and my feet are swollen and I'm feeling vaguely nauseous. All I want to do is eat Chef Boyardee ravioli and watch cable, neither of which you can get here." Yes, I was cranky, but I'd been socializing for the past several hours, and I had eight more days of it to look forward to.

Nine days. The nine day long ceremony of *Zi Gong Hu*, the

public introduction of myself as the mother of Jian Huo's children. I'd railed long and hard about how insulting I found the entire thing. I was little more than a walking womb. Jian Huo's children – I gave myself a mental shake – *our* children were not even born, but some of our guests didn't even bother to address me, they just spoke to my belly.

It was a healthy dose of culture shock. For some of the spirits, this was traditional. I tried not to take offense because I was the intruder here. There were others who disapproved of me; they treated me like a womb because while they had to acknowledge Jian Huo's children, they wanted to ignore my existence as much as possible. That made it hard to remain diplomatic.

Since the Shanghai contingent had been the last of the day's arrivals, I recited the lines welcoming our guests to the house and gardens like a good little marionette. Jian Huo took one look at my grumpy frown and escorted me to the empty bench I'd been eying.

I sank down onto it. Rather, I maneuvered my bulky form onto it. When we'd discovered that I was going to have twins, I had been excited. It was like double-the-pleasure, double-the-fun. Now, so near to term, my enthusiasm had waned. I felt twice as huge, twice as uncomfortable, and I was certain the birthing would be twice as long and twice as painful. Growing up, I'd heard all sorts of romanticized bullshit about women loving being pregnant and glowing and such. Now I knew it for what it was: propaganda designed to make sure the human race was propagated. Being pregnant sucked donkey balls. I just wanted it to be over.

But first, I had to get through my nine-day baby shower.

It didn't help that the ceremony was a thinly disguised test to see if I could behave for the duration. Anything I did wrong, any insult I offered, could cause a powerful spirit to curse our children. On the plus side, every being that I impressed had the choice to offer their blessing. It was like I was stuck in the fairy tale of Sleeping Beauty, seeing it from her mom's perspective. I was terrified of making the tiniest misstep. Again with the donkey balls.

Jian Huo bore the brunt of my unhappiness with draconic equanimity. Now, as I tried to find a position that would relieve my cramping muscles, his hands settled at the base of my spine, and he kneaded away the tension. I sighed and shifted so I could lean back against him.

"How much longer do we have today?" I asked.

"There is the banquet this evening, but you may stay ensconced on your pillows. For the next two days, all those who wish to address you will come to you." Well, that was a relief. I was a waddling cow, but as long as I could sit, I could attempt to be charming.

"On the fourth day the great spirits will arrive. We will greet them as we greeted the lesser spirits today." I pulled a face; he ignored it. "Then more banqueting. On the seventh day…" He drifted off, fingers stilling on my back.

"The seventh day?" I pressed.

"Traditionally, that is the day for Dragons to come and bless the children." He didn't need to give an explanation beyond that. Neither of us expected his siblings to make an appearance. He'd never gone into detail on why they'd exiled him, but I'd been here long enough to figure out that it was over my grandfather and the champion issue. It hadn't been quite as pretty a romance from Jian Huo's perspective, and I was torn between fury at my grandfather for forcing Jian Huo to leave Shambhala and annoyance at the other dragons for punishing their sibling for doing the right thing.

I grasped his hand, bringing it to my lips and then resting my cheek against it. One of the twins took a whack at my cervix. I moved Jian Huo's hand down to feel it. Thinking about the children always cheered him up.

We sat in quiet contentment as our guests mingled. It was the largest gathering of spirits I'd ever seen, and exhausting just for that; I'd grown accustomed to our hermitage. But there was still the feast tonight to get through. I needed to recharge my batteries. I shifted away from him. "Do you think I could manage to slip away for a bath before this evening?"

Jian Huo's hand had crept up to brush the underside of my breast. "I had hoped we might manage to slip away together instead," he said with a half-smile and a lift of one brow.

I shook my head at his one-track mind. "I'm as big as a house! I'm due any time here. I wouldn't be surprised if I popped in the middle of one of these formal greetings."

"Is it terribly wrong of me that I want you so much in this state?"

"I gotta admit that your thing for pregnancy sex is kinda kinky, but since I'm the one benefiting from it, I'm not going to complain." Another spasm hit my lower back, and I grimaced. "But if you want me to be on my game tonight, I think hot water is going to be better for me than hot sex."

Jian Huo's brow drooped, but there was sympathy in his smile as he smoothed my hair back. He helped me rise from the bench, and we made our way through the gamut of our guests. I let Jian Huo take the lead on pleasantries. Most of the guests had already blessed my womb, but a few more deigned to do so as we passed. I half expected my belly to start glowing like the Holy Grail.

I loaded my bathing things into a basket and made my way to the hot springs, anticipating a quiet hour to myself with the warm water soothing my cramping muscles. I didn't expect to run into someone else already bathing. I didn't recognize the woman, but I'd greeted so many people that I might have forgotten her. I hesitated at the edge of the grotto, still wanting my bath but reluctant to disturb her. She turned and smiled a welcome.

"Good afternoon, Lung Xin Niang. I am sorry if my presence is an intrusion. If you wish time for yourself, I will leave. Or, if you allow me to remain, I promise I will be undemanding company." Her words were so polite that they rounded the corner into mocking. She regarded me with sly, golden eyes that held just a hint of playful malice. Steam had darkened her hair, but dry it would be a russet shade near my own. How on earth had I forgotten her?

But had I? Something about her was familiar. "Do I know you?"

She inclined her head. "It may be that I am known to you."

That was all I needed. The woman might be unfamiliar, but I'd recognize that mocking head-tilt anywhere. My bath things went tumbling into the pool.

"Holy shit. *Huxian*?"

"Even so."

"You're... uh..." I gestured, not sure I was more thrown that she was woman-shaped or that she was naked. As long as I'd been here, the spirit world still had the ability to throw me on a regular basis.

"I am many things. Shall I leave you to contemplate them?"

I wasn't up for our usual sparring. "Look, if you're willing to be undemanding company, then I'd be happy to set aside our usual guest/host, spirit/human, trickster/trickee crap to just relax and chat."

I didn't wait for her agreement. I couldn't bend down to recover my bath things, so climbing into the pool was my only option. I shucked my brocade robe and slid into the heated water, groaning in rapture as my cramping muscles responded.

Her smile turned from sly to bemused. "I have always wondered what Jian Huo sees in you. I believe I begin to see it now."

She couldn't be talking about my body, not as pregnant as I was. Had to be something else. I was curious to see if she'd say what.

"Really? Do you mind sharing? Because it has always baffled me." I leaned forward, as if offering a secret confidence, and she responded as predictably as any human would, leaning in to catch my stage whisper. "Poor guy doesn't even mind that half the spirits here are laughing behind his back."

She pulled back and blinked twice. She had to know it was true, but I don't think she expected me to point it out.

"I believe you must have some fox in you, Lung Xin Niang."

I'd heard the honorific from our other guests, but I didn't expect it from her. The *huxian* was the closest thing I had to a friend these days. "I'm not good enough to be *Miqian* anymore?"

Her gaze faltered away. She shaped a bit of foam that floated on the surface of the steaming pool. "You are now *Lung Xin Niang*. It would no longer be appropriate for me to be so uncivil."

Ah. That explained the shift in her manners and the reduction in mockery. I outranked her.

"Then call me Missy, please," I said. "And maybe I do have some fox in me. It'd be British fox blood of course, but my grandmother had red hair, and people used to call her a vixen all the time."

"Missy," she nodded. "And you may call me Si Wei." It was a minor pact, this exchange of names, but at least now the fox-woman was meeting my eyes. "I have heard tell of your grandmother. It was she that your grandfather chose over Jian Huo, was it not? He gave her Jian Huo's pearls?"

"That's her." I wondered if this was some sort of huge insult, but Si Wei just nodded her head as if a puzzle had finally come together.

"Then she must have fox blood in her. No other woman could entice a man away from his dragon-lover." This conclusion eased whatever other reservations she had had about me. Probably because if I had fox-blood, Jian Huo's interest in me was more understandable. I was happy to take what truce I could get.

"You've known Jian Huo a long while, then?" I asked.

"I have known him since I first ceased to be a fox and became *Huxian*. It was shortly after his first altercation with his elders."

"Ah... the writing incident?"

"He has told you of how he defied his siblings the first time?"

"A little. He doesn't like talking about it much."

"I believe that if he had not defied them then to give the knowledge of writing to the peoples of China, or if the results of that gift hadn't turned out so badly – at least in the eyes of his siblings – then his more recent defiance of them would not have resulted in such a harsh punishment. But of course, he refuses to admit that the two events might be linked."

"I had wondered about that. It seems a bit extreme to exile him just for training my grandfather, but there are always so many nuances that I just don't get."

"You seem to be doing well in spite of it."

I smiled my thanks at the compliment. "What's funny to me is that he's so proud of it. The whole writing thing, I mean: as if it's proof that he's a man – or rather, dragon – of the people. I can't quite figure out how to tell him that giving people a written language with a gajillion characters isn't doing them any favors."

She laughed at this. "I believe his reasoning at the time was that they would only appreciate the results if they had to earn it."

"That explains so much," I groaned. I didn't expect her to understand the meaning behind my cryptic statement, but her foxy mind snapped right to it.

"Long courtship, was it?" she asked with another sly grin, but I sensed no malice in this one.

"You have no idea."

"And do you appreciate the results?"

I just smiled and changed the subject.

•••

The next several days were a slog, but I managed to make it through the informal conversations without insulting anyone, and I even managed to soften up some of the hard-liners. At least, they started talking to me instead of my belly.

Fang Shih, who I mentally referred to as Mr Dung Heap, took a particular liking to me. He took over Jian Huo's workshop, and I sat with him as he crafted dozens of little toys and trinkets for the children: schools of sunset-hued carp and phalanxes of hard-shelled turtles, a miniature army and a palace for them to guard. I anticipated a lot of hopping and cursing in my future when I ended up stepping on the tiny wonders.

While he worked, he made it his personal mission to drill me in my addresses. Every so often he would repeat my "dung heap" mistake and roar in what passed as laughter for him. We even made a game of his instruction, figuring out ways to mispronounce the honorifics so that they became horribly insulting. The realization that I was a diphthong away from calling Tiger a mangy, fig-eating herbivore did wonders for my pronunciation.

Si Wei and I also became good friends, much to Jian Huo's dismay. At first I paid some heed to his dire warnings that fox-women, Si Wei in particular, couldn't be trusted – that her friendship was a pretense for some other design. But I'd developed some keen insight into reading Jian Huo, and I suspected that his reservations were just the normal reservations of a guy who didn't want his current girl talking to his ex. It was cute in a normal kind of way, and after the first few dire frowns, I just smiled away his surly warnings, kissed him on the cheek, and waddled off to gossip with my new girl-pal.

I was more on my game by the time the Great Spirits arrived. I still suffered cramps, and I felt like a cow, but with several more allies in my corner I was able to greet our newcomers with gracious equanimity.

It was a good thing too, since I had to greet the other Guardians of China. Feng Huang was the Phoenix, Guardian of the South. Greeting her was easy enough since she was a regular visitor. I could navigate my awe at being in the presence of such a majestic creature. Lao Hu was the Tiger, Guardian of the West. Greeting him was more nerve-wracking. I got the impression that he might eat me even if I didn't screw things up. Gui Dai was the Tortoise, Guardian of the North, and that conversation ended up taking half the afternoon. I had all the time in the world to mentally rehearse my response while he was making it through his address.

The weirdest thing was having to greet Jian Huo as Lung Huang, the Dragon Guardian of the East, since Jian Huo's eldest sibling had not deigned to grace us with his presence. The traditional words flowed, but a large part of me wondered what would have happened if I messed things up. Would Jian Huo have cursed my womb simply because tradition and honor demanded it? I thought about asking Si Wei, but I left it alone. I didn't want to know.

Then there was the *qilin*. Viridian flames wreathed her slender body, and there was a wildness about her that diverted the eye, as if looking too closely, too directly, would send her fleeing. She woke my deepest girly-girl instincts regarding unicorns. I was ashamed to meet her in my pregnant state, even though I knew that Chinese unicorns didn't have anything to do with virginity or purity. I was reminded of *The Last Unicorn*, and Molly Grue's weeping accusation: *Where were you when I was new? … How dare you come to me now, when I am this!* For all that I was happy in my chosen life, meeting the *qilin* made me want to cry for the girl I hadn't had the chance to be. I never hated my grandfather so much as in that moment. I choked on my greeting; my eyes filled with tears. I was terrified that I'd messed everything up, but she just gave a delicate nod of her head and lowered her twin horns to rest on my belly: her promise that she would not forsake my children as I had been forsaken.

There was also another *huxian*, but this one was aged beyond time. She was Jiu Wei – nine-tails – and according to Si Wei, she was the first and most powerful of the fox spirits. Even with her advanced age, her amber eyes twinkled, and her silvered hair caught the eye of more than one spirit in attendance. I was utterly charmed by her, and I stayed up late into the evenings chatting and drinking far too much tea with her and Si Wei.

We were such a merry party that it seemed doubly strange that the morning of the seventh day should find us all so somber. After breakfast we gathered in the garden, as we had on the first and fourth days, to await our final guests. Nobody dared mention that it was an exercise in futility. Jian Huo sat on a bench near the entry gate, pensive gaze fixed on the mountain trail. I sat next to him, holding his hand against my belly. Not even that could chase away his gloom.

We waited well into the morning, the clear view into the far-below valley mocking our vigil. Our guests mingled uneasily, trying to show with their patience that they respected Jian Huo's pain over the great gulf that separated him and his siblings.

Finally, at no signal that I could tell, Jian Huo stood and walked away. The guests breathed a collective sigh of relief that the vigil was over. They began speaking amongst themselves. Si Wei ventured my way, but I waved her off. None of this was my fault; none of it was about me. Didn't ease my guilt any, and I preferred to wallow in solitude.

I gazed blindly down into the valley for I didn't know how long before I realized that a front had been building. Low clouds moved in to obstruct the clear view, roiling and rising at a much faster rate than was normal for a meteorological event. I stood, staring for a moment longer to make sure that I was seeing what I thought I was seeing.

"Jian Huo?" My voice wasn't loud, but the urgency in it silenced the low murmurs of our guests. He joined me, gaping down at the fog-shrouded valley.

Si Wei was at our side an instant later, her voice low and urgent. "My Lord, have you prepared her to greet them?"

"No. I didn't... I didn't think they'd–"

"Men!" She rolled her eyes in exasperation. "My Lord, without proper guidance your bride is certain to cause insult. I will offer myself as adviser. In return, you will forgive me the debt I owe you."

Debt? What debt? This was the first I'd heard of it. I was also a little insulted that they thought I couldn't hack a few dragons. I mean, I handled my own just fine.

Jian Huo closed his mouth, considering her offer. "The debt you owe me is great. What you offer in return is small."

"Yeah," I piped up. "Plus, I've managed just fine so far. How hard could it be?"

They both regarded me as if I'd sprouted two heads, and Jian Huo had a look of dawning horror on his face. He turned to Si Wei with a desperate nod: "Done."

The preparations that followed could never be termed frenetic – they were too meticulous for that – but there was a sense of harried urgency to them. Si Wei was in her element.

First, she declared that my clothes and hair were too casual for such an occasion. I tried to argue that the dragons were only minutes away, but Si Wei shushed me and told me that since they had kept us waiting, it was permissible for us to keep them waiting. Si Wei whisked me away to my rooms to dress me, roping in Jiu Wei and Song Yulan to help out. Between the three of them, they lectured me thoroughly on how not to insult the gods knocking at our gate.

Thus it was that an hour later, swathed in brocade robes

of green, red, and gold; red hair hidden by an elaborate headdress; face whitened with rice powder and features limned with black, I picked my way down the steps into the garden. My headdress wobbled with every step. I would have been embarrassed by my *hanfu*, but I was too busy concentrating on not falling down the long flight. Splatting at the feet of your guests was not in the standard greeting protocol.

At least I'd done this twice already. As Lady of Jian Huo's house, it would be my duty to acknowledge the new arrivals. Until I did they would not be considered guests of the house. Paying attention to Si Wei's subtle gestures, I maneuvered toward Lung Wang, the eldest among the dragons and the true Guardian of the East. Lung Wang had an agelessness that transcended gender. Of all Jian Huo's siblings, she looked the least human. Her face was a porcelain mask, her eyes deep pools of turbulent water, or maybe storm clouds chasing across the sky. I bowed low, awe replacing my nervous jitters. I'd grown so accustomed to Jian Huo that I forgot how striking and terrifying he had been on our first meeting. Now I remembered.

My fancy hat didn't go tumbling across the dragon's feet, which I took as a good omen. I parroted the lines of the formal greeting, and Lung Wang nodded her acceptance. I couldn't tell if she approved or disapproved. I'd learned to read Jian Huo, but my dragon was an open book compared to his eldest sibling. Whatever the case, Lung Wang stepped aside, and I moved on to greet Jian Huo's other siblings, so I suppose it didn't go too badly.

It was good that I had Lung Wang's acceptance, because my next greeting was to Lung Tian, and his disapproval was plain as anything. Everything about the Celestial Dragon was martial and masculine – in-your-face masculine. He sneered at my greeting, forcing me into more docile and feminine speech forms to assuage him. I got the feeling that he'd been hoping to get a rise out of me so that he could denounce me. Even Si Wei was bristling by the time Lung Tian accepted my greeting and moved aside for his younger siblings.

The next greetings were less fraught. Lung Jiao, the Horned Dragon, was rumored to be the most powerful of the guardians. He was also deaf, and he followed my greeting only by the shape of the words on my lips. He accepted it with the same, aloof nod as Lung Wang.

Lung Shen, the Spiritual Dragon, was the first of those I greeted to have taken female form. Si Wei had given me the gossip on her. She had been furious when Jian Huo had sided with my grandfather, and she'd been one of the strongest advocates for his exile, but in the intervening years she had taken a *laowai* lover of her own. Now she was in the glass-house quandary. While she wasn't likely to be giving me cheek-kisses any time soon, she was also not likely to give me too much grief. Lung Fu Cang, the Dragon of Hidden Treasures, was also in female form. I gathered from Si Wei that Lung Fu Cang preferred to be female. Both Lung Shen and Lung Fu Cang accepted my greetings with detached cordiality.

Lung Ying, the Winged Dragon, who often served as his siblings' messenger to the human world, gave me the first real smile I'd seen from any of them. He was double-take handsome – a younger, more roguish version of Jian Huo. Si Wei sighed beside me, and I fought back a grin. I wasn't the only girl around here with a thing for dragons. My greeting to Lung Ying lasted several minutes longer than any of the others because he kept changing the traditional phrasings so that we ended up bantering. It reminded me of some of my sessions with Fang Shih. With a rueful smile, I ended the exchange with a promise that we would speak at much greater length during the coming days.

As I faced my next and final dragon, I wished that the exchange with Lung Ying had lasted longer. Lung Pan, the

Coiling Dragon, glared at me with undisguised hatred. Si Wei had warned me that Jian Huo had been close with his youngest sibling, and that Lung Pan had taken her brother's choice as a personal betrayal. Her youth showed in the way that she was barely able to make it through the greeting. She had no facility with the complex verbal manipulations of Lung Tian. She growled her responses through clenched teeth while the other dragons and many of the spirits looked shocked at her overt rudeness. Speaking with her made me feel years older than her, even though I knew that she was older by aeons. I tried to play down the severity of her rudeness, but I think she recognized that she had lost face in our encounter, and that she was in my debt for not calling her on it. It only made her glower more.

With all of the dragons greeted, I turned to the assembled guests to announce that the gardens and house were open for their enjoyment.

Before I could, a shout from one of the guests drew everyone's attention: "Another is coming!"

Oh, god. No.

I wanted to groan, tear out my hair, hide my face deep in my robes. "Another" could mean only one being: Lung Di, Jian Huo's fellow exile. Si Wei and I shared an aggravated glance. Jian Huo looked furious, as did most of his siblings. Only Lung Wang and Lung Jiao appeared unconcerned, and with Lung Jiao I wondered if it was because he was deaf and hadn't heard the shout.

Jian Huo and his other siblings strode to the gates. I wished I could just follow the old mantra of never getting involved in family quarrels, but the formal greeting period had not been closed, and I was the arbiter of such things during the formal greeting. Sitting this one out would be a catastrophe in the long-term. Lung Jiao regarded me with studied indifference, and I wondered if maybe he did know who was coming up the mountain and was waiting to see what I'd do.

Taking another breath, I called out in carrying tones, "Stop."

Lifting my robes a fraction, I teetered through a startled throng, no longer quite as concerned about my wobbling hat. Everyone stared; even Jian Huo seemed to be looking at me as for the first time. I made it to the gate and looked down the path. Perhaps a hundred feet off stood a handsome man. Looking at him, I would never have guessed he was guilty of any of the things Jian Huo had described to me in our time together.

"Who comes to the House of Lung Huang and his Bride?" I called the traditional opening.

"It is Lung Di, Dragon of the Underground and brother to Lung Huang. I come to offer blessings on the womb of Lung Xin Niang," he responded.

I let a beat pass, then two. This was the moment when I would invite him to the house and the festival. I dared not glance around to see what I should do, not even to Jian Huo or Si Wei. This was my decision to make, and I had to make it myself or appear weak. Another moment passed, but I wouldn't let myself be rushed. I'd been performing for years; I knew how long I could hold a crowd before I began to lose them.

Of course, that knowledge didn't help me with my decision.

If I invited Lung Di to stay, then I could kiss any hope of a cordial relationship with my husband's other siblings goodbye. They would be livid and would take it as a sign of my poor judgment. But if I refused him entry then they might also take issue with my choice, condemning it as arrogance. Who was I, a human, a *laowai*, to refuse a dragon anything, even an honorless one? On top of that, there was the whole Sleeping Beauty issue. Smart people sucked it up and invited the evil fairy to the christening. Could I risk making an enemy out of Lung Di, when it might be my children who would pay the price?

The man below shifted; so did the crowd. Jian Huo looked ready to pop a vein. I was running out of time.

Would letting him into our home be so terrible, if it meant that our children might grow up in safety? Jian Huo would be furious. Even in their shared exile, he never sought out his brother. The one thing he had left, the one thing that kept him from despair, the thing that he held strong to and that differentiated him from his brother, was his honor. It was what made it acceptable for his other siblings to visit, even though they never had before this day. It was all he was. I couldn't invite dishonor into his house. I couldn't do that, not even for the sake of our children.

The crowd was beginning to whisper, but when I opened my mouth, they hushed.

"This is a house of honor. You have tired yourself to no purpose. You are not welcome here."

I had a brief moment to register the surprise and fury on Lung Di's face before I turned my back on him to face the crowd. Their faces also showed surprise, although I'm pretty sure that if Jian Huo weren't so stuffy he would have kissed me right then. Even Lung Tian and Lung Pan looked bowled over.

"Friends, I thank you for your greetings and welcome you to our house. Please feel free to make it yours as well until such time as we must say our farewells. May friendship and goodwill flow between us." And with those words, I was done. I swept back through the crowd and up into the house, Si Wei and the rest of my abbreviated entourage following in my wake. The last thing I saw before ducking through the doorway was Jian Huo's face, and the fierce pride and love in his eyes. Whatever the cost, I'd made the right choice.

"So, tell me about this debt you owed to Jian Huo."

It was after the banquet, and Si Wei and I had spent most of the evening learning a complicated drinking game from Shui

Yin, as Lung Ying had instructed us to call him. Part of the game called for the revelation of embarrassing confidences, rather like a Chinese version of Truth or Dare. I sucked at it, and I had spent most of the night spilling every awkward moment I'd ever lived, much to the entertainment and amusement of my two companions. I didn't mind because I was in full matchmaker mode. If ever two individuals needed to hook up, it was the fox-maiden and my husband's handsome young brother. Si Wei had cottoned on to this, but Shui Yin was proving to be oblivious as only a guy could be.

At my words, Si Wei caught her breath, and Shui Yin wouldn't meet my eyes, indicating that perhaps I'd overstepped the bounds of the game with my question. I'd finally won a round, and this was my only hope of getting the story out of anyone, so I just smiled and waved away their discomfort.

"Oh, c'mon. It's not like Shui Yin doesn't know, and probably everyone else here except me. Plus, the debt is forgiven now, so the water is under that bridge. And you know me, it's not like I'll understand any of the ramifications, or that I'll ever hold it against you. So what's the what?"

My unique butchering of Cantonese proved to be the *huxian*'s undoing. Si Wei smiled in spite of herself and nodded her assent. She opened her mouth, struggling to find the words. Shui Yin took her hand, and I tamped down on the urge to jump up and shout "Score!" Two birds and all that.

"It was many centuries ago. I was," she paused again, then forged on, "I was Ba Wei – eight tails. I had much power and was second only to Jiu Wei." Her voice grew quiet, and I could tell she was blushing even in the dim light. "I wanted to be first.

"There was a man, a powerful man. I went to him and courted him and made him more powerful. With my aid, he became Emperor. But he was also a cruel tyrant, and when I was with him I became one too. Together we developed new forms of horror to unleash on the world, but we went too far. His generals rose up against him. He lost the Mandate of Heaven, and I was discovered and cast out. The generals cut off my tails. They left me to die.

"I went to every spirit I knew, everyone who I had ever had dealings with, but in my quest for power, in my attempt to supplant Jiu Wei, I had mistreated them all. They turned their backs on me." She paused and became lost in reflection.

"All except Jian Huo," I guessed, when she didn't go on.

"I have never understood it. You know as well as I how highly he values honor–"

"He also values pigheaded stubbornness," I cut in. "I imagine that even with all you'd been through, even with everyone turning you away, you just kept going. Am I right?" She nodded, delicate brows knitted in thought.

"You think that this is so? I had always assumed he gave me shelter so that I would be in his debt. I always assumed that he thought little of me." Her mouth twisted somewhere between a frown and a bitter smile. "He was quick to warn you away from me."

"Naw," I brushed aside her concerns with a wave of my hand. "If he despised you, he'd have left you to rot. I doubt the debt meant half as much to him as it did to you, otherwise he wouldn't have let you off so easy."

Shui Yin laughed, and Si Wei's grimace gentled into wryness. "You think that guiding you has been easy?"

"Hey!" I cried in mock protest, glad for the lighter mood. I was also happy to notice that they still held hands. "As for the warnings, he's just nervous about me getting to know his ex. Who knows what we might gossip about. It makes him jittery. It's a guy thing."

"This I can confirm," Shui Yin said.

"Really?" Her smile was pure fox. "Perhaps you should keep that in mind if you ever get another question. It may be that I have a confession or two you might be interested to hear."

"Oh no. I will not court my brother's wrath by encouraging you two harridans to gossip." Shui Yin released the fox-girl's hand to scoop up the cups and pot, summoning a servant to dispose of them. He sat back and surveyed the bare table with satisfaction. "There. That should stop your mouths."

Si Wei looked bereft for just a moment, then she caught my encouraging wink and fixed him with a pout. "But now that you've taken away our game, what choice do we have except to gossip?"

Shui Yin was no match for the fox-girl's wiles. He stammered, looking to me for help. I shrugged; he was on his own. Si Wei had maneuvered herself closer to him, so that when he turned back to her he met the full force of her grin. "Perhaps you should find some other way to stop my mouth?"

I'll give Shui Yin this, he held it together a lot better than I would have. He only gulped once before meeting her smile with one of his own. He stood and offered her his hand. "Perhaps I should. Shall we explore the gardens while we discuss possibilities?"

As they walked away draped over each other, I allowed myself a tiny two-fisted victory gesture and a whispered, "Score!"

The success of my brilliant matchmaking scheme meant that I was left alone the next evening. Si Wei kept me company during the day while Jian Huo and the other dragons disappeared to who-knew-where, but as soon as Shui Yin returned with his siblings, the longing looks started. After five minutes of it, I told Si Wei to get lost. Jian Huo kept me company during the banquet, but then he abandoned me as well. I didn't begrudge him the time with his siblings; I snuggled into my cushions, watching the world go by.

That's where Lung Pan found me. The sour look hadn't left her face. "I see you are without your protectors," she said, interrupting my people-watching. Right on cue, my back spasmed. I grimaced, and the comedy of errors began.

"I am sorry my presence displeases you so." She crossed her arms and raised her chin, smiling for the first time since I'd met her. No. She wasn't sorry.

"Not at all." I struggled to sit up. Smiled as if my body wasn't ripping itself in two. "Your arrival has brought Jian Huo much joy. I have never seen such happiness as I see in him now that he has been reunited with his siblings. His joy is my joy." It was the proper sentiment for a wife to express, even though it made me want to cringe. I hadn't taken into account how much Lung Pan refused to accept me as Jian Huo's wife.

"You have no right to share his joy. You are a concubine in all but name."

I went cold, then hot. I'd been with Jian Huo for long enough to recognize the depth of the insult. She wasn't done bullying, though. "You have no right to call yourself *Lung Xin Niang*. It is a travesty that all have agreed to out of respect for Jian Huo, not for you. You are not worthy to be called wife."

"You are wrong," I said before I could consider my words. I should have just ignored her insults. What can I say? I was pregnant, and I was pissed.

"Prove it." The challenge came from another quarter. Lung Tian and several of the lesser spirits who most disapproved of me had been watching the altercation. My stomach sank as I realized I'd been set up.

"Wh– what?"

"The Lung Pan has made a statement; you have contested it. She will not yield. You must either concede the point or prove your own."

"Prove that I am Jian Huo's wife?" I asked, still confused. That would be easy enough.

"No." Lung Tian smiled. "Prove that you are worthy to be so named."

Well, crap.

Jian Huo, Si Wei, Shui Yin, and a crowd of others hurried over to see what the fuss was about, but they were too late. This was another mess I'd have to deal with on my own. My back spasmed again, and I wished all dragons to perdition, especially ones who impregnated me and had rotten siblings.

"And how might I do that?" I glanced back at the younger dragon. "To Lung Pan's satisfaction, of course."

Her mouth worked, and I hoped she would make some sweeping statement that I could never prove it to her satisfaction, which would have gotten me off the hook, but Lung Tian was cagier than his youngest sibling. He spoke before she could voice any impractical terms.

"The matter must be decided by a disinterested third party. I will offer myself as an objective arbiter, since I was witness to the challenge."

I smiled in acceptance of this, to mask my inward seething. Witness? Set the whole thing up was more like it. Lung Pan wasn't cunning enough to plan this on her own.

"The *Lung Xin Niang* must be accomplished in many ways, but most importantly she must have grace, wit, and honor." He twitched his robes close, as though my lack of these was catching. "Tomorrow we will have three trials to test these qualities in you. If you pass to my satisfaction, then Lung Pan will recant her words, and you shall receive the blessing of dragons."

To his satisfaction. Well, that nixed it right there. Like that was ever going to happen. I tamped down on the urge to wipe the smug look off Lung Tian's face; in his mind, he'd already won.

Instead, I rose. My cheeks ached from all the fake smiling. "I have every confidence that you will be a fair arbiter in this matter, just as I have every confidence of my own worthiness. Agreed."

Taking Jian Huo's arm, I forced him to escort me out of the room. Shui Yin and Si Wei trailed us. I didn't stop until we got to our private chambers. I needed to lie down before I fainted from the back spasms.

I sagged onto a long, low couch, lying back and taking deep breaths. It took a few moments, but the spasms subsided. The ringing in my ears and fuzzy whiteness at the edge of my vision went away. I cracked an eye; three alarmed faces looked back at me.

"I'm sorry. What did I miss?"

Jian Huo knelt beside me and took my hand. "Only me asking you a similar question. Several times. What happened?"

I grimaced and tried to rise, but he pushed me back down. Worried that the cramps might return, I obeyed. "I don't even know. I was just sitting there having some people-watching fun, and then Lung Pan came over, and I grimaced at the wrong time, and she decided it was because of her and not because I'm a *fucking pregnant woman,* and then she got nasty and called me a concubine, and I got defensive and told her she was full of it, and I'm pretty sure Lung Tian set the whole thing up anyways, and–"

"Does she ever take a breath?" Shui Yin whispered to Jian Huo.

"Not that I can tell," he muttered.

"I am so sorry, my Lord." Si Wei twisted her robe in her hands. "I should have been there to guide her–"

I couldn't let her take the fall. "It's not your fault, Si Wei. It's not her fault, Jian Huo. They knew what they were doing. They weren't trying to get me to insult them; that'd be dirty pool. They got me to put my money on a hustle. Pan set up the shot and Tian sank the ball. So it wasn't even Si Wei's responsibility to keep me out of this trouble. They tricked me into it fair and square."

"If I say I believe you, will you stop torturing the concept of metaphor?" Jian Huo asked. Si Wei sighed her relief, and Shui Yin looked impressed. "What happened is past, in any case. We are now left to determine how to get you out of this challenge."

"Uh... no. We need to figure out how I'm going to pass it." All three of them opened their mouths to argue, so I struggled to a sitting position. Note to self: nothing stops arguments faster than a pregnant woman flopping around on a backless couch.

"Lung Pan said some pretty nasty things, but she only said what everyone else is thinking, including all of your siblings, except for Shui Yin."

"And that is only because I find thinking to be very strenuous." At Jian Huo's glare, Shui Yin pointed at me. "What? She's the only one who gets to be inappropriately funny?"

Ignoring my new apprentice in comedy, I took Jian Huo's hands in mine. "Look, I know that this is ridiculous. I know that I am worthy to be *Lung Xin Niang*. I know this because I know you, and I know that you would never ally yourself with someone who wasn't worthy." I spared a brief glance at Si Wei. "I know that I can be graceful and witty and honorable." I glared at Shui Yin, and he closed his mouth on whatever smart-ass remark he'd been about to make. "And I know I don't have to prove it to Lung Tian or Lung Pan. I just have to prove it to everyone else, and then Tian's 'objective arbitration' won't mean squat."

Jian Huo considered this, then rose and sat beside me. "Very well, what do you need?"

Releasing his hands, I motioned the others to pull up some chairs. "Well, first I need to know what kinds of challenges I'll be facing, and then we'll need to figure out how I'm gonna pass them – and by passing, I mean nail them to the ground and dance on their dusty remains."

"Are you sure that you can do this?" The words were from Shui Yin, but they all looked varying degrees of skeptical.

"Are you kidding?" I flashed them my most brazen grin. "With 'Team Missy' at my back, Lung Tian doesn't have a prayer."

I didn't have a prayer.

I thrust open the door of my room and stripped off the complicated *hanfu* that 'Team Missy' had insisted I would need to wear for the first challenge. They underestimated how much Lung Tian wanted to grind me into little humiliated pieces. Rather than proving my grace through some "easy" trial like catching and releasing a live butterfly with chopsticks – Jian Huo and Shui Yin's pick – or writing some complicated calligraphy – Si Wei's choice – Lung Tian had challenged me to a dragon dance.

Which meant I was supposed to fight him. In my condition. Hence the quick costume change and the raging fury.

Unlike my teammates, I had expected something like this. Maybe not this extreme, but I didn't expect Lung Tian to pull any punches simply because I had a belly the size of a beachball. I let them talk me down because I trusted their knowledge of Lung Tian better than my own judgment. Now I knew better, and I knew that today would be even more difficult than we'd planned for the night before. I yanked my modified shaolin robes out of the wardrobe. I needed to calm down and center if I wanted to get through this. That's when the wetness whooshed down between my legs.

Oh, you've got to be kidding me.

I sank back against the wardrobe, staring at the spreading wet patch on the floor as though wishing would make it go away. It remained, a straw on the camel-high pile of problems I was facing. Was I allowed to call things off on account of having to give birth? I suspected Lung Tian would just love it if I asked.

One of the main problems about living with an exiled

dragon in a pocket spirit realm in the middle of China was that the pre-natal care sucked and birthing information was non-existent. Television and movies hadn't prepared me for the realities of being pregnant; maybe that meant they were similarly misleading about the labor part. I centered my chi and did a quick body check, trusting my own senses over what I'd been conditioned to expect. I didn't feel much different. I'd been having back spasms since the night before, but nothing I hadn't already decided I could cope with. It wouldn't be any worse than fighting through the pain of an injury, and I'd done that before.

Fine. I could do this. But if that bastard tried to make me run a footrace against a horse, I'd figure out a way to curse his family line with birthing pains. I had precedent on my side.

Taking a deep, centering breath, I cleaned myself up and donned my simple trousers and robe. I spent the walk back down to the garden going through the mental exercises necessary to make sure my chi was aligned. That in itself was a revelation. I sensed the energies flowing around my children. They were composed entirely of determination – probably to get out. I wove those energies into my own, bolstering the places where I felt weak. By the time I got to the top of the stairs, I was able to acknowledge and let go of the pain that blossomed with every back spasm. I doubted I could win, but maybe I could hold my own.

The assembled spirits watched me waddle down the stairs to the garden with varying levels of interest and excitement. The older dragons looked on with polite interest, but Lung Pan glared as if I would forget her dislike. Shui Yin gave me a surreptitious thumbs-up – somebody needed to take that boy in hand – and Si Wei gave an encouraging nod.

Lung Tian awaited me in the dragon circle, but before I could enter, Shanghai's guardian strode into the ring.

"This is preposterous," Song Yulan snapped. She shot a glare over her shoulder at Jian Huo. "Grandfather, if you will not stop this, then I will."

Grandfather?

I did a bit of glaring myself. Jian Huo folded his hands in his sleeves, impervious to all the dirty looks he was getting. "I have already tried to dissuade Missy from this path. It is her choice."

Song Yulan arched a brow at this side-stepping, but she must have known it was pointless to argue with Jian Huo when he was in hand-sleeve mode.

Grandfather?

"Then I will fight for her," Song Yulan said, lifting her chin as she faced Lung Tian again.

Whoa. I abandoned my glaring to step into the circle. "I can fight for myself."

She didn't break her staring contest to answer. "You're in no condition to fight."

Another cramp crawled its way from the small of my back around to my abdomen, making it harder for me to argue with her, mostly because I was trying to breathe through the urge to scream.

Lung Tian covered my silence. "This is a test of her fitness, not yours, Guardian. She must fight for herself."

"If I were her champion–"

"You are not." Lung Tian had to raise his voice over the collective gasp from the crowd. "Nor would it speak well of either of you if you agreed to such a compact for so frivolous a reason."

Frivolous. He thought sticking up for a pregnant woman and her unborn kids was frivolous?

What an ass.

But the cramp had passed, and I wanted to get started before another one came. I touched Song Yulan's arm. "Thank you. Really. But I'm OK. I need to see this through."

She glared at all three of us – Lung Tian, Jian Huo, and myself – before throwing up her hands and returning to her place among the lesser spirits and guardians.

I stepped into the place that she'd abandoned, facing off against Lung Tian. I was like Ralph Macchio standing up to the Cobra Kai bullies. Wax on, wax off, baby.

"Let's do this."

Lung Tian did not leave me much time to think after our initial bow. He slipped into Tiger, assaulting me with a barrage of strong blows and kicks. Given his superior strength and my condition, I didn't want any of those blows hitting, so I tried to flow like water around them, meeting his Tiger with Crane.

I danced aside from his strikes, using his own momentum against him, spinning out of his way so that he was left staring at the circle's edge, me standing behind him. I tapped him on the shoulder. When he turned to face me, I gave him my biggest, shit-eating grin. I heard several snickers from the crowd. Crane, with her innovation and sense of humor, was my best and favorite form, as I imagined Tiger was his. As long as he kept coming at me with fiery directness, I could keep away from him with watery creativity. He switched to Snake.

Snake was about patience: the wait and the strike. Lung Tian slid around the circle, waiting for me to exhibit a weakness. I matched his movements with my own stalking pace, not Tiger, but Leopard. I had to move us out of these forms. If I had another back cramp, it would provide the opening he was looking for. I attacked with a series of my own quick strikes to distract his analysis of my form. I wasn't strong enough to gain any ground, but as long as he was in Snake, I didn't need to be. I just needed to keep him off kilter so that he couldn't recognize that my cramps were coming with growing frequency and pain. I got the feeling that he didn't have much patience for the earth-bound Snake. He switched forms again.

That left me in a bind. Earth generates metal, and the form

that followed Snake was Dragon. That meant that in order to overcome him I'd have to become the fiery Tiger, and I didn't have the strength or the skill to beat him as Tiger. Instead, I transitioned to Dragon as well, figuring that if I could outwait him, I could transition back to Crane.

We stood in the center of the circle, our breathing deep and meditative. I was banking on him being more impatient than I was, on him wanting to kick my ass, and on the hope that I could transition to Crane before he could get a blow in as Tiger. What I had forgotten to bank on was that I was still in labor.

The muscles of my spine twitched in the beginnings of another spasm, this one much worse than the previous ones; it rippled from the small of my back all the way around to my abdomen, stronger than the worst menstrual cramp I'd ever had. I closed my eyes against it. Lung Tian transitioned to Tiger and lunged at me, but I'd dropped to my knees from the pain. His kick swept over my head, ruffling my wispies. I opened my eyes to see Lung Tian blinking at me in surprise.

"You yield?"

Now that the cramp had passed, I could think again. From the outside, it must have looked like I was conceding the contest.

Opportunist that I was, I nodded. "I do. I have seen the end of this contest. You are faster and stronger and more skilled than me. You would have struck me before I could have changed forms. There is no grace in drawing out a losing conflict, therefore I yield to you." I didn't add that I didn't need to win the fight in order to win the contest. I hoped the implication was clear.

Lung Tian's lips thinned; the muscles in his forearms bunched and unbunched, but there was no way he could gracefully continue when I had yielded. He nodded and stalked out of the circle. "The next contest will take place in the pagoda."

I struggled to rise, and I found myself surrounded by friendly hands offering their help. Jian Huo lifted me to my feet. His jaw clenched; the family resemblance to Lung Tian was strong.

"This needs to end. Song Yulan was right. You are in no condition to be fighting him. You are in no condition for any of these contests."

If I had been considering telling any of them that I was in labor, Jian Huo's words stopped me. He was two seconds away from ending the contest and throwing all of his siblings out. I couldn't let that happen.

I squeezed his hand. "It's fine, Jian Huo. The worst part is over. I doubt that the tests of wit or honor are going to involve a lot of physical exertion." Aside from the physical exertion of labor, but I kept that thought to myself.

I took Jian Huo's silence as concession.

He led me to the pagoda, where, as "Team Missy" had successfully predicted, Lung Tian had set up a game of *wei-qi*. I couldn't beat him. In all my time here I'd never come close to beating Jian Huo, and he was the bookish sibling. Lung Tian was the tactician. The best I could hope for was to acquit myself competently. As I took my seat at the table, Lung Tian threw the wrench.

"A person of true wit does not fill the air with incessant chatter. Therefore, you will remain silent during our game."

It was a not-so-complimentary testament to how quickly our guests had come to know me that Lung Tian's caveat caused everyone to go quiet.

In the pin-dropping silence, Si Wei's whisper was all the more audible: "She's doomed."

I glared at the fox-maiden, who spared me an apologetic grimace before going back to looking worried. Lips deliberately pursed, I nodded at Lung Tian, and we began to play.

The game lasted for over an hour, during which my contractions grew worse. I timed them by our moves, or rather my moves, since my opponent never paused to think more than a few moments before making his own. I assume that he intended for the hardest part of the game to be my required silence, but given that my contractions came more often and more painfully, it was easier for me than anyone would have guessed. The most difficult thing was controlling my breathing so that I didn't look like I was in unbelievable agony.

He trounced me. By the end, however, he was once again seething in fury. I had managed to remain silent during the entire game despite his many comments and taunts, most of which I was too preoccupied to hear. With a final decisive move he won the game, but he didn't look happy about it. He just glared at me and gestured for the game to be removed.

"Once again you have lost."

I glanced at the servants removing the game, not speaking until they were out of sight. "I have lost the game. Whether I have lost the contest is a different matter to be determined, and one that I would imagine cannot be decided until all the challenges are met."

His jaw worked, but he nodded his assent to this and forged ahead. "The third challenge will be one of honor. I will tell a tale of my most honorable moment."

And he commenced his tale. I listened closely, unsure what the challenge was supposed to be. This was not like anything "Team Missy" had predicted. Maybe I was supposed to catch on to some small detail in his tale and explain how the moment was honorable? He laid the tale out in bare bones: fact, fact, fact. I found myself several times editing his style, figuring out ways that I would tell it better, for greater impact.

By the time his tale marched to an end, even I was impressed. The story made me realize that Lung Tian wasn't a bad guy, just a bit old-fashioned and prejudiced. I could see things from his point of view. He was just looking out for his stupid younger brother, who had always exhibited more honor and pigheadedness than sense, especially when it came to his choice in lovers. Lung Tian's methods didn't endear him to me, but at least I could respect him for that familial love. Maybe it was just the labor pains and the hormones doing the wacky in my system, but by the end of the story, I was blinking back tears and my throat was tight, not because of anything that Lung Tian had done in the story, but because of what he was doing now. The light murmur of approval from the crowd pulled me back from becoming completely maudlin. Lung Tian had finished his tale.

"Now it is your turn."

My turn? Oh, crap. I was supposed to tell a tale of my most honorable moment? After I'd just listened to an epic saga and had been getting all weepy over what a great guy Lung Tian was? What kind of life experience could I draw from? I was in my early twenties, and my most interesting years had been spent in an isolated valley in Western China. As far as I was concerned, most of the people here had been witness to my most honorable moment when I chucked Lung Di down the hill, and my second most honorable moment involved a lot of heavy petting and me overcoming my libido. That didn't strike me as appropriate to the spirit of the challenge.

This was the trap, of course. Any story I told would make me look silly and petty and boastful. I glared at Lung Tian, hating and loving him at the same moment. Stupid dragons and their stupid family loyalty.

Then it hit me like a contraction, which, appropriately enough, was also hitting me in that moment. Taking a few deep breaths to let the spasm pass and collect myself, I launched into a tale. Not mine. His. I retold Lung Tian's tale as I had started to do in my mind. I made the epic more epic, the sweeping more sweeping. The maidens were more beautiful, the deeds braver. I took the swelling of esteem and admiration that I'd just felt for Lung Tian, and I let it flavor my entire tale. I told the story the way I would tell it to my kids when I wanted them to know just how badass and awesome their uncle was.

When I ended there were more murmurs of approval and a slight smattering of applause. Even some of the older dragons looked impressed, and for the first time I saw an expression I could read on Lung Wang's face. She regarded me thoughtfully.

"You but repeat the tale that I have told. How is this a story of your own honor?" Lung Tian's words were combative, but absent of his usual vitriol.

I smiled at the crotchety but increasingly lovable old fart. "There are many things that are honorable in the doing, but there are some things, some individuals, some acts so noble that they ennoble the world around them by their very presence. Hearing your tale has reminded me that to be in your presence is to know greater honor than any act of valor of my own could bring me. Whatever the differences that lie between us, and whatever may come, I am grateful to you for granting me such a gift."

The room had fallen silent, but many spirits nodded in agreement, including the other Guardians and most of Jian Huo's siblings. Only Lung Pan looked sour, as if she had been forced to swallow something that disgusted her. *Suck on it, kiddo.* I'd work on figuring out what was lovable about her at some later date.

Lung Tian regarded me for some time, and the sweat that broke out on my brow was only partially due to the increasing pain of my contractions.

"You have failed all three of the contests."

I nodded.

"You have demonstrated that you have neither the grace, nor the wit, nor the honor to match a dragon."

I nodded again. Lung Tian stood, and the look on his face told me it was all over. Lung Pan must have guessed the same because she was beaming in triumph.

"This, then, is my judgment–"

"A moment, brother," said Lung Fu Cang. She motioned to where Lung Wang and Lung Jiao conferred. Lung Jiao stepped forward and placed a hand on Lung Tian's arm.

"Such a judgment as you must make, brother, is a grave one and carries with it great finality. Surely it would be wise to deliberate carefully before making it. The shadows grow long and night is falling. The *Zi Gong Hu* is ending, and we must all make our farewells. When we return to Heaven, you will have the time and peace that you need to fairly consider the matter. It need not be decided just now."

Lung Tian looked as though he wanted to argue with Lung Jiao, but apparently decided against doing so in public. "What about the blessings?"

"Lung Pan will keep her blessing until the matter is resolved, and it might be prudent for you to do so as well, given that you are arbiter in this matter. As for any others who wish to offer their blessings, there is nothing in the matter that keeps them from doing so." Lung Jiao approached me and bowed low. "If I may, *Lung Xin Niang*?"

I nodded, dumbfounded. Jian Huo came to stand behind me as the most powerful of his siblings placed his hands on my belly and murmured ancient words in a language I didn't know. One by one the other dragons came forward, except for Lung Pan and Lung Tian. Shui Yin looked both proud and smug, while Lung Shen looked thoughtful, perhaps contemplating her own human lover. The most amusing moment was when Lung Fu Cang came forward. While her hands were on me, another contraction rippled across my belly. The flash of surprise across her features told me that she had felt it as well. On the pretext of whispering her blessing, she leaned in close, lips a breath away from my ear.

"How long?" she whispered.

"Since I went to change clothes this morning." She pulled back an inch, and one of her delicate brows arched in surprise.

"Since before the... and Jian Huo let you–"

"He doesn't know."

The other brow raised to join the first. "Then I will ensure that we vacate in all haste." She smiled and patted my belly, quickly finishing her blessing.

I smiled back. "Thanks." Let everyone else think it was the blessing I was thanking her for.

Lung Wang came forward. Looking on her still unnerved me; she was too ancient, too alien, too powerful. I could only imagine how minor my entire existence must be to her. And yet she placed aged hands on my belly, and in a low, melodious voice spoke the ancient blessing. Then she nodded, and within moments all of Jian Huo's siblings except Shui Yin were gone. The guardians and the other spirits followed, and I was left on my cushions, surrounded by a flabbergasted Team Missy.

"You did it. I can't believe you did it." Shui Yin's stunned statement wasn't the most inspired congratulation. I considered making his appointment to Team Missy provisional.

"I can," Jian Huo said with pride, though I thought this was a bit of revisionist history on his part. Si Wei just smiled and kept her mouth shut.

"Yup, I did it. Hoodey-hoo and woopdi-dee for me." Now that I could afford to be, I realized how exhausted I was. I also realized that another contraction was on its way, and I gave in to the luxury of venting my pain through my vocal cords. My three companions looked at me as if I'd transformed into some alien creature. Given the noises I was making, perhaps there was some justification for this.

"Is it time?" Jian Huo asked. "Are your pains starting?"

"Starting?" I cracked an eye, responding between hee-hee-hee, hoo-hoo-hoo's. "I've been in labor since... early this morning you... half-witted warthog!"

Shui Yin and Si Wei's mouths dropped in shock, though I wasn't sure whether it was from my revelation or the name-calling. Jian Huo just gave an "ah" of comprehension and summoned serving spirits to take me to my bed.

"Now I understand," he said, his mouth twisted in a grin of sardonic affection. "I'll admit that I'd wondered what power on this earth could keep you silent for an entire game of *wei-qi*."

NINE

What Happens in China

Now

The light of the *Kestrel's* explosion burned out my vision, and I came down harder than I should have, my knee screaming at the impact, though I bit down on any scream of my own. I tried to roll with my landing and got tangled up in my restraints for my efforts.

The more I struggled, the more I tangled myself up, until I recalled the knife in my satchel. It might look dull, but that blade had cut through worse things than a few nylon straps. I pulled it out and started sawing.

The flames of the burning *Kestrel* lit up the rolling plain in relief, coloring it orange and doing a fair bit to make it look like a Boschian Hell. It would get worse. The light was a clarion call to every nasty within eyeshot.

But also our way out. If I could get free. If I could find the others.

I cut through the main restraint and wiggled free of the straps. Without my weight for drag, the parachute billowed and rolled away like some terrestrial cephalopod. What would the Conclave make of that? My laugh turned into a cough as the tang of smoke reached me. Better question might be how long they would torture the parachute for information before realizing it wasn't alive.

Thoughts of the Conclave got me moving again. A disturbance like this would draw their notice. Worse than any stray, curious denizens drawn to the crash, would be the knights of the Conclave. I had to make my escape before they arrived. Once they had a scent, they were like bloodhounds, chasing a body even once it had returned to the light world.

"Tom? Mr Tsung?" The ever-present background chittering lulled to a hush before returning louder than before in a wave of sound like a cicada invasion. Bad idea to risk calling out, but what choice did I have? The flickering light and shadows set every hill on the plain to dancing like it was a mountain. I climbed one of those hills and spied a bladdered man-o-war struggling its twisted way along the dell below. I limped down the rise, hoping for the best, but there were no men being dragged along with the parachute. Just straps and flame-orange silk.

Hell.

I followed the tracks left by the chute, but the winds across the shadow plain blew the dust into whirling devils before I could follow far.

I climbed up another rise. The heat from the burning wreckage washed over me. Standing in the full light of the blaze, I called again. "Tom? Mr Tsung?"

The chittering quieted again. This time, it stayed quiet. And then came the sound of hoof beats.

I flattened to the ground. Double hell. Where had they gone? The wreckage was too hot to check, and the tangled chute meant Tsung at least had landed free. Perhaps he'd used the light from the flaming *Kestrel* to pull himself and Skyrocket back to the safety of the real world?

Lord knew there was nowhere safe in the Shadow Realms. Least of all lying prone on a rise in the light of burning wreckage with a troupe of Conclave knights bearing down to investigate.

Damn the risk. I had to make sure Tsung and Tom weren't nearby. I pushed up to a squat and half-ran, half-slid down the hill, closer to the light of the wreckage where the dark-sighted knights would be less likely to spot me. I glanced over my shoulder. Everything was shadow and flame. The brightness burned nuance away. The thunder of hoof beats crescendoed as a cloud of living smoke poured out from a valley between two hillocks.

I ducked around the side of the wreckage – mostly intact, though smaller chunks of burning and scorched debris scattered from the point of impact. Still no sign of Tom or David Tsung, neither in the *Kestrel* or on the plain.

The knights would be circling around, checking the area. Tsung must have gotten out, and taken Tom with him.

Did I really trust David Tsung that much to do the right thing?

More thunder of hooves. I had no choice but to trust. I couldn't stay here. If the knights spotted me, there'd be no escaping even to the light world. I'd do nobody any good if I got taken.

I clung to that thought as I grabbed onto the light cast by the flames and propelled myself out of the Shadow Realms.

I came across atop a slanted rooftop. It took a bit of scrambling to keep myself from sliding down the slope and tumbling to the street below. I hooked my arm around a pipe vent, braced my foot against an eave, and looked out across a rolling sea of slate-tile rooftops to the city beyond.

Shanghai.

It wasn't a postcard view of the city. I'd come across too far south for that – somewhere in the old Nanhui District, I'd guess. The city stretched on and on, identical rooftops broken by green spaces and the odd squat tower. The yellow haze of smog hung thick, the late afternoon sun setting it to glow in flame hues. An unsettling echo of the wreckage I'd just left behind, along with my companions.

A shadow hand emerged from the eave, groping towards the golden afternoon glow and my leg. With a bright enough light source on their side, the knights of the Conclave could reach across and drag things back across the veil. I couldn't stay here. I needed to find someplace well-lit and away from the shadows, or they'd follow me through the entire city.

I crawled away from the searching hand, over to the other side of the rooftop where the setting sun shone against the face of the building. Too high up to climb down. I peered over the edge and found an open window. Dropped down and swung into the apartment, nearly landing on an old man who gaped at me with toothless surprise.

"So sorry for the intrusion," I said in Mandarin, hoping he understood it in addition to whatever dialect he spoke. "Would you mind if I called a cab?"

Still gaping, he pointed at the phone, an old rotary dialer.

"Thank you." I retrieved my hat from my satchel and settled it firmly on my head, pulling forth as much shadow as I dared this close to the searching knights. First, get my bearings, then I could deal with finding Tom and David Tsung and rescuing China. But I'd had enough of this running around without a clue as to what I was doing. I struggled out of my jumpsuit, pulled on my coat, and slid the knife into my breast pocket. It was time to call on some old friends.

I'd say this for China: they were handling their enforced quarantine with unsettling efficiency. If the United States were faced with such a crisis, there'd be anger, paranoia, rioting in the streets, twenty-four hour news cycles urging the panic to soaring heights. Come to think of it, wasn't that the United States I had just left?

Not so China. Perhaps, having come through the upheavals of the twentieth century and the madness and violence of the Mao era, China was mature enough to deal with a little crisis like a magical wall of isolation. Or perhaps the existence or absence of such a wall didn't touch the lives of the majority of people. Perhaps we needed China more than they needed us. Whatever the case, things were business-as-usual in China's largest city.

The cab driver took me over the river and up the Hujin expressway, chattering at me in Shanghainese the entire time. I understood perhaps one word in ten, and none of them had anything to do with the New Wall. I couldn't very well ask without giving away that I was a foreigner, so I sat back and fumed as we crawled through the traffic past the outer ring and the middle ring and eventually onto the streets of the Huangpu district. Between the buildings we sometimes caught glimpses of the financial district across the river, shrouded in a haze of gold.

This was the postcard of Shanghai: the skyscrapers lit more by neon than by the setting sun. The world flashed with color and light. It was too much – too many colors, too many people, the air too thick with smog to properly see. "Crowded" was too tame a term to describe the teeming mass of traffic choking the streets. Bodies ceased to be individual things and became the circulatory system of some greater organism, surging forward in pulsing waves with every beat of the traffic lights. Everywhere I looked, Jumbotron screens flashed images at eyeblink speed, faster than I could decipher. I was glad for the protective cocoon of the car as we crawled along with the current of traffic. The chatter of the driver ceased to be confusing and became a comfort – meaningless syllables strung together, like some sort of crash course in meditation.

I'd visited New York a few times. I didn't like it. Too crowded. New York had *nothing* on Shanghai.

I wrested my attention from the passing street before agoraphobia could take hold.

"Everything is very well-ordered," I said. Perhaps with the shadows pulled about my face to hide my features, I could get away with asking a few questions under the guise of being a *hukou* provincial. No need to disguise my Mandarin; I'd never bothered to rid myself of my Sichuan accent.

The driver glanced back through the mirror, switching to something that might once have been Mandarin. "This is Shanghai," he said, as if that explained all.

"Other places are not so well-ordered," I said, an invitation for him to brag about Shanghai and condemn those "other places" – and pass along some news in the process.

He made a spitting sound against his teeth. "Hong Kong. No control there, and they weren't quick enough to quarantine the *laowai*. Too many *laowai* in Hong Kong. Here," he thumped his dashboard, "Beijing," he thumbed a direction I assumed was north, though it might just have been "up". "Every other city, the People's Heroes keep the peace, and the *laowai* are kept safe until the terrorists are caught."

"Well, but the students…" I trailed off. It was China. There was *always* something happening with the students.

Another tetching sound. "They want to get rid of KFC. I say get rid of McDonalds. KFC is good." A pause as he squeezed by a group of bicyclers. I closed my eyes, afraid I was about to see someone get sideswiped into a smear by the passing cab. "They should question the Japanese."

"The… Japanese?" Unlikely the "they" he was talking about were the anti-KFC students anymore.

"The Japanese. They did this. The Americans helped. You heard about the drones?"

I shook my head, and the cab driver proceeded to tell me about the secret technologies and schemes that the western governments had been developing for years to forcibly stunt China's emergence as a world power. The sad thing was, I didn't disagree with many of his observations. Eighty percent right was still twenty percent wrong. And the twenty percent was very, very wrong.

But at least I knew the visitors and tourists here were being kept safer than they likely would have been back in the States. The People's Heroes were China's state-sponsored answer to Argent. Trained like Olympians – and with a similar wash-out rate – they didn't number among the many hidden arms of Chinese bureaucracy. If the People's Heroes were involved, then China had decided that keeping foreigners safe was a matter of face.

The rest of the world might spin it differently, but I couldn't think of a better way to ensure the protection of the *laowai*. One could never underestimate the power of keeping face. Mark one for China.

The driver wove through a confusion of smaller streets and closes, dropping me in front of a row of *shikumen* terrace houses that had somehow escaped developmental destruction, a rarity this close to the Bund. I wished I dared give him a tip, but it would have marked me as a foreigner. I didn't want him calling the People's Heroes on me.

The teal-and-silver cab drove off, leaving me alone on a quiet street. For just a moment, standing next to the line of close-built brick townhouses, I could pretend I was back home, and that the world wasn't in turmoil.

Only for a moment. I couldn't leave the world hanging for longer than that. I drew in a breath, coughed at the twinge deep in my lungs from taking in all the gunk in the air, and passed through the stone archway.

The courtyard on the other side of the *shikumen's* outer wall was little bigger than a postage stamp. A mural covered the brick side of the building, artfully distressed to look older than it was. A red-lipped woman on the mural winked with her smile, welcoming me to Magnolia House. A guard stood to one side of the main door. His face remained impassive, but he shifted, stance widening, knees bending – ready for trouble.

"I'm here to see Song Yulan." And I hoped I was in the right place.

The guard said nothing, eyes fixed on a point somewhere over my shoulder, but before I could repeat myself, the door opened. A slender man of middling age bowed to me.

"Mr Masters." He ushered me in before I could run. I'd hoped to cling to anonymity for a bit longer. "You honor us with your visit. It has been a long time. What brings you to Shanghai?"

I held onto my coat and hat when he would have taken them. He couldn't be serious with that question. That was manners taken to a ridiculous extreme.

But just as ridiculous was my instinctual response to play along. "Business. Is Ms Song available?"

"For you, sir? Always." He led me into the club proper. I followed, trying not to gape. Mr Mystic had been active in fighting the Red Guard. I was supposed to have been here before.

Whatever the club had once been, it had changed since my grandfather's day. The steward led me into a Gibsonian cyber-cafe. Computers lined the walls. Neon and blacklights made me blink and cling to the shadows about my face. Kids – mostly kids, but a few adults on the younger side of the spectrum – clacked away at keyboards. Some of them wore ungainly contraptions about their heads, but most stared at screens featuring improbably-attired avatars and fantastically-colorful worlds. Many of them chattered into headsets, presumably to virtual people they only connected to through those other worlds. The recessed speakers blared a jarring *unh-tse, unh-tse, unh-tse, unh-tse*, complete with a juvenile female's voice wailing about how her love was forever.

I snorted. Nobody that young could possibly comprehend forever-love.

A woman detached herself from the bar. She was older than most of the customers, somewhere in her forties at least, but she carried her age well. In her tailored jacket and palazzo pants, she could have given fashion lessons to Marlene Dietrich.

So strange to see her out of the traditional robes. Her expression was as blank as her doorman's for all that her lips curved in a welcoming smile. Her eyes glittered cold and hard as marcasite in the techno pulse of lights coming from the monitors. "I get the feeling you disapprove," she murmured by way of greeting.

And I got the feeling she was fighting back a snicker. Well, that answered that question. However much my disguise might fool most people, Song Yulan saw through it. Perhaps Johnny had told her.

"Nothing so strong. Just feeling my age. Is there someplace quieter we can talk?"

"Of course. My office?" She led me through the main room of the club and down a back hallway. We stopped at another door, this one with an electronic keypad. Her nails clacked against the casing as she punched in the code. The lights blinked green, followed by an electronic buzz. She led me into an office that sported the colonial theme I'd expected to see in the common area, all oxblood leather sofas and walls of books and a half-domed globe sporting a tea set instead of the usual brandy or scotch. She shut the door behind us.

"There. Now you can remove that ridiculous disguise. Tea? I've just made a fresh pot." She moved to the service.

I stiffened. It was one thing to suspect she knew me, quite another to have my identity pulled out from under me. I stayed in character on instinct, fighting the urge to fidget. "At the risk of being rude, do we really have the time?"

"There is always time for tea." She sat and crossed her legs. Her long nails formed a cage around her teacup. She watched me over the rim of her cup but didn't drink. "Does it really fool anyone?"

And now I just felt silly. I removed my hat and released the shadows obscuring my face. My spine curved into a slump. I let my voice crawl back up to its natural pitch. "Yeah, seems to."

"Sit." I remained standing. She poured me tea. "I apologize for my abruptness. You caught me unawares. We weren't sure that you would come."

We? "Because I should leave China's business to China?" My jaw tensed. Just let her try to feed me that line of bullshit.

Song Yulan's brows rose in an expression that was so familiar it near broke my heart. Like grandfather, like granddaughter. "Because Lung Di wanted you to come."

I expelled a breath, my chest sinking inward. It was one thing to suspect that David Tsung was a lying bastard, quite another to have it so baldly confirmed. I fumbled for the chair and lowered myself into it. "I know. He sent your former apprentice with the two-by-four equivalent of a calling card."

Song Yulan tapped her nails on her cup. I didn't need to look at her face to know she was struggling over how best to tell me that I was an idiot. "*We* sent David, but that doesn't mean you should trust him. I'm still not convinced that he's sincere in this latest defection. He was quick enough to support the suggestion that you be brought in, but I can't tell if that means he's serving our interests, or Lung Di's... or his own."

"We can shut out Tsung if his motives are in question. I'm more concerned about Lung Di. Has he ever been this blatant?" It was one thing to work underground. Behind the scenes. The puppetmaster nudging his human tools. This New Wall wasn't his style. "Or am I wrong in thinking he's taken the other Guardians?"

"We are all in agreement that he's gone too far this time. It is one thing to meddle with humans, quite another to break *guanxi* with his fellow spirits."

Amazing that my teacup didn't shatter from the strength of my grip. I breathed in steam to cool my anger. It was OK to mess with humans, but heaven forbid Lung Di inconvenience his fellow spirits? "Perhaps he's hoping the rest of the Nine will respond?"

"The Nine have withdrawn from the world." The twist of her lips and the deadpan delivery as good as gave me her opinion on that decision.

"So it falls to us to fix his mess."

Song Yulan shook her head. "I am not so eager to include you as others are."

"Why? Because China's business is not my business?" I snapped, setting aside my cup. It clattered on the table, tea sloshing over the side. "Four Guardians – *four* – he needed to capture to create this ward, and not just some classroom turtle or little girl's pet chow."

Her lips formed the words "pet chow?", but I wasn't finished with my tirade. I stood, looming over her. "He had to develop the ritual, send instructions to Chinatowns all over the world, and get his people to execute the ritual simultaneously. Can you actually sit there and tell me that nobody suspected something was going on? Is he so damned powerful that he can keep something like this secret? Or was it that nobody wanted to go against him because they have *guanxi* with him, and going against him might damage your own interests? Until he went too far. And now you're saying you couldn't possibly have foreseen that he would do something this extreme? Well, you should have known better. You all should have known better."

Song Yulan didn't move through my tirade, her face frozen in a porcelain mask. She blinked. Took a measured breath. "David Tsung knew. He claims it was why he left me. To discover what his grandfather was up to."

It sounded like a concession. I chose to read it as such. "But you don't trust him." I resumed my seat, lifting my teacup and taking a sip. My own concession. "You said 'we' before. Who is 'we'?"

Song Yulan's jaw tensed. "It is complicated."

"Then use small words."

That earned me a chuckle. "The People's Heroes have been establishing order within the city–"

"So I've heard. I wouldn't expect you to ally yourself with them." The Cultural Revolution hadn't been kind to the more traditional spirits of China, and the PHC was the secular face of new China.

Song Yulan shook her head, blunt cut feathering along her jaw. "Much has changed in the past few weeks. It makes for strange allies. The PHC has taken control of most of the Shadow Dragon Triad's holdings, including Lung Di's sanctum. The only way to get at it is to go through them. We believe that is where Lung Di holds the Guardians."

"He's with them?"

"It is unclear. The wards are impenetrable."

"Not for someone who can pass through Shadow." Which left myself and Tsung. "So why didn't you send Tsung in?"

Song Yulan grimaced. "You think the PHC is inclined to trust him any more than you or I? But it is convenient that they don't trust him because it meant we needed you."

"Is there a reason I shouldn't go to the PHC?"

"There has been a coup among the Shadow Dragons. It would be best if you spoke to their new leader directly."

"You'd trust Lung Di's own network over the PHC? Why?"

"I believe the PHC will have few qualms about sending you in to fix this, but what if that is what Lung Di wants? The new leader of the Shadow Dragons may have ideas for a different approach. She understands how he thinks."

She. Interesting, though I didn't think I could trust anyone who understood the thought processes of the Shadow Dragons' former head.

I set my tea aside. "When can I meet her?" If I didn't agree with Song Yulan's reservations, I could always go to the PHC.

It sounded like we'd have to go to them eventually, anyways.

Song Yulan ducked her head, but I caught the flash of a smile. By the time she looked up, it was gone.

"I will take you to her now."

Song Yulan led me out the back way, into an alley so narrow that only a madman would try to drive down it.

And, of course, every taxi driver along the Puxi.

We flattened against a wall until there was a break. It was paltry as breaks went, but Song Yulan dove across the way, and I was left to follow. Horns blared, and the driver bearing down on me passed close enough to clip the tail of my coat.

Song Yulan didn't wait for me to catch my breath. She led the way down a built-over brick tunnel that had once been a space between buildings. Crumbled masonry littered the path. I held my arm over my face to ward off the stink of bodies and feces.

We came out on a busy thoroughfare. No dodging traffic here. We'd have to wait at the light like good pedestrians.

Song Yulan fidgeted and shot glances up and down the street. Her agitation attracted more curious glances than my shadowy presence.

I leaned close to be heard over the traffic. "Is there something wrong?"

"Let us hope not. The People's Heroes will know you're here by now. They have people watching the club. I think I've spotted four agents following us."

I closed and opened my fist. The light changed, and we flooded across the street with the rest of the crowd. "And you didn't think to mention this before? We could have been more circumspect."

"They knew you were here the moment you arrived. It's not their rank-and-file I'm worried about. We can handle them. Just so long as their commander doesn't show up."

"Let us hope," I muttered. Song Yulan was the Guardian of Shanghai. Big fish, by anyone's standards. I didn't want to meet up with anyone who she thought was trouble.

We hit the curb, and Song Yulan cut crosswise through the crowd, leading us into an open-air promenade: a cross between a futuristic shopping mall, a food court, and a stock exchange on steroids. The press around us lightened to something more in keeping with Times Square on New Year's Eve. My guide bullied her way past the other pedestrians, the only way to get anywhere in a city like this. She glanced over her shoulder, frowned, and pushed harder. I followed her backward glance. Four men shoved through the crowd. To the untrained eye they were nothing remarkable. Just a few businessmen with someplace to be, like every other businessman in the crowd. But my eye was trained. As was my escort's.

"I believe they've been instructed to delay us," Song Yulan said. She stopped, ignoring the curses of the people forced to eddy around us.

"Are things about to get interesting, Ms Song?"

"I'd say so, M– Mr Masters."

The men closed with us. After my recent experience with Lao Chan, I was careful to keep in mind that there could be more than just these four lurking somewhere in the crowd. Before the men could offer any threat – or even speak – Song Yulan struck out with a series of quick, precise punches at the fellow in the lead. The man blocked. He was good, but no match for my escort. I didn't have much time to make a more thorough assessment of anyone's style. The other three were upon us.

Two of the men came for me while Song Yulan was occupied with the others. One of mine held a black woolen sack open, as if I'd meekly submit to him slipping it over my head. Or not so meekly, I revised, as his friend lunged at me for a grapple. I ducked under his outstretched arms, grabbing his wrist as I slipped past. I used an elbow lock and our combined momentum to lead him around. Before he could get his bearings, I kicked at his shoulder while yanking back on his arm. The shoulder popped, and my opponent's face crumbled into pain.

The man with the bag flinched back at seeing his mate go down. I took advantage of this, tearing the bag from his hands and shoving it over his head. The drawstrings made a good garrote, and he forgot any training he might have had as he scrabbled at the rope constricting around his throat. He sagged to his knees, but I released my hold before his struggles had fully stopped.

I turned to help Song Yulan with her attackers, too late. She lowered a man's limp body to the pavement, laying him out next to his friend. She straightened and finger-combed her hair to smoothness. I tugged the brim of my hat lower.

"Come along. We need to hurry before their back-up arrives."

The crowd around us had paused when the fight started, moving back in a ring to watch with blank-faced interest, as if street brawls were a common thing in Shanghai. For all I knew, they were. They didn't bother to part as Song Yulan and I tried to leave. She was forced to shove her way past. I followed before they could close in her wake.

The exit from the arcade dumped us into a back alley warren, the gutters between high-rises. A few twists and turns left me more lost than I had already been. Song Yulan paused at a break along one of the walls, peering out through the gloom of twilight onto a small park wedged between concrete and glass.

A woman with the build of a linebacker stood in the middle of the park, beefy arms crossed over an ample chest and a frown on her round, sun-roughened face.

"Song Yulan and Mitchell Masters. You are in violation of Quarantine Directive four-five-three. Surrender now or we will take necessary action to secure you."

Song Yulan muttered something fit for a dockworker and

rolled back to lean against the wall.

"The commander, I take it?"

"Not that bad, but if she's here, he's on his way. I'm going to get some back-up of our own. Wait here, and don't let her get her hands on you."

"I'll do my..." She faded from sight, leaving me alone in the little alleyway. "Best."

I peeked back around the corner.

"I can see you. Come out."

"And who are you?" I called, playing for time. I pulled the shadows closer around me. If it came down to it and she closed the distance between us, I'd have to abandon the alleyway in favor of the maneuverability the park offered, but there weren't as many shadows. Better for movement, horrible for cover.

"I am Hekou Yangtze," said the woman. It translated roughly into "Mouth of the Yangtze". So, not a given name. A title, like Skyrocket or Mr Mystic.

"You're with the People's Heroes."

"And you are spy of the Argent Corporation." She dropped her arms to her sides and approached my hiding place. Stay and fight, or run and evade capture? But if I ran, where would I run to? And would Song Yulan be able to find me?

So, compromise. Stay and evade.

"I'm afraid you're mistaken. I broke off my affiliation with Argent many years ago." I slid around to the other side of the wall after I'd spoken. A basic ruse, but it worked. Her attention was on where I had been.

"Liar. You arrived with one of their men. The flying one."

That almost surprised me out of the shadows. Skyrocket? How did she know about him?

And did that mean he and Tsung had safely made it out of the Shadow Realms?

She rounded the corner, and I didn't dare ask. I snapped a kick out of the shadows, going for the back of her knee – on top of my usual aim for low casualties, I didn't want to offend the People's Heroes by permanently disabling one of their agents. Yangtze grunted and stumbled, but she didn't go down. It was like kicking a sack of rice. She just kind of... shifted.

Then she turned to face me.

Hell.

Yangtze swiped for me. I rolled under her arms. At least, that was the plan, but she spun about faster than I would have expected for someone of her size. She caught my ankle and dragged me out of my roll and into the park. I tried rotating my ankle out of her grip, but there was no gap between her fingers and thumb – her hand was so large, my ankle so thin in comparison, that her digits overlapped by a healthy bit. No freedom to be found there.

I kicked her with my free leg, but this time it was more like kicking a side of beef than a bag of rice. She grunted, and I ignored the pain of impacting an immovable object when I was nothing like an unstoppable force. She grabbed me above the knee with her other hand and choked up her grip, lifting me high above the ground. I twisted about, dangling by the one leg. My hat tumbled to the grass.

"You are a liar," she said, shaking me. Her face swam in and out of view as I swung about. "And you are also not very smart."

I was almost glad Song Yulan wasn't there to agree with the second bit. That would teach me not to listen. "So I have been informed on numerous occasions," I said, hoping the guardian would arrive with that back-up. With the way the blood was rushing to my head, sooner would be better. "Now that we have found some common ground, I would very much appreciate it if you would set me down so we might talk."

Yangtze laughed, a hearty alto that would have made Wagner weep. "I have nothing to say to you. You are the reason for this attack on China. We know of your alliance with the Shadow

Dragons. We have your master trapped, and now we have you. Perhaps if I killed you, that would break this spell."

She grabbed my other leg and pulled like she meant to tear me in twain. She was strong enough that I feared she might manage it. I curled up and grabbed at her wrist, trying to break her grip as she pried me into upside-down splits. Without any leverage and my body being gumbied into a shape it wasn't meant to take, my struggles were as effective as a fly pinned by a bully.

"Yangtze. We have our orders. Release Mr Masters."

The strain on my inner-thighs eased as Yangtze stopped prying me apart and turned to the new speaker. "He will get away if I do."

"No, he will not."

I twisted to catch a glimpse of my savior, just in time to witness him fling a ribbon of paper at me. It hit like a floodlight. I flinched and squinted as the park was illuminated from all sides like Madison Square Gardens. There didn't seem to be any source to the light. It was just *there*. Sorcery. The People's Heroes were more comfortable with its use than their western counterparts. Damn. There would be no escaping into shadow now. Even my face was unshielded.

Unshielded, and probably beet-dark. It was hard to hear my captors' conversation for the ringing in my ears.

"Song Yulan got away." Yangtze told the newcomer.

"Doesn't matter. Mr Mystic is the one we want. Put him down. You both look ridiculous."

"He tried to kick me." But she put me down. I lay on the grass for a moment, letting my circulation regain equilibrium. The other speaker picked up my hat and held it out to me. I sat up, taking the hat and settling it back on my head. I pulled the brim low. With the magical floodlights, it was impossible to coax even a wisp of a shadow to cover my face. I popped my collar in a vain attempt to make up the difference.

"My apologies for any discomfort, Mr Masters, but you really shouldn't have tried to kick Yangtze. You are the visitor here, after all."

The man eschewed the dark suits of the other People's Heroes I'd seen, favoring instead a monk's garb: loose peasant pants, grass sandals, and a dun-colored short robe that was all folds. His legs bowed out in a gentle curve, and his head was shaved bald.

"You're the Commander?" Hard to imagine Song Yulan being afraid of this man, until I recalled the little strip of paper that had turned on the floodlights.

Monks were tricky like that.

The man laughed and helped me to my feet as a dark sedan pulled up to the stone archway. The alley was too narrow to open the doors anywhere else.

"No sir. I am Seven Lotus Petals Falling, the Incense Master for the PHC in Shanghai. But our commander is very eager to meet with you. Will you come quietly?"

"He will." Yangtze gave me a look that said I'd better.

I dragged my feet all the way to the car, keeping my face buried in my collar. Between Yangtze and the floodlights, what choice did I have?

"I suppose that I will," I said, ducking my head as I was helped into the car by the monk and the woman. Yangtze climbed in beside me. As we scraped our way down the alley and onto the busy streets, her hand closed around my wrist.

Who needed handcuffs when you had China's answer to Brunhilde?

Once free of the monk's sorcery, I was able to coax forth my disguise of shadows. We drove past the cluster of hotels that lined the Bund, heading for the tunnel under the Huangpu. Traffic thinned to nothing as police diverted every car but ours. We came to the barricaded entrance to the tunnel and were waved through without being stopped. I glanced over my shoulder as we entered the falsely bright tunnel. The air compression, the white tiled curve of the walls, the brightness of the lights that emphasized just how constricting the tunnel was, all contributed to create a claustrophobic miasma. There were no other cars or noise to break up the impression that we were entering an inescapable labyrinth.

"Why close down the tunnels?" I asked, wondering if they'd done the same for the bridges. They were the main arteries for commerce between the Puxi and the Pudong. It seemed a new one was being built every year.

"Public safety," Seven Lotus Petals Falling said. "The tunnels are unsafe, so nobody wants to use them."

Unsafe? Or was that just the Party line? Control of the tunnels meant control of the city. I turned forward to ask the monk when Yangtze's hand squeezed around my wrist hard enough to make me wince.

"We have a problem," she told Seven Lotus Petals Falling as the tunnel behind us glowed with a red-gold light. I shielded my eyes, disoriented for a moment. It looked like the setting sun catching the opening, but the sun had set already, and there was too much city and smog in the way.

Also, the glow was getting brighter.

"Drive faster," Yangtze urged the driver. She strained against her seatbelt, as if that could add to our momentum. I was pressed back into my seat as the car surged faster. The driver's knuckles were white on the wheel.

"We can't outrun her," Seven Lotus Petals Falling said, twisting around to look behind us. I turned as well, as much as Yangtze's grip would let me.

I couldn't look directly at the light. It blossomed in our wake like a fireball, overtaking us in a dizzying flash of dancing lights and shadows, and then surging ahead. It burst out of the tunnel and exploded into the road beyond. The car swayed as the driver flinched and covered his eyes.

I pressed forward alongside Yangtze, both of us straining against our seatbelts. The light had resolved into a dragon, red and gold and longer than any of the puppets I'd seen in New Year's parades. Her serpentine coils blocked the rounded tunnel exit. She'd taken out most of the tunnel lights with her passage, leaving her the only bright spot at the end of our darkened path.

"She'll move," the monk told the driver. "Don't stop."

"No! Don't hurt her!" Like hell was I going to let him play chicken with the dragon blocking the tunnel's mouth, but we were too close to stop, and tile walls curved up on either side of us.

Gripping the edge of my seat, I pulled the entire car through to the Shadow Realms. The engine sputtered a quick, noisy death. The car fishtailed. A bump in the terrain that hadn't been there a few moments before flipped us. What should have been a long coast to stopping became a whirligig of terror. Rolling world, dark sky, and darker land, and Yangtze's face wide-eyed and screaming. Metal groaned, safety glass shattered over us in a spray. My head was jerked about on my neck, my legs flopping in front of me, though I kept my grip on the seat. I closed my eyes until the car settled.

Before I could get my bearings, someone grabbed me by the lapels and pulled me back into the light of the world.

"I've got her. Let's get out of here." I knew that voice.

"Tsung?" Impossible.

And then another voice, so heart-breakingly familiar that I forgot all about Tsung. "Get the others."

"We don't have time to–"

"Get them. I'm not leaving them in that place."

I opened my eyes as David Tsung tore a wound between the worlds, using the shadows cast by the dragon's light. He pulled out Yangtze, the monk, and the driver, all still dazed from the crash.

Red-gold claws clasped around Tsung and myself. The dragon took to the air before my captors could collect themselves. I shrieked and held on for dear life. Shanghai passed below us, the Huangpu River a dark strip between the lights of Pudong and Puxi. My wig whipped about my face. I'd lost my hat somewhere in the crash. I tore the wig free and shoved it into my pocket. Above me, the dragon's body caught the lights off the Bund. Looking up at her gave me vertigo. I swallowed and closed my eyes until I felt solid ground under my feet. She'd landed in a familiar garden with fox statues lurking behind every bush. A cobbled terrace led up to a temple.

Her whiskers quivered as she gave me the draconic equivalent of a grin.

"Mei Shen?" I must have hit my head in the crash. But no, I'd seen her *before* I'd ripped the car into the Shadow Realms.

"Hello, Mother," the dragon chirped. She folded in on herself and became a pretty teenage girl in jeans, a red top, and gold-spangled chains. She hurled herself at me, and I met her with a crushing hug.

"I think Father was right." She sniffled into my shoulder. We were both crying. "I do get my ability to find trouble from you."

TEN
Chasing Tails

Then

Idylls are measured by moments of difficulty, and difficulty never came to Jian Huo's realm unless it was brought from the outside. A dozen years passed, and I became teacher as well as student, filling in certain necessary cultural gaps in my children's education. Good thing I could recite *The Princess Bride* from memory. Jian Huo claimed their brilliance was due to their draconic heritage, and he was probably right, but I cited my genetic contribution anyway. And they were brilliant. Lung Mian Zi Zun could challenge his father at *wei-qi* before he could walk, and Lung Mei Shen Mi was constantly testing the boundaries of how much trouble she could get into.

They were never sick, rarely cried or fussed, and the time passed without note beyond the usual markers of raising a family: first words, first steps, first accidental transformation into a big serpenty critter. I woke every morning surrounded by a dark curtain of sandalwood-scented hair and pestered by laughing imps. I spent my days in loving domesticity. Each evening I told my children tales of heroes and villains, just as my grandfather had done with me, and shooed their nurse away to tuck them in myself. Every night my senses were set aflame by my dragon-lover, and I slept sated and content in his arms.

It was those same arms, more or less, that cradled us now as we soared high above the spiritual reflection of Shanghai. Of all of us, I took the most geektastic joy from flying, *whoo-hooing* like a madwoman. Mian Zi and Mei Shen couldn't fly far in their dragon forms, and they found being carried, compounded by my unbridled enthusiasm, embarrassing as only soon-to-be teenagers would. Even so, Mian Zi smiled into the wind, and Mei Shen laughed as rain spattered her face. Jian Huo thrummed with a deeper, quieter sort of contentment, and my whooping was cut short on a breath-catching moment of intense happiness. A heroine in a story might have recognized this as a warning of pending disaster, but we'd been so happy for so long that I'd ceased expecting anything to go wrong. I should have remembered that dragons think of time on a different scale.

We landed in the courtyard of a temple. Jian Huo's arrival had been preceded by a rainstorm, which cleared away the Shanghai smog into something breathable. The air was still thick and warm, but it smelled clean, and it was heavy with moisture. The gardens rolled out before the temple with studied simplicity, like a lady's robe dropped at her feet but not yet kicked away. Statues of slender foxes, one paw raised just so, dotted the grounds. Tiny shrines peeked out of grottoes and nestled between tree roots. It was less like a temple, more like a den. I spied a flash of white standing near the door of the temple – Jiu Wei, greeting Song Yulan and the hulking form of Fang Shih. I grinned, anticipating much teasing from him about my grasp of spirit speech… or lack thereof.

Jian Huo transformed while still holding the children, setting his squirming passengers down so they could rush forward to meet those coming to greet us. Shui Yin, as roguish and carefree as when I'd first met him, bent to swoop up an adoring Mei Shen. Mian Zi cast a disapproving glance at his sister's outrageous flirtations before greeting Si Wei with a proper little bow. The fox girl greeted him back with equal solemnity, but her fingers plucked at the brocade edges of her sleeves, and the back of her robes twitched. Squeezing Jian Huo's hand, I smiled my greeting to the couple.

"Shui Yin, it's good to see you again. Si Wei, you look lovely." And like she might snap any moment. I shot Shui Yin a glare that he missed because he was busy tickling his niece.

"Jian Huo, why don't you and the children go with your brother. Si Wei and I need to catch up. Jiu Wei can greet any latecomers." I nodded to the ancient fox-spirit who stood at the doors of the temple. She nodded back and waved me off. Before anyone could protest, I grabbed Si Wei's arm and dragged her into the gardens.

"Whew." I collapsed on a bench and motioned for her to join me. She did, looking nonplussed. Whirlwind Missy, at your service. "You look almost as awful as I felt during the *Zi Gong Hu*."

"I do?" Slender fingers flew to check her perfectly-coifed russet hair. If I took myself more seriously, I would have been insulted. Stupid non-aging friends being prettier than me. I chuckled away any jealousy.

"No. Not at all. You look perfect. You just seemed anxious. I figured you could use a break before you found a convenient bell-tower."

She sighed and slumped. Since I'd never seen her with anything other than perfect poise, my alarm-meter jumped to Code Mauve.

"I should have no fear of this," she said. "I've proven myself. I've passed all the trials. I've done this before!" She slapped her palm against stone, then sighed and closed her eyes. "Shui Yin says that I am being silly and just want more attention–"

"Whoa. He said that? That is *way* out of line." I glanced around, hoping for his smirking face to appear so I could smack him one. She opened her mouth to defend the rogue, but I silenced her by taking her hands and given them a stern shake.

"Si Wei, it's all right to be nervous. You have every reason to be nervous. Not because you don't deserve this or because anything's going to go wrong. You do and it's not. It's just that the last time you didn't have anything to prove. You'd done the time, passed the trials, and it was all gravy. This time, people are watching you. Maybe they haven't questioned you for a century, but this is like a big neon sign reminding them that you used to be dangerous. They're going to be sizing you up, looking for signs they missed last time. It sucks, but there it is. But you know what?"

"What?" Her butt wasn't doing the four-tailed mambo anymore. Maybe she'd just needed reassuring that she wasn't crazy.

"I'm not looking at you like that. And since I'm the most important person here, that's all that matters."

"You?" She sputtered at my outrageous claim, a grin tugging at her lips. "I think there might be some who would argue with that."

"Let them." I squared my shoulders and lifted my nose. "I'm *Lung Xin Niang*..." I deflated. "OK, well, provisionally until Lung Tian unbunches his panties. Just give it another few centuries."

She shook her head, but her willow-strong posture had returned. She was looking lovelier and more composed by the second. This was a good thing because I had some curiosities that needed sating.

"So, this whole gaining your fifth tail and becoming Wu Wei... is it, like, a surgical procedure, or do we actually get to play 'pin the tail on the *huxian*'?"

I didn't even try to duck her swipe.

For all Si Wei's anxiety, the ceremony went off without a hitch. It was simple and beautiful, without a lot of the elaborate pomp I'd come to expect from the various traditional Chinese rituals I'd seen. Russet-furred foxes and russet-haired women filled the temple. Many of them wore masks, and most of them wore robes of various shades of russet silk. If I squinted just right I could make out the blur of white-tipped tails. I stopped squinting when Jian Huo reprimanded our daughter for doing the same thing. Apparently it was rude. Who knew?

Jiu Wei stood out in robes of palest cream, her silver hair flowing free around her. She anointed Si Wei with water from a silver basin, while Si Wei's sister-foxes disrobed her, replacing the russet silk with robes a shade lighter. Then Jiu Wei led her into a chamber beyond the main temple, all the fox-women following behind. The guests were left to our own devices.

"That's it?" Mei Shen looked around, confused. The ceremony was over before she could start fidgeting, which said a lot about its brevity.

"No." Mian Zi's response held the all-knowing disgust that only a sibling could muster. "The ceremony continues for the rest of the night, with each fox maiden saluting Si Wei – now Wu Wei – and bringing her to her pleasure in turn."

The hall had emptied out, so there was only our little group left to gape at my son in shock.

Shui Yin collected himself the quickest. "R–r– really?" he sputtered.

"Nuh-uh," was Mei Shen's skeptical rebuttal.

"Where did you learn that?" Jian Huo's tone, curious but not surprised, clued me to the possibility that all-night lesbian fox orgies might not be a factoid that my son had pulled out of nowhere.

I tamped down on my appalled shock and went for dire motherly suspicion. "Yes. Where *did* you learn that?"

Mian Zi shrugged. "Everyone knows that."

I got the impression that his interest in the topic had only ever been academic, not prurient. He slid off the bench and followed his sister, who had already grown bored with the conversation and was running toward the gardens. That left the three adults glancing between each other, and the formerly innocuous-looking doorway at the rear of the temple, with renewed interest. Shui Yin still sported a shell-shocked expression, and I couldn't help but smirk.

"I didn't know that." He turned to us, "Did you know that?"

"Of course." Jian Huo's smirk matched my own. He set a hand at the small of my back to escort me out to the gardens. Shui Yin was an amateur rogue compared to his brother. "Didn't you hear Mian Zi? Everyone knows that."

It took forever to coax the children to sleep. The day had been a long one, what with the excitement of the flight and the requirement to be on their best behavior. Their eyes were over-bright and their imaginations too active. Their latest ploy – after the usual requests for water, snacks, stories, songs, windows open, windows closed, and questions about lesbian fox orgies that I was *not* going to answer – was to tell me that there was something shifty about the nurse Jiu Wei had provided.

"She was clipping her toenails just before you came in. I heard her. She's inviting ghosts to come and kill us in our sleep," Mei Shen said. I didn't want to discount the superstition, but I also knew my daughter's penchant for tall-tales and exaggeration.

"Was she?" I pretended concern but glanced at Mian Zi, who ran every statement he made through a rigorous process of logic.

"Maybe," he hemmed, trying to give his sister the benefit of the doubt. "I was nearly asleep. But Mei Shen wouldn't lie about something like that. And the nurse is foreign. Who knows what primitive magic she might have?"

My son, the budding racist. I was going to have to work on that cultural elitism – not easy, when all the spirits he met were one step away from worshipping the twins as godlings. Still, it was odd that a foreign spirit should be taking care of them. I stole a quick glance at the nurse, who sat in a chair near the brazier, carving a bit of wood with a dull-looking knife.

"Excuse me?" The old woman glanced up when I spoke to her. Sure enough, her apple-granny features had a distinct Western cast. "How long have you worked in Jiu Wei's house?"

"Not long my Lady," the old woman responded. Points against her for that, but at least she was honest about it, "Si – Wu Wei brought me here to care for your children. We are old friends." And opinion swung back in the nurse's favor. The fox-girl would never bring harm to me or my children. I nodded thanks to the old woman and turned back to Mei Shen, whose chin was jutted out as though her point had been proven.

"There, you see! You see! She said 'si'. Everyone knows that is an ill-omen. It means death."

I raised an eyebrow. "Everyone knows that was Wu Wei's name until a few hours ago. It's not her fault that the number four is ill-omened." Maybe my first instincts were correct, and this was another bedtime-resistance ploy. Mian Zi was already out, his serious little frown softened into a snoring rosebud. However, soothing Mei Shen's worry would be no small task. I considered for a moment, then reached into the folds of my robe and pulled out a package wrapped in red, green, and gold silk.

"Here." I placed the package on her lap. "Open it. I was going to give them to Wu Wei as a gift, but I don't think she'd mind if you wore them tonight. They'll protect you from ghosts and death-omens and evil nannies."

Mei Shen gasped at the pair of carved jade combs in the package. I took one from her and fixed it in her hair. She kept the other clenched in her fist. "There. Is that better?"

Mei Shen nodded. It was grudging, but already her eyes were unfocusing. For all her worry and resistance, she was as exhausted as her brother.

"Good. Then sleep tight. And don't worry, Maybug. I would

never let anything harm you." I tucked the covers around her chest, kissed her on the forehead, and bid the nurse goodnight on my way out.

The hallways of Jiu Wei's temple were unfamiliar, but I managed to find my way from the nursery back to our rooms. I found Jian Huo there with Shui Yin, who had decided that he was not cool with the all-night lesbian fox orgy portion of the ceremony. He was deep in his cups and declaring a pox on all red-haired temptresses.

"I hope that doesn't include me. I'd hate to have a pox. Of course, if I'm not included then I think my feelings will be hurt. Don't I rate high enough to be a temptress anymore?"

Shui Yin glared at me for several moments before grabbing his wine bottle and stalking off, muttering that know-it-all human red-haired temptresses were the worst of the lot. I laughed. Tormenting him was such fun.

"Did the children go down all right?" Jian Huo pulled me onto the low-backed couch. I nestled into his arms. "I was on my way to join you, but my brother insisted on stopping by to inform me what a trial fox-women are – as if I didn't know myself – and how lucky I am to have met a sweet and biddable woman. The wine seems to be affecting his memory."

"Biddable? He actually called me biddable!" I made a mock move to rise and hunt down the offender, but Jian Huo pulled me back.

"No you don't. You've done enough, encouraging them as you have. I won't have you adding to his misery."

I pouted at being foiled, but he kissed it away and settled me more firmly on top of him. I propped myself up on my elbows so I could continue babbling at him. Resigned to this from long experience, Jian Huo ignored me in favor of undoing my robes.

"He really does seem bothered by it, doesn't he? I wouldn't have expected it." I paused and Jian Huo hmphed, freeing me to continue. "I mean, sure, they've been together for over a decade, but they always seemed so casual." I knew from long conversations over tea and plum wine that the fox-girl's feelings were anything but casual, but I also knew from observation that they had never seemed to be fully reciprocated.

Jian Huo's response echoed those observations. "She is his concubine."

"I hate that word." I growled, no longer distracted by his hands. He stopped to brush my wispies back from my cheeks.

"I know. But until now he – they both – have let that term define how they behave with one another. But you are right. Shui Yin is much more disturbed than he should be. I think after tonight that Wu Wei will no longer be his concubine."

"Wife?" I asked. A lifted brow communicated the unlikelihood of that. "Some indeterminate in-between state, then." My words skirted the unresolved issue of our own relationship; he tensed beneath me. I smiled and copied his gesture, sliding my fingers through the hair at his temples. "I can live with that." Jian Huo relaxed and resumed fiddling with my robes. I looped back to his original question.

"As for the children, I've met political prisoners who've behaved more compliantly." My voice took on a mocking, sing-song quality: "It's too loud; it's too quiet; we're thirsty; we're hungry; tell us a story; sing us a song; it's too hot; now it's too cold; our nurse is an evil, ill-omened hag who is plotting our deaths."

"That is a new one," he chuckled, but by the way he was nuzzling my throat, I was pretty sure he was only half paying attention. I started to stop paying attention myself.

"Mei Shen's invention. Still not the winner of the day, what with Mian Zi's anthropological knowledge of all-night lesbian fox orgies." I felt more than heard the thrum of laughter in his chest. My last question emerged breathy and distracted. "How exactly did you know about that?"

His lips smiled against mine. "Didn't you hear Mian Zi? Everyone knows that."

Whatever response I might have made was lost in his kiss.

The moment I woke up, I knew something was wrong.

I'd like to claim a mother's instinct or something equally arcane, but the truth of the matter was that I hadn't slept late for over ten years, ever since the twins had mastered walking. My mornings started early with two imps bounding onto the bed, tangling themselves in the covers, and getting tickled near-to-gasping by their father and myself for their pains.

Diffused sunlight greeted my eyes as I cracked them open. I stretched against Jian Huo's warm length, the silk of his hair sliding along my skin as he shifted with my movement. Magic hair. It never tangled or got caught underneath your arms or in your mouth. It entranced me. I reached down to grasp two long coils of it, intending to wrap myself in the silken warmth, when the wrongness of the morning hit me.

The children.

I sat up, rubbing away sleep, and looked around the room. Maybe it was some new, inventive game designed to send me into a panic. Jian Huo sat up as well, sensing my growing distress.

"What is it?" His hand rubbed up my arm, a futile attempt to soothe. I shrugged him away.

"The children. They're not here. It's late, and they didn't wake us up."

It was a testament to how regular our idyllic days were that he also recognized the wrongness of this. I scrambled from the bed, reaching for my robe. He rose more fluidly, eyes serious and pensive, seeking a rational explanation as he donned his own robe.

"The nurse?" he offered. "She doesn't know them, or us. In all likelihood she wouldn't let them leave the nursery. I have sometimes wished that our own nurse was half so diligent."

I started to agree with this. We were in a strange place. The nurse wouldn't know how much we indulged our children. It must have been a mighty struggle for her to keep them in the nursery. Even so...

"Since when would they let a little thing like that get in their way?" I asked.

He held my gaze for a beat. We broke, scrambling for the door and rushing down the hallway.

The strangest tableau greeted us when we burst into the nursery. The nurse was nowhere to be seen, but Mian Zi and Mei Shen sat in the middle of the chamber, playing a game. He laid down a set of colored sticks, which she studied intently before picking them up in reverse order. Then she laid them down, and he picked them up. They played with a level of concentration usually reserved for *wei-qi*, humming a tuneless drone. I'd seen Cronenberg films that creeped me out less.

They didn't notice our entry. I don't know how long we stood there watching them with growing horror.

Jian Huo interrupted the game. "Mian Zi. Mei Shen. What are you doing?" His words were quiet, his normally rich baritone strangled. I couldn't even bring myself to speak. The children finished the round, stopped humming, and stood.

"Hello, Father; hello, Mother. Are we ready to go home now?" Normally the more reticent of the two, Mian Zi stepped forward. Mei Shen cast her eyes to the floor in proper feminine deference. There was no sign of the jade combs I'd given her the night before. Their skin was swarthier than it should have been and oddly grainy, their movements jerky and wooden, and when they looked at us, there was something wrong behind their eyes. I let out a choked gurgle. Pod people. My children had been replaced with pod people.

Tears welling, I wrenched my gaze away from these imposters. My eyes fell on the chair near the brazier, the one that the nurse had sat in the night before. Wood-shavings from whatever she'd been carving lay in a scatter; the dull knife sat abandoned amidst them. I stared blindly at the knife for a moment, then back up at the things pretending to be my children. Years of bedtime stories and folk lullabies had supplied a catalogue of dangers to warn them against, but some of those warnings weren't meant for children. They were meant for parents.

Mei Shen and Mian Zi weren't pod people. They were changelings.

Jian Huo started forward in fury. I rushed at him, grabbing his arm before he could strike the imposters and make it that much harder to get our own children back.

"Jian Huo. Wait!"

He turned to me. "Missy, these aren't–"

"I know," I interrupted. "Bring me eggs."

What?" His fury had turned to surprise and suspicion. He had to be wondering if he had three pod people on his hands instead of just two.

"Please. I can't explain, but I… I know what to do." I choked on the words, doubt creeping up in conviction's wake. I glanced at my children. Not my children? They were so wrong, everything was wrong. What if I was wrong, too?

And even if I wasn't, that didn't mean I knew better what to do than Jian Huo, who'd always lived this life. But he'd been about to strike the imposters. His hand opened and closed in impotence. Maybe basing my children's recovery on instructions gleaned from a folk song was madness, but it had to be better than violence.

I shook Jian Huo's arm. "Eggs, some kind of bread, milk – preferably spoiled – and rice with as much chaff as possible." Thank god we were in Shanghai. Half the ingredients would have been impossible to get in Huanglong. "Oh, and a pot with hot water. I'll need that for the brewing."

His mouth worked as he struggled through a thousand questions, but then he just clamped his jaw, nodded, and stalked from the room. I walked over to the shavings and ran my hands through them, taking a moment to collect myself. The knife I picked up and slid into my robes. With a deep breath, I rose and turned back to the imposters, smiling brightly through my fear.

"So, my darlings. That is an interesting game you were playing. Why don't you show me how to play it."

The waiting was horrible, made more so by having to watch the two changelings go through the motions of being my children. Whatever intelligence animated them was rather dim. On the one hand, it made things worse because my own children were so brilliant. To see Mian Zi's copy confounded by the stick game, to see Mei Shen quiet and deferent – I wanted to shake them, strike them as Jian Huo had been about to. Still, it gave me hope that they would be easy to trick. In the tales, changelings were always so cunning, but, if these two were anything to judge by, then just maybe my folk magic had a shot of working.

Before my patience could snap, Jian Huo returned with several servants and the items I'd requested. Jiu Wei, Shui Yin, and Wu Wei were with him, the latter looking as if all she wanted was to be left alone to commit ritual suicide. A small part of me wanted to assuage the tortured guilt in her eyes, but a much larger part of me was furious that she'd been so careless with my children's safety. Part of that fury was misdirected – it was my fault for not taking Mei Shen's worries more seriously – but it was easier to blame Wu Wei.

"The nurse has slipped away. She was brought here in repayment of a debt." Jian Huo glared at the fox-girl. "She expressed an interest in meeting the dragon-children. Si Wei thought her harmless. Apparently, Si Wei was mistaken."

Even I shivered at the coldness of Jian Huo's tone, but I'd already figured most of that out while I waited. My attention was caught by the one unexpected element.

"Si Wei?" I asked.

"I have forsaken my claim to my fifth tail. To be so duped, and to such ends, proves that I have not earned it." The fox-girl managed to look me in the eye. "I am so sorry."

My anger ebbed, but rather than dissolve into tears and accept the comfort I knew they would all give me, I beamed a big, fake smile at her and thumped her on the shoulder.

"What for? Everything's fine!" I ignored the shocked looks and, quelling my revulsion, I grabbed each pod-child by the hand and led them over to the brazier and the pot of steaming water.

"Now, my darlings, we're going to go home, but first we need to brew the parting glass. We'll drink the beer with our friends, and it will give us all luck until we see each other again." Which was utter nonsense, but that was the point.

I hummed as I added ingredients to the pot, half to steady myself and half to keep the song's instructions in mind. First I broke the eggs, tossing out the whites and yolks and putting the shells into the simmering pot. Next came the bread – little golden bing that didn't have the crusty bits I needed. I did the best I could, picking out the charred pieces to toss in the pot and discarding the rest. Everyone gathered watched me with rapt fascination, although the adults all shared a similar look of concern over my apparent madness. The children's jaws were slack, though in the Mian Zi imposter I discerned a bit of growing skepticism.

I kept humming. Next came the milk. Holding my breath, I skimmed off the curdled film at the top and dumped it into the pot. I gestured for a servant to take the rest of the milk away; I didn't want to gag from the smell and ruin the entire process. Once the milk was gone, I stirred the unlikely ingredients together. Skepticism now lighted both of the changelings' eyes.

"We're supposed to drink this?" Shui Yin's *sotto*-voiced question held similar skepticism, and a level of disgust. Jian Huo and Si Wei both shushed him. With trembling hands, I reached for the final ingredient. Please, I prayed, please let this work.

I sifted out the chaff from the rice and added it to the pot, throwing aside the whole, unbroken grains. I heard a snort of disbelief behind me and turned to face Pod-Mian.

"That's not the way to make beer."

"Of course it is!" My smile was at full wattage.

"No," he countered. "It isn't."

I floundered. This wasn't how things were supposed to go. So far, his skepticism was similar enough to Mian Zi's that it didn't count as an admission of his charade. My smile dimmed. "Maybe it isn't how you make it here in China, but it's how we make it back home in San Francisco."

Pod-Mian's eyes narrowed, as if he'd never met a simpler creature than me. "You stupid woman. I've traveled the world and lived over two millennia, and I've never seen anyone make beer that way."

Not to be outdone, Pod-Mei's voice was similarly dismissive: "I've traveled as far and lived as long, and neither have I."

This time my smile was real, and full of triumph. I upended the pot, dousing them both with the stinking contents.

"Eggs and crumbs and milk and grain, bring my baby back again!" I shouted the final line of the song in English, the first I'd spoken in years. The Shadow Realms shifted, regurgitating *something* back into this world, but other than that, there was little outward sign that my spell had worked. One moment the two pod- children were washed over by the hot, stinking liquid, and the next moment Mian Zi sat clutching his sister in the middle of the steaming muck. Mian Zi blinked up at me, a look of fastidious disgust on his face at the smell and the mess.

Heedless of the stink, I rushed forward to hug them both, and our little group was soon enveloped in Jian Huo's arms. Our relief was short-lived. Mian Zi struggled against me, and I pulled back, confused.

"Mother!" He loosened his hold on his sister and she thunked to the floor, a lifeless wooden doll dressed in Mei Shen's clothes.

"Mei Shen?" Terror ripped through me as I reached out to touch rough wood. "Mei Shen!" I snatched up the wooden effigy and dove for the nearest shadow. Mian Zi had come back that way; Mei Shen had to be there too. I didn't care if it was dangerous, if I might lose myself. I'd had years to grow stronger, and I had to try. I could sense the shadow landscape just across the edge of light. I called out for Mei Shen. All I heard in response were nightmare echoes, and all I saw were shifting shadows.

Before I could submerge, something yanked me back with physical force. I lost hold of the wooden stock that had been Mei Shen's double. Jian Huo's arms circled me in a subduing hold as he hauled me back from the wooden stock sitting in shadow, back into the light of the room. I kicked at him, would have bit him, pulled his hair, anything to get free and go after Mei Shen.

"Missy, stop!" he said, but it wasn't his command that stopped me. Mian Zi huddled where he'd been soaked, knees pulled tight to his chest and lips white as he bit them to keep from crying. I wanted to collapse, to shove Jian Huo away and try again, but I had to get my shit together for my son's sake. I sagged in Jian Huo's grip. He held me for a moment longer to make sure it wasn't a feint.

"Let me go," I whispered. He did. I dropped to my knees in front of Mian Zi, pulled him into my arms. "I'm sorry."

"There was something in the spell, Mother. We could hear you. He laughed and said he only had to send back one of us, and that it would be more fun to keep Mei Shen." Mian Zi gave a little hiccup, and I realized that as hard as it was for me to lose my daughter, it was harder for him to lose his sister. They had been inseparable since birth. I stroked eggshells from his hair, while Jian Huo stroked mine. "What did you do, Mother? Why didn't he have to send her back?"

"It's an old folk story about making the fairies return children that they've stolen away. It goes 'Eggs and crumbs and milk and grain, bring my baby back again.'"

Speaking it aloud, I knew where I'd gone wrong. In the story, the faeries hadn't taken twins. In the story, the mother only pleaded for the return of one child.

"You said baby." Jian Huo said, confirming the failure I'd already realized. "He was only forced to return one of them."

"Who?" I asked. Who could wish harm to my children? Stupid question, but I'd had a rough morning. Jian Huo waited for me to connect my own dots. "Lung Di." The insulted dragon had come home to roost.

"We'll get her back," Jian Huo promised. "I'll get her back."

Sitting there, rocking my son back and forth in the mess of my partially successful spell, I could only worry how much damage Lung Di would do in the meantime.

Whereas before time had flown, now it crawled. Jian Huo spent every day meeting with allies and friends across the breadth of China, looking for some way to force his fallen brother to parlay. Mian Zi and I spent our days in the room he'd shared with his sister at Jiu Wei's Shanghai temple. We passed the time talking or reading or playing desultory matches of *wei-qi*, which Mian Zi let me win. Often I would sit holding him close and turning the dull woodcarving knife over and over in my hands while we both tried not to stare at Mei Shen's empty bed. I was powerless to do anything for my daughter. All I could do was hold my son and hope Jian Huo's allegiances were enough to let him get her back before I did something stupid.

Again, I forgot to take into account draconic time scales.

I snapped three months after Mei Shen was taken. Jian Huo had returned after an absence of several days, and he was describing to me as best he could the complex network of *guanxi* he was massaging to win Mei Shen's freedom. It sounded like it would take years to get our daughter back, and I said so.

"These are the ways of our kind," he explained, as if I hadn't been living in an eternal spirit-realm for the better part of my adult life. "Care must be taken to preserve the balance of power. Such arrangements take time."

He reached out a hand to comfort me, but I jerked away.

"Jesus, does everything always have to be about face and *guanxi*? Can't you people just do things for each other because it's the right thing to do? Why does every action and friendship here have to be reduced to use-value? No wonder Marx called it Oriental Despotism!" I slammed my fist into a support beam, letting the pain soak away some of my white-hot fury. Better to hurt myself than continue lashing out at him.

Jian Huo regarded me for a moment, and then demonstrated that not all interactions were social economics by taking my throbbing hand and pulling me to him. I curled into his arms and turned my face to his chest, wishing I could find comfort in hiding from the world. But I couldn't, not as long as that monster had Mei Shen.

"It didn't take Lung Di this long to arrange Mei Shen's kidnapping." My last sally was weak, barely a whisper.

"It took him twelve years, and I am only beginning to uncover the web of alliances he made to accomplish it. The breadth of his power is... unnerving. There are many who would now move to protect him, because to do so protects their own interests. If I do not take similar care to retrieve her, the results could be disastrous. The balance of power between my siblings must be maintained for the good of all realities."

Jian Huo rarely made mention of the role that the Nine played in shielding reality from what was outside – their true purpose in the grand scheme of things. I was so concerned over my daughter that I ignored the import of anything else he had said and went straight for the bit that concerned me.

"*Twelve* years?" I pulled back from the cocoon of his arms, shaking. "No. Please. There must be some quicker way. Some Gordian-Knot solution. Why all the machinations? Why can't you just round up a posse and take her back?"

"Unless he is a great fool, my brother holds Mei Shen in his own realms. No mortal creature may enter or leave such a place without his permission, just as none may enter or leave Huanglong without mine. And for all that she is my daughter, she is also *your* daughter. She bears mortal blood."

"What can we do, then?"

"I could force him to relinquish her, but in doing so I would offend many of our mutual allies. Or I could offer him something in trade, but anything he deemed acceptable would strengthen him and weaken me."

"And that matters more to you than the safety of our daughter?"

Jian Huo sighed and released me when I tugged away. He folded his hands into his sleeves, face gone expressionless. "I have lived a long time, Melissa Masters, and my relationships with the other spirits are deep and complex. I will recover our child, this you may trust, but it will take time."

"And by that *time*, after all the *time* she has spent with your brother, what are the chances that she'll still be our little girl?" I asked, not expecting an answer. The ghost of a flinch passed across his face, and the satisfaction that welled inside me was warm and ugly. I turned and stormed out of the temple before I could do more damage.

A dozen years in Minshan had taught me to appreciate the panoramic vistas of nature. Now, staying in Shanghai, I felt trapped. The gardens outside Jiu Wei's temple were just a tiny stamp of green among lights and noise and towering buildings. I had no desire to brave the crowds I suspected teemed outside the garden walls. I sat on the bench at the back of the garden.

The rains of Jian Huo's first arrival had frozen into snow – not the magnitude of the blizzards we got in Sichuan, but a cold dusting of hoarfrost that bleached everything in the garden to bone. The bare branches of the trees were black against the white snow, reminding me of my daughter's dark hair and pale skin. The sky was an improbable blue, almost as blue as the Masters family eyes that Mei Shen had inherited from me against all logic of genetics. All it needed was for me to prick my finger and drop some blood on the frost at my feet for the fairy-tale trope to be complete. But nothing in nature could reveal my daughter's true charm: her ready laugh, her adventurous spirit, her smiling mischief. Also, Mei Shen's lips weren't blood red; they were cherry-blossom pink. Spring was a long way off.

The switch from Snow White to Persephone was no comfort. It terrified me, the thought of what Lung Di, the Underground Dragon, could do to her while she was in his keeping. Terrified me more to realize that by not acting fast enough, by going through official channels and petitioning the gods, Demeter doomed her daughter to live six months out of every year with a rapist husband. I had used to find the whole Hades/Persephone myth kind of sexy. Not anymore.

I toyed with the nurse's carving knife, turning the blade in my hands and fuming over my own impotence. A scrabbling at the edge of sight and hearing distracted me. I looked up, trying to place it. At first I couldn't see anything, but then my eyes caught movement from one of the shadows beyond the brick archway that led to the world outside the walled temple garden. A gnarled hand beckoned me. Glancing around to make sure nobody – namely Jian Huo – was watching, I gathered my robes close and made my way across the garden.

Some thread of caution kept me from entering the alley. The figure hunched in the doorway across from the garden entry was the nurse who'd stolen my children. She wore a hooded cloak that disguised her and let her blend into the shadowed opening, but that did little to disguise what she was. The apple-granny mien had rotted; it was pinched and withered now. Why the hell hadn't I paid attention to Mei Shen's misgivings?

"Where's my daughter?" My voice shook. I wanted to sound cool, in command, but what was the point? We both knew the truth.

"Come closer," she beckoned. "Come let us speak."

I approached the boundary of the archway, but then good sense asserted itself. Jiu Wei's temple might have some of the same protections as Jian Huo's realm. "You can just say whatever you have to say while I stand right here."

The old nurse chuckled and settled back into the doorway. She lowered the cowl of her cloak, and I caught a flash of jade in her ratty hair. My grip on the knife tightened.

"Told him you wouldn't fall for something that obvious, but my master insisted it was worth a try." Her tone was wry... conversational, even. Here I was, brewing up a good pot of fury, and she spoke like we were having afternoon tea.

"Oh, so we're going to be cordial?"

"Would you rather we were insulting?"

"I'd rather rip out your heart with a meat hook, but in the absence of that, sure, I'll be cordial. Where's Mei Shen?" I met her gaze and waited for her to introduce the terms of the game. I didn't have to wait long.

"Just like that?" she sighed and tsk-ed. "You know it won't be so easy. Lung Di sent me here, it is true, but I've not seen your children since I took them. I'm only his emissary to places where he is not welcome."

"And what message were you sent to bring?" I asked, entering the game.

"Lung Huang has nothing that Lung Di wants. But you might. My master says he will only parlay with you, but only if you come alone, and only if you bring an offer worth his time. Something of true value." The old woman's smile at the end of the speech made me wish for my meat hook solution. Instead, I drew out the conversation.

"What guarantee do I have that Lung Di won't just take me captive too, or that he will honor anything we agree to?"

"None." She cackled. "But it's the only chance you have of recovering your daughter, so you'll take a gamble and do it."

My eyes narrowed. I hated her cackling. I hated her certainty. She reached out a gnarled hand, expecting me to accept no matter the terms.

"Go to hell." The shocked look on her face was small satisfaction. I turned and stalked back into the gardens before I weakened enough to take her hand. Perhaps if I told someone she was there, they could catch her before she got away.

"If you change your mind, just come across the river," she called after me. "Lung Di's sanctum is easy enough to find."

My steps faltered. I looked back over my shoulder. "You'd tell me where it is?"

The hag sank into the shadows, so that even I had trouble tracking her. "As I said, it is hard to miss. Just look up." And she was gone.

I continued into the temple, chewing on the old woman's poisoned bait. She knew where Mei Shen was. I had given the jade combs to Mei Shen as protection. The magic of that gift was like Dorothy's silver slippers; no-one could take them from her unwilling. Mei Shen must have known her nurse was being sent as a messenger, but the comb was Mei Shen's message to me. The hag knew where my daughter was.

Across the Huangpu? Had she lied about that, too?

My step quickened. Let Jian Huo play his games of debt. I'd save Mei Shen myself, but I'd be doing it on my terms.

I returned to our temporary rooms and pulled traveling clothes from my wardrobe. Jian Huo had brought the entire thing when I made it clear that I wouldn't return home without my daughter. My old knapsack sat wadded in a heap at the back of the wardrobe. I shook it out and began filling it. I sighed over the cracked and tattered remains of my Doc Martins, Union Jack emblazoned on each side, but tossed them into my pack for luck. I settled on flimsy slippers to go with my Shaolin robes.

Rooting through my jewelry, I found little worth taking. Not that the jewelry didn't have value, but it was just gold and jewels and craftsmanship. All gifts from Jian Huo, and nothing that would interest Lung Di. Except... I extracted my grandmother's pearls: Jian Huo's gift of love. More than just a symbol; they warmed to my touch and smelled of sandalwood.

It was a risk, taking them, but if I worked things just right, Lung Di would never get his claws on them. I tucked the pearls into one of the deep interior pockets of my pack along with the nurse's carving knife.

Pulling out a small writing desk, I sat on the bench at the foot of the bed and composed the note that might end everything. I wrote in English because my frantic mind and hands could not properly construct the Chinese characters into coherence. A gajillion characters. I snorted at yet another example of Jian Huo's slow-moving pedantry. Give me a good old 26-letter alphabet any day of the week.

I sealed my hastily-scribbled note with a bit of wax and set the writing desk aside. Then I hefted my pack over my shoulder and headed to the nursery.

Mian Zi had crept up onto Mei Shen's empty bed and fallen

asleep. I hesitated over waking him. He was too like his father; he'd try to stop me from going. I brushed the hair over his brow and kissed him on the forehead, then I propped the note on the end of the bed.

I accosted one of Jiu Wei's servants on my return to the gardens and commandeered a candle, a lighter, and a handful of sparklers. Then I returned to the gardens, to the archway opposite the one where the hag had accosted me. A few steps out into the alleyway was probably far enough, but I ventured out until I could hear the noise and smell the smog of the city beyond, just in case. Before sense could return and stop me from what I was about to do, I stepped off the path and into the Shadow Realms – the one place Jian Huo couldn't follow.

The shock of entering the Shadow Realms after so long left me staggered. Had the place always been this chill, this empty, this echoing with the howls of pain and grief and despair? All around me was gloaming; the dark pressed against my skin like a living thing – which in this place it very much was. I stood on a vast plain that stretched bare in all directions save for the odd tree, twisted of limb and stripped of leaves. A hollow-voiced wind rushed across the plain, whipping clouds of shadow dust into whorls and eddies. Some of those eddies took life and form of their own, crying in rage as they tried to flee from the cutting wind. None of them made it more than a few paces before they were shredded back into dust.

Everything was devoid of color, and even the gradients between hues were muted. I was grateful that I had opted for undyed silks. I would have felt like a neon sign in the middle of Kansas if I had worn my usual clothes.

As it was, I still felt like something was watching me. That was always the case in the Shadow Realms, and it was usually true. No one who came here escaped the notice of the Conclave for long. I didn't have time to get dragged into their war. What I needed was a guide who could take me quickly and surreptitiously to my destinations. When you're looking to skitter unnoticed through the shadow, there's only one creature to call.

"Ghostbusters," I whispered to myself with a nervous laugh. I closed my eyes and concentrated on a dark, sleek shape about the size of a small dog, with beady, black eyes and a nervous air. I heard a scrabbling of claws in the dust and opened my eyes to see the imagined shape darting from twisted tree to shadow-whorl to rocky outcropping, nose a-twitch for the slightest hint of danger. I smiled. It had been so long since I'd last seen my friend.

"Heya, Templeton."

"Missy? Missy, it is good to see you!" His twitching rat-nose snuffled over my legs and torso as if to verify that I wasn't an illusion. He jerked like he'd received a shock and looked at me warily. "You smell strange," was his verdict. He sneezed. "Like foreign magic."

"I've been living in a pocket spirit realm for a while. I guess it'll take some time for the residue to wear off."

"You had better take care. If the Conclave lays their hands on you, they may be able to scrape off enough magic to open a portal to that realm."

"I'd like to see them try." The Conclave was high on my list of people I wouldn't mind seeing get theirs, pretty much right after Lung Di. "Something tells me they'd be biting off more than they could chew."

At Templeton's confused look, I smiled. "Let's just say that only a fool beards a dragon in its lair." The rat nodded, despite his lack of comprehension.

But I had little time for, or interest in, sniping at the powers-that-be in the Shadow Realms. "Let's try to avoid Conclave attention. I'm hoping I won't have to be here long, it's just that there are places I need to go, and this is the only way I know how to get there without being caught."

"You would like me to guide you?"

"I know it's asking a lot." I rummaged through my pack. "I don't have much I can offer in return–"

"I will do it. Of course I will. You are my friend. You gave me my name. You don't need to give me anything more. I will be happy to help."

I stopped rummaging and shot him a stunned look. Despite my recent barbs flung at Jian Huo, I had forgotten there was a time when my life wasn't ruled by debt and counter-debt. When I had friends who would help each other out because we could. I sniffled back a few tears, leaned down, and squeezed Templeton into a grateful hug. He squirmed with ratty indignation.

"Thank you," I whispered, releasing him.

"Of course. Where do you need to go?"

Where first?

"Well," I began, thinking as I did best – on my feet. "The first thing I need is another guide. You know your way around the Shadow Realms, but I need someone who knows Shanghai."

"I do not think I know anyone like that," Templeton said, confused.

"No, but I do. And I know where to find her. And she owes me big. She'll help me, one way or another."

"I cannot help you. You cannot ask me to." Si Wei's initial shock at seeing me emerge from the shadows of her living room, accompanied by a dog-sized black rat, had turned to stubborn refusal.

"Can't, or won't, Si Wei?" I demanded. She'd come to visit me at the temple a few times, given me her address in the city – a *shikumen* terrace house owned by Song Yulan – in case I needed company. In case I decided to forgive her. I don't think she expected me to come begging her aid to go behind

Jian Huo's back. She looked at me as if I'd somehow usurped her friend.

"Does it matter if the result is the same?"

"You know what Lung Di can do to Mei Shen in however long it's going to take Jian Huo to get her back. I was the only one who didn't blame you for falling for the nurse's trick, but now I need your help. Who else can I go to?"

Her amber eyes shone with unshed tears, lovely and forlorn. If it weren't my daughter at stake, I would have taken her in my arms and hushed her tears away. As it was, I remained implacable. Let her cry a thousand years of salt tears on me, she could not erode my resolve.

"Please. Lung Huang knows you have left to seek Mei Shen on your own. He has sent messengers to all his allies, telling us to turn you away or warn him of your movements. Shui Yin has promised to forsake me if I choose to honor my friendship with you over my debts to his brother."

"I thought that debt was forgiven," I countered. Guilt had knocked Si Wei off her game. Manipulating her was too easy.

"You do not understand our ways. I allowed Lung Huang's children to be taken, and he did not slay me for it. That is the debt I now owe."

"They're my children, too."

She winced, twisting her fingers, but didn't contradict me, however much she might want to. I knew what she wouldn't say; my entire plan depended on it being true. I was Schrödinger's wife until Lung Tian dispensed his judgment. I had no claim on what was Jian Huo's, neither responsibilities nor debts – nor our children. As infuriating as I might usually find this, at the moment it was a blessing. Jian Huo would not be embarrassed by any action of mine. His precious balance of power would be preserved.

"Fine," I snapped. "I suppose I'll have to get help from someone who isn't kissing dragon tail. Come on, Templeton. There's nothing more for us here." I turned away, my rat friend cowering at my side from the charged argument he had just witnessed. With one final, angry glance at Si Wei, I fell into the Shadow Realms.

Standing on the other side of the veil, I lit my candle, using the meager light to peer across the thin membrane and watch Si Wei.

Templeton stood at my other side, shying away from the light. "I am sorry about your friend, Missy. What do we do now?"

"Now? We wait," I murmured, my attention only half on him as Si Wei rushed around her room.

"But... I know you had hoped your friend would act as your guide. How are we to find our way to your other allies now?"

"I said she would guide me," I assured the rat as the fox-maiden left her home. I stepped along the same path, trailing her through the Shadow Realms. "I never said she would do so knowingly."

Following Si Wei through the shadows was not hard. The most difficult part was avoiding the dangers of the Shadow Realms: ancient nightmare monsters of void and smoke; patrols of shadow-knights serving the Conclave; scars across the landscape that bubbled and oozed with unformed horrors. The darkness crawled against my skin, seeping in bit-by-bit through my nose, my eyes, my mouth, my very pores. I had never stayed long in this awful place, and now I recalled why. I tamped down on a surge of nostalgia for my happy home in the mountains of Sichuan and concentrated instead on trailing a sad and forlorn fox-spirit who was carrying a warning against her will. My hatred of Lung Di in that moment knew no bounds. The shadows around me fed upon it and grew darker, more daring.

"Missy..." Templeton ventured, nose twitching at the growing miasma around us that was beginning to take on life of its own.

"It's fine. We're here." I wrenched in my emotions and

waited for Si Wei to deliver Jian Huo's warning. She was quick about it, and before long she had been shown to rooms for the night to rest before the next leg of her journey. I smiled at the convenience of the slow-moving wheels of Chinese hospitality. I would not have to rush through my meeting in order to catch up with Si Wei as she led me to those she thought would be most likely to help me. I waited in the shadows until my quarry was alone, puttering around his workshop, then lit one of my sparklers and blew out my candle. The flare of burning phosphor was enough to shred the darkness taking form around me. Templeton squeaked. I grabbed his ruff and yanked him through into the light world.

"Hello, Mr Dung Heap."

Fang Shih gaped row-upon-row of sharp teeth at me in his version of a smile. He didn't roar his roaring laugh at me, an indication that he understood the seriousness of the situation.

Our friendship had grown since the birth of my children, and he was one of the few spirits I'd met who was *my* friend. As a lesser spirit, he found Jian Huo's elevated company to be somewhat discomfiting, always worrying that he would somehow make a faux-pas or offer insult. My early mistake and my regular missteps since then caused him to regard me with the indulgence of a more-experienced uncle. He enjoyed the novelty of it.

Still gaping, he approached me with a series of bobbing bows.

"Miss Missy. You are welcome here. You and your friend." He nodded at Templeton, who twitched his whiskers in greeting.

"Are you sure?" I was feeling guilty over how I had manipulated Si Wei, and now I was having qualms about getting Fang Shih in trouble, too. He worked so hard to avoid the squabbles between the greater spirits. "I know you've been warned off from helping me."

"Perhaps I can help you," he said, swaying before me. "Perhaps not. But always am I happy to see a friend. Come.

Sit. We will have tea and talk as in happier days, and we will be friends. After. After, you may ask me your favors."

He pulled me to a little table strewn with odds and ends. Fang Shih was an alchemist, a craftsman at heart, and his home reflected this. He gathered up the scraps of half-finished projects onto a linen square and bundled it away before laying down cups and putting an old cast-iron kettle on to boil. Templeton and I sat as he puttered, nattering on about inconsequentials. It was so normal as to be soothing. The shadows that draped about me in a stranglehold loosened and bled away in the warmth and light of Fang Shih's presence. I drank deeply of the tea he offered, and the rhizomatic warmth chased the last remnants of bitterness away.

I contemplated the green depths of my cup for some time, letting Fang Shih's genial chatter wash over me. Templeton sniffed at his cup before deciding the strange, bright green liquid might be safe and slurping away at it.

"You should have offered this tea to Si Wei when she arrived," I observed. My original plan had been to trick Fang Shih as I had tricked the fox-girl, but I couldn't go through with it. In fact, now that my impetuous anger was draining away, my entire plan was undergoing a massive overhaul.

Fang Shih paused in his banter. His wide mouth drooped into seriousness. "She would not have accepted a brew from my leaves. She is still too full of recrimination. Perhaps if others were to forgive her, then she would begin to forgive herself. Until that time, I fear she will not feel welcome to enjoy tea with friends." There was no accusation in his tone, but I nodded my understanding. If I wanted his help, I needed to come clean with Si Wei. I needed to find some other way to locate my possible allies.

"But our own hour for genial companionship draws to a close, and you have weighty concerns. How may I aid you, *Lung Xin Niang*?"

I straightened and took a deep breath, glad to put aside the shifty terrain of guilt-ridden contemplation to focus on my mission.

"I do not come to you as *Lung Xin Niang*," I said, grateful for once that Lung Tian hadn't yet passed down his judgment. It freed me to do what I needed to do. "I am Melissa Masters – Missy – and I come to you because you are the greatest artisan that has ever lived. I need you to craft me a jewel. A jewel to tempt a Dragon."

Half an hour later, I stood outside Si Wei's door. Once I had described to Fang Shih what I needed, once I'd explained the details of my still rough plan, a mad fervor had lit his eyes and he had gone to work. No artist can resist the challenge of the impossible. I'd seen taggers nearly kill themselves trying to get at a bit of pristine underpass. Fang Shih was no different at heart.

Nothing was left but to discharge my debt, and Fang Shih had made it pretty clear how I should do that. I'd never realized he had such a soft spot for Si Wei. It made me reconsider how I had pushed to match her with Shui Yin. Fang Shih might not be much to look at, but he was solid. Didn't he deserve some hot lovin' and domestic bliss?

I shuddered at the idea of the Muppety-looking spirit getting some hot lovin' and decided that it would be best if I laid off the matchmaking for a while. I had enough worries on my plate.

Like admitting I was a manipulative ass to a dear friend.

I knocked on the wood support next to the thin, rice paper door. Something rustled, and a moment later I was looking into the wide, amber eyes of the fox-maiden. A robe of russet silk wrapped loosely around her, and the rumpled covers on the empty bed behind her indicated that sleep was eluding her.

"M– Missy?"

"Hello, Si Wei. Can I come in?" Without waiting for her

answer, I entered. She had no choice but to close the door behind me. She turned to me, mouth still working.

"How... how do you come to be here so quickly? How did you find this place so fast?"

"Yeeeaaah..." The word was long, drawn out, and twangy – a complete Americanism amidst my Cantonese. Obnoxious sound. I vowed never to make that particular noise again. "It's like this. I tricked you. I played on your worry over your debt to Jian Huo, and then I followed you here because I knew that the first thing you'd do would be to warn all my potential allies that I was coming, and I needed to find Fang Shih."

"Oh." She sank down onto the rumpled bed, hands loose at her sides as she worked through her mistake. Poor Si Wei. It must have been quite a blow to her *huxian*'s pride to be duped so thoroughly and in such quick succession by so many non-foxes. I sat next to her on the bed and took one limp hand in mine. It was cold. I rubbed the warmth back into it.

"I'm sorry. I don't want to get you into any more trouble with Jian Huo. I don't want to mess things up between you and Shui Yin. I just want to get my daughter back, and I guess I went a little crazy. I thought the easiest way to get what I needed was to play on your guilt." This was what Jian Huo was always on about: the how and the why of doing things. Some hero I'd turned out to be.

"You are within your rights to do so." Her hand remained limp in mine, her voice strained and distant. "I am to blame for your loss–"

"No." I took her by the shoulders and gave her a rough shake. She was so fragile in her distress, I might have been shaking a doll. "You're not to blame, and neither am I, or Jian Huo, or anyone else except Lung Di. He's the one who did all this. Sure, we all knew it was coming; we knew what he was and what he was capable of. Maybe we should have taken more care, but he's the one who did this. He spent years planning it. If not this way, he would have found some other way to get at Jian Huo."

She wouldn't meet my eyes. I had to try another route. "We can't let him use this to tear us apart. Because you know that's his goal, as much as anything. There were a dozen ways he could have infiltrated that nurse into Jiu Wei's house, but he chose you because he knew what it would do to you, to me, to all of us. Hell, for all we know, his real intent was to break things up between you and Shui Yin, and kidnapping Mei Shen was just the cherry on that sundae."

"I think you and I both know this is not the case," she said, but her amber eyes were beginning to burn with their old warmth.

"You never know. There're a lot of guys with the hots for you. Maybe Lung Di hopes he can get you to go all retro-tyrannical and help him rule the world."

She surprised herself with her own chuckle and sagged against me, giggling harder than my joke warranted. Relief. Had to be.

"Oh, *Huxian*," I cried in a mock voice that in no way resembled Lung Di's. "Show me who's been a bad Dragon. Whip me with your heavenly tails!"

"Shut your mouth, wyrm. Cower before my might!" She pushed me back onto the bed and loomed above me, her cruel frown spoiled every time she snorted or snickered. "Who's your *kitsune*? Say my name, bitch!"

I lost it for good then, and Si Wei joined me. Every time the laughter ebbed, one of us would catch the other's eye, and we'd be off on another round. We were left lying side-by-side, limp as noodles and groaning over our aching bellies.

"I am forgiven, then?" she asked, rolling to her hip and propping up on one elbow.

"Yes. Of course." I reached up and smudged away the tracks of tears that ran down her cheeks. These were from our hysterical laughter, but they weren't the only tears she'd shed recently. It was a simple gesture, motherly, like I would have done with Mei Shen or Mian Zi when they cried. There was nothing sexual intended in it, but when I stroked her cheek, Si Wei's breath caught. She leaned closer.

"Promise?" she whispered against my lips.

Her lips were warm, firm, yet petal soft. Her mouth tasted of spice and chocolate, rich and sweet. She pressed me into the bed, her hand skimming up my side to cup at the base of my neck, the perfect combination of aggression and deference, and I let her because I was busy trying to figure out when we'd gone from joking to serious, and when exactly we had become kissing friends, and why hadn't we become kissing friends a *long* time ago? The edges of her robe parted, revealing a line of ivory-pale flesh. She pressed against me, the heat of her body slipping through the thin silk of my robes. My nipples tightened at the feel of her breasts pressed against mine, and I fumbled for something to hold on to. To make sense of this. I dislodged the sticks holding up her hair, and it slid around us in a curtain of russet silk, smelling of ginger. I inhaled deeply. Wrong color. Wrong scent.

My libido stumbled at the thought, and I pushed back from her. I slid up the bed until I could be free of the heat of her body and the lure of her kisses. She crouched over my legs like a vixen over its prey. I gulped a deep breath and was again assailed by the scent of ginger.

"Jian Huo's on his way, isn't he?" I already suspected the answer, but the question gave me a moment to get my bearings. "You sent a message that I might be coming here, and he told you to stall me if I did."

She sat back on her heels, her pretty, oh-so-kissable – stop that! – mouth twisted into a moue. "First I am tricked by you, and now I cannot even seduce you. Perhaps I should forfeit all my tails." One slender hand trailed up my leg. I scrambled from the bed.

"Trust me," I panted, trying not to look at my friend with newly-opened eyes, and wishing like anything for a cold shower, "if it weren't Mei Shen at stake, I don't think there's a power on this earth that would stop me from–" I gulped, and inched toward the door. "Uh. Yeah. Well, you know." That's me, glib to the end. I got to the door and fumbled it open. Si Wei crouched on the bed. She didn't seem inclined to chase after me. I suppose she could assure Jian Huo that she'd used all her wiles and still failed.

"Tell Jian Huo I love him, even if he does play dirty. Oh, and tell Shui Yin he's an idiot if he lets you get away."

"I will. And Missy? After this is all over?" She cocked her head to one side, and her hair slid across her shoulders with a whisper of silk. The scent of ginger wafted toward me. She slid off the bed and closed the distance between us in a few quick steps, leaning close enough that her lips brushed my ear. "Perhaps we will... talk."

"Vixen," I grumbled as I pulled away and jogged down the hallway. Behind me came the sound of her light, teasing laughter.

My jog became a sprint as I neared Fang Shih's workshop. Like most spirits, time for him was more of a suggestion than a hard and fast rule. He had assured me that it wouldn't take long – relatively speaking – to make what I'd asked. But that same convenient temporal malleability meant that I didn't know how long I had before Jian Huo arrived. Why, with all this bendiness of time, did it threaten to take years to get Mei Shen back? Yeah, I didn't get it either. Zen *koans* were easy compared to the complex relationship that spirits had with time.

I shot into the cluttered workshop to find Fang Shih polishing his masterpiece with a soft, black cloth. He glanced up when I came in, folding the cloth around my prize and hiding it from view. He teetered over to me, scooped up my knapsack, and slipped the black-wrapped package inside. He handed me the bag with a worried look at the door.

"It is done as well as it can be. It will be up to you to make him want it. Don't let him look too closely, or all will be revealed. And take care you do not harm yourself on it. There are dark magics woven into it that blood is sure to awaken."

"I won't. I won't. Thank you." I bent to give him a quick hug, which he tolerated with a grudging *humph* of breath.

"Templeton?" I called out, looking around. A sack under one of the workbenches rustled, and the rat came tumbling out in a stream of multicolored gems.

"I have found them, Missy. The very best of the lot!" His whiskers twitched with excitement. I eyeballed the pile of stones around him, sparkling with rainbow fire. I doubt he'd ever seen such an array of colors in all his ratty life in the Shadow Realms. He held out trembling paws, which were clasped around three stones. I bent down to inspect his prizes. Slowly, as if worried they would be snatched away, he opened his paws.

The first bauble was a bit of coral, violently pinkish-orange and twisted into an agonized shape of bony knobs and hollows. The second was a misshapen fire opal, the fractured face alight with licks of green, blue, red, and violet flame. The third was a thick chunk of bottle-green glass, edges softened by years of immersion in saltwater, thick bubbles of imperfection frozen forever under its liquid-clear surface.

I glanced again at the pile of cut diamonds, rubies, sapphires, and emeralds that surrounded him. A dozen types of lesser stones – topaz, amethyst, aquamarine – winked at me as well. Templeton shook his paws with an exasperated grunt, as if unable to understand how I could tear my gaze away from his treasures to look at the dross beneath him.

"You're... sure?" I asked.

"Yes. These are the best. The very best." He tore his earnest gaze from mine to look in wonder at the baubles. "I have never seen anything more beautiful," he whispered.

"All right then," I said with a conviction I did not feel. It only mattered that Templeton thought they were. The baubles were just part of the pledge in the bit of sleight-of-hand I was putting together. I turned to our host with a resigned sigh. "Fang Shih?"

While we inspected Templeton's treasures, the other spirit had cocked his head to one side, as if listening to some distant sound. Now he turned back to me, eyes wide. "Yes. Yes, take them. Only go. Now!"

My response was cut off by a loud, angry roar. It reverberated through the entire workshop, coming from everywhere and nowhere at once. I cringed away from it. Templeton squeaked and jumped about five feet straight up, nearly losing his death grip on his baubles. Even Fang Shih flinched.

"Go," the spirit urged.

"Right. Thank you. C'mon Templeton." I reached down to grasp the rat by his scruff and took two steps toward a shadow cast by a large brazier. My move put me in line-of-sight of the door; without thinking, I glanced down the hallway.

The building shuddered with another roar. Lung Huang – I could not imagine this ancient, angry god as Jian Huo – snaked down the hall in a rush of wind and wet. He filled the entire passage. The scales of his sinuous red, green, and gold form shredded the thin paper walls, digging long furrows into the wood supports. Tiny storm clouds roiled around him, complete with miniature chains of lightning. His eyes burned with rage.

"MISSY!" he roared, closing the distance between us. With an apologetic grimace, I tightened my hold on my rat and my pack and stepped into Shadow.

"I do not think your monster is coming, Missy," Templeton said, so quiet, and with so many huffs leading up to it, that I wondered how long he'd been gathering up the courage to tell me what I already knew.

"It's not a monster, Templeton. It's a *qilin*," I explained through gritted teeth.

"You've said it is a creature of shining light?"

"And purity, yeah."

"Sounds like a monster to me," he muttered. I guess the shadow rat had a point.

I shoved away from the deadfall log I'd been sitting on. Templeton didn't deserve my frustration. I'd frittered away the night in a futile attempt to salvage my plan. The sun was coming up, and I hadn't managed anything more effective than fiddling with my pearls. I could have done that just fine at Jiu Wei's temple.

"I think you're right," I conceded. "I don't think she's coming."

"Then we can leave this place?" Templeton's paws clenched around his baubles, his whiskers twitching with enthusiasm for this new plan that didn't involve monsters of light.

"This place" was a clearing in a nature park somewhere in southwest Shanghai, unremarkable and indistinguishable from a thousand other city parks except that it seemed more earnest to me – but that just came from too many viewings of *It's the Great Pumpkin, Charlie Brown!* on my part. We had passed the night here uninterrupted. Dawn threatened in the east, greeted by the calls of herons and the chirp of crickets.

Without my plan to follow Si Wei, I was pretty much floundering. The earnest park clearing was my A-list material at this point, and I didn't have a B-list. The extended solitary time – Templeton didn't count – hadn't worked to my benefit. I'd fretted away any peace I'd found at Fang Shih's table. If pearls weren't so resilient, I would have worn away all the nacre on mine.

I stalked to the edge of the clearing, kicked at a bit of moss. It tore from its moorings, disintegrating it from a lush, green furze into a lump of black dirt and roots. I crossed my arms to keep myself from shredding every leaf from every bush surrounding the clearing.

"Dammit," I whispered. "Why won't you come? You promised me. You were supposed to protect her. You were supposed to keep her safe." I didn't know whether I was more angry at the *qilin* or myself. *Why* hadn't I listened to my daughter?

I took a deep breath past my guilt and fear. Then another, and another. Each breath came easier. I'd hoped for a back-up, a safety net, but that didn't look like it was going to be an option. I had all the aid I was going to get. If I waited any longer, I'd never screw up my courage. It was time. Untwisting my pearls, I reached up and fastened them around my neck.

"C'mon, Templeton. If she was willing to come, she'd have been here by now. We're as ready as we're going to be. Let's go." The rat clutched his baubles to his chest and trundled to my side on three paws. I took one last, deep breath and stepped once more into Shadow, leaving nothing in our wake but the shirring chirp of crickets.

ELEVEN
Outlaws

Now

"I see you've found each other," Song Yulan drawled from a stone bench as Mei Shen helped me limp into the temple. My daughter had hushed my sputtered *how... what... whys* with a wary glance at the sky and a shake of her head. David Tsung might have helped her support my battered body, but I scared him off with a glare.

I wasn't much happier with Song Yulan. "You could have said Mei Shen was here."

"I could have." She uncrossed her legs and rose from the bench. "She asked me not to."

"I wanted to surprise you," Mei Shen said. She couldn't stop bouncing, and I couldn't stop hugging her. She'd cut her hair into a bob similar to Song Yulan's. So modern. A typical Shanghai girl, if you ignored the dragon thing.

"Your father must be worried sick," I grumbled, smoothing her hair. "Is he... here?" I wasn't sure which answer I dreaded more. A yes, or a no.

"No..." Her gaze drifted from mine. She pushed my hands away.

"What aren't you telling me?" Fear slammed my stomach into the floor. I swayed on my feet. "He's not one of the trapped guardians?"

It had to be one of them, and Jian Huo made the most sense, but I'd hoped...

I don't know what I'd hoped.

Mei Shen caught me. "No! It's not that. Mian Zi..."

Worse. I exhaled and couldn't breathe again. A tremble started deep in my bones. He'd taken my daughter, and now he'd taken my son.

I turned to march right back out that door. Fuck them all. I would go to the People's Heroes and make them let me through into Lung Di's sanctum.

"Mother, wait–"

Before she could pull me back, light flashed through the windows, golden as a summer afternoon and green as a bamboo forest. The temple doors blew open. I shielded my eyes against the bright assault. The flames passed, leaving a lean figure in silhouette against the afterburn.

I blinked. Stumbled forward. The young man caught me before I could fall.

"Hello, Mother."

He was safe. I smoothed his hair like I had Mei Shen's. Still long, like his father's. Mian Zi frowned and squirmed, just as his sister had, which made me sniffle some more. Some adventure hero I was. "She said you'd been taken."

Mian Zi stiffened, his head jerked up so he could glare at his sister. "So he's got you lying now, too?"

Mei Shen huffed. "I didn't say that. She misunderstood."

"Who's got what lying now?" I pulled back to look between them. Mian Zi stood stiff and cool and distant in a suit that bore a little too much resemblance to a Mao suit for my taste. Mei Shen leaned forward, fists clenching and unclenching, chin thrust up. Begging for him to throw the first strike.

Mian Zi never went physical when a cerebral attack would do. "Mei Shen didn't bother to mention that she's taken over leadership of the Shadow Dragon Triad?"

I glanced at Song Yulan. She shrugged. I probably should have put it together earlier, but I'd never expected... Mei Shen.

Mei Shen took a step toward her brother. "Well, somebody had to do something besides sitting on their ass pushing papers all day."

Mian Zi met her halfway, his posture a mirror of hers. "I'm protecting China–"

"You're playing *wei-qi* with people's lives."

"And you're infatuated with a collection of murderers and thieves."

"The Outlaws are heroes–"

"You mean *hanjian* –"

"*Enough!*" They both shut up. Mom voice. I still have it.

I ran my hands over my hair, still braided tight enough to give me a headache. Or maybe that was a combination of the crash and the reunion and my children fighting. This was Lung Di's doing; it had to be. Mian Zi and Mei Shen had been devoted to each other as only twins could be. Only someone as insidious and manipulative as Lung Di could change that.

"What's going on with you two? Do I have to find out where your rooms are so I can send you to them?"

Two sets of Masters-blue eyes wouldn't meet mine. Mei Shen twisted the gold foil hem of her blouse. "No."

Mian Zi stretched his neck as though his collar was too tight. "That will be unnecessary, Mother."

"OK then." Not a resolution. Just a truce. Whatever had come between them dug deep. I shouldn't have left, shouldn't have stayed away for so long, no matter how much it hurt.

"I want to know what's going on. Why did you take over the Shadow Dragons?" I asked Mei Shen, then turned to her brother. "And why aren't you helping her since she did? Who does Lung Di have hostage, if not one of you or your father?"

I held up my hand when they would have both spoken at once. "One at a time. You first." I pointed at Mei Shen, since she'd explode with impatience if she didn't go first. Mian Zi wouldn't mind; he preferred taking the rebuttal.

"You were right," Tsung whispered in aside to Song Yulan. "She's good."

The Guardian sighed. "Perhaps we might finally get a reasonable conversation between them."

Mei Shen planted her fists on her hips. "Mian Zi realized the Guardians were in trouble when Feng Huang stopped visiting. I knew it had to be uncle, so I came to Shanghai. I met David, and he confirmed everything."

"Just like that?" I cast a glare in Tsung's direction. How convenient.

Mian Zi had waited long enough. "You see? Mother doesn't trust him either. You are the only one he has managed to fool."

I flinched. No wonder Mei Shen was being obstinate if that was the reception she was getting.

"Has David given us any reason to distrust him? He brought the key. He brought Mother, just as he said he would."

"It was his suggestion to bring her."

"It was my idea."

"At his suggestion."

"If you would have let him into Lung Di's sanctum, we wouldn't have had to find somebody else you approved of."

I stepped between them to cut off their squabbling. "Why is it Mian Zi's fault that you can't get to Lung Di?"

"He–"

"I–"

Mei Shen flicked a hand for her brother to explain.

"Because when Tsung helped Mei Shen take over the Shadow Dragons, I had no choice but to take charge of the People's Heroes to stop them."

I froze. Blinked. He said it like it was no big deal.

"You took over the People's Heroes."

"Of course."

I sputtered as I tried to make sense of that. My son, who had lived his entire life reading and playing *wei-qi* in a valley in Sichuan, was the head of one of the world's most powerful private armies. A dragon was the Commander of China's shining example of the modern secular state. I gave up trying to come up with a coherent response to that. "Of course," Mian Zi had said, and who were any of us to argue with such clarity of purpose?

My kids scared me sometimes.

"You." David Tsung tensed when I turned to him, his expression closing off. "Where's Skyrocket?"

"Safe. Jiu Wei is tending to him."

I wasn't sure if leaving the boy with a *huxian* constituted "safe", but it was safer than being left in the Shadow Realms. "What happened?"

"He was out when I found him. No injuries I could see, but the Conclave knights were approaching. I assumed you could take care of yourself, so I got us out of there."

So the rescue on the bridge hadn't been a fluke. He knew the Shadow Realms well enough to fear the knights, and he'd saved Skyrocket when he could have left the Ace behind.

I dropped my head into my hands. I needed a shower and an aspirin and possibly a shotgun to the head. I pressed fingers hard against my browbone. "If you're Lung Di's blood, his protégé, why help us? Why betray him?"

"Because some things are more important than power."

I raised my head to catch him looking at Mei Shen in a way that made me wish for that shotgun even more.

"She's your *cousin*."

"Mother!" Mei Shen wailed.

"Distant." Tsung took my daughter's hand.

"She's underage!"

"Is she?"

Mei Shen threw up her hands. "I can't believe you. You're as bad as Mian Zi."

And then it clicked. All this squabbling and sniping and sibling rivalry. David Tsung was the wedge that had come between Mei Shen and Mian Zi. The question was, had he done so of his own choice, or at Lung Di's behest? I hoped for his continued health and well-being that it was the former.

I looked to Song Yulan for help. "What do you think of all of this?"

"I think that it distracts from the larger issue, which is perhaps exactly what Lung Di intended." She raised a brow at Mei Shen, who thrust her chin up and stepped closer to Tsung. Mian Zi shifted to stand at my shoulder.

Lovely. A face-off. I stepped away so that I stood between them. An arbiter rather than an ally. We still had a common foe. "Have either of you bothered to sit down and talk?"

"I do not see the point–"

"He won't listen."

"*I* will listen." I turned to Mei Shen, who presented me with the same mulish chin she'd been giving Mian Zi. "I am not wild about the idea of confronting your uncle again, especially since that seems to be what he wants; however," I included Mian Zi in my glare when he snorted. "Nor am I so quick to trust Mr Tsung's motives. So we will sit down and I will listen to your arguments about how we should take down the barrier, and whatever I decide is what we'll do. Agreed?"

Neither of them seemed inclined to agree, but Mei Shen nodded under my glare. Mian Zi remained stiff.

"My people are already on their way here," he said.

"The more the merrier."

The knowledge that he would not be alone on his side of the table seemed to relax Mian Zi. He held out my hat to me. "Then perhaps you will need this? I recovered it from the crash. They are expecting Mr Mystic."

I took the hat and groaned. Mitchell Masters seemed as far

away as a dream at the moment. Song Yulan saved me, taking my arm.

"Come along. We'll see if we can get you a shower at least, and perhaps you'll want to check in on your flying fellow?" I thought it was just a delaying tactic, but Song Yulan was wilier than that. "David, why don't you go and let Jiu Wei know that we'll be needing somewhere to hold our little war council?"

Neither of my kids looked pleased when they realized this would leave them alone with the other, but David Tsung slunk away under the commanding gaze of the Guardian of Shanghai.

I followed Song Yulan out of the room. "You're good."

She sighed. "I'm passable. If I were good, I would never have allowed things to come to this pass. Come along. Let's see if we can give you a moment to breathe."

The space to think was a little less welcome when it turned out to be the same prison of misery I'd stayed in the last time I'd been to Shanghai. The decor had changed, and Jiu Wei had added the modern amenity of a bathroom, but I'd stared at these walls for too long to mistake them.

Was I seriously considering bearding the dragon in his lair? Again? With less of a plan than last time?

I avoided answering that question by staying in the shower until my fingers were pruny, only leaving when the hot water gave out.

Song Yulan was waiting for me. With a fresh suit, so I was less inclined to tell her to get lost.

She remained silent as I dressed. I could only take it for so long. "Any advice on how to get them to see reason?" I asked as I settled before the cheval mirror. I hated braiding my hair when it was wet, but it did make for a tighter braid. I winced a few times when the wet strands clung to my fingers. Someday, I was just going to cut it all off and have done.

"You assume that they aren't seeing reason. Perhaps it

was unreasonable for you to expect that they would always remain devoted to each other. They are Yin and Yang. Conflict was inevitable. Here, let me do that. Watching you makes my scalp hurt."

I lowered my arms and tilted my head to give her better access. She was right, but that didn't solve anything. I was going to have to convince them to do things my way with something stronger than a *"because I said so"*.

"You think this is silly, don't you? Mr Mystic, I mean."

"I wonder why you think it is necessary." She grabbed a hairband from the pile of pins I'd removed before my shower. She was too good at this. I suspected she'd done time as a boy during her long tenure as Guardian.

I took my wig from her when she would have pulled it on. She sat on the edge of the bed and crossed her legs, leaning forward to watch my transformation with avid interest.

I didn't even let Shimizu watch this. I turned my back on Song Yulan and tried to ignore the discomfort that came with such intimacy. "It made sense at the time. I'd just gotten back. Nobody was taking me seriously. It drove me mad. Everything that I'd gone through, everything I'd learned, it started to feel like a dream. I joked to a friend that I felt so old, more like my grandfather than myself. She said that at least my grandfather commanded respect. And she was right. From that conversation, Mr Mystic was reborn."

As I spoke, I deepened my voice, lengthened my vowels, let my Rs recede and my consonants become crisp to the point of being clipped. Mr Mystic's voice, coming from deeper in my chest and sitting richer and fuller in my mouth. A voice made for drawling and considered words.

"It is an impressive transformation," Song Yulan said. Quite a compliment, given that she had a front seat for the process.

I paused in the act of tying a half-windsor. "How well did you know him?" I asked her reflection.

Her nails clacked together. "Hardly at all. I'm afraid I have no secrets to share, if that's what you're after."

I lifted my hat, ran my hands along the inside to smooth out bumps, both real and imagined. It smelled a little scorched, possibly from the car crash. I'd taken more than my share of knocks these past few days. "I find myself less and less interested in learning his secrets. It is only that I wonder what he would have done in this situation."

The clacking stopped. Song Yulan rose and took the hat from me, flicking dust from the brim. "He would have walked away. Your grandfather was Lung Huang's champion. He avoided confrontation with Lung Di at all costs."

The more I learned about him, the more I wondered just how much of a hero Mitchell Masters had been. Perhaps he and Argent were more suited to each other than I'd thought.

I retrieved my trench coat and checked the pocket. The silk-wrapped knife was still there. I pulled it out. Looked up at Song Yulan. "I wonder if you might do me a favor."

She set my hat atop my head and tapped the brim with one long nail to give it a rakish tilt.

"Depends upon the favor."

After sending Song Yulan on her errand, I quizzed a few fox ladies and found my way to Skyrocket's recovery room. Jiu Wei was tending him herself, her white hair rolled up in a rat-and-snood, the back of her white nurse's uniform twitching as she bustled around his bed, plumping pillows and straightening covers.

At least somebody was amusing herself in the midst of all this.

She stopped fussing as I entered, amber eyes laughing as she sashayed out the door. "Don't tire him out."

I watched Skyrocket watch her depart.

"Now that is one pretty little lady."

Oh lord. Make that two people amusing themselves. I felt compelled to give him some kind of warning. After all, Sylvia had put him in my care. "Down boy. She's old enough to be your grandmother." And far older than that.

Skyrocket sighed and tore his gaze from the empty doorway. "Always did like a lady with a little bit of mileage."

I pinched the bridge of my nose. On his own head be it.

"Speaking of. How's the *Kestrel*." From the forced cheer, I had a feeling he already knew. Asking was pro forma.

I perched on the edge of the bed. "I think I'm required not to tell you. For your health. No sudden shocks and all that. How are you feeling, my boy?"

"Like Samson after a trip to Supercuts. Can't even say the other guy looked worse. Sorry I let you down, old man. Don't know what happened. One moment I felt fine, the next, like I was flying through molasses. Knocked out by a crash landing." He shook his head. His color was still off – a peaked grey under the sun-kissed skin. "My rep'll be in the can after this."

"I won't let it get about."

"Still leaves the other fellow. Tsung."

"He won't let it get about, either." I'd make sure of it.

"So, what's the sit-rep?"

Always the soldier. No. Always the hero, even when he was down. Hard not to be inspired by that. "I'm heading into a sit-down with the two big power players here. One group wants David Tsung to go in and take down the New Wall. The other supports me. I'm going to listen to their pros and cons, and they've agreed to abide by my decision."

"Seems like a no-brainer to me. I trust you a lot more than that other fellow. Even if he did haul my ass out of hell."

"But you are not Chinese. We are the intruders here. Just because I *can* be the one to go in doesn't mean I should be. 'The wise man prefers the left; the man of war prefers the right'."

"Mind putting that in plain speak for me?"

"My apologies. The Tao helps me think. It means that peace favors the creative solution, and the creative solution often leads to peace."

"The Tao. I get that. It's Johnny Cash for me."

That surprised a laugh from me. "There's a good deal of crossover between the two, now that I think on it. What do you think Mr Cash would say about this situation?"

"Something 'bout the guy on the right and the guy on the left and the guy in the back being a Methodist. Which means don't bring in politics when you're starting a folk band."

I laughed and shook my head. "A very sage man is Johnny Cash."

Mian Zi met me at the door to the conference room, gave me a once over, and sighed with only a minimal brow twitch – just as his father might have done.

"I might say the same thing about your costume," I drawled. He didn't rise to my baiting – likely a good thing, since we were supposed to be on the same side. "Have your people arrived?"

"Some time ago. They're waiting inside." He opened the door and gestured for me to precede him. Yangtze and the monk from my earlier capture rose at our entry, along with several other men and women in near-identical suits. "Where is Mei Shen?"

I paused on the threshold. "Last I knew, she was glaring daggers at you."

Mian Zi frowned. "She went to get you when they arrived. Ten minutes ago, at least."

That didn't sound good. Jiu Wei's temple wasn't that big, and I'd left a string of *huxian* in my wake who knew I'd gone to visit Tom.

"Bollocks," I muttered, because I had a fair idea where she must have gone and who she must have taken with her.

As if on cue, several phones rang. The suits answered, buzzing into them. Mian Zi didn't need to know the details to figure out what was wrong.

"She lied." He spun and charged back towards the front doors of the temple.

"Mian Zi, wait." I hurried after him.

"For what? She promised. She said she would abide by your decision. Do you see what she has become? What her association with that man has made her?"

"This is pure Mei Shen, and you're upset because you should have guessed she'd do this. We both should have." When hadn't Mei Shen been one to take advantage of opportunity? She was a tactician where Mian Zi was a strategist. I should have known better than to trust that docile nod. What better time to make a run on Lung Di's sanctum than when Mian Zi was away and occupied? "We still need to talk–"

"No. I have tried talking. I have been reasonable. The longer I delay, the greater the chance that she will make herself more of a tool of that man and our uncle. Now is the time to put a stop to this for good."

He thrust open the temple doors. With a flash of green and gold, he took to the skies, leaving me with the queasy certainty that his "for good" would not be to anyone's good at all.

I turned to find the ranking agents of the People's Heroes arrayed behind me, gawking at their commander's departure.

"I don't suppose any of you have a way to get across the river quickly?"

Seven Lotus Petals Falling lowered his phone long enough to answer. "We have cars."

Of course. And I'd already been given a firsthand demonstration of the traffic issues in Shanghai. By the time we arrived by car, the fight would be decided. And what would David Tsung be doing while Mian Zi fought Mei Shen? He wanted to get into Lung Di's sanctum, that was clear. Whatever the reason, I had to stop him. Had to get there first.

Song Yulan flowed into being in the midst of the confusion,

and a moment later, Fang Shih trundled through the half-open temple doors. The suits fell back before the squat spirit with grunts of surprise. Yangtze huffed and crossed her arms, and the monk bowed to Fang Shih.

"I feel like we might have missed something," Song Yulan said, as she took in the muttering agents.

"Mei Shen and David Tsung decided to use the delay to have a go at Lung Di's sanctum. Mian Zi left to stop them," I said.

"That girl." Song Yulan sighed and shook her head.

We could commiserate later. I bowed to Fang Shih, who gaped and blinked at me. Had Song Yulan neglected to explain my guise? Lovely.

"The knife?" I prodded, hoping that getting to business would distract him from giving me away.

"Oh. Yes. Yes." He held it out to me atop its wrappings of silk. "It is as it always was. There is no new magic on it that would make it a key. And such a purpose wouldn't settle easily on it in any case. It's a tool of deception, not of warding."

I ground my teeth to keep back all the curses I wanted to give vent to, because most of them would have been directed at myself rather than Fang Shih or the others. Deception. I should have known. I *had* known, and I'd worked with Tsung anyways.

I didn't know his game, but I knew how to stop him. I took the knife from Fang Shih, wrapped it back up in the silk, and pocketed it.

"Song Yulan, I need you to find Tsung and guide me to him. The rest of you, take the cars and head to Lung Di's tower. Except for you, Seven Lotus Petals Falling. You follow me."

He obeyed, glancing back at his fellows as I led the way through the temple. "Where are we going?"

"To see a man about a ride," I said, pushing open the door to Skyrocket's room.

•••

Skyrocket couldn't carry the both of us. "Not even on a good day, and this ain't one of those," he said with a shake of his head as Jiu Wei helped him on with his pack in the courtyard of the temple.

"I promise you, I'm lighter than I look—"

"Not a matter of weight. It's a matter of grip. Only got two hands. Something goes wrong, I don't want to drop you in the river." He cocked his head, grinned a strained version of that Colgate grin. "Well, maybe you, Old Man. But not the other fellow. He seems pretty decent."

At this rate, it might have been wiser to take the cars. "Fine. After you drop me off, come back for him." I turned to Seven Lotus Petals Falling. "Be ready. I'll do my best to delay Tsung."

The monk bowed. I took a deep breath to prepare myself for this new madness. "Let's go."

"Aye, sir." And then Tom surprised us all, save perhaps for Jiu Wei, when he bent the nine-tailed *huxian* back in a classic first-ashore kiss. She came up giggling. He tapped her nose and scooped me up beneath my arms.

"Always wanted to do that."

"I am going to go back in time and castrate Sa- aaaahhhhh!" My scream rose in pitch and register as Skyrocket took off, before I recalled that perhaps such a howl was a tad unmanly even for myself. I clamped my lips tight and resisted the urge to jerk my legs up every time we passed over a building taller than two stories. My protests aside, I didn't particularly want to be dropped in the middle of the Huangpu.

Lung Di's tower curved into the sky with a gentle, serpentine twist, smoke-glass windows glimmering like scales in the nighttime lights of Shanghai.

"That's quite a light show."

No mistaking what Tom was referring to. Red, gold, and green explosions burst around the serpentine twist of the tower like a localized storm, breaking my heart with every flash.

"Not our problem," I yelled over the wind and the noise of Skyrocket's jetpack. As much as I wanted to stop the battle, I didn't want to attract Mei Shen's attention. She'd only stop me from dealing with David Tsung. I spied Song Yulan at the base of the building, next to an open service entrance. "Down there."

I stumbled as Skyrocket released me without touching down himself. Song Yulan caught and steadied me. Tom streaked off again before I could tell him to hurry.

"Tsung?" I asked Song Yulan as she led me into fluorescent-lit hallways.

"Already at the basement ward. The PHC troops slowed him down a bit."

"No idea what he wants?"

"Other than to beat you to Lung Di's sanctum?" She shook her head. "You should save your breath. It's a long way down."

We slipped into an atrium. The peaked and faceted glass roof slithered up and around the building's core like a constrictor. I broke out in a sweat, my little mammalian hind-brain sending all sorts of conflicting signals – *freeze, run, hide, fight!* – as it bought into the illusion that I was trapped and immobile until the serpent could consume me. For all my bravado, I didn't feel up to facing off with Lung Di. At least the last time I'd had a plan. Now, I was just a mouse in his coils, scrabbling to get free of something too big to grasp.

Bursts of flame and smoke broke the cobalt darkness of the night sky beyond the atrium. Water rained down and spattered against the glass, breaking the light into fractals of reflection and shadow.

Maybe my death would heal the rift between my children. Bring them together against their common foe. Except I didn't think Lung Di wanted me dead. He was too complicated a villain for something so straightforward.

"I want an easier nemesis," I muttered

"Pardon?"

"Nothing. Just wishing for horses."

Song Yulan didn't bother to answer, didn't pause to gape at the battle above. She hurried across the empty lobby, feet silent on the marble. Only her palazzo pants made any sound, the silk swishing against itself. I pulled my hat lower and followed. We rounded a corner to the elevator lobby at the same time a contingent of four guards burst out of one of the bays. I ducked back as they raised their rifles, but I needn't have bothered. Song Yulan pulled out a prayer strip from somewhere and threw it at them. The curling ribbon of paper burst into a cloud of dandelion fluff that drifted down onto the guards. One of them had a moment to get off a yawn before all four collapsed into a snoring pile.

Song Yulan skirted the pile and avoided the elevators in favor of the stairwell.

The sounds of fighting reached us long before we reached the bottom floor. My thighs and calves burned from clattering down so many flights, and my knee was not terribly happy, but at least we were going down rather than up. Song Yulan didn't bother with the stairs. She just popped to the bottom of every flight and waited for me with nails clacking against the railing. I was starting to resent her as much as I did Johnny Cho.

I came down hard on the bottom landing; we'd been descending for so long that conditioning made my body expect there would be another step beyond. I caught my stumble before it could turn into a roll. Song Yulan helped steady me.

"Your friend has arrived with Seven Lotus Petals Falling."

"Go. Get him. I should be fine for a few minutes."

She arched one brow but faded from view without comment, leaving me in the stairwell with the sounds of fighting coming from the room beyond.

Time to give the PHC a hand.

I opened the door quietly, hoping to have a moment to assess before I was dragged into the fight. David Tsung was surrounded by five men in black suits, but he still seemed to have the upper hand. Several more bodies lay unconscious or dead where they'd fallen, and at least two of the standing fighters were limping. The room had poured concrete floors and the same cinderblock walls and fast-flickering fluorescent lighting as the stairwell. I felt another headache coming on. Centered on the far side of the room stood a portal made of darkness: the entry to Lung Di's sanctum, ebony frame carved with even darker sigils that had no meaning I could discern beyond being really fucking creepy. I snorted. God, he was such a melodramatic hack.

Now that I had seen it, I could sense that door like an itch in my brain. Calling Shadow here would be a Very. Bad. Idea.

One of the suits noticed me and was wise enough to back off. The others followed his example, and Tsung turned to face me.

"Give it up, Mr Tsung. Mei Shen was your only ally, and she's busy."

"Masters." He paused, perhaps to catch his breath, perhaps calculating the value of giving up my identity. I wasn't worried. I had no doubt that Mian Zi could ensure the silence of the people in this room – without killing them.

Tsung must have realized the same. He continued without giving me away. "I won't let you be the one to go in there."

"Why not? Just give me a good reason." I stepped around him. Not enough time to go for the door before he could catch me, and that didn't even get into the danger of crossing over in this place where the level of nasty on the other side of the veil was even worse than the things that waited outside Jian Huo's realm. "But you could have done that at the meeting at Jiu Wei's temple, which tells me there isn't any good reason."

"You're quick to assume I'm the bad guy."

"You left Song Yulan to work for Lung Di. It's a pretty damning association."

"Three years ago, there were stirrings among the Shadow Dragons. Something big. Something hidden. I needed to find out what he was up to, and going to him was the only way to find out."

Three years ago. I'd been gone from China for three years. "You can't believe he trusted you."

"My defection was useful to him. My purpose didn't matter."

"So you know he's playing you."

"I like to think we're playing each other."

"And now you're playing the rest of us. You really expect me to buy all this?"

"I don't care what you buy. Mei Shen trusts me. You should trust your daughter. Or is it only Mian Zi whom you trust? The rationalist. The boy."

He might as well have just come out and called me a hypocrite. "And you think an *ad hominem* attack is going to help you make your case? Have you told Mei Shen whatever it is you won't tell me?" He flinched. I nodded. "I didn't think so. Mei Shen doesn't trust you. She just knows that I shouldn't go. You're her unpleasant alternative. My daughter is wiser than us all."

"And yet you're ready to ignore her concerns and play into Lung Di's plans?"

"Because Mian Zi is right, too. He knows that whatever's going on, I'll do what's best for everyone. You'll do what's best for you." We'd stopped circling, each of us equidistant from the door. I waited for his next sally, watched for an attack. Where the hell were Song Yulan and the monk?

"I suppose if that's how you feel, the meeting was pointless from the beginning." He tensed, but not for an attack as I'd expected.

My stomach flipped with nausea, and a chill washed over me like a bucket of spiders dumped over my head – the familiar feeling of shadow being brought forth. No. He wasn't. Not *here*.

Nobody was that stupid.

Creatures more void than shadow pulled themselves up off the ground into hulking shadow-behemoths. Snakes of darkness slithered out of the pockmarks in the cinderblock walls and dripped down from cracks in the ceiling. The background whispers and chitterings of the Shadow Realms crescendoed in volume somewhere between a cicada swarm and an alien invasion.

The People's Heroes cried out as the dark shapes formed from nothing. One man cowered in the space between the door and the open wall. Bad call. Tendrils of inky black slid out from under the door, the thin space alongside the frame, the spiral grooves of the hinges. He slapped at them, a grown man and trained fighter as terrified as young Billy Westmont from Potrero Hill. He had more cause. These shadows were sharks compared to the guppies I usually called.

"No," I whispered, watching the shadows multiply. No matter how many I tried to send back, there would be more. That was the nature of unformed, uncontrolled shadow. I tried anyway, but it was as I'd feared; the shadows eluded me. We were too close to Lung Di's sanctum. These monsters had another master. A stronger one than either Tsung or myself.

"You are fucking insane." Even if I shut the door to the stairwell, the shadows would break free and be loosed into Shanghai. So many. So awful.

"And you should probably deal with this rather than call me names." David Tsung strode to the portal. The sigils on the frame writhed, the darkness of the ward rippling like oil.

I lunged for him, knowing I'd be too late to stop him. I flinched as a flash like sunlight streaked past me and hit Tsung mid-back. He grunted, stumbled, hit the ward–

And bounced back off of it. We collided and tumbled to the ground. The shadows around us hissed and recoiled from the light.

I glanced back over my shoulder. Seven Lotus Petals Falling rushed through the doorway, followed by Song Yulan and a peaked-looking Skyrocket wielding a gun that would be completely useless against the shadow-threat.

I pushed Tsung's limp form off me, and Song Yulan hauled me to my feet. "Go. Quickly."

Already, the shadows were amassing, their pulsing tendrils and wisps coming together to form larger, more threatening shapes. "I can't leave you here with them."

"Can you banish them?"

I shook my head. "They only answer to one master."

"Then better that you go and finish this business with the New Wall. Hurry. We'll hold them here as long as we can."

Seven Lotus Petals Falling stepped up beside us and tossed a prayer strip in the direction of the man cowering in the shadow of the doorway. The strip uncurled in a burst of warm yellow light, driving the shadows back from the poor man. One of the other men slammed the door shut and grabbed his friend, pulling him into the small knot of defenders forming before the doorway.

"Go!" Song Yulan shoved me towards the portal. "Do not fail."

TWELVE
Enter the Other Dragon

Then

The hag had been correct. The moment I stepped out of the shadows on the Puxi side of the Huangpu, I knew which building housed Lung Di's sanctum. It fit into the eclectic skyline of Shanghai's financial district by standing out: a glass serpent twisting up from the earth to challenge the heavens. The smoked glass sides were limned with violet-blue neon.

Nobody stopped me as I entered the building and headed for the elevators. I wasn't even sure the lobby guards noticed me. The car took Templeton and me down no matter how many buttons I pushed, so at least one person had noticed me.

I don't know what I expected when I stepped out of the elevator and into Lung Di's realm – some dark corner of hell, crawling with vermin and rife with human suffering, I suppose – but reality didn't comply. A passage from the elevator lobby led to a series of large, water-smoothed caverns. Phosphorescent algae grew along the rivulets of water that trickled down the arching walls. Most people would have thought themselves in pitch blackness, but I had an affinity for darkness. The light from the algae was as bright to me as starlight in the desert. It played off the colors of the stone, jewelling the cavern in glowing viridian greens, cobalt blues, and shadow-spars of deepest amethyst. Templeton and I both drew breath in wonder at the beauty.

"I am happy to see that my realm pleases you."

The voice emerged from a pocket of shadow so deep that not even my eyes could pierce it. A figure stepped out of the shadow, and I had to force myself not to take a step back. Templeton cowered between my legs.

It was the first time I'd seen him in over a decade, the first time I'd ever seen him up close. During the *Zi Gong Hu*, I had been so anxious and flustered that I'd hardly registered his looks, beyond a generic handsome. Now I had to revise that impression.

He was taller than most Chinese men I'd met. Long face, high cheekbones – classic Han features. He could as easily have passed for a hero as a villain. He wore a tailored suit of charcoal grey, a crisp, white dress shirt, and a tie of cobalt blue. A tie-tack of smoked platinum winked at me in the dim light of the cavern. I had to do a double-take. The contemporary clothes were so out-of-keeping with the life I led – the world I'd thought he inhabited – that they made me self-conscious. I tugged at the hem of my Shaolin robes, which I'd been wearing for almost two days. I hated that he could make me feel so awkward.

"It's lovely," I conceded, then couldn't keep myself from adding: "Like a shiny apple with a worm inside."

He surprised me again by laughing – a real laugh with no menace whatsoever. Oh, he was good.

"You mean to be insulting, but it is no more than the truth. A worm. It is not much of an improvement over a pig or a carp. The inventiveness of mortals when it comes to our ancestry never fails to amuse me." He was smiling.

"Yeah," I grumbled. "We're a hoot. Where's my daughter?"

His laughter ebbed. His dark eyes glittered, but I couldn't tell if it was from humor or anger, or just a reflection of the algae.

Templeton wisely continued to cower.

"Come, Missy." He stepped closer, nudging the edge of my personal space. I held my ground. "You know that there are formalities that must be observed. You know how we spirits love our little rituals. Won't you indulge me? Nobody will anymore."

"I guess you should have thought of that before you became a murdering, thieving psychopath."

"I believe the proper diagnosis would be sociopath." He took another step closer, breaking into my comfort zone. Once again I ignored the urge to step back.

"Look." I was tired of the baiting. "I could care less about your mental issues. I just came for my daughter."

"You don't care to know why I took her?"

It was a trap – or a game – but the bait worked. With that question, my curiosity stirred. "Revenge?"

"Against whom? You? You overvalue yourself. Jian Huo?" He lifted his hand to the pearls at my throat. No more holding my ground. I flinched back before he could touch me. Or them. It made him smile. "He knows better. I wonder that he said nothing to you."

"Fine." I bit out. "I'll listen to whatever you have to say. But I want to see Mei Shen first."

"Of course you do. I expected no less. But it will cost you."

"I already said I would listen to your megalomaniacal ravings."

"And therefore I have a vested interest in allowing you to stay as my guest. Access to your daughter will cost you more."

I didn't like the way he was looking at me. I crossed my arms to indicate that some things weren't for sale at any price. "What do you want?"

"You have things of great value with you, I am sure. Gifts from my brother?" He gestured to my throat. "Your pearls, for example. They will suffice."

That was more what I had expected. I snorted like any

haggler confronted with a first offer. "Jian Huo's pearls? Just to see Mei Shen? Pfft. I thought you'd have a sense for how these things are supposed to go. You're blowing your wad too soon. Templeton." The rat wasn't cowering quite as much, but he jerked when I brought attention to him. I put my hand out, still holding Lung Di's eyes. Nothing happened. I broke eye contact to glare at the rat. He held the baubles clutched to his chest.

"Templeton!" I jerked my open palm. His beady eyes darted between me and the dragon, then slowly, reluctantly, he reached out and placed the bit of coral in my palm. I turned to Lung Di.

"Here." I thrust the coral at him.

"I was hoping for something more."

"Well, that's all I'm offering for now. Take it or leave it."

He looked askance at the knobby chunk of sunrise-colored calcite before taking it. He inspected it with a sneer, then tucked it away in his breast pocket. Templeton whimpered.

"I can see I'll get nothing in the way of civil conversation from you until you have your way. Very well. Follow me." He took my arm and placed it in the crook of his. I tried to pull away, but his grip was like steel. I ended up stumbling beside him as we walked through subterranean passageways. Even with my enhanced vision, the pathways were treacherous. Not rocky – they'd been smoothed by aeons of trickling water – but uneven, with hollows and rises hidden by deep shadow. Lung Di's grace moving over them was preternatural. Even Templeton seemed to be doing OK with his three-pawed trundle. Me, not so much.

The corridor opened into a large cavern. A bank of flat screen monitors covered one cavern wall. I made out the obscured speakers of a – I did a quick count – 6.1 surround sound system. Sleek black couches in leather and chrome sat waiting to swallow me whole, and carpets of black, cobalt, and pale dove-grey covered the floor. Even the cave walls had been carved into strange, abstract murals; in the recessed lighting they swayed and shifted like rich draperies.

A skylight of thick glass loomed above us, revealing a murky sky and wavering stars. It took me several moments to realize that it wasn't a skylight at all. We were under water, and the "stars" were the lights of the city.

I must have gasped. The dragon at my side slid closer and said in a voice that was too intimate: "Shanghai. It is by far the best view of that city."

"We... we're under the river?"

"We are." His hand ran up my arm, and I recalled myself enough to pull away.

"Where's Mei Shen?" I demanded.

He leaned over the coffee table – a modern monstrosity of steel and glass – and plucked one remote from the collection that sat there. He pressed a series of buttons, and the entire wall of screens flashed to life. He spared me a brief glance to gauge my reaction, but he didn't get much for his trouble. Apart from my pregnancy, I hadn't missed TV during my years with Jian Huo, and high-tech gizmos were never my thing. He glowered when all I did was raise a brow. The glower slid into a malicious smile, and he pressed another button.

Mei Shen's image flashed up on the screens, dwarfing me with her size. I sank onto the couch, hugging myself to contain my trembling. I wasn't among friends; I couldn't afford to break down. Mei Shen was safe, that's what mattered. I don't know what situation I'd feared to find her in, but seeing her sitting in the middle of a room that was an altar to gender norms, in every shade of Barbie pink, was not it.

Mei Shen hunched over a small bamboo cricket cage, ignoring the Toys 'Я' Us collection around her. It was an artful display of blissful innocence, but I knew my daughter's ploys as if they were my own. She knew she was being watched.

She knew the toys were there to beguile her into complacency. Ignoring it all to play with a cricket was her way of being ornery. I wiped away tears and darted a glance at Lung Di. He only had eyes for Mei Shen, and he looked distinctly put out. He noticed me watching him and turned away from the screens.

"As you can see, she is happy and well-cared for in my keeping."

I set aside all the censure I wanted to heap on him about his attempt to poison my daughter with western consumerism and misogyny. Mei Shen was fighting that battle very well on her own. Instead, I loosed my building anger at his literal interpretation of our bargain.

"You know that this isn't what I meant when I asked to see Mei Shen." I motioned to the monitors, where she was still speaking to the cricket. He'd even left the sound muted.

"Do I? Forgive me. I gave you what you asked for. In the future, you will have to be more specific."

My mouth worked as I tried to come up with some counter to this, but I had nothing. He was right; I would need to choose my words more carefully.

"Fine," I bit out. "If literality is how you want to play this, then that's how we'll do it." I leaned back on the couch, crossing my arms and legs. I tried to hold my gaze steady on him, but my eyes kept darting to Mei Shen's image, which rather ruined the effect I was going for. "I believe you had a manifesto you wanted to deliver?"

He flicked a button on the remote and the screens went dark. I jerked but held back my protests.

"In due time. You're dirty and your clothes smell and you haven't slept." He reached down and pulled me to my feet. I resisted with my dead weight, but he was strong. "I will play the good host whether you wish it or not."

He propelled me out of the room and down another hallway, this one carpeted and illuminated with recessed lighting.

Templeton's claws scrabbled for a moment on the polished stone floors behind us, before being muffled. I glanced back to make sure my shadow was keeping up.

Lung Di stopped at a set of black-lacquered doors with silver fittings. He released my elbow to open them with a grand gesture. The suite beyond rivaled the décor of any Ritz or Waldorf penthouse, right down to the wet bar and cabinet mini-fridge. Only the watery cityscape, gloaming through the skylight, gave a hint that this wasn't a hotel suite in any major city around the globe.

"Take a shower," he instructed with a sniff. "Take a nap. Ready your wits. We will dine together, and I'll deliver my 'manifesto', as you called it. Then we may begin negotiations in earnest."

With another lascivious look, he shut the heavy doors in my face. I knew without trying that they'd be locked, but I made the attempt anyway. They were so well-made that they didn't even rattle. Templeton huffed and sniffed the seam of the door.

"I don't trust him," the rat observed with a shudder.

"I don't either," I said.

"What was that you said earlier about facing a dragon in its lair?"

I thought back. Yesterday seemed far away. "That only a fool does it."

"But you have a plan, right?" He looked up at me. "Right?"

"As much a plan as I ever have." Turning away, I headed deeper into the suite to examine my new prison.

"Oh," Templeton whispered behind me. He gave the door another half-hearted nudge.

It took me an hour of dithering to get over the idea that Lung Di could be watching me. He didn't have to be. His demonstration with the screens was enough to set me to self-surveilling. Just make me think that he could be watching, and I'd do the rest of the work myself.

All lascivious looks and suggestive physicality aside, I wasn't under the delusion that Lung Di wanted me. He just wanted me to know my place. He'd already evidenced a strong predilection for stereotypes – the Bondian Batcave he lived in, the Pink Princess Palace where he'd cloistered Mei Shen. I wasn't going to let him turn me into the rope for a sexual tug-of-war with Jian Huo. That whole "sleep with your brother's girl to get at your brother" thing was bullshit. No way was I going to yield him that kind of power.

With these rationalizations buttressing me against the specter of surveillance, I got over myself enough to strip out of my dirty clothes, though I kept my pearls on.

In keeping with the rest of the suite, the bathroom was enormous. The shower had a multi-setting showerhead that I would have killed for during my student days with Jian Huo. Not that I'd be making use of it here and now. I shut the opaque glass door and steamed up the place the good, old-fashioned way.

By the time I got out of the shower, my clothes were gone. I wrapped myself in a thick, terrycloth robe and went in search of a more suitable replacement. I found Templeton hiding in the shadows under the coffee table, checking over his remaining two baubles. He was sitting on my knapsack.

"Servant?" I asked.

"Shadows. Two of them," he responded. "I would have tried to stop them, but I thought your bag was more important."

"You did right." I patted his head and checked the pockets of my knapsack. All present and accounted for. The bones of my plan remained undisturbed. "Did they give you much trouble?"

"They fear me." His voice was tinged with surprise at the novelty. "I am the only shadow here that he does not control."

"Well, that's something. I'm glad to know I can leave the bag and its contents in your excellent care." I gave him a smile and another scratch behind his ears. His tail twitched in guilty pleasure.

I left the rat to his baubles and went in search of clothes. Sure enough, the wardrobe in the bedroom was filled with designer clothes and underthings, all of them hyper-sexualized in one way or another. Good god, this guy needed a Bond girl to get his adolescent fantasies out of his system. I thought of my giggle-fest with Si Wei and had to stifle a laugh. Maybe we hadn't been that far off the mark.

The aborted giggle turned into a yawn. I couldn't face wedging myself into one of those slinky ensembles just yet, so I lay down on the bed and rationalized a nap. After all, it had been almost two days, and I did need my wits about me.

I fell instantly asleep, and almost as instantly, I dreamed.

I stood in a pagoda of widely-spaced bamboo beams. They stretched above me like interlaced, golden bars. A pretty reflecting pool rimmed with well-polished stones sat in the center of the pagoda, and a giant cricket, its metallic carapace burnished blue-green, stood beside me. Twin antennae twitched, shining with a pearlescent light. It regarded me with patient, viridian eyes. I'd been the subject of that gaze before.

I was still in my bathrobe, pearls around my neck. Figured. At least I wasn't naked.

"Forgive me, *Lung Xin Niang*, for not coming to meet you earlier when you called. I did not think you would desire me to leave my charge," she said, though on reflection I was pretty sure all I heard was a cricket's chirp.

"Mother? Mother, is that you?" Mei Shen's face pressed up against the bars, ten times larger than it had been on Lung Di's big screens. The *qilin* chirped a warning.

"Hush, Lung Mei Shen Mi. Do not alert your nurse. Your mother is here, but she cannot walk these halls. If you wish to speak with her, you must practice subtlety."

Subtlety was not my daughter's strong suit, any more than etiquette was mine. Watching Mei Shen trying to school her features into nonchalance, I felt a momentary sympathy with

Jian Huo's pained forbearance when he had to watch me bungle through the complex social rules of our life.

"Oh. Yes, I can do that. Hello, Mother," she said in a whisper as loud as a yell, though that might have been a matter of perspective, what with my reduced size. She poked a finger through the bars, as wide and long as my leg. I hugged it anyways, and kissed the bend of her knuckle. No one can rival the weirdness that is my life.

"Oh, Maybug. I'm so glad you're all right. I'm so sorry I didn't believe you about the nurse." I wanted to babble more apologies, but the words came too fast, choking against one another.

"It's all right, Mother. I'm fine, but I have been bored, even with the *qilin* to keep me company, and I miss you, and Father, and Mian Zi. It's no fair that he got to leave and I didn't. I hope he is as bored as I am. He had best not be having any fun. Father promised to show us how to fly kites when we returned. He better not have shown Mian Zi without me. I will never forgive him if he has."

More than anything else, Mei Shen's torrent of words convinced me that she had come to little harm. I sent the *qilin* a grateful look of apology. I should never have doubted her.

"Are we going home soon, mother? I should like to go home." Mei Shen ran out of words, blinking at me with trust that I hoped wasn't misplaced.

"Yes, Maybug. I've come to take you home." I reached out to touch the shadows, but everything beyond the cage was smudged in a cocoon of viridian fire. I glanced again at the *qilin*; her antennae waved at me.

"He cannot know I am here," she said. "Or that I've brought you here in your dreams. You must find your own way to us."

"That's OK," I said with a shrug. I'd have been disappointed if things ended up being that easy. Really. "I have a plan. Mei Shen, I need you to tell me everything about your nurse."

I spent the next hour plotting with my daughter. It was a strange sort of mother-daughter bonding, and I had to engage in logical gymnastics to keep her from launching a dozen ill-conceived plans. My respect for Mian Zi vaulted to new heights, given that it often fell to him to keep her out of trouble. The *qilin* sat apart from us, watching with many-faceted eyes. I wondered how many of Mei Shen's plans she'd had to foil in the last several months.

The world grew fuzzy around the edges. Mei Shen's whisper-shout receded to the edge of hearing. I tried to answer but couldn't speak. The *qilin's* voice resounded throughout my skull.

"Our time here is done. I dare not bring you again. Do not fear. I will do as I have pledged. That which is Lung Huang's will come to no harm while in my care. Wake, and remember."

The fuzz cleared into darkness. I opened my eyes to a ceiling patterned with spiraling tessellations. It was hypnotic. I forced my eyes away. The bedroom was still empty, and I was still in my robe, but I imagined I could hear Templeton snoring in the other room. Poor rat. I'd run him through the wringer, and we weren't even half-done.

Padding over to the wardrobe, I opened it and regarded the contents with a heavy sigh. Spandex and sequins winked back at me. I was getting too old for this shit.

"You look lovely," were Lung Di's words when he came to collect me an hour later. I said nothing and kept my face impassive. If we were going for literal interpretations, then I wasn't giving him any more than I'd agreed to. I'd chosen a dress because I didn't have a choice. I'd listen to his manifesto. But for the rest of his games, he was on his own. He escorted me down the carpeted hallway in silence, back to the room with all his toys.

"I imagine it must be nice to wear something that doesn't

take an hour to figure out how to get into," he offered as his second sally. It was, but I wasn't about to admit that to him. I just pursed my lips with a non-committal grunt and let him seat me at a table set for two.

In keeping with the rest of his businessman-playboy shtick, the dining area was furnished in chrome and glass, just off the main room. Above us, the underwater skylight continued to shift with the murky glimmers of the Shanghai skyline.

My brief perusal of the wardrobe had yielded a blue silk wraparound dress as the least sexualized of the offerings, but I was revising that opinion. When I sat down, the damn thing kept sliding open along the line of my thigh, revealing way more of that skin than I was comfortable showing to anyone but Jian Huo or a gynecologist. After a few futile attempts to tug it into obedience, I gave up on subtlety and bunched it closed between my legs, clamping my thighs shut to keep it that way. It would wrinkle the silk, but I didn't care. I wasn't trying to impress anyone.

Lung Di fell silent again as two waiters served us the first course. They looked mortal. I didn't know whether to be more surprised by them or by the plate of food they placed before me.

"Tuna tartar with persimmon chutney," Lung Di said, in response to my raised eyebrows. He flipped a napkin into his lap and lifted his fork. I couldn't help staring. I hadn't seen a fork in ages. "You should eat. I imagine it has been a while since you've eaten, and much longer since you've had anything this good. If ever."

I wanted to be pigheaded, but I was hungry, and the food looked edible. It reminded me of Jack. A reluctant smile tugged at my lips. I fumbled with my own fork, trying to recall how to use one, and took a cautious bite. It was delicious.

"It's good," I conceded. "What did you do, seduce away the Shanghai Marriott's executive chef?"

"Hilton, actually. The owner's brat insulted his pea puree. It was either come work for me or waste away in a Hong Kong prison for poisoning her morning Weetabix."

I stopped chewing. Poison hadn't occurred to me.

Lung Di smiled. "Please don't concern yourself. If I wanted you dead, you'd be dead."

"Well, that's comforting," I muttered. I took another cautious bite. We continued to eat in silence. It would have been unnerving if the food weren't so good. Who was I kidding? It was unnerving as hell.

The salad course came next, some kind of tomato and salmon thing.

"Grilled heirloom tomatoes and goat cheese." Lung Di said. I goggled. I hadn't had cheese in... God, too long. Like most Chinese, Jian Huo wasn't a fan of cheese.

I paused with the fork halfway to my lips. Remembered that the first bite's free. Set it back down and struggled to recall my purpose.

"I believe you had a manifesto to deliver?" I said, as the waiters placed the next remove before us. I took a sip of wine – when had I been given wine? – and tried to look stern and businesslike.

Lung Di regarded me for a moment over his fork. He placed the bite of food back on his plate, untouched. "Do you really want to disturb this lovely meal?"

"Yes. You're being charming... or at least, not threatening. The food is good, and somewhere along the way I acquired a glass of wine. I don't trust any of it, and I'd rather be reminded of that."

He smiled. "Hardly an argument designed to encourage me to speak."

I leaned back and folded my arms, ignoring the siren call of whatever that was on my plate. Some kind of shrimp lime salsa on fried bananas, though I imagined there was a fancier name for it. Lung Di regarded his own plate with a sigh.

"Very well. You are as pugnacious as your daughter, you realize."

"You can skip the compliments."

He hid a smile behind his napkin. "What has my brother told you of me?"

I frowned, unsure what angle he was trying to play. There was no question in my mind that he had an angle. He mistook my expression for reticence.

"Oh, come now. He must have told you all manner of horror stories, or you would never have risked my wrath by refusing me entry that day on the mountain. So, what am I guilty of, according to my little brother?"

I tucked away that little tidbit for later consideration. I knew that Jian Huo was older than Shui Yin and Lung Pan, but I hadn't realized that he was younger than Lung Di. I didn't know what to make of that.

"He told me that the two of you used to be inseparable. You'd ditch heaven to go down to earth and mess around with mortals; innocent stuff, mostly, which is why your older siblings let you get away with it. After Jian Huo got busted for the whole writing incident, they cracked down. He tried to get you to stop sneaking down the mountain, but you wouldn't listen. You mocked him for being a kiss-ass. You started going off on your own, started manipulating people just to see what would happen. At first it was small stuff like theft and rape and murder, but you kept pushing. You started wars to see who would win and how. You stacked the deck in favor of one side or another to see how people would react. You loosed plagues and natural disasters to watch how humans dealt with the suffering."

I took a sip of wine. I was good at playing ignorant about my lover and his family. Easier than dealing with the knowledge that they were gods. It was hard to comprehend the scale of havoc that Lung Di had wreaked. It was like reciting facts out of a history book. I tried to imagine all the individual faces that had been affected, but it was just too big. I took another sip of wine and waited as the waiters brought in the next remove. My appetite had deserted me.

"Jian Huo was the one who discovered what you were doing," I forged on. "He tried to talk to you, to understand why you were doing it. He tried to stop you, but you were too far gone. When the others found out – when Jian Huo told them – they exiled you. Since then, you've involved yourself even more deeply in mortal affairs. Most of the atrocities of this past century – Mao, the Red Guard – you were involved in all of that."

"Ah yes. The Long March." He smiled fondly, as though that terrible exodus were a happy memory. "But later, the good chairman took exception to my existence and decided my kind needed to be eradicated. He was remarkably dedicated in his efforts, if ultimately ineffectual. The Triads were a useful buffer."

Ineffectual, he called it. Hundreds of thousands dead, ancient monasteries and cultural sites destroyed, a whole nation terrorized for half a century and still recovering from the impact of Mao's policies, and he was able to shrug all this off. Jian Huo was right. Lung Di was a monster.

He ignored my look of revulsion in favor of digging in. When I didn't continue after a few moments, he set down his fork again. "An interesting version of the events."

"Are you going to try to deny it?"

"No, no. It's all true. Much less damning than I expected. It appears my brother is loath to admit just how reprehensible I am. Or maybe he still harbors some affection for me." Lung Di looked up and scratched his jaw. "No. It's almost certainly the former."

He leaned back again and favored me with a lazy smile. Here it came. Manifesto time. I steeled myself.

THE DRAGONS OF HEAVEN

"I'm going to make an intuitive leap and guess that you're not an 'ends justify the means' sort, are you?"

"No. Because they don't. In the doing of a thing, the how and the why matters."

"Now, where have I heard that before?" he drawled. I shifted uncomfortably. Just because I was parroting Jian Huo's words didn't mean I didn't believe them.

Lung Di's smirk dimmed. "But how does that work when you're up against something that has the power to crush you without a thought? Worse, something that will use your weakness to further its agenda? You can't just defeat such monsters with hugs and positive thinking. Your Gandhi and your King, their peaceful protests succeeded because they were already part of the elite classes. They were equipped with the weapons of social capital and rhetoric. But what about those who are not? What about those for whom the only recourse is desperate violence? Like your Middle Eastern terrorists, or those Zapatistas in Central America? Or your own Irish people a century ago? Your philosopher, Nietzsche, observed that if you fight monsters, you become a monster yourself. What if it is more than that? When the monsters are so much more powerful, your *only* hope to defeat them is to become a monster. But it *can* be done. That's what I've learned in my centuries of pitting humans against each other. It is something that none of my siblings is willing to admit about humans, not even Lung Huang, who knows you best. You lot can be more powerful than gods, given the right incentive."

I gaped at him, blinking to make sure I understood. "That's it? That's your justification? You've been doing us some kind of cosmic service, testing us to prove that we can be as powerful as any monster that we face? So that we can take their place and become our own monsters?" I threw my napkin on my plate. "That's the crappiest manifesto I've ever heard!"

"You know nothing about monsters."

If I'd been smarter, I would have taken heed of the warning in his quiet tone. But I'm not that smart. "Oh, I think I'm learning," I said, glaring.

"You. Know. Nothing." He jabbed his finger into the table with each word, rattling the dishes and making the wine slosh in the glasses. "I will tell you about monsters. The fabric of reality is weakening, did my brother tell you that? Your access to the place you call the Shadow Realms is proof. In the beginning, the Nine Guardians set ourselves to protect reality, all realities, from what waited beyond. We hold back all that was separated out from reality when the cosmos came into being – all that is not-being. But we are weakening. For centuries now, things have been crawling through the spaces between the warp and the weft, getting past our guard. Monsters beyond your imagining."

"Just because they're from outside our reality doesn't make them monsters. I don't believe in othering just for othering's sake–"

"You idiot girl! This isn't some hippie, water-your-plants-with-menstrual-blood, save-the-whales, love-thy-neighbor crap. I'm talking about entities that cause reality to unweave by their very presence. You mortals interpret it as horror and madness because your minds can't comprehend the unreality of it. This isn't a case of 'can't we all just get along'. These monsters *unmake* reality."

I tamped down on the urge to defend my hippie roots. Instead, I went for skepticism. "And you want to stop them, great humanitarian that you are?"

"No. I want to prepare you so that *you* can stop them."

"Huh? Me?"

It was his turn to throw down his napkin. "Not you, personally, you silly girl. Humanity. The Triads. The People's Heroes. Your Argent Aces. It's past time we took the training wheels off. Past time you mortals learned to do for yourselves, rather than letting us do it for you. You're more than capable. And if you aren't, or if you act like stupid, short-sighted monkeys and end up either trying to have a love-in with the void, or trying to take its power for yourselves, well, then you'll all get exactly what you deserve."

And this was how he justified all that he'd done? "Everybody's the hero of their own story," I muttered.

"I never claimed to be nice or good or honorable. Let my siblings cling to those notions. They took exception to my methods, and their solution is to exile me. They would rather endanger all reality than admit I might be right."

I was on firmer ground here. "No, there's got to be more to it than that. Maybe the others, but not Jian Huo. He cares for mortals."

"Take the blinders off, Missy. Jian Huo's the worst of the lot. Just consider how he has used you."

I stilled. We'd been speaking in such general, big picture terms that I had stopped expecting Lung Di to get personal. I should have known better. I crossed my arms as though that could protect me from anything he might say. "Jian Huo loves me."

He shook his head. "You are so naïve."

"He does."

"Unquestionably." He favored me with a pitying smile. "Insofar as a being who predates existence, who transcends the boundaries that separate realities, can love a silly mortal girl with more hair than wit. Do you really believe it? Have you never questioned it? How can a being like Lung Huang love one like you in any way save as a pet – a momentary distraction to a consciousness that spans both infinity and eternity."

With the inconvenient timing of waiters everywhere, the two servants came and removed our plates. Mine was still untouched. In place, they set down ramekins of crème brûleé with glazed peaches. The sweet, heady scent of the peaches hit me, and the last remnants of my appetite disappeared. My stomach churned, and I had to choke back sudden tears.

"You're just trying to make me doubt him, to drive a wedge between us," I said when I could speak again.

He cracked the caramelized top of his dessert. "In my experience, the truth works far better as a wedge than any lie ever could."

"Maybe you're right that my life for him is just a brief flash, but that doesn't mean that he doesn't love me. He could have ignored me, or sent me on my way. He didn't. He courted me. He chose me to be his bride. He wouldn't do that unless he meant it."

"You were convenient." Lung Di waved his spoon. I curbed the urge to knock it from his hand. "Your connection to the Shadow Realms made you marginally more useful, but any one of a thousand girls would have done. You made it easy for him. He didn't have to trouble himself with looking. You came to him. You offered yourself to him. You offered him something of value, and he repaid you in kind. It was a bargain, like any other, and Lung Huang honors his bargains. You got what you wanted – the approval of dragons – and my brother got what he wanted."

I hugged myself tighter. "Oh really? And what was so valuable that he would make such a bargain?"

"Children, Missy. You gave him children." He spoke as if talking to a child himself. "The children you bore him are a more valuable trade than you yet realize."

"What do you mean?"

"Dragons – true dragons, which is to say we Nine Guardians – cannot breed true offspring. We are creatures of eternity and infinity. There always were nine and there always will be. You might even say that we are not separate beings, but one constant with nine faces, at all times self-aware and aware of our own place in the cosmos, in all iterations of the cosmos."

He pushed away his half-finished desert and steepled his fingers, settling in to lecture mode. His mannerisms were similar to Jian Huo's. Uncomfortably so. "Like a mathematical equation, the only way to quantify us is to add a limiter. Infinity must become infinity minus one. We achieve this by dallying with creatures ruled by time and limited by space. The offspring of such unions carry the limitation not only in their blood, but in their metaphysical beings. They're half-breeds. Mongrels. They are no real threat to the status-quo because they are not true dragons. They become heroes or guardians, and eventually they go the way of all mortal creatures.

"The Nine are not mortal. My siblings exiled me because there was little else they could do. If they had the choice, they would remove me from existence, but doing so would alter our systemic being. It would break our power and create a wound in the cosmos more terrible than even we can imagine. The monsters that only trickle through now would be able to pour through in unstoppable numbers.

"Lung Huang has discovered a way around this. In his hatred of me, he has been most dogged. As I said, there have always been and will always be Nine, but with the birth of your children, it is no longer certain just who the Nine will be."

"But wait," I interrupted. "I thought you said they were only half-bloods, not true dragons."

"Individually, yes, but my brother wrought them well in the crucible of your womb. They are complementary – female and male, yin and yang, twins. They share one soul, and they touch multiple worlds: the mortal world, the spirit world, and the place you call the Shadow Realms. One day, and not too long off by my reckoning, they will have the choice to burn away the limitation of their humanity and incorporate into one being – a being of eternity and infinity. A true dragon. When that day comes, one of the Nine will be supplanted. Jian Huo means for it to be me. I intend for it not to be."

He leaned forward, a cruel smile playing about his mouth. "That is what you have given him, Missy. That is why I sought to take your children. They are something not even your grandfather could give Jian Huo, though my brother chose exile so that he might try. How could he not have some love for the vessel that has bred the instrument of my destruction?"

I swallowed down nausea. The over-sweet smell of the peaches was making me sick to my stomach. Really, it was the peaches. Lung Di leaned back again, his smile self-satisfied. "Nothing to say? No witty quips? When you are so renowned for your chatterbox charm?"

"I... I want to be alone."

"Of course."

I stood and walked away from the table.

Being alone was the last thing I needed, but it was better than the alternative. For all Lung Di's civility, I got the feeling that he'd love nothing more than to cause me some serious physical pain. I didn't want to test the possibility that if I knocked that knowing smirk off his face, he'd indulge that urge.

Instead, I paced my rooms and fumed. I hated feeling so powerless, but that was old hat. This anger was all new, and it was directed at a certain dragon who had been lying to me since I met him.

The crappy thing was, Lung Di's accusation was plausible. I hated to admit to myself that Jian Huo might use me like that, but I could even understand how he wouldn't see anything wrong with what he'd done. From his perspective, everything was justifiable. Looking back with this new knowledge tarnished every memory I had of our time together. Even his fascination with my pregnant body took on a more sinister cast. I wanted to rail against it, but in some ways I'd been waiting for the other shoe to drop since the moment Jian Huo welcomed me into his home.

I just didn't expect it to be a five-inch spike heel through my heart.

I stoked my anger as a means of keeping the pain at bay. I didn't have time for breaking down. I made another round of the room, sat down to fidget before springing back up and charging into the bedroom. I rooted through the wardrobe, looking for something else to wear, something that didn't remind me of that dinner. The selection ranged between desperate housewife and vamped-out power attorney, with little choice in between. I settled on black slacks and a cobalt blue silk shell. The silk was so thin that the lace details of my bra stood out in relief, but it was the best the closet had to offer. Muttering imprecations against Lung Di and his sartorial manipulations, I turned back toward the sitting room and promptly tripped over a black, furry form.

"Templeton!" I snarled, harsher than I had any right to be.

"I'm sorry, Missy." His speech was muffled. He cringed back as though he expected me to kick him. "I didn't mean to get in the way."

I took a deep breath, then another. "You're not in the way, Templeton. It's my fault for running around like a headless chicken." I sighed and pushed my heartache back to a deep corner of my psyche. Later. I'd deal with this later, after Mei Shen was free.

"What's a chicken?" His question took me so off guard that I surprised myself with a choked laugh. I swallowed it before it could become a sob.

"It's not important. Someday, if we get out of this in one piece, I'll show you what a chicken is," I promised.

"All right." His response was still muffled. His cheeks bulged.

"Templeton, what's in your mouth?" I asked, not sure I wanted to know. In answer, he spat out his two remaining baubles. They glistened with saliva.

"It is difficult to hold them and walk," he said, as if carrying them in his cheeks was a reasonable solution to this problem. "And this way I can keep them safe."

He fondled them a moment longer, then popped them back in his cheeks. "So," he slurred, "what's next?"

I shook my head at my strange companion and strode to the door, motioning him to follow. The door opened without resistance. I might be a prisoner, but my warden wasn't worried about letting me wander. I suppose that should have concerned me more than it did. I smiled down to the rat at my side.

"Stage two," I answered and slipped into the corridor.

I wandered to get a feel for the place. The corridors wormed about and double-backed upon themselves in a spatially impossible mess. I'd have to find a way to cut through this tangle if I wanted to get Mei Shen out of here. Templeton was right about the shadows, too. They felt strange. Alien. I could tell they led somewhere, but it wasn't the Shadow Realms I was familiar with. These shadows led to a darker and more frightening place. There'd be no stepping sideways into one with Mei Shen in tow.

They might have unnerved me, but the shadows shied away from Templeton as if they were afraid of him. I'd never seen the rat walk in so much light. The novelty tickled him, and every so often he would lunge toward one just to see it flinch away.

"Templeton," I snapped when he would have gone chasing one shadow down a side corridor. "Leave the local kids alone. They're more afraid of you than you are of them."

"I know. Isn't it great!" he exclaimed, missing my sarcasm. He did refrain from doing more than snapping at the shadows when they ventured too close.

I returned to the main room. Dinner had been cleared away, and Lung Di was nowhere to be seen. I fiddled with the controls on the bank of televisions, but all I got was a blue screen of death and one weird game show where the participants had to put live eels into their pants and see who could stand it the longest. Their only reward was additional time on a timer. I switched it off before I could learn what they needed the time for. I had my own live eel to put in my pants.

OK, bad metaphor. Terrible metaphor.

"So, where's my host?" I muttered under my breath.

Templeton left off sniffling at the shadows to point his nose toward one of the cavernous exits. "That way. In his office."

I did a doubletake. "How did you know that?"

"They told me." He nodded at the shadows.

"I thought you said they served Lung Di. Why are they being so helpful?"

Templeton shrugged. "They fear the Conclave more than they fear him. They serve here at the Conclave's behest." He snapped at another shadow, which bled into a puddle and scuttled away. I wondered if I'd just witnessed the shadow equivalent of pissing oneself. I tried to focus on how this turn might be useful.

"And they're afraid of you because you serve the Conclave?" He nodded. "What about me?"

"You're a lightwalker." With a flick of his ears, he dismissed me as someone of little importance in the shadow hierarchy.

"Can you 'convince' them to take us to Mei Shen? Or lead us out of here?"

He exchanged a few uncanny whispers with the shadows. Dim memories of childhood fears crowded to the fore. The things that had lived under my bed and in my closet made those sounds, I was sure of it. My grandfather always assured me that I was imagining things. Now, I wondered if he was just giving me the only protection he could. Denial is sometimes the only ward against the things that live in the dark.

"They are barred from where your daughter is being kept, but I believe I could make them show us the way out. They are cowards." He stretched and preened, as if he didn't spend the majority of his time cowering between my legs. I smiled in spite of myself.

"Well, that's something. All right, let's go. We've got some more bargaining to do."

Templeton's body sagged. His eyes widened and he gulped audibly, but the bulges in both cheeks remained. I patted his head in sympathy. My stalwart shadow rat companion. I couldn't have asked for a better helper.

At Templeton's urgings, the shadows led us to another set of black-lacquered double doors, similar to my own rooms. I knocked once, then tried the door. It wasn't locked. It opened into the offices of a corporate CEO. The walls were a neutral dove grey, the carpets a thick Berber in cobalt, black and grey. A large, misshapen chunk of hematite graced a recess in one wall. Opposite that was an amethyst geode almost half my height. Both were lit from above by recessed lighting.

Lung Di sat behind a huge desk of black-lacquered wood, working on a laptop. Two client chairs were set in front of the desk, the kind that were designed to be stylish and uncomfortable. He looked up impatiently, as if I'd actually interrupted him in the middle of work.

"What, no executive assistant?" I asked to fill the silence.

"I had to let the last girl go. She refused to bring me coffee, and she kept demanding better 401k benefits. Also, she was stealing office supplies."

I shrugged, "That'll teach you to hire humans. 'Anything that isn't bolted down,' that's our motto."

"I believe, 'that's why god invented boltcutters' is a corollary," he countered with a smile. We were bantering. Dammit. Why couldn't he just be evil? Things were so much easier when I could dislike a person. I thought about Mian Zi sleeping forlorn and alone in Mei Shen's bed, and then it wasn't so hard to recall my purpose.

"I want to see my daughter. And by 'see', I mean speak to,

touch, interact with, be in her actual presence for an extended period of time."

He closed his laptop. "Why, Missy. It sounds like you expect me to deal unfairly."

"You're the one who set the tone of our negotiations. If you're going to take me literally, then I'm going to be careful. Fool me once, and all that."

He conceded the point with a one-shouldered shrug. "Have you thought at all about my 'Manifesto' or the other things I told you?"

"Huh. It completely slipped my mind."

The smile dropped. "I would like to know your thoughts on those matters."

"Is that what you want in exchange for letting me see Mei Shen?"

He shook his head. "Consider that as payment for your continued presence as my guest. For Mei Shen... I suppose it is still too early to request your pearls? You don't appear to have much else of value." His eyes traveled my body with a suggestive lift of a brow. I ignored the suggestion. Maybe the smarm was chronic.

"Appearances can be deceiving." I put my hand in front of Templeton's mouth. He whimpered and scrunched his eyes, but spat one of his baubles into my palm: a fire opal covered in rat-saliva. I strode across the room and dumped it, slime and all, into Lung Di's lap. He glared at me before using his silk pocket square to pick it up.

"Your rat must love you dearly to keep sacrificing his treasures for you."

"Is it enough?"

He wrapped the opal in the silk and set it on the corner of the desk. "It is, for now." He pressed a button on a sleek black console that must have been some kind of phone system. "Bring the girl to my office."

Lung Di turned back to his computer, effectively dismissing me. Templeton pouted. I pretended to examine the amethyst until I heard the door open behind me. I turned in time to take a daughter to the gut. I squatted and clutched her close until she squirmed for release.

"Mother! You're here! I'm so glad to see you!" I resolved to spend some time in the future teaching Mei Shen how to lie better. Her pip-squeak cheer was a beacon to my paternal senses, indicating in neon, capital letters that SOMETHING was going on. Lung Di watched us, but he didn't have the same paternal warning system that I did. The nurse hovered nearby, as shifty and pinch-faced as she'd been that day in the alley.

"Have you come to take me home?" Mei Shen asked. "I should like to go home."

"Not yet, Maybug. Soon, but not quite yet." I earned a raised eyebrow from my nemesis for that promise. I glared at him.

"I'd like to speak to my daughter alone."

"You stipulated no such condition."

"Oh, for the love of– Fine," I bit out. "You can stay, but the nurse leaves."

"Then your rat leaves as well."

I waved my arms at the office. "What do you think I'm going to be able to do here? Against you?"

Lung Di leaned back in his chair. "It isn't about that. It's about making sure that you don't get away with more than what was promised."

I glowered, but turned to the rat. "Templeton, could you wait outside?"

"But, Missy–"

"Please, just do it." He shuffled out the door, the nurse following in his wake. She shot a smirk at me over her shoulder as the doors closed.

"Why 'Templeton'?" Lung Di asked in a musing tone.

"Huh?"

"Why name him Templeton?"

"He didn't strike me as the Reepicheep type."

"Ah." He nudged the silk-wrapped opal with a finger. "I believe you were mistaken."

"I think you might be right."

"Who's Reepicheep?" asked my ever-curious daughter.

"Who's Reepicheep!" I sputtered in mock outrage. "Why, only the most heroic mouse ever to have lived."

"A heroic… mouse?" Her skepticism was as exaggerated as my outrage. I shot Lung Di a forbidding glance and herded her to the far corner of the room. He snorted and went back to his work.

It told Mei Shen about Reepicheep and Narnia – how had I ever missed that particular hole in her education? I told her how much her brother missed her, and a lot of the things I'd said already in the *qilin's* dream. Once she got into it, Mei Shen was better at playacting that we hadn't already spoken. Unfortunately, she was so into it that I couldn't determine whether she'd done her part. It was probably better that way. From the angle of Lung Di's head and the lack of keyboard clacking, I was pretty sure he could hear every word we said.

After too short a time, Lung Di approached and put his hand on Mei Shen's shoulder. She started to protest, but I shushed her with a warning glance.

"So soon?" I complained, because I knew he expected it. "You hardly gave us any time at all."

"I gave you half an hour. Nurse," he called. Within moments the hag was back. Templeton sulked by the door. "Take Lung Mei Shen Mi back to her rooms and help her get ready for bed."

The old woman grabbed Mei Shen and whisked her away before I could do more than squeeze her hand in farewell. I gazed at the door long after it shut behind them. I could feel Lung Di's eyes on me, but he had a dragon's patience. I broke the silence.

"You're wrong, you know."

"About what?" He gestured toward the desk and the uncomfortable client chairs, but I stayed where I was. It was his choice to remain standing or sit at his desk and shout across the room at me. He chose to remain standing. Point for me.

"Everything." I flicked a glance at him, then looked back at the door that had closed on my daughter. "Well, maybe not everything. You're right that mortals need to learn to fight our own battles. We also need to learn the consequences of getting in over our heads and of messing with powers we don't understand."

I turned back to him and crossed my arms. "But we don't need to become monsters in the process. You're the one who decided that for us, and you're the one making it happen. I don't know if it will make us stronger. I don't know if it's the best way to prepare us. I doubt it on both counts, and I think it's the kind of thing we should figure out on our own.

"What I do know is that out of all of your siblings, *you're* the hypocrite. They cut the apron strings. They retreated into Heaven. They *have* been letting us fight our own fights. Even Jian Huo tries to keep his nose out of things most of the time. You're the only one who stayed down here, meddling with us, because you think you know better." His face remained impassive, but his fists clenched at his sides, knuckles white. I stopped before my words caused him to forget his hospitality. The last thing I wanted was to be backhanded across the room.

He twitched a moment longer, then chuckled. If it weren't for the tightness still around his mouth, I would have thought him unaffected. "You are blind to the complexity of the matter."

"Probably. Undoubtedly. Half the time, I'm not even sure what's going on right in front of me. But I know you're wrong about what you're doing. And about Jian Huo and me."

"You know nothing. You've convinced yourself what you want to believe, simply because you want to believe it."

"Maybe, but you didn't manage to convince me that the how and the why don't matter, and you never will. And doesn't that just stick in your craw?"

One fist jerked up. I flinched back. That'd teach me to let my mouth run off in the presence of an angry dragon. Jian Huo was a bad influence on my common sense.

"Get out. Now. Before I forget that you are my guest and recall that you are less than nothing to me. Before I decide that killing you will be adequate to my purposes, and I put an end to your irritating little existence."

I wanted to believe that it was an empty threat, but that fist hadn't lowered, and his knuckles were still white from clenching. I bowed my head and forced myself to walk – not run – from the room. Templeton trailed behind me. I didn't stop until I reached the questionable safety of my own rooms. Only when the doors were shut did I allow myself to give in to my fear.

I didn't stop shaking for an hour.

"Missy. Missy, the shadows say he has finally left."

It was late the next day – or, at least, I assumed the lighter murky green of my skylight indicated daytime in the city above. I'd spent a fitful night and a restless day. I didn't dare leave my rooms until I'd given Lung Di some time to calm down.

"You're sure?" I asked, more out of anxiety than doubt.

"They're sure," he corrected.

"Right. Right. OK." I glanced around the room, as if any surveillance devices Lung Di had left would be visible. I was gambling on his overconfidence being his weakness, and hoping that my faith in my friends wasn't mine. In the end, it all came down to Templeton.

I took a deep breath. No use wasting worry over my paranoia. It was now or never. "So, what did the nurse say? Did Mei Shen convince her? Will she do it?"

"She's worried that your word won't be enough to protect her from the wrath of Lung Di and Lung Huang. She said that she'll only accept the second comb as protection."

I sighed in relief. "So then, she'll do it?"

Templeton hesitated. The rat had no respect for my blood-pressure. "Ye-es. But she said that if the comb was protection, she still needed payment. She wanted something more, so I..." he plucked up his hairless tail, worrying it between his paws. My stomach dropped even further. He hadn't given up the entire game, had he?

"Templeton, what did you do?"

"I... Igaveheryourboots," he confessed in a rush.

"My what?"

"Your boots. The ones in your bag. I was trying to find something in there to offer her, and she saw them, and she said they would do."

"My... boots? Why would she want those?" I couldn't fathom a reason. They were destroyed, the leather eaten away by—

"Demon blood," Templeton answered a split second before I came to the same realization. "That's what she said – that she could do a lot with the lifeblood of such a powerful demon."

I tucked away my concern over the implications of that. I'd deal with it later when it came to bite me in the butt. Templeton misinterpreted my silence.

"I'm sorry, Missy. I didn't mean to give away your boots. I hope I didn't mess up the plan."

I shook my head and gave him a reassuring pat on the shoulder. "No, you did good. I just brought them along for luck. I guess they worked." His nose twitched in what I'd come to interpret as ratty happiness. There were times when I envied how easy his moods were. "So, she agreed to do it, then?"

"She... she wanted her knife back, too. She said it was sympathetic to the kind of magic that makes people see what you want them to see. But I told her it wasn't possible, that you didn't bring it," he assured me in a rush. "She said she might be able to make do with something else, but it will be a shoddy copy. The illusion won't last long."

"I don't need it to last long. Just long enough. Did she say when it would be done?"

"Tonight."

"That doesn't give us much time. Let's hope Lung Di gets back before then. Otherwise, we'll have to go with Plan C."

"What's Plan C?"

I frowned. "There isn't one."

The wait was interminable. I puttered. I changed clothes. I tried not to be irritated at Templeton as he crouched on top of my knapsack under the coffee table, whispering in the shadow-tongue to his final bauble. I forced myself to sit still on the floor near him. I concentrated on the incomprehensible whispers, letting the shadow speech chase away all my other fears. In my laid-back acceptance of the rat, I often forgot that he was formed of raw shadow, shaped only by the name I'd laid upon him. Just below the surface was a quiescent mass of primal terror – scrabbling on the floorboards, chittering in the darkness of the night. Plague, death, decay. If I concentrated, I could just make out those darker notes on the edge of my senses. I let the fears wash over me, clearing away my lesser anxieties. I meditated on Fear, and let my own go. Welcome to the dark side of the Force.

"Templeton," I said after a time. "After the final trade, whatever happens, you're free to go. In fact, I want you to go. Take my bag and meet me back on the plain where I first called you."

He raised startled eyes from his bauble. His whiskers twitched. "Won't you still need me? To guide you out of this place?"

"It will be too dangerous. We'll just have to hope the shadows will follow your instructions after you've gone. If things go according to plan, Lung Di will be furious. I don't think he'll kill me, but there's nothing to keep him from killing you."

I leaned forward and placed a hand over his, covering the chunk of glass. "Thank you, Templeton. I know it's been hard for you. I couldn't have asked for a truer friend."

"I will always be a friend to you, Missy."

I said nothing. Templeton, not Reepicheep. I had inscribed avarice into his nature when I named him. I knew it. Lung Di knew it. But Templeton demonstrated that he was oblivious to that fact when he handed me his final bauble.

"I want to put Mei Shen to bed."

"I beg your pardon?"

The shadows informed Templeton the moment Lung Di returned. We made our final preparations in silence. Even our goodbye was no more than a wet nose snuffling against my cheek as I hugged him a little too tightly. I left him giving the shadows firm instructions to help me or fear his wrath and that of the Conclave. I hoped it worked. I hoped it all worked. I left my room in search of my nemesis. I found him in an alcove off the main room, looking through thick windows into the murky waters of the Huangpu.

"I said, I want to put Mei Shen to bed: tuck her in, get her a glass of water, all of the things I normally do when I put her to bed. And I want to do it without you or the Nurse hovering nearby. An hour of quality mother-daughter alone time, that's what I want."

"Are you sure? Even with your rat's treasures, you have little left to trade. Shouldn't you save what you do have for something that matters?"

I crossed my arms and shot him a challenging look. Let him think I was losing patience with his games. It wasn't far off the mark. "This matters. To me. To both of us. And you and I both know that the next time we bargain, it will be for Mei Shen, and you won't be accepting any baubles. I just want to have one last bedtime with my daughter." My voice cracked, and it wasn't entirely playacting.

"And what are you offering in trade? Your pearls?"

I shook my head and handed him Templeton's third bauble, the water-softened chunk of glass. He took it and favored me with an enigmatic smile.

"We could just end this charade now, you know," he said, taking my arm and pulling me deeper into the shadows of the alcove. "I would give you Mei Shen in exchange for the pearls. We both know it, just as we both know that you'll do it – that you've already decided you'll do it. Why keep stalling with these games?"

"You would just give her up for the pearls? Here and now?"

"Yes."

"Why? If she's one half of the weapon that will lead to your destruction, why give her up for anything?"

"And paint myself the villain in her eyes?" He arched a brow. "Anything I did to her would only make her will stronger, or turn her against me. Better to keep her for a short time, demonstrate what a 'swell guy' I am, and then let her leave as soon as her mother comes to get her. But you and I both know the truth of what I'm giving up, and I won't give it up for nothing."

"Why do you want the pearls?"

"I could sleep with you instead. It would do nearly the same damage, but…" He shook his head and turned again to gaze out the window. "No. Jian Huo could always deceive himself into thinking that you were unwilling. Forced. The pearls offer less in the way of visceral pleasure, but they are symbolic. He will know exactly what you've spurned in exchange for your daughter."

"So, why not just take them, then? I'm here at your mercy.

Why haven't you just taken them?"

"And how would that be different from forcing you?" He aimed his question at my reflection in the glass. "You'll give them to me, of your own will, to save your daughter. I will not have them by force or guile."

"If he doesn't love me, if he's just using me, then what makes you think it would even matter to him?"

"Honor, Missy. There's nothing he prizes more." He turned to face me. I shrank back against the curve of the wall. "I think you're different. Honor is something that's useful to you, but also negotiable. Malleable. That's what I'm betting on – that you value your child more than some misguided sense of honor."

"You're wrong," I whispered, but my voice wavered. I swallowed and tried to strengthen it. "I'll never give you Jian Huo's pearls."

"I think you'll reconsider. You really have no choice."

"No. You don't get it. You pegged me when you delivered your manifesto." I straightened, my face inches from his. "The ends don't justify the means. Not ever. How and why you do something is as important as what you're trying to do. That conviction is what Jian Huo and I have in common. It's why your manifesto is crap. It's why your claim that Jian Huo used me is crap. And it's why I won't ever give you my pearls. Now stop fucking with me and let me put my daughter to bed."

He pulled back, but no flash of amusement or irritation crossed his features. He'd dropped the pretense that I was anything but a tool to him. I wasn't worth getting worked up over. That was fine by me. We both were at our end-games, and my strategy was too complicated to muddle with emotions.

Lung Di pocketed the glass. "Very well. You may have your hour. Follow me."

He led me through more serpentine corridors until I was lost. The symbolism was clear: he held my daughter trapped in his coils. Another set of black-lacquered doors opened onto the Barbie palace. Mei Shen sat on a chair next to an empty cricket cage, feet kicking as they dangled. The nurse was nowhere to be seen.

"An hour." Lung Di said. Before he could grow suspicious, I entered and shut the door in his face.

Given my previous encounter with the nurse's work, her changeling was better than I'd expected. It was too quiet by half, but the questions it did ask were intelligent, more like things my daughter would say. Perhaps spending so much time with the original had helped the nurse to improve the quality of the doppelgänger.

I went through the motions of putting my false daughter to bed, lingering over the experience not because I enjoyed it, but because I had no doubt I was being watched. I needed to give the nurse as good a chance as possible to spirit Mei Shen away.

I was singing an old sea shanty to the sleeping changeling when Lung Di returned for me. I left without too much fuss, playing off that I didn't want to wake my sleeping daughter. We were both quiet as Lung Di escorted me back to my own rooms. We stopped before the doors.

"There are no more moves for you to make." His words made me pause on the threshold. "It is time to bargain in earnest."

I shook my head, and there was little artifice to the weary droop of my shoulders. "In the morning. Then I'll be ready to bargain."

"Putting it off will not make the outcome any different. Only more painful."

He sounded almost sympathetic. I ignored him. "I'll see you in the morning," I said and shut the door.

Leaning back against the closed doors, I took a deep breath. The only light in the room came from above the wet bar. Everywhere else was deep in shadow. I scanned the rest of the room, but there was no sign of Templeton. He'd done what

I'd asked and vacated. I was relieved, but also saddened. Who knew if I would ever see him again?

I did one last sweep of the rooms – hotel habits die hard – then took a deep breath and stepped into shadow.

The terrain on the other side was like no shadow landscape I'd ever entered. The ground was slick and black: featureless. It fell away from beneath my feet, and no horizon marked where it bled into the black sky. I looked up and then couldn't look away. Void yawned above me: a gaping crack in reality that reached down to brush at me with oily, black tentacles. Nine shining threads, strained near-to-breaking, were all that held the wound closed. Nine threads. Nine Guardians. They were stretched thin with weakness, so inadequate against the void that pulsed to break through. I shied away from the questing polyps that had made it past their guard, swaying with vertigo. The world spun into a mad twist of laughter. I collapsed to my knees and scrabbled at the slick ground, seeking some kind of secure purchase. The void pulled at me, stretching me like taffy into a shape no human was ever meant to take. I sobbed, or maybe I laughed. Or screamed. There was no difference here. They were sounds in a place of not-sound.

Oh, God. What had I done in coming here?

My wail was answered by a soft chittering. Underneath that, the scrabbling of claws.

"Help me," I whisper-screamed. The chittering grew louder. I shut my eyes. I didn't want to see what was making that noise. The blackness behind my lids, comfortable and known, helped anchor me. I recalled why I was in this place, what I needed to do.

In the name of Templeton, lieutenant in service to the Conclave of Shadow, I command you to come to my aid.

Had I spoken? Through the madness, I couldn't be sure. Perhaps it was all in my head – fifteen years living a fever dream of dragon-lovers and ancient gods; thirty-odd years of an insignificant life, a monkey trying to make sense of the cosmos. Might as well hand me a typewriter and ask me to write the works of Shakespeare. Life's but a walking shadow. Perhaps the Judeo-Christians had the right of it: to hear the Logos, to look into the face of God, was to invite madness. But if the void was God, then why lock it away from us? The tentacles of darkness tugged at me, urged me to reach out and pluck away the threads that strained to hold the wound closed. Guardians? What were they guarding against? The void that strained against them whispered of the completion of annihilation, a return to the primordial womb before the Big Bang of creation. Not Guardians. Wardens, and Creation was our prison. They kept us from reuniting with God.

Something closed around me, caught my reaching hands and drew me back from the wound in the void. I fought against it, but I was stretched too thin between Self and Otherness. Resistance was futile. I couldn't recall why that was funny, but I laughed, and the thing pulling me back caught hold of that laughter, wrapped me up in it, used it to give me shape and voice. It named me... *Missy*... in a dozen chitters that were all echoes of Templeton's voice

I felt cold, slick ground beneath my cheek, like obsidian. The chittering around me grew louder, blocking out all other sounds. I cracked an eye. Shadow-shapes darted around and above me – a plague of Templetons. They blotted out the void, the landscape, everything. The shadows nudged under me, forcing me at first to my hands and knees, and then into a low crouch. Above me, the void strained against its cage and called to me, its daughter, to free it. Only I could do it. I swallowed and kept my eyes focused on the ground as I ran.

A few of the shadows darted forward a short distance, then back to me. I stumbled in the direction indicated, and soon we were making our halting way across the obsidian-dark landscape. After an eternity, they stopped, milling about my feet as if they could go no further. In normal circumstances, I would have shown more gratitude, but I couldn't wait to be quit of this place. Lighting a crimson sparkler, I fled the void.

Sight, sound, and sanity returned in an overwhelming rush. I fell to my knees again, dry-heaving. The cave entrance turned to brick maybe ten yards ahead of me. Beyond that, the lights of nighttime Shanghai flashed so brightly after the never-ending nothingness of the voidlands that it set my eyes to tearing.

"Mother? Mother, are you all right?" Mei Shen crouched at my side. I gulped the thick air in deep breaths and struggled to get my stomach under control. I was still trembling as I sat back and looked into my daughter's face. I sensed movement to my right, and then the nurse stepped into my line of sight. She stood between us and the light beyond the cave's mouth. Her shadow stretched out toward me, and I flinched away before I realized that it was just a shadow.

"You are either very brave or very stupid," she observed.

"A little of column A, and a little of column B," I muttered, rising to my feet. Mei Shen steadied me, stronger than she had any right to be. I spared a moment to check her over, but I had no doubt it was my daughter. I spared the nurse a nod of gratitude.

"I thank you for what you've done. It will go far to ensuring that Lung Huang does not seek vengeance against you for the wrong you did him."

"Hmph. The combs'll see to that," she grunted. She smoothed her matted thatch of hair, where two ornaments of jade now gleamed, and then hitched at a tangle of strings slung over her shoulder, my Docs dangling from them. "And I know a few places where these'll fetch a pretty price. Places a world away from here. Figure it'll be healthier for me to leave China for a while. If you see your rat again, give him my thanks. Few're willing to deal with the likes of me, much less deal fair."

With a nod, she spat over her left shoulder, spun three times widdershins, and disappeared in a fall of autumn leaves.

"Oooh. Mother. Can you teach me to do that?" Mei Shen asked.

"Later," I promised, distracted by a building rumble beneath our feet. "We need to get out of here. Now. Run, Mei Shen."

We started forward. The rumbling grew with every step. Mei Shen's legs were too short to keep up, so I scooped her up and booked toward the mouth of the cave. The walls smoothed from stone to smoke-blackened brick. Little crumbles of masonry rained down on us as the tunnel collapsed in our wake. I ducked and rolled, shielding Mei Shen with my body. Indiana Jones would have been proud.

Coughing, I raised my head and squinted against the cloud raised by the rubble. Still a few paces to go until we were free, and a few more across the alleyway to the fox temple gardens. I struggled upright and carried my daughter those last few feet.

As I passed through the archway and into the flashing neon of the Puxi at night, Mei Shen tumbled from my grasp as though yanked by invisible strings. I turned to grab her up again. Lung Di stood amid the rubble of the cave, an affable smirk on his face. From the temple across the alleyway came a roar like thunder.

"Mei Shen, hurry," I said, trying to pull her across.

"I... I can't." She strained forward, but it was as if some invisible force held her back. For the first time, I saw fear in her eyes. "Mother, I can't!"

I stopped tugging, kneeling and calming her with a few hushed words. Lung Di approached, stopping an arm's reach away from us. A rush of warm air at my back blew my hair and Mei Shen's into tangles. I spared a quick glance over my shoulder. Jian Huo had already reverted to human form, and he looked none-too-pleased. I returned his glower. If he'd been honest with me, we might not be in this mess.

If he'd been honest with me, my children might not exist.

Mian Zi spotted Mei Shen and clambered down from his father's arms with a glad cry, but Jian Huo held him back from rushing to greet us.

"She can't leave, you know." Lung Di's words called my attention back to him. "She has been in my realm. Once a mortal creature has entered, they may not leave save by my will."

"I left."

"I allowed it." He spread his hands. "Marvel at my generosity. Still, it was quite amusing, watching you go through all your machinations. Did you really think you had me fooled, even for a second?"

"Let her go, you bastard," I whispered.

"Now, Missy. We both know what I want in exchange for that." He reached into his breast pocket and pulled out a strand of pearls. Their nacre gleamed dim and familiar. I stiffened, and behind me I heard Jian Huo growl.

"How did you get those?" I demanded.

"Your rat. You should never have left him to guard them while you put your fake daughter to bed. He was quite happy to trade them in exchange for his little trinkets."

Mei Shen pushed again at the barrier that held her back from family and home, whimpering when it did no good. I shifted beside her so that I could see Jian Huo as well as Lung Di. Standing beside his father, Mian Zi looked just as miserable and frightened as Mei Shen. My children and I, caught in a war between two gods

Time for some magic.

"All right." My shoulders slumped. "You win. You can have them. Just let Mei Shen go."

Jian Huo jerked, and a defeated shudder ran through his entire body, but I only had eyes for my nemesis. Lung Di smiled a slow, malicious smile.

"Of course," he said. "She is of little interest to me until she grows up. At the moment, I much prefer this prize."

"So, she is free to go as she pleases? In exchange for those?" I nodded to the pearls in his hand, holding my breath. He stroked them lightly, possessively. I tried not to let my anxiety show.

He paused, seeming to consider the pearls, but he was enjoying everyone's distress too much to really look at them. His eyes passed over the jewels in his hand to meet mine.

"In exchange for these? She is." He looked beyond me. I followed his gaze to Jian Huo. I had never seen my lover look so... I couldn't find a word to encompass all the emotions – anger, betrayal, disgust, despair. Everything that I'd felt on hearing Lung Di's revelations. I wanted to take it back, to go back to a time when I didn't know I was being tricked, but it was too late for that.

Mei Shen hurtled past the invisible ward with a cry of "Father!", and all the hatred on Jian Huo's face drained away as he bent to catch her in his arms. Mian Zi was swept up too. I couldn't swallow past the tightness in my throat, to be on the outside of the family I'd worked so hard to bring back together. If I could just survive the next few minutes, then maybe Jian Huo would listen long enough for me to explain, maybe he'd have a good explanation for me. Maybe everything didn't have to be broken.

"What a happy sight." Lung Di crept up beside me. I hadn't thought skin could crawl, but mine gave a good approximation. I stepped away, and I imagine the look I gave him was similar to the one Jian Huo had given me, minus the betrayal. I'd always known what Lung Di was. He'd only acted true to form.

"I thought you said you wouldn't take those by force or guile." I nodded to the string in his hand.

"And so I didn't. They were yours. Your rat had no right to give them up. It doesn't matter who held them. They were still yours until you gave them to me." He laughed his own triumph. "Instead, you bargained for your daughter, thinking you had nothing to lose. Such a shame. If only you had known better... were a little more patient. If only you belonged to this world, you might never have lost my brother's love." He twined the pearls around his fingers, and again I held my breath. Nothing happened. I felt a moment's panic that I had been too clever for my own good, but I stifled it. My plan had worked. Please, let my plan have worked.

Jian Huo shifted to dragon form and bundled the children close. I had hoped for better circumstances to reveal everything – something more conducive to me not dying – but if I didn't act now, I might never see my family again.

"Wait!" I lunged for him, hoping also to put some distance between myself and Lung Di before I said anything more. Jian Huo ignored me, and the dragon at my side caught me by the arm before I could escape.

"Let it go, Missy. You've ceded his love to me. His pride is all he has left."

"No. Jian Huo!" I called again. I yanked my arm, but Lung Di held fast. I hoped that bruises were the only injuries I'd have suffered come tomorrow. "I never gave him your pearls. I swear!"

"I already told you–" Lung Di began, but then Jian Huo swung his head around and stalked toward us, the twins still cradled in his grasp. A face full of draconic ire was thrust at me. His head was as tall as my whole body. I shied back a step, but Lung Di's grip kept me from retreating further.

"It doesn't matter, does it? Your intentions mean nothing, Melissa Masters. He has them now. I gave you the most precious gift I had to give, and because you could not trust in me, you squandered it. My siblings were right. You are not worthy to be my bride." His head drooped and he turned away. In his claws, Mei Shen and Mian Zi huddled wide-eyed and silent. "I suppose, at the very least, I owe you my thanks for rescuing my daughter."

Oh no. He did *not* get to make me the bad guy. "Will you listen?" I reached for him. The muscles of his hind quarters bunched as he prepared to launch into the sky. "They're not your pearls, you self-righteous lizard!" I shouted. "They're fakes!"

Jian Huo's head whipped around again. Before I could decipher the look on his face, Lung Di laughed.

"Really? Fakes? How stupid do you think I am?" Lung Di demanded.

"That's a rhetorical question, right?" I asked, anger turning me into a smartass. He growled and shook me by the arm he still held. He thrust the pearls into my face.

"These are real. I can taste the magic on them. Your rat gave them to me in exchange for his precious baubles, and you yielded them for a pittance."

"Mei Shen isn't a pittance, and Templeton did exactly what he was supposed to do. Sure, those are real, as far as that goes, but they're not Jian Huo's pearls. You've been had."

Lung Di sneered, but before he could respond, we were interrupted.

"She speaks truth."

A warm wind washed up the alleyway, smelling of spring rain. The lights of Shanghai dimmed until there was only the deepness of night, the cold stars in a clear sky, and the rabbit-filled moon. The speaker picked her way over the rough pavement on a beam of silver moonlight, snowdrops and mossy green turf sprouting and spreading wherever she stepped. I shook my head, sure that I could hear the sound of crickets chirping.

The *qilin* was strange and wild and beautiful, but that was where her resemblance to the beast of western legend ended. Her head was more reptilian than equine, and her sinuous viridian body was smooth and hairless, wreathed in blue-green flame. She looked more like a slender, long-legged dragon than she did a horse. The unicorn comparison had to be based on the two corkscrew-spiraled horns that crowned her brow. The exterior of each horn was roughened and black like the outside of a mussel, but the insides shone violet-blue with nacre. A strand of pearls twined around one horn, glowing with a reflected sheen.

Jian Huo jerked when he saw the pearls. It was Lung Di's turn to go still and silent. The *qilin* walked up to me.

"I believe these belong still to you," she said, lowering her head. The pearls trickled down her horn like heavy dew, pooling in my waiting hand.

"Those... those are..." Jian Huo's words faded on a breath.

"Your pearls." I finished. Despite the *qilin's* words, I wasn't sure whether I should return them to him or not, given the circumstances.

"You gave them to the *qilin*?" Jian Huo's question rang stilted and harsh. I flinched.

"In a dream. But she never yielded them to me," the creature said when I couldn't respond. "She asked me to guard them so they would not fall into... unwanted hands."

"You..." Lung Di spun me to face him. His expression was twisted into an inhuman grimace. The false-pearls twined through his fingers. His fist clenched around them, and the illusion that Fang Shih had worked into them broke. They sliced deep into his flesh. As blood welled in the cuts and bathed the pearls red, they shimmered and became a dull woodcarving blade.

Lung Di uttered a cry of pain, dropping the knife. A necrotic cancer spread from the wound, engulfing his hand and moving up his arm. He released me to grasp at his forearm, stemming the necrosis with a grunt of pained concentration. Even though Fang Shih had warned me, I was so stunned by the turn of events that it didn't occur to me to use that opportunity to make my escape. Instead, I stood watching in dumb wonder as Lung Di's hand withered and blackened from the knife wound.

I was startled out of my stupor when his head whipped around to pin me with a glare. Before I knew what was happening, he was unfolding on himself, transforming from the suave businessman I'd spent the last few days conning into an ancient serpentine god. His blue-black coils tumbled down the alley, and the earth shook beneath us.

"You *BITCH*" he screamed, his withered claw coming around to strike me with the mother of all backhands. The blackened tissue broke on impact, and I went flying in a spray of blood and pus, hitting the far wall surrounding the temple and landing at its base in a crumpled heap.

I imagine things happened after that, as things are wont to do, but I wasn't too concerned about them until Mei Shen and Mian Zi's faces swam into view. I blinked. The stars swirled behind them like a Van Gogh painting, or something else. I struggled to remember the proper term for a skylight when it was underwater. Surely there was one.

"Mother? Mother, are you all right? Please be all right." The twins alternated between being four beings and being one. I blinked again. Looking at infinity was making me dizzy and a little sick to my stomach.

"My pearls?" I said. I couldn't recall why it was important, but it was.

"They're still in your hand, Mother," Mian-Mei replied. I wanted to hold them and tell them it would be all right, but I couldn't seem to make my body work. In the background I could hear strange sounds, like an earthquake... or a great thunderstorm.

"What's happening?" I asked.

"Father is fighting Lung Di." Mian-Mei seemed to be crying, but I couldn't figure out why.

"Good," I said. "I hope your father kicks his ass." Speaking was difficult. My jaw hurt for some reason. My mouth was filled with cotton, my vision rimmed with white fuzz, and a high-pitched whine sounded in my ears.

   I must be at the dentist, was my last thought before the world
dissolved to white.

THIRTEEN
People's Hero

Now

The first thing I saw when I entered was the dragon.

And I mean *dragon*. Blue-black serpentine coils tangled beyond undoing, lined with parallel fringe the violent blue of irises. A rainbow sheen played across the twists and bends, like light off the surface of an oil slick. It took me a moment to realize the light came not from without, but from within.

I took a step back, bumping into the door. This side wasn't shadow. Just door. Very solid door. Which meant I was trapped here with a dragon. The last time I'd tangled with him, things had not turned out well for me. Seeing him in his true form – or as true as any form he chose to take – reminded me just how badly they'd turned out.

But those great claws of obsidian lay quiescent in the gouges they'd dug into the stone floor. I took a tentative step forward, then another. He didn't stir. Maybe he was sleeping? Comatose? Dead?

No such luck. One great eye slid open, pale nictating membrane parting underneath. The iris narrowed; the great eye rolled toward me. I was Frodo in Mordor. There was nowhere to hide.

The eye fixed on me. He blinked. Slowly. A sluggish lizard

too long in the cold. Except it was mild down here; there's a reason sommeliers use caves for storing wine.

He yawned with a jaw-popping crack that echoed like cannon fire. To my credit, I didn't try to retreat again. Wanted to, but didn't.

"Missy Masters. Come to save me from my own hubris. My hero."

Yeah, he was just as annoying as I remembered. It was almost a comfort. At least he was predictable.

"I didn't come for you." I edged further into the cavern. It was hard to see beyond his bulk, but I'd caught a flash of vibrant plumage when he'd opened his jaws. Not in them. Beyond them.

"I am bereft."

"I just bet you are."

His coils shifted, sliding against each other like a nest of eels. Past the constricting knot, I caught another flash of color. Feng Huang, the Phoenix, sat hunched in a gilded cage, head tucked under her wing. If she were here, the other Guardians must be.

I continued to circle him. The great eye tracked my progress. The bearded tendrils streaming from his maw twitched in amusement.

"And you are a liar. Of course you came for me. I created an international crisis and upset the balance of power in the spirit world." He shifted again, uncoiled a bit, stretched. "I would be disappointed if I went to such trouble and you didn't come for me after such a blatant invitation."

"Has anyone explained the concept of 'overkill' to you?" I spied a flash of orange: Tiger in another golden cage, curled up tight as any house tom. His tail draped over his nose, tip twitching as he tore apart some doomed creature of his own imaginings. He should have been cute, but I found myself in sympathy with the dream creature.

"No. Perhaps you'll indulge me, though you may not want

to waste the time. It took you longer to arrive than I'd expected. Much longer, and I might never have awoken."

"Getting here was a bitch."

"My apologies. If I had made it too easy, you might have suspected something."

"Next time you might as well make it easier, because I'm always suspicious of you. When are you not up to something?"

He yawned again. "And yet you came anyways, and jumped through all my hoops. I suppose we should take a moment to mourn the death of the little idealist who wouldn't trade her pearls for her daughter."

"I'm still an idealist."

"Idealism is just a series of compromises waiting to happen. How many compromises did you have to make to get here?"

That hit close to home. I struggled for a good comeback. "Yeah. Well... so's your face." Not the best retort in my arsenal. He looked pained.

"At least you are not rubber and I am not glue. That is something, I suppose."

It had taken a bit more circling – I didn't bother being sneaky about it, and he didn't make a move to stop me – but I finally spied the third cage, golden bars set into the ground, arching over an emerald pool. The darker jade of Tortoise's shell just broke the surface, water lapping against it to some distant tidal rhythm.

"Well, you've got me here now. The compromises are my business to deal with. So what's it going to take to get you to release the Guardians and let down the Barrier. Let's bargain."

"Everything I want from you, I already have. All that is left is to release the Guardians and seal the matter."

"Just like that?" Seal what matter?

His eyes slid closed. He looked like he might go back to sleep on me. "You requested easy, and now you complain. You're an extremely contrary woman."

"I'm the one who's contrary. Right." I nudged a coil with my foot. "Wake up."

His eyes opened a crack. "I apologize. Maintaining the ward takes much from me. From all of us. Here."

He uncoiled, and I saw that he was curved around something besides himself. An altar with all sorts of junk on it – symbolic implements I didn't know the purpose of, so junk to me, at least. Red candles in tall brass holders flanking an etched brass ewer, jade tea cups ringing a silver basin, a huge wooden rice tub painted red, with several banners on poles jutting up out of it. The inscriptions were just as arcane as the rest of the implements: the Three Dots Society, the Three Harmonies, Red Eyebrows, and White Lotus. If there'd been a banner for the 4-H club, it wouldn't have looked out of place to me.

"Take the banner above the door. Burn it. Mix the ash with the wine."

Banner above the door? I glanced that direction. A long sheet of paper with the characters for *"Lung Xin Niang"* hung above the lintel. And other characters I didn't recognize. *Lung Bao Hu Zhe?*

It took me a moment to translate; I was rusty. Dragon protector? As if. "Aw. You made me a banner. Is there a cake?"

"I'll get you one later. You brought the knife?" I pulled it out, unwrapped it from the protective silk. Something flickered through Lung Di's half-lidded eyes at seeing it. His left claw clenched against the stone. It looked well and whole, but still emaciated compared to his other claws.

"Good. I can't tell you what a disaster this would have been if you'd forgotten it."

"So, Tsung is still working for you?" Poor Mei Shen. She'd be devastated. Assuming she didn't refuse to believe it.

"David works for himself, which makes him easy to predict."

"He tried to come here instead of me."

"Of course. He wants badly what I'm about to give to you.

But I was confident that you wouldn't let him stop you. You could say I counted on it, your need to be the hero." His eyes drooped shut. I recognized that state. It was the "just for a moment" level of tiredness that led to semis crashing on the Grapevine in the early morning hours.

I snatched the yellow paper banner from above the doorway, crumpled it into the empty silver basin, and set it alight with one of the candles. It burned quickly. I grabbed one of the banners from the rice tub and used the end of its pole to tamp down on the cinders and crush the thin filaments to ash. The brass ewer was so heavy it took both hands to steady it while I poured. The ashes sloshed about in the dark wine.

Lung Di's head curved toward me as if to watch the proceedings, but he hadn't opened his eyes again. In fact, he was doing something that sounded suspiciously like snoring – his breath came hard enough to blow my trousers flat against my legs.

"Hey." I nudged his chin with my toe. Then nudged harder. "Wake up, you useless lizard."

"Hmm?" He raised his head an inch, his lids opening only a few inches more. The nictating membrane underneath barely parted. "Ah. Good. Now dip the knife in the wine and slice your finger with it."

I looked at his claw again, half-tucked under his length and still not fully healed.

"No fucking way."

"As amusing as it would be to see my wound visited upon you, that is not my intent. The mixture nullifies the necromancy of the blade. Your blood on the blade is the key."

"What key?"

"To the cages. Above each is an inscription. Read the oath, use the knife on the lock, and the Guardians' magic is returned to them. Missy saves the day. There'll be a parade, I'm sure. And cake."

"You're lying." And I'd had enough of playing along. I squeezed past the altar and held the blade of the knife to the joint below his jaw. His moustaches quivered again, a reaction I'd always read as amusement with Jian Huo. "We've seen what this did to your claw. Wonder if it'll do the same to your head. Now stop screwing with me. This whole thing has cost you. Mei Shen rules the Shadow Dragons now. Everyone else is pissed at you. And you want me to believe you captured the guardians and raised the New Wall just to free them and take it down? What's the point?"

"The point was to bring you here to free them. Only that knife will do. Only the blood of a Shadow-born will do. Even if you use that knife on me, I am immortal. The ward will stand, the world will fall, and you will be trapped here."

"But why me? Why this big, Rube-Goldberg scheme to get me here? I'm nothing to you. I'm not even a good pawn anymore."

"You are a lousy pawn. You bested me before because I mistook you for one. Just a concubine, I thought, when you had the makings of a champion, like your grandfather. Well, now you are one, or will be. Mine."

I jerked – away, luckily, or I might have nicked him. "Bullshit. I'm not your champion."

His shoulders rolled, the movement rippling all down his length. "You will be, as soon as you speak the oaths and free the others. They'll be furious, I imagine. Your first duty will probably be to defend me from them. Lucky for you they'll be weakened as I am."

One claw – the thinner one – lifted and curved possessively around my ankles. "Once *Lung Xin Niang*, now *Lung Bao Hu Zhe*. Not quite my brother's bride, now my champion."

I was shaking so hard I could barely keep hold of the knife. There's no worse feeling in the world than helplessness. It had been years since I'd felt this *used*.

"I won't do it."

"Of course you will. This isn't like that debacle with the pearls. This is a game I've controlled from the start."

"But why me? You said yourself: I'm a lousy pawn now."

"Against my brother, yes. Against your children? There's none better. Will they try to supplant me if it means they must kill their mother to do so?"

"Get bent. What happens if I just let them kick your ass anyways when that day comes?"

"Then your honor would be ash in the wind, and your word dust on your tongue. Lung Tian would have reason to deny your status as *Lung Xin Niang*. Mei Shen and Mian Zi would no longer be fit to be Lung Huang's heirs. They would no longer be a threat to me."

My everything went numb. The knife clattered to the floor.

"You fucking asshole." He would pick now to develop a taste for poetry.

"I am seeing to my own protection. Remember, Missy, that I am not the one who arranged for them to be a threat. For that you must look to my brother. I am merely assuring a *détente*. If Mei Shen and Mian Zi do nothing, then nothing will ever come of this. I may even come to your aid to ensure your safety. Now that I have a vested interest in your continued existence."

His head settled back to the ground. His eyes slid shut again with a sigh that blew my hair back.

"So now we will see... what is your opinion on doing the wrong thing for the right reasons, Missy? Because I am not asking you to betray anyone this time," he murmured. "Except yourself."

I don't know how long I watched him sleep, frozen in my helplessness. I could try to break the cages some other way, but I was no sorcerer. Card tricks and parlor magic were my forte. What if I just made things worse? The cages glimmered gold, but with a brightness and energy like no metal I'd ever seen.

I couldn't even leave, unless I wanted to brave the voidlands without the plague of Templetons to save me. And every moment I delayed was another moment the world grew more chaotic.

In the end, I stooped down and picked up the knife. Dipped it in the mixture of wine and ash. Brought it to my hand.

Idealism was a series of compromises waiting to happen, he'd said. He'd managed to manipulate me into one I was willing to make.

I approached Tortoise's cage first. He was slow. Of all the Guardians, he was the one I could probably take in a fight.

The barest touch of the knife sliced my finger, deeper than I'd intended, almost as though intent to cut were enough. Shades of the Subtle Knife. No necrotic cancer crawled up my arm, but the cut still burned as though unclean, oozing blood as I pulled my finger away from the christened blade.

A strip of yellow paper fluttered above Tortoise's cage. There was no door I could see, but a plain, solid plate sat at waist height. The kind of place where a keyhole should be if this were a normal cage.

On impulse, I tried touching the knife to the plate without reciting the words. All I got for my trouble was a shock. I yelped and swapped the knife to my bleeding hand, fingers going to my mouth on instinct. The heat didn't help. I pulled my hand away; my fingers were already blistering.

He could have just made the key-plate not work rather than giving me second-degree electrical burns, but no. He was an asshole, and this was his reprimand.

Gingerly, I swapped the knife again. I could make out the inscription easily enough. I almost wished I didn't understand it. Then I could pretend to myself that on some level this wasn't my choice.

"I stand as *Lung Bao Hu Zhe*. This I swear on the freedom of the Guardian of the North."

I touched the knife to the plate.

There was another jolt, but this one didn't burn me. It traveled up the bars of the cage, which began to sizzle, then to melt. They trickled down themselves like a candle burned too long, into a puddle around Tortoise, and then into the Guardian himself.

His shell brightened to jade fire. A beaked snout poked out one end, myopic eyes blinking like a newborn. Four webbed feet, sharp claws curving back, also emerged.

Really sharp claws. A beak that could sever a limb, and a shell harder than the stone it resembled. Why had I thought he would be the easy opponent?

He lifted his head over the lip of the pool, looking past me at his captor. With a heave of those powerful legs, he wedged himself up over the edge of the pool and lunged for Lung Di.

He moved faster than I remembered, faster than any newly-awoken creature should. What if Lung Di had been lying and the Guardians weren't weakened by their captivity? Maybe this was just a pointlessly elaborate plan to end me.

I caught Tortoise by the edge of his shell as he barreled past me.

"Oh no you don't! I need him alive." With a heave of my own, I flipped Tortoise onto his back.

There's something horribly cruel about watching a turtle struggling to right itself from being overturned and doing nothing to help. He looked how I felt: trapped and helpless.

"*Lung… Xin… Niang…*" He stopped trying to use his head as a lever when he caught sight of me. Recognized me. He twisted for a better view. "Why are you helping that villain? Turn me over. Let me have my vengeance."

"Gui Dai," I set my palms together and bowed. "I would love nothing better than to let you rip him a new one, but if he gets hurt, all of China suffers."

"What do I care for that?" Tortoise snapped. I took a step back, just in case his neck could stretch farther than I'd estimated. "He imprisoned me and stole my power. I will drag him into the deep waters of time until I have extracted repayment."

Why had I thought Tortoise was the mildest, most considerate of the Guardians? Looking at him now, even comically overturned, I realized he was closer in mind and body to a great crocodile. Or a dinosaur. One who didn't care about me one way or another.

"You aren't taking anyone anywhere like that. I'll flip you back over, but only if you promise to leave here without attacking Lung Di or dragging him anywhere."

"You assume the role of his champion?"

It was still hard to accept, but every compromise made it a little easier. After all, it was too late now. I'd shed the blood and spoken the oath.

"Yeah. I guess I do."

Tortoise stilled, considering this. He considered a long time.

"Very well. You have freed me from the cage of my own power. For that, I will spare your master. Today. Now, right me."

He could have been lying, but I doubted it. The oath of a spirit was a binding thing. I crept forward and grabbed the edge of his shell. Any moment he could snap out and I'd lose my blistered hand.

It took more effort than flipping him into this position had. The curve of his shell worked against us, but eventually we righted him.

He looked to the other two Guardians, still locked in their golden cages.

"You intend to free them, too?"

I nodded. "Yeah. It's why I came here."

Tortoise trundle-scraped back to the pool. "Then one of them will succeed where I have not. I wish I could wish you luck in defending your master, *Lung Bao Hu Zhe*. But I do not."

He slid back into the viridian pool with a splash that sloshed water over all sides, and disappeared into the depths.

I turned to the other two Guardians. Phoenix and Tiger. Tortoise was right. I was screwed.

I approached Phoenix's cage, mostly because thinking about facing Tiger set large parts of my mind to gibbering in abject terror. Anything to put that off. Phoenix would just burn me to a crisp and have done, but Tiger was a cat. He'd play with me first.

"I stand as *Lung Bao Hu Zhe*. This I swear on the freedom of the Guardian of the South."

There was another surge as I touched knife to plate, but instead of melting to a puddle, the bars imploded into a fiery ball. I jumped back as Phoenix was bathed in bright gold flames, nearly dropping the knife for the umpteenth time. My hand was killing me.

Phoenix's long, sinuous neck untucked. Her wings spread, and she launched aloft with a cry. She circled once, twice, reveling in her freedom. Then her head craned down, and the flames shifted from the gold of exaltation to the red of pure fury. She dove down at Lung Di's sleeping form, flames rising to fill the room.

"Oh no you don't!" I hopped a dragon coil and snatched the full basin from the altar, dousing the Phoenix a scant meter away from ground zero.

The flames sputtered out, and she fell the last few feet in a graceless tumble. She squawked, a sound more in keeping with a surprised chicken than a creature of legend. Her bedraggled feathers dripped wine and ash. She managed a spark or two, but the flames of a moment ago were beyond her, at least for a little while.

"*Lung Xin Niang*?" She cocked her head, carnelian eyes still shining with an inner flame. "Why are you protecting this louse?"

"Because I'm his champion. Long story. Look, I'd take it as a kindness if you could just let the vengeance thing slide for today? I really don't want to have to fight you."

I'd only met Tortoise the one time, but Phoenix was a regular visitor back in my days on Minshan. Granted, she'd been Jian Huo's friend, but that connection had to count for something, right?

Not much, given the darkening of her eyes and the hiss she let out. I'd read once that a full-grown swan could break a man's arm with a beat of her wings. Phoenix had a similar wing-span. I considered setting a few dragon coils between us, then realized that Lung Di hardly made a good shield.

"You have fallen far, *Lung Bao Hu Zhe*, if you have taken up with this one. But you have freed me, so I will spare you this once."

Another spark, and another, like someone trying to light a Zippo that was out of juice. But with the third, she sparked to life, flames burning away the wine in a sour-smelling cloud.

She launched aloft again. "I cry for your children, to have such a mother."

She didn't pause her momentum as she reached the roof, dashing against it and sending a cloud of flame roiling out from her point of impact.

It died with nothing to fuel it. Phoenix was gone, leaving me alone with the dragon.

And Tiger.

I approached Tiger's cage with all the trepidation it deserved. Actually, a lot less trepidation than it deserved, but there was only so much I could muster. I was reaching exhaustion point.

On reflection, maybe saving him for last hadn't been the best of ideas.

"Hey, kitty, kitty," I whispered to give myself courage. He was asleep. What was he gonna do?

The bars of the cage burned fallow gold, crosshatching

his stripes with their light. The inscription over the bars was predictable at this point. At least I'd have a few moments grace while he woke and stretched.

"I stand as *Lung Bao Hu Zhe*. This I swear on the freedom of the Guardian of the West."

Only as I touched the knife to the plate did I notice that little shift in his haunches – the one that told you a cat wasn't sleeping at all, but was merely biding its time to pounce.

"Oh, shi–"

The cage dissolved too fast for me to react, separating into motes of dust scattered on an invisible ray of light. Tiger launched at me through the cloud, the dust coating his body.

I was down before I could do more than turn, my chin knocking hard on the stone floor as four-hundred pounds of Tiger pressed me to the ground. My hands twisted under me, palms stinging from where the stone had gouged my skin when I tried to break my fall.

I wormed my hands into a better position, ignoring the additional scraping. If I could just get a little leverage, I might be able to throw him off before he ate me.

"*Lung Xin Niang*. No. It is *Lung Bao Hu Zhe* now." Tiger's breath blew hot against my ear. His whiskers brushed my neck. They tickled. I cringed.

"You know?" I was having trouble breathing from the weight of him.

"I know." He settled on top of me, front paw patting at my head. It should have been a comforting gesture – his claws were retracted, after all – but I'd seen enough cats play with small objects to know the difference.

"*Lung Bao Hu Zhe*. Do you think I take the form of a cat by chance? Cats are never so asleep that we do not know what goes on in the waking world, nor ever so awake that we do not also walk in dreamtime. I know because I watched your 'battles' with Tortoise and Phoenix and your conversation with my... host. You will not have things so easy with me."

He rose and stepped off of me. I scuttled up to my knees, turning to face him. He looked almost demure, tail curled about his feet, golden eyes watching me with the patience of a predator who knows his prey has nowhere to run.

"You have freed me, so I will offer you this. You may choose to continue this fight now. I am still drowsy and weak. Maybe you will best me because of this. But if you do not, I will devour you, and your master, and chase your friends through his tower until I tire of the game. Or, you may put off our battle for another time, when I am strong and you have no chance of winning. But your master and your friends will be safe. Which is it to be?"

There wasn't really a question. There'd be no trick for defeating Tiger, not like with the other two, and I still had a Wall to dismantle.

"Later," I said.

He nodded, as though he expected nothing else. Rising back to his feet, he turned and stalked off into the shadows, orange-and-black-ringed tail flicking.

I used a nearby coil to haul myself to my feet, then slumped over it. Lung Di slept on, unconscious. The final Guardian. There was no cage around him that I could see, but...

I picked up the knife and lurched towards the door I'd come through. Sure enough, there was the blank gold key-plate, just as with the others. I didn't need an inscription to know what to say.

"I stand as *Lung Bao Hu Zhe*. This I swear on the freedom of the Guardian of the East."

I touched the blade to the plate. Every particle of air in the room charged. My hair stood on end, my bones and teeth itched with a vibration like one of those turn-of-the-century electrocution carnival games. A sharp stench, like ozone, permeated the space.

Lung Di opened his mouth, breathing it all in with a cavernous yawn. His coils toppled over themselves in great rolls, the dragon equivalent of a stretch. The charge dissipated, and his coils compressed themselves in a mind-breaking demonstration of non-Euclidian geometry. Within moments, I wasn't looking at a dragon at all. In his place was a tall Chinese man wearing a dark blue business suit, violet tie held in place with smoky topaz, and a smug grin.

"As I said when you arrived. My hero." He smoothed the lapels of his suit, straightened the glove that covered his left hand. "Now, let us see about cleaning up this mess Mr Tsung summoned onto my doorstep."

He gave me a wide berth as he passed. It was almost like he knew I wanted to kick him in the shins.

FOURTEEN
The Time Between

Then

No conversation in the history of relationships that has started with the words "We need to talk" has ended well.

I found Jian Huo in the pagoda. Since stairs were still a challenge for my wobbly vestibular sense to navigate, it was the best hiding place he could have picked. I had to commandeer Mei Shen and Mian Zi – they refused to be parted after their long separation – to keep me steady on my hobble down to beard the dragon in his pagoda.

I shooed them off at the arch. Kids shouldn't witness their parents fighting. I'd read that somewhere.

"We need to talk," I said to Jian Huo's back. I marveled at how strong and steady my voice sounded, almost as if I wasn't speaking from a churning diaphragm and a strangle-tight throat. Almost as if I hadn't been muffling great, wracking sobs into the pillow of my recovery bed as I relived over and over my dinner with Lung Di and the truths he'd revealed in his manifesto. I'd watched my kids' reunion, hating... not them, but the way their closeness cultivated the seed of doubt that asshole had planted. I knew the truth. I just needed to hear it confirmed from another asshole's lips.

Jian Huo set his teacup on the low table at his side, giving me a glimpse of his face in profile. Darkness shadowed his cheek from temple to jaw. Not shadow. I knew shadow. A bruise. Lung Di had given us a matching set.

That which doesn't kill us... But I didn't feel stronger. I just wanted to cast myself across Jian Huo's lap and use his chest like I'd been using my pillows.

"You need to talk. I have little to say to you." He turned back to the sea of clouds covering the world. Any urge to water him with tears was banished by those smooth, cold words. He was pissed at me?

Aw, *hell* no.

"Are you seriously still mad about the thing with the pearls?" I rounded the tea table and planted myself in front of him so he couldn't stare off into the distance and pull his ancient, mystical dragon shit. "I told you, the *qilin* told you, you saw. They were–"

"Fakes. Yes. You fooled us all." Jian Huo stood. I thrust out a hand to stop him if he meant to escape, but he squared off against me. "You should be very proud of yourself."

"I am. I got Mei Shen back. And I didn't ruin your *guanxi* or lose your pearls."

"Or get yourself killed?" He grabbed my shoulders. He was trembling. We both were. "He could have killed you, Missy, or trapped you as he trapped our daughter. And me left helpless to do anything for you. You just left, without talking to me, without sharing your plan so I might help you. And I am glad – overjoyed – that you succeeded, but you treated me as though I was nothing to you. And he could have *killed* you."

Meteor showers cascaded through the black of his eyes. I'd never seen Jian Huo distressed like this, not since that first time I'd been sucked into shadow, and I didn't want to see it now. He dared take me to task over the way I'd treated him?

"He doesn't want me dead. Dead, I'm a heroic martyr, and Lung Tian wouldn't be able to wriggle out of naming me

Lung Xian Niang." I brought my hands between us and swept my arms in an arc, breaking his hold. I hobbled out of range of his hold or his concern. "Seems Lung Di isn't down with that scenario."

"What do you mean?"

I pressed my hands to my cheeks to cool them. It was warm here in Jian Huo's realm, always spring, but fury had me flushed beyond that pleasant warmth. "Did you have kids with me to supplant your brother in the cosmic order of things?"

Said aloud like that, it sounded ridiculous. So ridiculous, I almost laughed. How had Lung Di ever convinced me to believe something so–

"Ah. So he told you." Jian Huo took a step back from me, hands disappearing into his sleeves.

I gaped at his assumption of that reserved mien, like he couldn't possibly be in the wrong. "You son of a bitch!"

"I am a son of the Tao."

Fucking pedant. "Well, the Tao is a mother fucking bitch. You *used* me. I… I can't even…" I hobbled back and forth, needing movement, needing to escape this confirmation. I felt ill all over again, the same nausea that had taken me when Lung Di revealed that I was being used. I wanted to flee, but my own injuries and Jian Huo's tall form in the archway blocked any easy escape. He kept his hands in his sleeves, his face devoid of any emotion. The distress of moments before had been packed away. I guess the lie of his concern was no longer needed now that I'd confronted him with the truth.

I barked my shin on the corner of the tea table. The pain shot up my leg, deeper than bone, clearing away all confusion. I knew what I had to do, what self-respect and self-preservation demanded. I kicked the stupid table aside and lurched past Jian Huo. "I'm out of here."

"Missy–"

"NO!" I evaded his attempt to catch me, stumbling into

the arch post for support. I didn't want him touching me, not ever again. "I got what I wanted from you. You got what you wanted from me. We're done. Good luck ousting your brother." I pushed away from the pole and made my unsteady way down the path toward the Dragon Gate. Oddly, I really meant that last sally. Not that I didn't mean all the others, but that last?

Yeah, I wanted Lung Di to go down. And I wanted my kids to be the ones to do it.

Shit. My kids. I hesitated just past the Dragon Gate. Even a few steps out of Jian Huo's realm, my teeth were chattering from the cold seeping through my silk robes and into my core. Not even fury could warm me against it. I glanced back at the gardens. My kids were up there. I couldn't stay because of Jian Huo, but I couldn't leave because of them. Not like this, not like Mitchell had left, without a word of explanation.

But if I stayed to say goodbye, could I force myself to leave at all?

"Missy, we are not finished." Jian Huo had followed me. He stood at the head of the path, and, gods, he was beautiful, even with half his face shadowed purple with bruises.

Home. Husband. Children. I'd built a life here, beyond any original intent I'd had to come and study and leave again after... when? A few weeks? Months? Gods, I'd been so fucking naïve. How could I leave this, even after learning the truth? This was my life now.

"We are. We are finished." I wanted to charge back into the gardens, find Mei Shen and Mian Zi, drag them with me. But Jian Huo would never allow that. Worse, Mei Shen might be willing to come, but Mian Zi would resist. And they'd both be miserable. I couldn't do that, tear them apart, make them miserable. Better to contain the misery to just myself.

"It's all... finished." I turned my back on my home and hobbled down into the cold and piling drifts.

Jian Huo caught me a few steps down. Not the man. The dragon. His claws closed above me in a loose, golden cage. Snowflakes landed on his red and green scales, diamonds among emeralds and rubies before his heat melted them into wisps of steam. "I will take you down to the temple. You will never make it on your own. You are not recovered."

He wasn't even going to ask me to stay? No, of course he wasn't, and I hated myself that I wanted him to. I hesitated. Nodded. This way, I wouldn't be tempted to turn around and trudge right back up the hill when the cold ate away my anger and my resolve.

Jian Huo scooped me up and launched into the sky. I huddled in his grip and tried to tell myself I wasn't leaving my heart behind with my stomach.

Jian Huo approached the temple at the head of the Huanglong valley in a roiling fog meant to hide him from curious tourists. It burned off within moments of landing, but that was fine. I wasn't standing beside a dragon anymore. I was barely standing beside a recognizable Jian Huo. He'd dumped the fancy *hanfu* for a simple set of monks' robes. He still had his bruises, though, and his hair. It coiled behind him, the end dipping into the aquamarine waters of one of the travertine pools.

I wanted to fish it out, just for an excuse to touch that hair one last time. I clasped my hands behind my back to keep myself from showing such weakness.

"So."

"So."

A shriek from the temple interrupted any attempt at awkward goodbyes. "Missy?"

A distantly-familiar *laowai* woman with lean limbs, sun-kissed cheeks, and salon-streaked hair jogged toward me, waving and beaming. I had to root through memory to place her. "J-Jill?"

And the man coming up behind her. "Jim?"

She reached me and yanked me into a hug. "Oh, thank god you're OK. And you made it back down just in time. It took a few days–"

"And more international roaming minutes that I care to calculate," the man behind her drawled.

"–But we found another bus that can take us back to Chengdu." Jill released me, but only enough to inspect my face and clothes. She flinched. I wasn't sure if it was due to the bruise or the fact that I wasn't a fresh-faced eighteen-year-old anymore. "You look... different." Her gaze dropped from my face, settled on something less troubling. "Is this silk? God, I *love* this! Jim, look at the embroidery!"

Jim seemed more interested in Jian Huo than the embroidery. He glowered at him like a protective older brother, even as he spoke to me. "Where did you go? We tried to tell the temple monks and the tour guides about you, but half the time they pretended not to understand, and the other half they said you would be safe as a guest of the mountain. Whatever the hell that means."

Jim might as well have been a midge for how much effect his glare had on Jian Huo. "It means me. And I have brought her safely back to you."

As weird as it was to see Jian Huo in anything but his ostentatious robes, it was even weirder to hear him speak perfect, received-pronunciation English.

English. He spoke English. We could have been speaking English this entire time. I glared fuck-yous at him.

Jill remained oblivious to my fuming, hugging me again. "The cousins are going to be so relieved. And Gunther. We've all been kicking ourselves for letting you go off on your own."

I couldn't speak past the surreality of the meeting. Who *were* these people? I'd only known them for a week, and that had been fifteen years ago.

I wormed out of Jill's embrace. "If you could just... I just need to have a quick word with..." I gave up on coming up with a good excuse and grabbed Jian Huo's sleeve, dragging him across a nearby bridge that spanned the pools so I could rip him a new one in solitude.

I stopped halfway across. "What. The hell."

He gave me a curious look. "Was that a question?"

I glanced back at Jill and Jim, who were casting us equally-curious looks. Two older ladies joined them, hands clamping matching sunhats to their snowy hair. I couldn't remember their names, but I recalled they were from England. Norfolk? Suffolk? One of the folks.

I released Jian Huo's sleeve like I was flinging off a bug. "Explain," I commanded, crossing my arms.

For several seconds, I didn't think he would, but then he tucked his hands in his sleeves and sighed. "I do not know that I can give you what you wish. There is no great need for explanation. You are an intelligent creature. If you have not already deduced what I did, then you soon will."

"You worked some spirit mojo with time so that everything that I thought took place over fifteen years actually took place in a moment of real time," I said. I didn't understand all the nuances, likely never would, but I'd gotten that much at least. I touched my cheeks, looked at my hands. I didn't *feel* any different. I didn't feel like the clock had been turned back fifteen years. "You couldn't have stopped me from aging?"

"I could have, but then you would never have changed, never grown, never been able to..." He flattened his lips against his next words, as if I couldn't guess what he'd been about to say.

I would never have been able to bear him his fucking master plan.

Screw explanations. I'd been right to leave. "You are unbelievable."

He caught my arm when I would have walked away. "I thought you would have been pleased to return to a world unchanged."

"Oh, is that what you thought? And you didn't consider that I might be upset to learn that it was all a dream? That none of it was real?"

"What do you take me for? Do you think me some kind of charlatan, that the only realities I can spin are illusions? It was real. The life we led was as true as anything in this world."

"Don't you see? It's meaningless now. You've given it back, and it's like it never happened."

"How is it so? Mei Shen and Mian Zi are alive and well. You retain all that you've learned. The friends that you've made are still yours." He snorted. "As are the enemies. You believe I've wronged you by compressing all of this into a moment, but perhaps you wrong me by denying the significance of that moment."

I couldn't. I couldn't stand here and listen to *him* tell *me* how I'd wronged him. Not without wanting to shove him over the bridge railing and into one of the travertine pools that had brought me to the Huanglong valley so long ago.

A few days ago?

I covered my face, scraped my fingers back through my hair, feeling every one of my thirty-three years, and fighting back the exhausting realization that I wouldn't be able to share my loss with anyone. The friends I'd left behind were no longer family; the family I'd built, I had to leave behind.

"Missy–"

I stepped back from him before he could touch me. "Leave it. It's done. I guess at least I won't have to deal with missing persons reports and whatever you have to do to come back from the dead." I laughed so I wouldn't cry. My visitor's Visa wasn't even expired.

"We can still–"

"No. We can't. *I* can't. I came here to learn to be an adventure hero. Guess I should get around to being one." I forced myself to meet his eyes. To not care. "Goodbye, Lung Huang."

Turning away, I crossed the bridge back to a world I didn't belong in anymore.

FIFTEEN
Fallout

Now

A knock sounded at my bedroom door. I rolled over and pulled the covers over my head. "Go away."

The door opened. "No."

Shimizu. I parted the covers just enough to give her a baleful glare. "Why can't you respect my need for privacy?"

"Because the last time you were like this, you made me promise to never let you go more than three days without showering. You're on day two, Masters."

The last time I'd been like this. The last time I'd returned from China. In many ways, this time was worse. Last time, I'd just felt disconnected from my life and everyone in it. This time, everywhere I looked I was reminded of my failure. It was made all the worse by almost everyone insisting that I – or Mr Mystic – was the hero of the day.

Fucking Skyrocket. What a blabbermouth.

"If I had just let David Tsung go through that ward–"

"Then he would be Lung-whatshisface's champion." Shimizu yanked away my covers and poked me until I sat up. "And Mei Shen would fight even more with Mian Zi to protect her boyfriend. Probably end up working for Lung-bad-guy, and definitely end up with a broken heart."

Her no-nonsense assessment, no matter how insightful it might be, did little to make me feel better. Neither did her bustling. I batted her hands away when she tried to smooth my sleep-rumpled hair. "I could have done something else–"

Shimizu huffed and planted her fists on her hips. "You stopped World War III, and that's not enough for you? I give up. Wallow all you want. I just came in to tell you that there's someone here for you."

She was letting me go back to wallowing? I crossed my arms. It was a trick. "There is no one in this world or any other that I can imagine wanting to see."

But she'd perked my curiosity. Who would cause her to brave my surly hermitage? Not any of the housemates. Not Jack, who'd already left me dozens of messages about everything from private security contract offers to movie deals. Not Johnny Cho, who would just barge in himself if he wanted to see me.

"Who?" I took the yoga pants she handed me.

"I guess you'll have to go up to the parlor to see." She left me with a wink and a grin.

She was too cheerful for it to be anything but a ruse to get me mobile and back in the world. I almost climbed back into bed. Dressing seemed like too much of an effort, even to satisfy my curiosity. It better not be Sylvia Dunbarton or anyone from Argent. But no, they wouldn't know to look for Mr Mystic here, even if it was his old house turned intentional living co-op.

OK, maybe I was curious enough to get dressed. I pulled on the yoga pants, pulled my dirty hair back with a hairband, and shuffled upstairs into our rarely-used parlor.

I froze in the doorway. Never in a million years would I have guessed this visitor.

"I'll just give you guys some alone time," Shimizu said. She squeezed my hand on the way past and shut the door behind me.

Jian Huo dressed as he always had, in rich robes out of some *wuxia* fantasy. He should have looked out of place standing in the Victorian parlor, but he was one that made the parlor look out of place, a cheap, gaudy stage for something out of legend. Light from the stained glass windows dappled his robes with roundels of blue and violet.

I sat on a nearby fainting couch before I could faint across it. "I suppose you came to yell at me?"

He moved away from the window and sat next to me, his knee touching mine. He took my clammy hands in his warm ones. I stared at his hair, the long tail snaking across the Turkish carpet to coil in the stained glass sunbeam. I couldn't look him in the eyes.

"Do you wish me to yell at you?"

"I screwed up. I got cocky."

"You found yourself in an untenable situation, and you did the best you could."

"You trained me better than that."

He released my hands to lift my chin, forcing my gaze up. "I have not been your teacher in some while. You are a student of the Tao, remember?"

"Is the Tao going to show up and yell at me?"

Jian Huo choked on a laugh, which made me grin despite the grimace yanking on the corners of my mouth. I frowned harder. Everything was ruined. I shouldn't be smiling. He shouldn't be laughing.

"Last time, you learned that my brother could be bested. This time, you learned that he cannot *always* be bested. In the final balance, I still trust that you will prove a better student than he has."

Strange, how such a simple absolution could make me feel better about the whole mess. As long as Jian Huo didn't lose faith in me, maybe I didn't entirely suck.

"About last time..." I started, and then wasn't sure where

to take it. I wasn't talking about Lung Di anymore. He knew that, right?

"Yes. About last time. I did not say what I should have said."

"Which is?"

"You asked me if my purpose in our union was to supplant my brother."

I held very still. "Well... it was." And it had Lung Di scared enough that he'd pulled out all the stops to arrange his *détente*. I had to give Jian Huo props for effectiveness.

Jian Huo's hands rested over mine. "Perhaps, but it was not my *only* purpose. And I should have told you. I can plot against my brother and still love you. The two are not exclusive. I am sorry that I did not share my plans, that I did not allow you a say in the decision, that I left you doubting my love. That is what I should have said."

All the things he'd been pissed at me for doing to him when I went after Lung Di on my own. I sighed and twined my fingers with his. "Yeah. Me too."

I watched the sunlight move across the carpet, then dim as a cloud passed over the sun. I didn't want to break the fragile moment, but one of us would have to, eventually. "How are Mei Shen and Mian Zi?"

He grimaced. "Not speaking. You may soon hear more than you want to of Mei Shen's side. She has declared her intention to move here. To be close to Mr Tsung, no doubt. Mian Zi... does not approve."

That made two of us. Three, because I couldn't imagine that Jian Huo approved, either. I sighed.

Jian Huo brushed my hair back. "Mei Shen and Mian Zi are young," he said. "They must grow apart before they can come back together."

I leaned into him; his arms came around me, chin resting on my head. I closed my eyes and breathed in sandalwood.

"I've missed you," I whispered. Maybe I should have been

stronger. Nothing had changed between us. Except that time had given me some perspective. I was right to leave him. It didn't mean I had to hate him.

"I cannot stay."

"I know. But I've still missed you." A breath warmed my scalp as he buried his nose in my mussed hair. I probably stank from days of wallowing. Damn Shimizu for not making me take a shower.

"I have something for you." He pulled back and dug through his robes, drawing out a familiar strand of gleaming pearls. "You didn't take them when you left."

For so many reasons. I didn't want the reminder of Jian Huo; I couldn't face the possibility that I would give them to someone else as my grandfather had done. I'd kicked myself ever since for leaving them behind. "It didn't seem right, given... everything."

"And how does it seem now?" he asked, still holding the pearls out. I wondered if I only imagined that hitch in his voice, the slight tremor of his hand.

I took the pearls, fastened them around my neck. "Like a second chance."

Acknowledgments

No writer creates in a vacuum, and I am deeply grateful to all the people who supported, encouraged, inspired, or just plain put up with me through this journey.

First, thanks go to my family, and especially to my grandmothers Diane (a librarian) and Bettie (an English teacher). If love of books is genetic, I got it from them. Special thanks go to my mother, Conna, who is my biggest (and least discerning!) fan and supporter, and to my brother Devon, who taught me that the bonds between brothers and sisters might get a little bendy, but they never break.

Second thanks go to the players in Jason Pisano's Sunday Afternoon Comics Stack game. You guys helped me crawl out of some pretty dark shadows, dragging Missy behind me. Thank you to Emily Dare for the use of Skyrocket. The story wouldn't be the same without Tom's Colgate grin. I'm only sorry to all of you that I wasn't able to work in a reference to Dr Chaos' favorite charity: Orphans. Orphans with Diseases (see what I did there?!).

The support of my found family of writers and friends was vital to keeping me going during the revision and submission process. I'm grateful to my littermates of Clarion West 2012 for grounding and centering me through all the angst and uncertainty, and to the extended Clarion West community for helping me achieve and celebrate my victories.

This book went through many permutations before reaching its current form, and it would be a lesser creation if not for the beta readers who offered critique throughout the various drafts. Thanks to Marie Brennan, Jason Pisano, Avery Liell-Kok, Emily Dare, Claire Balgemann, Henry Lien, Georgina Kamsika, David Higgins, SL Knapp, and the folks in my WisCon Writers' Workshop for all their helpful comments. Thank you to my agent, Lindsay Ribar, for giving me wonderful feedback and multiple chances to get it right.

I feel so lucky to be an Angry Robot author, and my deepest gratitude goes to Michael Underwood for running around the World Fantasy Convention at Brighton in an attempt to slam me into Amanda Rutter. Thanks to Amanda for being Mr Mystic's first official supporter, and thanks to the rest of the Angry Robot team – Marc Gascoigne, Phil Jourdan, Caroline Lambe, and the rest of the staff – for the hard work you've put into making my book shine. And to Amazing15 for that wonderful cover, thank you. It feels trite to call you amazing, but it's true!

Finally, thank you to my foundational authors. To Anne McCaffery who made me into a dragon-girl. To Mercedes Lackey who fed my id on a diet of pure squee. To Meredith Ann Pierce who skewered my perception of how fairy tales are supposed to end. To Katherine Kurtz who saved my life, inspired me to take up Highland dance, and taught me that villains have valid perspectives. To Jessa MacBeth, who provided me with a whole host of friends and guides. And to Connie Willis, who taught me that feminist can be the least scary word in any story.

I'm certain I've missed folks, and it isn't for lack of gratitude. This has been a long journey, and I neglected to take notes on who helped me along the way because when I started, I had no idea where I was going. I'll do better next time!